A MEMBER OF THE FAMILY

A MEMBER OF THE FAMILY

NICK VASILE

A TOM DOHERTY ASSOCIATES BOOK
NEW YORK

A MEMBER OF THE FAMILY

Copyright © 1993 by Nick Vasile, Donald Bain, and Anthony M. Tedeschi.

This book is printed on acid-free paper.

A Tor Book
Published by Tom Doherty Associates, Inc.
175 Fifth Avenue
New York, N.Y. 10010

Tor® is a registered trademark of Tom Doherty Associates, Inc.

Design by Diane Stevenson—SNAP·HAUS GRAPHICS

Library of Congress Catologing-in-Publication Data

Vasile, Nick.
    A member of the family / Nick Vasile.
        p.   cm.
    "A Tom Doherty Associates book."
    ISBN 0-312-85349-1
    1. Private Investigators—Washington (D.C.)—Fiction.
  2. Organized Crime—Washington (D.C.)—Fiction. 3. Mafia—
Washington (D.C.)—Fiction. I. Title
PS3572.A83M46M 1993
813'.54—dc20   93-17432
                                                  CIP

First Tor edition: August 1993

Printed in the United States of America

0 9 8 7 6 5 4 3 2 1

To my wife, Bea, and to my daughter, Brenda, my son-in-law, Ray, my daughter, Fern, and my three lovely grandchildren, Elizabeth, Ray Jr., and Katherine.

I'd like to thank my good friends Donald Bain and Tony Tedeschi. I would also like to thank my good friend and editor, Robert Gleason, and to give a special thanks to my agent, Ted Chichak.

THE CHARACTERS

THE BENEDETTI CRIME FAMILY

Vincent Benedetti—*The Family Head*
Santo Benedetti—*Vincent's younger brother and family underboss*
Tommy Guardino—*Vincent's driver and bodyguard*
Genaro Orsini (Gerry Orson)—*Santo's son-in-law*
Lucia (Lucy) Marcantonio—*Santo's daughter and Genaro Orsini's wife*
Marco Marcantonio—*Lucia's deceased husband*
Gina Benedetti—*Santo's wife*
Joe "Joey Balls" Bellisimo—*Family soldier*
Jake "The Ape" Cohen—*Family soldier*
Big Dom Piaggio—*Santo's bodyguard*
Johnny Morelli—*Family* capo

THE GOVERNMENT

J. Edgar Hoover—*Former FBI Director*
Stanley (Stan) Simonsen—*Attorney General of the United States*
Willard Thornton—*Assistant Attorney General*
Tom Whelan—*FBI Special Agent*
Fred Wozinski—*FBI Special Agent*
Joe Diggs—*DEA undercover agent*
Mr. Saunders—*IRS informant*
Clark Mason—*FBI Director*

THE LAWYERS & ACCOUNTANTS

Ed Milstein—*Accountant to the Benedetti Family*
Sal—*Attorney to the Benedetti Family*
Carl—*Attorney to the Benedetti Family*
Burton Carter—*Vincent Benedetti's personal attorney*

THE DRUG DEALERS

Raphael Tierranueva—*Washington D.C. drug lord*
Macho Man—*Tierranueva's driver*
Mambo Jenks—*Jamaican drug dealer*
Carlos—*Washington D.C. drug dealer*
Willie Johnson—*Drug dealer*

THE "GANG" AT CUFFS

Paul Dante—*Owner of Cuffs, former cop, and part-time private investigator*
Shelly—*Cuffs's manager*
Julio—*The chef*
Pete—*The bartender*
Sol—*The waiter*
Lucette—*The waitress*

THE OTHERS

Isabel—*A prostitute*
Fionia Smith—*A prostitute*
Angelo Andreotti—*A restaurant owner*
Carmela Andreotti—*Angelo's wife*
Jimmy "Too Tight" Titone—*Topless bar owner*
Ginny—*Topless dancer*
Barbara Dante—*Paul Dante's former wife*
Julia Croce—*Ballet dancer, professor, and Paul Dante's current girlfriend*
Lisa—*A Cuffs regular*
Jimmy Rooker—*A* Washington Post *reporter*
Cal Williams—*Dante's former partner at Washington MPD*
Cindy Williams—*Cal's wife*
Doris Sawyer—*Atlantic City casino cocktail waitress and Genaro Orsini's mistress*
Paddy Provenzano—*Atlantic City casino manager*
Jorge Belmondo—*Argentinian hit-man*
Angela Rinaldi—*Vincent Benedetti's private secretary*
Victor—*A factory owner*
Donnie Tenaglia—*Insurance scam artist*
Charlie Pietrosanti—*Rogue former IRS agent*
Carla—*Pietrosanti's former girlfriend*
Millie McGuire—*Pietrosanti's former girlfriend*
George McGuire—*Millie's son*

i

September—Washington, D.C.

"He didn't balk at coming here?" FBI special agent Tom Whelan said to DEA undercover agent Joe Diggs.

"Nah. I told him I only do business at home. He said fine, he'd show." Diggs was tall and lean. That his father had been a black man was evident in his features and coloring, although not too evident. In his fourteen years undercover, Diggs had passed for Spanish, or Colombian, or Puerto Rican. He'd infiltrated drug gangs and set up unsuspecting drug buyers in South America, New York, Los Angeles, and Houston. But never in Washington, D.C., which was why he was brought in two months ago for what he was told was a crucial assignment. Little chance of being made in D.C.

"Ten-thirty?" Whelan asked.

"Right."

"I still would have preferred a hotel."

"It would have spooked him. He's not the smartest wop on the street but he's no *cafone*, either. Besides, he needs the deal. It's not like he can keep scoring with the Colombians, not with his *goombata* whackin' them all. He's still got his snowbirds out there but no shit to sell them."

"How much does he think he's buying?"

"Two kilos."

11

Whelan knew the answers to his questions but asked them anyway. You could never be too sure of anything. They were interrupted by an FBI audio specialist who wasn't happy with the quality of sound being picked up by a trio of tiny microphones hidden in the living room. An eight-by-eight portion of the large master bedroom had been partitioned off to conceal audio and video tape recorders manned by technicians from the Bureau, the DEA, and the Washington MPD. The carpenters had done a good job. Unless you were familiar with the room in its original configuration, you'd never know the separate space existed. The work had been completed months ago in the hope that it would one day justify the expense of creating and maintaining the apartment. It hadn't—until now. But if all went as planned this night, those who'd backed the idea would smile with smug satisfaction.

A video camera in the living room was housed in what appeared to be a gold-and-silver sculpture of a cat hammered into shape by a Ming dynasty artisan. In truth, it had been molded especially for the camera by a DEA agent whose hobby was metal casting. It sat on a marble table in a corner, its red jeweled eyes fixed on a conversation area in the center of the room created by couches and a coffee table. The camera's sensitive lens was behind the cat's right eye, an incessant observer of everything that took place on the couches. Provided, of course, that no one pulled the plug.

The apartment, just off Dupont Circle, had been decorated and furnished in lavish, gaudy taste. It looked and felt like a rich drug dealer's crib where prey could be set up in style. Most of the dozen men getting things ready for that night's sting did not know who would sit on the couch and expose himself—or herself—to the tall, athletic black man named Diggs who'd put things into motion earlier that week.

He'd arrived in Washington driving a Mercedes sedan from a pool of cars in New York confiscated from drug dealers by the DEA. His thirty-thousand-dollar Rolex had come off the wrist of a dealer, the ropes of gold chain from a dealer's neck. Twenty thousand dollars in marked bills, most of which were hidden in a pouch created in the underside of the leather driver's seat, had been plucked from a busted dealer's pocket. The two weapons Diggs carried—a Smith & Wesson

.44 Magnum, which he kept with him; and a Beretta 9 mm semiautomatic handgun, which he hid in the Mercedes—belonged to him.

Diggs checked his Rolex. "I have to call him," he told Whelan. He'd withheld the apartment's address from the patsy to avoid having him check it out earlier in the day.

Whelan poked his head into the bedroom. "You about finished?" he asked.

"Looks like it."

"Let's move," Whelan said. To Diggs: "We'll be out of here in a few minutes, except for the crew behind the partition. Okay?"

"Yeah," said Diggs, smiling. "This guy was easy."

Whelan, who seldom smiled, did. "I know. You said that after he bit."

"That's what desperation does, huh? That black hooker was smooth, too. Beautiful fox. She put us together real easy." He laughed. "Man, I'd be less than honest if I didn't admit wanting to taste a little of her once she did her number."

Whelan only grinned.

"Still not going to tell me why so much interest in this dude?"

"Love to, Joe, but can't. Strictly need-to-know."

"I got to admit I'm curious. This is going down like a big number, but I read the guy as meaningless street shit."

"You ever know a dealer who wasn't?"

"More to it than that, buddy. My gut tells me this particular piece of shit is your ticket to a promotion. Director, maybe?"

Whelan's smile turned to a laugh. He slapped the tall black man on the back. They made an interesting pair. Diggs was swarthy and handsome, his flashy clothes defining a Colombian drug baron. Whelan was short and slender. Horn-rimmed glasses covered pale blue eyes set in a face the color of unbleached flour. He wore what he always wore, a white button-down shirt, muted paisley tie, and tweed sport jacket. "Joe," Whelan said, "one day we'll sit down in a nice restaurant and you'll know everything I know. For now, let's just make sure this thing flies tonight. Until then, thanks. They said you were good. I'm a believer."

ii

Two Months Later

Vincent Benedetti stepped from a black Lincoln Town Car into the reddening November morning. He placed his hands on his hips and arched his back. Car rides tended to stiffen him these days; it took longer to get his body cranked. A tiny moisture cloud from his breath lingered in the still air as he noted the twisted sticks of bare trees coming into soft focus against the early morning light. In the distance, a vintage wooden Chris-Craft sat at the end of a finger pier, a motionless silhouette against the reflected fiery red of the sun on the lake's slick surface.

A crow the size of a truck tire balanced on the highest limb of a naked maple tree, its discordant cry shattering the quiet. As the shrill call of the bird dissolved into the steady idle of the Lincoln's engine, Benedetti's aging driver and bodyguard, Tommy Guardino, held out the suit jacket Vincent had removed at the start of their journey to keep it from wrinkling. The Mafia don slipped his arms into the jacket, now a slightly snugger fit than when he'd kept his middle-weight physique in fighting trim. He folded the lapels smoothly against the jacket.

"*Grazie*, Tommy," he said.

"*Prego.*"

Vincent glanced at his reflected image in the car window and ran flattened hands over his temples where widening patches of white and grey had taken control of hair once as black as the crow in the tree.

14

A MEMBER OF THE FAMILY

Two Mercury sedans had accompanied the Lincoln from Baltimore and flanked him, their engines idling.

Driver, limousine—accoutrements of stature as a birthright, favors that had long been a part of Vincent Benedetti's life. He had achieved the highest position of power within the family of families before his fortieth birthday, and had done it with brains as well as brawn. Educated in international business at American University, he'd developed the tools to talk to the Anglo-Saxons in their language, using their inflections, and demonstrating their refinements. Leaders of government and industry listened when he spoke. He was knowledgeable, and spoke well. A formidable foe who preferred negotiation to conflict, but who had never hesitated to abandon rhetoric for the more direct message of force when words failed.

His younger brother, Santo, emerged from the other side of the Lincoln. The Benedetti brothers had aged differently. Vincent, the taller of the two, had remained slender, but his body now curved forward, like a tree buffeted by too many years of strong north winds. His hairline had receded, although he'd retained much of it. What had not changed was the sadness in his eyes, which gave him the look of a man dismayed with the human dilemma as he perceived it, a man who could cry for humanity were he allowed to do so. A patriarch.

Santo, fifteen years Vincent's junior, was shorter and more compact, more muscular. His face was as square as Vincent's was elongated. Santo had lost none of his hair, at least not yet. It remained a black helmet surrounding the heavy ridges of a face whose prominent bones above dark eyes might have resulted from too many blows had he been a fighter. There was an energy to Santo that Vincent now lacked.

News on the radio had rankled Vincent during the ride. "This President keeps making speeches against banning assault weapons," he'd growled. "The *schifosi* in the ghettos play with them like they're whacking guys in a Nintendo game. Like real life." Santo shook his head in a show of supportive disgust but said nothing. The brothers had more immediate concerns this morning.

They'd entered the compound through a gate three hundred yards behind. Now, they stood in front of an oversized log cabin built as if to withstand a missile attack, its timbers two feet thick. Located in the center of forty-acre Camp Rappahannock, in the Virginia woods, the lodge had been the mountain-lake retreat of an intelligence advisor during the Coolidge administration. A childless widower, he'd willed the property to the Justice Department which, after the death of its benefactor in 1939, turned it into a small conference center/stress-release getaway for department functionaries—and a place to meet unnoticed with people like Vincent Benedetti. A safe house. Secure and private.

The door to the cabin opened and two men wearing the requisite stone faces and dark suits of white-collar law enforcement emerged. "Mister Benedetti," one said to Vincent, gesturing him inside. "Please." There was a note of impatience in his voice.

"They always act like they're in a hurry," Vincent said to his brother, sotto voce. "Nothing good is ever accomplished in a hurry."

"We'll be here," Santo said to his brother. "If you need us."

Vincent walked slowly and deliberately up the stairs and, without a word or greeting, went inside.

The cabin's main room was warmed by flames in a massive fieldstone fireplace. Above the hearth, glassy-eyed deer heads gazed down from their resting places high on the wall—the exaggerated trophies of a sadly uneven competition. Seated behind a large desk—the top a cross-section of a single oak polished to an agate finish—was a jacketless man wearing a red-and-white striped shirt, red suspenders, and a tie boasting a coat-of-arms that picked up the red of his shirt. "Coffee, Mr. Benedetti?" he asked. The rose-tinged blush on his alabaster cheeks would have made any mother beam.

"Please, Mr. Thornton," the don said, lowering himself onto an oversized, lumpy sofa.

"Early morning meetings a problem?" Thornton asked through an insincere smile.

"Not at all. I'm an early riser," Vincent said, painting a matching smile on his face. "You know what they say about worms."

Thornton grunted and allowed his smile to fade. Vincent scrutinized him. A competitive man, he thought. Which was true. Willard Thornton loved contests. He was powerfully built, his body regularly honed in the better health clubs inside the Beltway to forestall what

16

could become a weight problem. Although in his late forties, he enjoyed outdoing the younger men of the department in tests of strength or endurance. He'd finished in the top ten percent in the last two Marine Corps marathons, the best showing of anyone from the Attorney General's office. Just as well for his juniors from the office who'd also entered the race. Thornton didn't deal easily with losses.

One of the two men who'd escorted Benedetti into the cabin placed a tray with a steaming pot of coffee, china cup and saucer, crystal creamer and sugar bowl before him. The man poured three quarters of a cup and left the room. Vincent preferred his coffee black, no sugar. He filled the rest of his cup and lifted it in the direction of his host. "*Salute,*" he said.

Thornton barely lifted his cup in response. "Well, Mr. Benedetti," he said, "you asked for this meeting. The floor is yours."

"Yes, I asked to meet. It is about the understanding."

"What about it?"

"There now seems to be *mis*understanding."

Thornton grunted. "It's worked well for thirty years."

"But not lately." Benedetti raised his cup, blew lightly across the surface of the black liquid and sipped again. He replaced the cup in its saucer. Piss water, he thought. He liked his coffee strong. "The change has been occurring over time, Mr. Thornton. Each year, we honor the arrangement. But you and your people seem less inclined . . ." He chose his words carefully. "Perhaps a little history would be in order."

"I don't need a lesson in history," Thornton said.

"Indulge me."

"All right. Go ahead," Thornton said with a gratuitous wave of his hand. "But I've got a meeting downtown. I have to be out of here in thirty minutes."

"Thirty years ago," Vincent began, ignoring his host's impatience, "Mr. J. Edgar Hoover let it be known to my people that he had something on his mind, a proposal, an arrangement, an understanding—call it what you will. I was told it had the blessing of the Attorney General, Mr. Robert Kennedy, and that he spoke for his brother in the White House. The terms were simple. No narcotics. No drugs. In addition, I was to keep our business out of Washington. In return, your people would allow us to operate laissez-faire, outside the district. An early form of deregulation?"

More like a license to steal, Thornton thought. Immunity from prosecution for the so-called victimless crimes of gambling, prostitution, loan-sharking, and other activities from which the Benedetti family derived most of its livelihood. The family would be allowed to engage in those pursuits from Atlantic City to Atlanta—except in the nation's capital. "Go on," Thornton said.

"Mr. J. Edgar Hoover was a visionary man," Benedetti said. "He saw what had happened with Prohibition. And he saw what was about to happen with drugs. Before I entered into my agreement with Mr. Hoover, drugs were a jazz musician's disease. Blacks. The Chinese used drugs. But not middle-class white people. Do you agree?" He cocked his head at Thornton, who said nothing.

Benedetti continued. "But then in the early sixties it changed. It seemed like everybody would use drugs, the hippies, men, women, kids. Middle-class America. And Mr. Hoover thought of Prohibition and he saw La Cosa Nostra selling the drugs like the whiskey, killing for territory, making markets, earning millions—billions. So—and he was a visionary man—he said to us that if we would not deal in drugs, he would allow our business to grow in other ways. It was, Mr. Thornton, a sensible arrangement, one that has endured for thirty years."

"Maybe, maybe not," Thornton said in the tone of a person unsure how to respond.

Benedetti sensed that the large man behind the desk wasn't comfortable. A good time to press harder. "Now, however," he said, "for the past few years there have been problems. My family has had to stand by as the growing drug trade disrupts the peace. Drug dealers from South America and opportunists in the black community have built a criminal empire within Washington, with no attempt at enforcement by the authorities despite our arrangement. We've stayed out of the city itself because we gave our word. You have allowed others to come in and prosper with their cocaine and heroin. It is not right."

Initially, this new crime cartel hadn't been considered by Benedetti and his people as constituting a direct threat; narcotics had never been part of the family's criminal mix. But as this new breed of criminal lord grew rich and powerful through drug money, he expanded into other areas that were in direct competition with the family.

Clearly, federal law enforcement had lost its war with crime within the District. Or, as Vincent Benedetti and his inner council had decided in recent meetings, it had allowed the growth of this new criminal organization at the expense of the Benedetti family—in direct violation of the spirit of "the understanding."

Now, thirty years after the agreement with Hoover had been struck, Vincent Benedetti sat in a Virginia log cabin with Willard Thornton, an assistant attorney general, and asked for enforcement of the treaty.

When Benedetti finished, Thornton said, "As far as I'm concerned, we've kept our part of the bargain. No one has put pressure on you or your activities, Mr. Benedetti. You're sitting here, aren't you? Others like you around the country are sitting in less accommodating quarters."

Benedetti did not like the inference, but the bureaucrat was right. The deal with Hoover was the envy of other heads of criminal families across the United States, many of whom were now doing time under racketeering laws. Those in jail were, for the most part, the thick-headed ones who'd refused over the years to pay for Vincent Benedetti's services as a lobbyist of sorts with the federal government on behalf of La Cosa Nostra. Vincent viewed himself that way, as a lobbyist in the truest sense of the word. After all, that was what he had built since striking his deal with the director of the Federal Bureau of Investigation. Nurturing such contacts at all levels of the government was a special skill, one that he was not too modest to acknowledge he possessed. It cost money too, lots of money. His lobbying fee was reasonable, he believed, considering the good that could come from it. Two million dollars a year from each family was money well spent. A legitimate business expense, like any other American industry buying the services of a well-connected and shrewd lobbyist in the nation's capital. It didn't buy blanket immunity, but it did buy consideration, as well as respect. It was the direction in which the families had to move, Vincent had decided long ago. He'd guided the Benedetti family away from the more violent and distasteful crimes that had built its fortunes in earlier days, to a position more in the mainstream of American free enterprise. Lobbying was as important an ingredient as paying lawyers and accountants, buying raw materials, and setting up distribution networks. He had little respect for those who insisted upon doing business the old way, and who dismissed the need for the sort of services that only Vincent Benedetti could provide. Those languishing in jail had gotten what they deserved. Stupid, short-sighted men.

Couldn't they see the advantages of establishing ties with influential members of the federal government? They had only to look at the Benedetti family itself to see the benefits to be gained. Vincent, Santo, and their inner circle had been relatively free for thirty years to run the family business without fear of undue federal interference—as long as they stayed out of Washington and narcotics.

"If there's been any misdirections in the arrangement," said Thornton, "there isn't much we can do about it, at least for the moment. There are other priorities."

"Your 'misdirections' cost me a nephew last week," Benedetti said coldly. "My cousin's kid."

"My condolences."

"It was in Jessup, on a family street, a nice neighborhood on *our* side of the understanding."

"It was a drug deal. Your nephew was a user. He'd been in and out of rehab."

"He was family."

"It happens."

"Do you know how it happened, Mr. Thornton?" He didn't wait for a reply. "The Colombians call it a Colombian necktie. My nephew's throat was slit. His tongue was pulled through the slit like a tie. A calling card to make sure we knew who had killed him."

"Drugs are a brutal business," Thornton offered.

Benedetti heaved a sigh. His stomach burned. He would be happy to leave, but there was more to say, more to place on the table. "These scum who operate freely in the District are over the line, Mr. Thornton.

They buy up politicians faster than distribution networks for their drugs. We have been prohibited from doing business in Washington, but that is not the case with them. And the cancer spreads. Their pollution rains down everywhere, on my family. We want assurances that—"

Thornton stood; Benedetti hadn't realized how large a man he was. He placed large, red-knuckled hands on the desktop and leaned toward Benedetti, his steel blue eyes pinning the mafioso like a lepidopterist spearing a butterfly. "There can be no assurances," he said. "Our budget has been cut, and there is a hell of a lot to do with what we've been left with."

"Such as prosecute these people? Do you mean you intend to prosecute them?" Benedetti's gaze was unflinching. He was a master of eye contact; it was a necessity in his business. "You place these people on trial but they walk away because they know the right people to pay. It was my belief that we knew the right people too, because *we* have lived up to our obligations. We expected the right people would live up to theirs. For many years, you did. But no more. Assurances, Mr. Thornton. We must have assurances."

Thornton went to the fireplace and leaned against it, posed actually: a magazine photograph. He said wearily, "Mr. Benedetti, when you reached your 'understanding' with Mr. Hoover thirty years ago, times were different. We must adjust to the times. All of us. *Capice?*" He pronounced the Italian word with a demeaning accent: "Kah-peeesh."

Benedetti stood, too. "No," he said. *"Non capisco.* We have been accommodating you for too long. It's time we protect our interests, not yours. *Our* interests. That is my responsibility to my people."

"Meaning what, Mr. Benedetti? You're not threatening me, are you? You still understand that your business 'license' still does not include the District. Correct?"

"Maybe. If it suits *our* needs. And maybe we no longer provide services to our partner in this arrangement."

"Services?"

"Need I remind you of those times when it was more convenient to hire us for chores that would have been—well, let's say awkward for the government to perform? Chores with a high potential for recriminations. We've always stood ready to serve our country, Mr. Thornton. Evidently, our country no longer wishes to serve us." Benedetti approached Thornton and smiled. He was markedly more relaxed. "Thank you for your time this morning." He extended his hand. Thornton was caught off guard by the gesture. He took it tentatively. "Next time, you call me," Benedetti said.

"What do you mean by that?" Thornton said as the stooped leader of the country's most powerful crime family walked slowly from the room and closed the door behind him. "What the fuck do you mean by that?" Thornton repeated to the only creatures left to answer him—the deer above the fireplace.

As Benedetti walked out into a warming fall day, the troika of vehicles moved toward him. Tommy emerged from the driver's door, took Vincent's jacket, folded it neatly and laid it on the front seat. The don got in the back alongside his brother.

"For a big man, his handshake is like wet pasta. Not like Hoover's," Vincent said.

————

Afternoon sun through venetian blinds penciled charcoal grey stripes across the face of Willard Thornton, who sat across the desk from his boss, Stan Simonsen, Attorney General of the United States. Simonsen was taller than Thornton but half his weight. His face and body seemed to have been created of a series of right angles. Everything was pronounced—nose, cheekbones, shoulders, and arms. He wore round rimless glasses through which peered watery green eyes that seemed never to blink. Impossible, Thornton knew, but as hard as he tried, he never caught his boss with his eyelids down. The attorney general's voice was thin and grating, as though the channel through which his breath moved was constricted. Not a likable man but, Thornton reasoned, being liked was not a requisite for becoming attorney general. Not in the job description.

"Is it an idle threat?" Simonsen asked.

"Not this time. I think the bastard's about to do something."

Simonsen sighed. "Your best guess?"

"Not sure. Pop some of the top drug people is a possibility. A strong possibility. Looks like they've already started. The Diaz people took out that hophead, Benedetti's nephew. They call it a Colombian necktie. Jesus, these people are animals. They slit the kid's throat and pulled his tongue through it. The war's already started. Reports I've been getting point to that. I heard just before I arrived here that a couple of Colombian dealers have disappeared. I know how the mob thinks. One-of-yours-for-one-of-mine crap."

"We don't need this," the attorney general said. "War in the streets. People in the neighborhoods may see it as the mob doing a job we can't handle. That could be embarrassing politically." He poured himself ice water from a silver pitcher, then offered his assistant a glass as an afterthought. Thornton shook him off. "I get to take *that* news to the President?" Simonsen added.

"I don't think you'll have to carry any bad news to the President, Stan. Things are progressing nicely with the Partridge."

"Fill me in. What stage is it at?"

"Everything's falling into place. Here." He pulled a sheet of paper from his briefcase and slid it across the desk.

Simonsen scanned the two typewritten paragraphs. "You think it will happen this quick?" he asked.

Thornton smiled. "I guarantee it." Simonsen fed the piece of paper into a shredder next to his desk as Thornton continued. "When this Partridge scheme was proposed, I didn't have any faith in it. But I'm a believer now. That DEA undercover agent, Diggs, did a hell of a job. No hitches. Went like clockwork." He snapped his fingers three times in rapid succession. "And it's still right on track. As we agreed, I met with the old guinzo this morning to see what he had to say. I didn't like what I heard. I think it's time Vincent Benedetti was put out of commission for good. Partridge will do that for us."

Simonsen grunted. "They're primed for a fall," he said in his reedy voice. "They're not as strong as they used to be. We can get Benedetti under RICO, provided the case is properly built."

"It will be, Stan. We're taking it in stages, using Partridge. We'll start hammering Benedetti from every direction. It may not take too much. The tax setup is already in progress. If that doesn't do it, we'll keep building our RICO case. Somewhere along the way, we'll have him."

Simonsen went to a window and gazed out on a smear of red taillights heading home for the day. Thornton joined him. "Sometimes I wonder if it's worth it," Simonsen said to the windowpane. "Sometimes I wish I were with them." He jutted his jaw toward the window to indicate the cars outside. "Nine to five. You show up for work on time, do what you're paid to do, then leave it and head home."

Thornton chuckled. "Sounds dull to me," he said. "Besides, they'll be in traffic for the next two hours. You should have been with me this morning, Stan. Benedetti acts like he's a diplomat. Very formal, very stiff, stilted speech. Christ, when you think about it, he's nothing more than a guinzo mobster telling *us*, the U.S. Government, how to treat him and his goddamn family. I was thinking after he left about what a sham he is. It's like my kids. They foul up. When I come down hard on them, they say, 'At least we don't use drugs.' And I tell them that I don't *expect* them to use drugs. I don't give them points for not using drugs. It's the same with Benedetti. Because he and his goons don't push drugs, they think they're model citizens who ought to get some freaking medal from the government. I mean, who the hell does he think he is? What balls. He cuts a deal thirty years ago with J. Edgar Buddha and thinks that protects him and his dago friends for life. I'm really going to enjoy taking him down, Stan."

Simonsen had continued to look out the window while Thornton expressed his feelings. When Thornton was finished, Simonsen said, "I'll have to clear everything up top. You understand."

"Of course."

"Benedetti has bought lots of people in this town over the years. I don't want to bring this thing to a conclusion and then have somebody come out of the woodwork and kill it."

"That ball's in your political court, Stan. I'll take care of my end."

"Keep me informed every step. No surprises. No cracks for anything to fall through."

"It'll be seamless. Count on it."

Simonsen turned and faced his stocky, red-faced assistant. "Thank you for all the good work, Will. Go get caught in traffic and enjoy the weekend. At least what's left of it."

Thornton picked up his briefcase from where he'd left it next to the desk and went to the door. He placed his hand on the knob, turned, and said, "You should do the same, Stan. Get out of here. Go home and enjoy the weekend."

Simonsen had already returned to his desk and sat behind it, his feet propped on its edge. He leaned back, rubbed his eyes, and said, "Good night, Will."

The Following Friday

A smartly dressed couple stepped from a silver Lexus sedan into the rain and prepared to dash for the restaurant. But their path was blocked by a black woman in soggy tatters who pushed six drooping red tulips at them. A valet car-parker wearing a hooded maroon American University sweatshirt bounded from the entrance, stepped between them, and took keys from the man.

"Any scratches in the paint job, Richie, I break your fingers," the man said to the valet, slapping him on the back.

The boy opened the driver's door.

"And close that door before the seats get wet."

The flustered valet drove off, narrowly missing a car approaching from the opposite direction.

"Jerky kid," the man muttered to his woman.

Above them, an antique neon sign with threaded glass letters glowed red, white, and green. It had once read "Angelo's," but the *o* had been blackened by some chemical failure, transforming the name of the restaurant to "Angel 's," as if in recognition of the black and Hispanic elements that now dominated what had once been a mostly white, blue-collar residential section of Washington. Customers no longer came to Angelo's, or Angel 's, to be seen—or not to be seen—depending upon whom they were with. They still came out of loyalty to a reputation built on quality. Despite the deterioration of the neighborhood, those who had patronized Angelo's for years knew it still served the best peasant Italian food in D.C.

The couple seemed too elegant for the setting. He wore a dark blue chalk-stripe suit with an Italian designer tie and matching pocket square. She was in an elegant silk Armani of a unique periwinkle shade.

He was fortyish, a large man, with square shoulders that rotated in the swagger of a youth spent at hard knocks. He had jet black wavy hair, still allegiant to the wet look, and eyes that were small and dark and peered at you through a perpetual squint, as though constantly assaying a potentially dangerous situation. His appearance said "dandy"; at the same time, it warned you to keep your distance.

His companion was lovely of face and figure, a little overweight in the hips, perhaps, which was more a factor of her thirty-eight years than a diet left unchecked. She moved with a touch of uncertainty that was out of synch with the statement made by her clothes. There was something naive and unguarded about the way she carried herself. While she appeared a woman of few pretensions, she was not necessarily a simple read. There was a depth to her demeanor that stopped just this side of mystery, not born of calculation but rooted in hurt.

They were greeted inside by a short, roundish Italianate man with a bald pate edged by pure white hair cropped closely to his temples. Angelo Andreotti had been standing just inside the door as if waiting all evening for their arrival. "Signor Orsini," he greeted. *"Come va, sta sera?"*

Orsini wiped his shoes on the doormat. "Not bad, Angelo. You?"

"I coulda complain, but who listens?" the elderly restaurant owner answered. It might have been small talk but for the tired look of his eyes, and deep creases in his yellowed jowls.

"You remember Lucy?" Orsini asked.

"Of course. Signora Marcantonio. *Come vai?*" He bowed and kissed her hand. "And how is Santo?"

She nodded.

"I don't see your father so much no more. Give him my respects when you see him. He don't come so much no more, not like when he and your uncle were younger, and when your husband . . ." Angelo's jaw went slack in response to Orsini's hard look. "I'm sorry, signora," he said penitently.

Lucia Marcantonio's husband, Marco, had been dead for six years.

The woman stared straight ahead, as if oblivious to the old man's words and gestures. Angelo coughed nervously and said to Orsini, "We've prepared your regular table."

"Good," Orsini said. "How is Carmela doing?" he asked as they followed him to the table.

"What can I say?" Angelo said over his shoulder. "You know how it is with these things."

Orsini pulled a business card from his pocket and handed it to Angelo. It read: *Gerry Orson, Investment Counselor/Insurance Representative.* Although his name was Genaro Orsini, he'd used the Americanized form for a long time. Better for business, he'd decided. "Call me," he told Angelo. "Maybe I can help."

"Thank you, Signor . . . Orson. I appreciate your concern. I know Carmela will, too."

The restaurant looked as though it had grown old with its owners, tired and demoralized, but not to the point of surrender. The room was sparsely populated; a half-dozen couples sat at tables in the main dining area. The buzz from them was quiet, polite.

There were still vestiges of what Angelo's had once been. An antipasto table at the center of the room overflowed with cold seafood, artistically sliced raw vegetables, cold cuts in reds and pinks, aromatic cheeses and fresh breads. But on the dining tables where once had stood unopened bottles of Piedmontese wines personally selected by Angelo during trips to the town of his birth in Italy, now only their shells remained, filled with dried flowers.

"I send over Corrado," Angelo said when they were seated. "Enjoy your dinner." He spread white napkins in their laps, handed them menus, placed a wine list next to Orsini, and left.

"He's so damn formal," Orsini said. "Signor! Signora!" he

mimicked. "He's been in this country fifty years and he still thinks he's in Piedmont. He should look around the neighborhood and he'd know this isn't *La Bella Italia*. You step over junkies getting out of your car, the whores lean on the flower pots by the front door, and bag ladies shove dead flowers in your face." He stopped himself. A smile swept over his face. "What am I going on like this for? Times change, huh? Not always for the better. But what does it matter what's outside? What counts is here inside." He placed a hand over his heart. "You and me are together, Lucy. That's what counts." He placed the same large hand over hers. She slid her hand out and folded it with her other hand in her lap. "I want tonight to be special, Lucy. Very special."

Most people called her by her given name, Lucia, but he used the Americanized version, as if once again applying his own signature to a matter of importance.

A short, squat, round-faced man in a grey pin-striped business suit emerged from the men's room still rubbing moisture from the back of his hands. He noticed the couple and came to their table. "Gerry Orson, how are ya?" he said. "The celebrity table. You must have pull with the old man." He winked at Lucy.

"That's right, Tenaglia. We go way back."

Orsini retrieved a box of English cigarettes from the inside pocket of his suit jacket, flipped out a long, white filter-tip, and lit it with a gold Dunhill lighter. "How's things in the insurance business?" he asked.

"Well, we haven't blown the actuarial tables—yet," Tenaglia replied, laughing at what he considered an inside joke. He laughed alone. "My clients are trying hard enough, though. They keep dyin' on me. I mean, *some*body's gettin' rich on all this."

Tenaglia waited for an introduction to Orsini's guest. When none was offered, he shifted his weight, fiddled with his tie, and politely excused himself.

"Friend?" Lucia asked.

"A business acquaintance. I use his company as a source of capital for some of my deals. I used them last year to refinance a nuts-and-bolts company for a coupla blacks doin' work for the Navy. They had some problems with back taxes. Hey, who doesn't these days,

huh? They had lousy accounting advice when they were starting up."
He took a long, deliberate drag on his cigarette. "They were so grateful
they made me their controller. Who can figure *tootsoons*?" He smiled
and stubbed out the cigarette, just two drags into its length.

Corrado took their drink orders, a Glenfiddich and soda for Orsini,
a glass of house red for Lucia.

Orsini studied his companion as her eyes shifted about the room,
alighting momentarily on everything from customers to wall hangings,
but all with an odd lack of focus.

"Lucy?" Orsini prompted.

"Yes?"

"Are you all right?"

"Of course." She removed her hands from her lap and folded them
on the white tablecloth. His hands took a position on top again. "Why
do you ask?" she said.

He paused. "I need—I mean I'd like to ask you something
important."

"Yes?"

"I was talking to your father the other day." Orsini had been a
soldier in the Benedetti family for a little over a year, a low-level
operator who generated sufficient money for the family to be considered
an up-and-comer.

"Oh? My father likes you."

"I know, and that's very important to me." He lit another cigarette,
took a drag and ditched it; it broke in half in the ashtray. "Marco has
been dead for like six years now."

Her large dark oval eyes seemed to recede into her skull.

"It's time for you to move on with your life."

She entwined her fingers into a prayerlike bundle under her chin.

"Your father. He agrees."

She stared at the wall behind him as she said, "I wouldn't do
anything without his approval." Her voice was barely above a whisper.

Orsini took a long swallow of his drink and stared at the empty
glass. Corrado, who'd been watching from the waiter's station, started

toward their table but Orsini waved him off. "I know the importance of your father's blessing," he said to Lucy. "That's why I went to him first."

"First?"

"Yes." He peered into her lovely, placid face. "I asked him if he would object if I asked for your hand in marriage."

Her facial muscles tightened. "And?" she said.

"He said no."

"No?" Two creases formed in the space between her arched eyebrows.

Orsini smiled. "He said no, he would have no objection."

She visibly relaxed.

"Don't you want your wine?" Orsini asked. "You haven't touched it."

"Oh yes," she said, and took a small sip.

Orsini regarded her. "And you?" he asked.

"Yes?"

"What do *you* think, Lucy?" His tone had a touch of unintended annoyance.

She pursed her lips, closed her eyes, opened them, looked directly at him, and asked in carefully composed words, "Do you love me, Genaro?"

"Do you have to ask?" He sounded hurt. "Of course I love you. What do you think this is all about, huh? What do you think the last two months have been all about? Why are we here, in this restaurant? You have been listening, haven't you?"

She smiled and reached for his hand. "When Marco had his accident, I was sure I would never marry again. He was my strength. He took charge of my life. He was a big, beautiful man. Like you, Genaro. Then, when I got over my grief, I vowed I would never make myself vulnerable like that again. I've been doing well at it, Genaro. I've been a stronger person the past few years. Stronger, but not happier. You've changed that. You've changed me. You make me happy."

"I'm glad," he said. "That's my pleasure. To make you happy."

Her eyes glistened, not lubricated by tears, but brightened by the warmth she now felt. "You do, Genaro," she said. "You do make me happy."

"Well, then?" he said.

"Of course I will marry you. My God, I can't believe I said that. You're the only one I've met who could make me say that since Marco, may God bless his soul. I never believed I would even think that again. Now I say it. Yes, I will marry you."

Orsini waved for the waiter. "Corrado, a bottle of champagne. The best you have."

"Si, Signor Orsini."

"And Corrado," Orsini added loudly, "pour a glass for everybody in the room."

Other patrons looked up from their dinners. One couple understood what had happened and burst into spontaneous applause.

"To my *inamorata*," Orsini said when the champagne had been poured. "The lovely lady who will be my wife."

———

Much later that night, after taking Lucia to her town house on Twenty-eighth Street NW, in Georgetown—which would soon be his house, he mused—and sealing their engagement with a tender kiss at her front door, Orsini drove downtown to where two topless bars stood side by side. He entered one of them, waited until his eyes had adjusted to the darkness, then walked past the small stage where a naked young blond woman writhed in a pool of red spotlight. Orsini knocked at a door at the far end of the room. "Come in," he heard.

The club's owner, Jimmy "Too Tight" Titone, sat behind a battered, cluttered desk. Seated on a bar stool between file cabinets was a slight, orange-haired black man. Two tiny gold drop earrings dangled from his left ear. "Hello, Gerry," Titone said. "Hey, baby," the black man said. His name was Willie Johnson.

Orsini returned their greetings and pulled out a cigarette, lit it and said, "We got business, Willie."

"Yeah, baby, I know."

"You want a drink?" Too Tight asked. He was a fat, sloppy man with a four-day growth of beard. His eyes were watery and looked as though they might close at any moment. He was called Too Tight because he was cheap. His greatest pleasure came from not tipping, especially when service had been excellent.

"Later," Orsini said. "You got it, Willie?"

"Yeah." Willie reached into the inside of his suit jacket.

"Not in here," Too Tight said. "You know dat."

Orsini circumvented the desk and opened a door with a heavy bar across it that led to an alley. Willie followed him outside. "Gimme," Orsini said.

Willie handed him an envelope fat with cash. "You got the delivery tonight?" Orsini asked, placing the envelope into his jacket pocket.

"Yeah. No sweat."

"You got a little extra for me?"

Willie smiled as he pulled two small plastic bags of cocaine from another pocket and handed them to Orsini. Orsini opened one of the bags, poured a tiny mound of cocaine into his palm and inhaled. He'd taken a hit just an hour before in the car after dropping off Lucia. "Okay," Orsini said, pocketing the bags. "Everything okay with you?" he asked.

"Yeah, man. Everything right. Keep those spic motherfuckers away from me and everything cool."

"It'll stay that way. See you next week."

Too Tight had nodded off in his chair. "Wake up, you fat fuck," Orsini said. He laughed and slapped his hands on the desk. "You fall asleep, those whores outside will steal you blind. See you next week."

The blonde who'd been dancing when Orsini arrived had been replaced by another dancer. Orsini went to a table in the dark recesses of the room and ordered a drink from a waitress. A black dancer on her break came to the table and sat next to him. "Hello, poppa," she said, her hand casually brushing his crotch. "Buy me a drink?"

His hand clamped on her wrist. "Get lost," he said. She got up and slowly walked away, her hips moving in exaggerated defiance.

Things had changed for Orsini. It wasn't long ago that he would have bought her a drink and allowed her to do him there at the table. He liked black women, found something sexually special about them. He kept that penchant to himself, of course. His friends didn't share that preference. But these days, he stayed away from black whores. Instead of being sexually aroused by them, they sent him into a rage, which was to be expected after what Fionia had done to him. The thought of her caused his body to tense. His hands curled into fists. "Bitch!" he muttered. "Black fucking bitch."

The blond dancer took the seat vacated by the black girl. "Hi, Gerry," she said.

"Hey, babe." He waved for the waitress, who promptly returned with a bottle of "champagne" and two glasses. Orsini told her to bring him another vodka. He said to the blonde, whose name was Ginny, "I got a little something for you." He handed her one of the envelopes of coke, which she tucked into a skimpy red satin bra that strained to contain her white breasts.

"Thanks, Gerry," she said.

"Yeah. It's okay."

"You want . . . ?"

"Yeah." He held up his watch to read it in spillover from the spotlight. "I gotta get out of here. Do it quick, huh."

She lowered her head beneath the table. Five minutes later, Genaro Orsini, aka Gerry Orson, was in his car and headed for home.

The Following April

He wasn't enjoying this as much as he'd thought he would.

Paul Dante got another bourbon on the rocks—single barrel Blanton's; Santo Benedetti always stocked the best. He stuffed a buck into the bartender's glass and walked out onto a spacious, lushly landscaped patio.

It was one of those lovely evenings in early April, a touch of a chill in the gentle breeze. Enjoy it now, Dante knew. It would soon turn to a long summer of hot, soggy D.C. days. A trade-off was how most people viewed Washington's weather. You sweated in the summer, but you didn't have to shovel much snow in the winter. Just some ice storms which turned the streets into skating rinks, and sent the city's careless drivers banging into each other. All the government big shots were driven to work. When they had to drive themselves on the weekend, they didn't know what they were doing. What had a former President's wife said? That if her husband wasn't reelected and had to return to private life, she wouldn't get in a car with him because he hadn't driven in four years. Smart lady.

Dante was happy for Lucia, now Mrs. Genaro Orsini. They'd grown up together; she'd been a kind of adopted kid sister. No common blood between them, which meant it was all right to have had a short-term crush on her before she married her first husband, Marco.

Now they were friends although they'd grown apart, as adult friends often do as the years pass. She'd suffered the loss of Marco too long. When his car skidded one night on icy pavement and plowed into a light pole, they'd been married only two years and had begun to plan a family. At the funeral, she'd been a ghost of pasty white in a black suit, and had that faraway, empty look in her eyes that would become a trademark. Too much suffering; Italian opera suffering. Nobody was better at it.

She'd quickly grown introspective and introverted to an unhealthy degree. Too much time in church. Finding God again was one thing. Living with him in his house all day was not a life—unless you were a nun and married to him. Santo, her father, had kept Dante up to date on his daughter's activities, but there hadn't been many to report. She didn't go out much, and seemed never to be present when Dante visited Santo and his wife, Gina, at home.

But, for the past five months since her engagement, Dante had heard happier things about her. Angelo Andreotti told him that Lucia and her fiancé came to the restaurant often, and Dante heard that she'd made a few day trips with Orsini up to Atlantic City. She'd begun to open up since becoming engaged. Dante had seen evidence of it only last week when he bumped into her at Tower Records on George Washington University's campus. There was light in her eyes, and a new blush to her cheeks. And she was buying up compact-disc collections of Sinatra and Bennett, those newly packaged, digitally remastered, lifetime collections, hours and hours of music. A good sign.

Seeing her happy again made Dante happy. But now that he'd met Genaro Orsini—who was inside reveling in the lavish reception Santo was hosting for the newlyweds—Dante suffered mixed emotions. It was one of those elusive things, hard to pin down. He didn't like the guy. Just that simple. Something about his eyes, the cut of his mouth. Lips too big and fleshy. Arrogant. I usually read people pretty good, he thought, and I give Genaro Orsini a bad review.

"Will you please get off it, Paul," Barbara, his ex-wife, would say. "You've got a rotten opinion of everyone. Nobody's any good. Even me sometimes. It makes you a real pain in the ass to live with."

To which he would respond: "Not true, Babs. I'm a cop, remember? I know what people are like when they crawl up out of their holes and into the light."

Actually, he was an *ex*-cop, with a private investigation agency that gave him all the work he could handle, and a small bar and restaurant that wasn't big enough to ever make him rich, but that generated a pretty good cash flow, most of it from mobsters and cops who comprised his steady clientele. Still, there never seemed to be enough money. What's enough? he often asked himself. More than you have, was his stock answer.

He'd continued to send money to Barbara even though he had no obligation to do so under the terms of their divorce. Both of their daughters were out of school and finished with universities that had swallowed thousands like a kitchen disposal unit. But that was okay with him. He'd kill for his kids. Probably for Barbara too, if it came down to it.

He took another swallow of bourbon, one more deep draught of the sweet evening air, and rejoined the crowd inside.

There weren't as many people as had been at Lucia's wedding reception with Marco. For that one, Santo had hired the ballroom of the newly redone Shoreham Hotel, adjacent to Rock Creek Park near Embassy Row. This time, the guest list was smaller—only a couple of hundred—and the party was in Santo's home. Dante smiled as he looked around. "Home" didn't seem an adequate term for this place: barony, duchy, would have been more appropriate.

Santo had built the place in 1967, and almost immediately people started calling it the Benedetti White House. Business had boomed during the years since Vincent and Hoover had reached their understanding. Everything seemed to be working, and the Benedetti brothers had begun to think of themselves as mainstream. Why not? Vincent and the top cop had shaken hands on it. The brothers' new status demanded certain symbolism. For Santo, it was a large and luxurious home.

Living in such luxury was only possible, of course, because of the unique relationship the Benedettis had forged with Hoover and the government. Other family leaders, in other parts of the country, had to live in relatively modest surroundings in order to bolster their claims that their income was minimal. In New York, the media had had a field day with John Gotti, reputed head of the Gambino family, and the modest income he claimed on his income tax returns as a plumbing supplies salesman. His home was appropriately unpretentious to reflect his lower-middle-income salary.

But for Vincent and Santo Benedetti, it was an insult to think that despite their business acumen, they were forced to live a blue-collar lifestyle. They were entitled to the good life like any other successful entrepreneur and businessman prospering under the American dream. They'd worked hard, and their families had sacrificed much to help ensure their success. No, there would be no modest house in a development of tract homes. Their homes would make a statement about themselves. It was their right. Their tax returns reported large incomes from an import-export business of which Vincent was chairman and CEO, Santo the president. Enough to keep the IRS at bay. Mainstream. Except that the Benedetti brothers never complained about the taxes they had to pay, as most mainstream Americans do. They paid with what could almost be construed as a sense of pride. And, of course, with the knowledge that millions from their other business dealings would never be examined under the harsh light of an audit, not as long as the legion of highly paid accountants and lawyers did their jobs.

Which had been the subject of recent meetings. A breakdown in communications concerning the laundering of revenues from their gambling interests had come to the attention of one of many permanent IRS agents assigned to the Benedetti account. If true, it could be damaging to Vincent. The lawyers and bean-counters were working around the clock on that one.

To an Italian, Santo had told Dante back in '67, his home really *is* his castle. Dante could appreciate that. He'd just returned from Vietnam where even the castles were broken. The first person he'd gone to see after his mother and sister was Santo Benedetti.

Dante had grown up in the same Baltimore neighborhood where Santo had spent his childhood. Although they were twenty years apart in age, Santo had become friendly with the kid who came each day for milk and Stella D'oro cookies at his mother's house, while Dante's own mother went off to work to support Paul and his younger sister, Laura. Dante's father had dropped dead of a heart attack at a painfully young age, and the pension the family got from the longshoreman's union didn't cover the rent.

At first, Santo wondered what this ten-year-old kid named Paul Dante was all about. Although he would never admit it, he was slightly jealous of his own favored, youngest-son position with his mother. But Dante answered Santo's mother's need to have a child around her again, and Santo grew to enjoy the boy's brashness, toughness, and surprisingly analytical mind. Santo knew you needed all three to survive on the streets, just as you needed them to succeed in business. Any business. Including mob business.

When Dante was a teenager, Santo started bringing his daughter around with him on visits. Lucia was an only child, and Dante could see even then that she was the love of Santo's life. Her birth had been life-threatening for her mother, Gina, and although Santo had desperately wanted a son—an heir—he could not in good conscience risk his wife's health for one.

Lucia Benedetti was a beautiful child with Mediterranean looks. She had dark hair, black eyes, and olive skin. Even though she was younger—and a girl—the young Dante liked playing with her. She never displayed any childhood arrogance because of the monetary and social advantages she enjoyed over him: her father's position and power; that she *had* a father and he didn't; that this was *her* grandmother's house, *her* grandmother's yard.

Dante appreciated that. On the other hand, he knew that when push came to shove, Lucia could be a classic daddy's-little-girl. She had that innate female sense of how to manipulate her father, and to use him to manipulate others. Not often. Just now and then. Like any savvy daddy's-little-girl.

When Dante joined the Marines at seventeen, Santo initially was not pleased. "You're just getting old enough to where you can help your mother out, bring in some money," he'd said, his jaw set just this side of outright anger. "Now you run away from your responsibilities."

"I thought I was running *to* my responsibilities," Dante answered. "To my country. I thought you'd be proud."

"Your first responsibility is to your family, Paulie," Santo had said. "Don't ever forget that. Don't ever let anything get in the way of it."

Dante's face lost its muscle tone. "I'm sorry, Santo," he said, "but I gotta do what I gotta do. Our country is in trouble. The Commies are moving again, taking over in Asia. We got candy-ass pinko bastards here in the U.S. marching all over the place and making the rest of the world think we live in some kind of nuthouse. I wanna show the world we're not all fucking draft dodgers."

Santo saw by the look on the boy's face that he'd gone too far. The kid now had doubts about what he was doing; a kid going off to face an enemy's bullets shouldn't have doubts. "You're right, Paulie," Santo said. "You're doin' the right thing."

"I feel bad about my mother and Laura but . . ."

Santo slapped him on the arm. "Don't worry about them, kid. They'll be taken care of."

Santo drove Dante, his mother, and sister to the bus station for Dante's trip to Parris Island. Lucia came along too, and provided him with a going-away kiss that was different from those of Mrs. and Laura Dante. All the women cried, and Dante had to fight back his own tears. The last words said to him as he boarded the bus came from Santo: "Remember what I said, Paulie. Don't worry about things here. You worry about saving your ass over there so you come back. Right?"

"Right," Dante said. "Thanks."

Dante was no letter-writer, but he managed an occasional note to his mother. Her letters were more frequent and certainly longer. She often spoke in them of how kind Santo had been. There was never a problem with necessities. Santo had given her a used Ford Grenada that the business was getting rid of—"It was just heading for the compactor," he told her when she protested his generosity. Far from being grist for any hydraulic press, the car had been kept in immaculate condition by the driver in charge of it. The engine purred.

Santo even saw to it that Mrs. Dante and Laura were included on the guest list for Benedetti social functions. Once, he sent by messenger two center-section seats for a Sinatra concert at the Kennedy Center, an Italian-American fund-raiser for Catholic charities.

When Dante won his Silver Star for taking out a Vietcong machine-gun emplacement, and a Purple Heart for having his right leg ground to chop meat by shrapnel, he received his only letter from Santo: ". . . well, Paulie, if you went there to do yourself proud," it said in part, "you've done it. We're all proud of you. I'm sure your country is proud of you. Now get your ass home in one piece."

When Dante was discharged and returned home, Santo suggested there was a future in the Benedetti family business for a man of Paul's intelligence and guts. It was apparent that Dante had become a man in Southeast Asia. The gangly kid was now a strapping, imposing figure, his six-foot physique filled out and developed the old-fashioned way—hard work and hard knocks.

Dante respectfully declined Santo's offer of a job. While he'd been turned down by the Baltimore Police Department before signing up for Nam, he was now a sought-after recruit for Washington's Metropolitan Police Department, and was excited at the prospect. He also knew his decision had the potential to create a delicate situation with Santo. He had no illusions about how the Benedetti family made its living.

But Dante reasoned he'd be a cop in Washington, not Baltimore. As far as he knew, the Benedettis did little business in D.C. Vincent, the family head, and Santo only ventured to the District for social events, or an occasional meeting with a government mover-and-shaker.

His concerns were relieved when Santo openly supported his decision.

"Just make your mother proud," he'd said. "Like you did in the Marines. You want to be a cop, Paulie? Be a good one."

———

Dante drifted back to the bar, one of four in the main room, ordered another Blanton's, and surveyed the room. It was enormous in a house that was enormous, a replica of the great manor houses of Tuscany. It was rumored that it had cost Santo four million, even *with* his connections in the construction business.

The corners of the room were dominated by Doric columns resting on a floor of Carrara marble. The columns rose to a vaulted ceiling decorated with frescoes that might have been stolen from the Sistine Chapel. ("The artist is one of the best Renaissance art restorers alive today," Santo had told Dante when he first visited the home.) The room was so large that Santo and Gina had had trouble finding furniture big enough to occupy the space. A huge mahogany table that seated thirty-six which ordinarily dominated the center of the room had been carefully disassembled and removed to the basement, replaced by twenty round tables from the area's oldest and most coveted catering service, Avignon Frères.

With the house packed for the wedding of Lucia and Genaro Orsini, the room appeared to finally be serving the function for which it had been created. It accommodated the large crowd nicely.

A twelve-piece contingent from the fashionable Gene Donati society orchestra, Washington's Lester Lanin, played "Just in Time" as Dante made his way across the room to where Santo and his new son-in-law held court with a knot of guests and family members.

". . . women like Lucy are rare in today's world," Orsini was saying. "I feel very lucky. You just don't find a woman with old-fashioned values anymore, somebody who'll keep a home for a man and let *him* go out and bust his—rear end every day for the woman he loves. Am I right?"

They nodded.

"You also don't find many men like you, Gerry," Santo chimed in. He noted Dante's arrival. "For anybody who don't know Paul Dante, let me introduce you."

He went around the circle reeling off names and an occasional business affiliation, few of which registered on Dante; maybe he'd better go lighter on the bourbon, he decided. He did notice that Vincent Benedetti, the family's leader and senior member, did not look well. He'd heard rumors of IRS pressure on Vincent; deep, dark circles beneath his eyes lent credence to the gossip. Vincent hadn't smiled much during the wedding of his goddaughter, a further indication that he was not at ease in his world. Of course, Vincent was getting old,

Dante reasoned. Maybe the family head was simply growing weary of wondering how much longer he had.

Earlier in the evening, Dante had asked Santo about another guest, a willowy redhead who stayed pretty much to herself. "Julia Croce," Santo had told him. "She's a dancer. Got a dancer's set of gams." He was about to lead Dante to her when someone spirited him away.

"Anyway," Santo continued to the group surrounding him and Orsini, "Paulie here is probably the closest thing I've ever had to a son. That is, until today." He slapped his son-in-law on the back.

Dante studied Orsini's face, whose expression indicated he wasn't pleased with being compared to Dante. Dante didn't take much pleasure from the comparison, either.

"Well, you know how *I* feel about family," Orsini said when Santo had finished. "Family's sacred, huh, even when you open it up to take in an outsider."

"Well, you're not an outsider anymore," Dante said to Orsini.

"I wasn't talking about myself," Orsini said, adding a laugh for effect. A stage laugh.

"Everyone, please, enjoy yourselves," Santo said. "My house, the music, the food, the booze—all yours. Go on, dance. That's what I pay the band for. Since when do musicians get paid so goddamn much? They look like they're having fun on my money. Come on, get out there and shake it. Give me my money's worth."

Dante debated whether to stay. He was alone and vaguely uncomfortable with that. He turned to leave and was face-to-face with Julia Croce, the redheaded dancer, who stood like a lonely pedestal in an empty space.

"Paul Dante," he said, extending his hand.

"I know," she said. "Mr. Benedetti told me." Her look was firm, but not hard. Thoughtful, pale blue eyes were friendly.

Dante looked down at legs protruding from beneath a short green cocktail dress. "Santo is right," he said. "You have a dancer's gams."

"Gams?" She laughed. "I thought that expression went out with World War Two."

"It comes from *gamba,* the Italian word for 'leg.'"

"I minored in Italian," she said.

"I majored in war," he answered. "Vietnam. You weren't one of those women sticking flowers into National Guard gun barrels, were you?"

"'Fraid so."

Dante grinned at her honesty. "Well," he said, "time heals all wounds, like they say. It did mine."

"You wearing some scars I should know about, Mr. Dante?"

"Not unless we get a lot more friendly."

"Time . . . opens up endless possibilities."

"In that case," he said, placing his hand on the small of her back and ushering her in the direction of the bar, "you'll let me buy you a drink."

"They're on the house."

"It's an expression."

"Of what?"

"You don't give much, do you?"

"Rémy," she said. "Neat."

Drinks in hand, they stood to one side of the bar. "I don't know many people here," Julia said. "Lucia and Mr. Benedetti. That's about it."

"I don't know that many myself," Dante said. "I've known Santo for more than thirty years, but not many of his business associates and friends. He was like a stepfather to me a long time ago, and Lucia was like a sister. I've never gotten to know Santo's brother much. We come from the same beginnings, but our lives took different directions."

"Mr. Benedetti told me you were a private investigator, Mr. Dante."

"Call me Paul."

"And?"

"Yeah, I own a private investigations business . . . and a bar."

"Interesting combination."

"My mother got me used to eating."

Orsini walked by with a group of capos from the upper echelons of the Benedetti family businesses, glad-handing, slapping backs, playing the groom. Dante watched him for a moment, then said to Julia, "Through those double doors is the nicest patio you'll ever see. At least it's the biggest. I staked it out earlier."

"What are we waiting for?" Her smile was coquettish.

They sat on a marble bench and he drifted into telling her about himself. ". . . I bought this bar with a couple of friends after I left the MPD. They were silent investors. Cops can't own bars. We bought the joint because we used to go there for beers after shift, and because the place was about to go bust. We changed the name to Cuffs 'cause that's what it used to clamp on our paychecks. I bought the other two guys out pretty quick. I was in a better position to run the day-to-day business, and I needed an office for my PI work. Anyway, the romance of being in the bar business had already worn off for them. Hanging out in a joint is one thing, balancing the books is another. My wife never liked the whole idea of me owning a joint any more than she liked me being a cop. It was one of the nails in our marital coffin."

"I'm sorry."

"Ancient history. And the true love in your life?" Dante asked.

She took a sip of her cognac. "My husband was just your garden-variety shithead," she replied.

He didn't expect her to be so direct. "You a feminist?" he asked.

"I'm a female. That makes me a feminist."

"Go on," he sighed.

"Met him in college. Married me for my . . . 'gams.' He was going to create all kinds of big showcases for my talents, write musicals and bring me to Broadway. I was young. I liked the sound of it. Showcase. Musicals. Broadway. Heavy stuff." She took another delicate sip. "He's on his third set of gams. That helps. I mean, I know I wasn't the only jerk to fall for his line."

Dante was not displeased with her story. "Jerk?" he said. "You? I don't think so."

"We learn from experience."

45

A burst of laughter filtered out to the patio, but for Dante, the wedding now seemed as if it were going on in another country. "How do you know Santo?" he asked.

"Actually, I met him through Lucia. She took a course in interpretive jazz dance I taught for a year at U of Maryland's continuing ed program. Lucia and I hit it off. She even helped out in the dance theater I've been running in the black community. Mr. Benedetti is one of my benefactors. His support has been important, crucial actually. The kids there need something to show them life is more than crack vials and Uzis. It's amazing how they glorify the bastards who ruin their lives. One of the worst, a Jamaican named Mambo Jenks, was gunned down right outside the theater last week. They called him a kingpin. Nothing kingly about scum like that."

"I read about it," Dante said. More accurately, he'd heard Santo talk about Jenks and the threat he'd posed to a project in which Santo was interested. Now, he understood.

Dante could see by goosebumps on Julia's arms that she was feeling the chill of the waning April day. They went back inside.

The music died in a dissonant chord as Santo raised his hand and took the center of the floor. "I haven't made any speeches yet. I left that to the best man. But now it's time for me to say something personal."

He drained his glass and handed it to a bodyguard, who crouched low to stay out of a video cameraman's line-of-sight. "This is a very special evening for my daughter," Santo continued, "and that makes it special for me. Tonight, I welcome a new member of my family, Mr. Genaro Orsini."

He paused for the cheers and applause.

"Family is important to life. It is important to everyone in this room. It is especially important to me. I visited my mother, rest her soul, every week, usually two, three times, in that house in Baltimore she wouldn't leave until she passed away. I've been in business with my brother, Vincent, since we counted nickels from our newspaper routes. And I've built everything I own so that I could pass it on to my daughter, and to the grandchildren she'll give me one day." He paused and smiled. "With a little bit of help from my new son-in-law, of course."

Everyone laughed. "Gerry is a man of old-fashioned values. He treasures the things that count. I expect him to treasure my Lucia, who's always been a treasure to her mother and me. Please welcome my new member of the family."

The bodyguard raced across the floor with a fresh drink for Santo, which he raised high above his head. "*Salute,*" he said. "*Salute,* Genaro and Lucia."

The crowd responded with a chorus of "*Salute,* Genaro and Lucia." A beaming Orsini walked halfway to where his father-in-law stood and took an abbreviated bow. "Thank you," he said. "Thank you very much. I love you all." He was obviously out of words. "Thank you," he repeated as he retreated into the crowd.

"The formalities are over," Santo said. "Everyone should enjoy what's left of the evening, and drive safely home."

Together, Dante and Julia Croce went to wish Lucia the best—he felt like they were a couple—and to drop their envelopes into her white silk bag. She looked radiant in a wedding dress that had cost twenty thousand dollars. The big smile was back.

"Thank you, Julia," Lucia said. "Thank you so much. Now I can dance again."

"You know where to find me," Julia said, kissing the bride on her cheek.

"And Paulie, look at you in that tux. You're a knockout. Shoulda grabbed you while I had the chance. Thanks for being here, big brother."

"I would have missed this, Lucia? Come on. You know I live to see you smile."

"Don't you just love this guy?" Lucia said to Julia.

They were edged out by the next well-wisher.

"You didn't answer her," Dante said as they waited for a maid to retrieve their coats.

"The question was rhetorical."

"Don't use big college words around me."

"Okay. To answer the question. She said 'love.' That takes me longer to get to. At least the second time around."

"But it's lovelier. That's a song."

She broke into a laugh.

"You set me up," he said. "A straight man. Woman."

The laugh turned into a giggle.

"Broads," Dante said as he helped her into her coat. He was sorry he'd used the term.

"The hard-boiled cop," she said. "Well, it's not something a ballerina gets every day."

"You need a lift?" he asked when they were outside.

"I've got my car, but thanks for asking. Call me." She took a card from her purse and handed it to him.

"Businesslike," he said.

"It's my home number. That's my calling card, not my business card. One of the refinements of a classical life. But if business is more convenient—" She wrote a second number on the back of the card.

He took her hand. "Okay," he said, "enough sparring. Meeting you was the highlight of the evening." Feeling the comment might be insulting to the bride, he added, "The highlight of a very special evening for Lucia."

"Me, too," she said.

He walked her to her blue Toyota Camry.

"How 'bout you buy me dinner at Cuffs some night?" she said. "You do trust the food there, don't you?"

"Sometimes. It's nothing fancy."

"No problem. Sometimes I like to slum it, get down and dirty."

"Thanks," he said. "How about tonight?"

"Too full of wedding cake. Another time." She kissed him politely on the cheek and he watched her drive off.

On the way back to D.C. and home, Dante's thoughts were a jumble. He liked having met Julia, but was not happy about Santo's new member of the family. Orsini continued to give him a bad feeling. He tried to explain it away as jealousy, but that didn't play. He loved Lucia like a sister, never as a potential lover.

Let it go, he thought. Lucia is a lovely girl; what's not to love? She could soften a stone. And if she couldn't, anyone who treated her badly would have to deal with her father, something Dante didn't wish on his worst enemy.

But there was also a vague recognition factor about Orsini that bothered him. He hated it when he knew he knew something, but couldn't remember what it was he knew—or where he knew it from. A sign of aging? The first thing that goes is the memory. And the legs.

Dante carefully maneuvered his Buick into the alley that ran alongside Cuffs, a shoehorn fit for the big car. One of his patrons once suggested he get a little Honda, but Dante had looked him in the eye and said, "I don't buy Oriental cars. Jap. Korean. None of them. Their cousins in Nam tried their best to kill me. I buy American cars only. If you want to drink here, you'll do the same."

"You're just kiddin', Paulie, right?" the customer said.

Dante didn't answer, and never saw the man again. Not the best way to build a business and keep customers happy. Politics, religion, and bars don't mix. Why should he care what people thought, as long as they paid their tab and didn't cause trouble? Because he was— hardheaded. That's the word he preferred to describe his behavior. All the others were worse.

He let himself in the back door, which opened directly into his office. The place smelled damp, of old food fumes, cigarettes, and sour beer. He liked that smell. His ex-wife hated it. He pulled his bow tie loose and went into the restaurant where the bar was standing-room only with off-duty cops and wiseguys, frustrated and disenchanted house-wives, and middle-aged cheaters hitting on them. The dinner crowd was gone. It had been a slow food night, the bartender told him, which accounted for the sullen look on the face of Sol the waiter. Less dinners served, less tips. Of course, Sol was never happy no matter how many people came into the place. Too many years on his feet serving pastrami on rye in New York Jewish delis before moving to D.C. to live with his widowed sister, and ending up waiting tables at Cuffs. Sol was fat and sweated a lot. His tuxedos, always purchased at local thrift shops, looked like lumps had been sewn into the fabric. A few remaining strands of hair dyed black were brought up from the back and pasted onto his dimpled bald head. He could be short with customers—even nasty at times—but they seemed to enjoy his dour sense of humor and caustic quips.

In contrast, the waitress, Lucette, was unfailingly bubbly. Short, pert, and blond, she worked to support her teenage daughter and an old dog she treated like a baby. What Dante liked most about her was her French accent. She came to the bar and ordered, "One Heineken, one Beef-eee-teur." Dante smiled, said to her, "What was that order?" She laughed and repeated it: "Beef-eee-teur." She knew he loved hearing her say it. Nice lady. Gives the joint a touch of Continental class, he often thought.

He looked around the place that had been his for all these years. Getting ratty at the edges. The black vinyl pad along the edge of the bar was slit in places, rubbed to the wood in others. He'd been meaning to have the canopy out front replaced but hadn't gotten around to it. You could still read "Cuffs" on it. That was good enough.

The place could use new chairs, too. And tables. And glasses and dishes and forks and spoons. But nobody seemed to notice except him. Aside from the occasional tourist couple who wandered in, his clientele was made up of regulars, none of whom was there to write a review for *Food and Wine* magazine. The place was worn but comfortable. No pretensions. Drinks poured from the right bottle, the food straight ahead and lots of it on the plate, the trios he booked now and then willing to play dumb songs for the musical tin ears. He smiled. He liked it just the way it was.

Dante knew most of the people at the bar and considered drinking with some of them. Instead, he begged off invitations, took a bourbon back to the office, drank it, suddenly felt exhausted and headed upstairs to his apartment that occupied the second floor of the small building. What a life, he thought, looking at himself in a mirror over a large dresser. Some days, he considered himself handsome, in shape. He'd never had a problem attracting women, who seemed to find his muscular six-feet-two-inch body appealing. When he was younger, he considered his prominent hooked nose to be a detriment, like acne. But as he aged, he grew into his nose. Now it seemed to enhance his appeal to members of the opposite sex, like a penis on a face, he sometimes mused. The nose went with him, was as distinctive as the heavy brows that hooded dark, sensual eyes—bedroom eyes, he was told.

Most days, he was happy with the way he looked and who he was. This night, however, as he viewed his image in the glass, he felt overweight and ugly, beyond his prime and on the downhill side of his life.

He'd feel different in the morning. With a vision of Julia replacing the floaters in his eyes, he plopped on the bed and fell asleep, a tuxedo for pajamas.

The wedding party at Santo Benedetti's house was breaking up. Santo was stationed at the front door with Gina wishing guests a safe journey home. Across the street, two FBI agents in a nondescript car watched the exit of the invited. Earlier, they'd noted the license plates of every automobile that had arrived for the event. Now, yawning, they wanted it to be over so they too could go home.

Behind the house, Vincent Benedetti stood in the six-car garage. A dark green Ford Mustang containing two Benedetti soldiers—Joe Bellisimo, known as "Joey Balls," and Jake Cohen, "The Ape"—sat idling. Joey Balls was a compulsive talker and giggler; Cohen didn't like doing jobs with him because of it. The Ape was irrefutably the strongest man in the Benedetti crime family, a brute of a man with a shaved head, tiny black eyes, and with what seemed to be an inability to smile, as though the gene that controlled that human trait had been missing at his birth.

"You do him if you can," Vincent said. "If there's people around, forget it. No scenes."

Jake and Joey Balls stared into Vincent's sad face. They had to assume he meant what he was saying, that they should go through with their job only if it could be done without fuss. Both men knew that if sent by the family head to kill someone, to fail was almost certainly an invitation to their own funerals. But they were off the hook on this one. If he meant what he was saying.

Vincent read their thoughts. A hint of a smile crossed his waxen face. "It's okay. Do it if it looks right. Here." He handed Cohen a fat envelope. "Ten grand. If you do it, take off for a coupla weeks. Florida. Ditch the car and go someplace. All right?"

They nodded.

Vincent stepped back and Joey Balls drove the Mustang from the garage and up a long gravel driveway leading to the front gates. "Look at those fuckers," he said as he spotted the FBI agents across the street. "Fuckin' numbnuts, huh?" he said, giggling. The Ape was stone-faced. "Sit on your fuckin' ass all night. Some fuckin' way to live, huh? Fuckin' assholes." He was tempted to flash his middle finger at the agents but contained the impulse.

They drove to the Adams-Morgan section of Washington where the bars and restaurants were open and doing big business, a diverse and lively ethnic mix of residents and visitors spilling out onto the streets. Joey turned into a narrow, poorly lighted street and stopped in front of a hydrant. Across the street was a small store with two bare bulbs barely illuminating a red and yellow sign that promised groceries, cigarettes and newspapers.

"That's it. Right?" Joey asked.

"Yeah. That's it."

"Maybe he's not in there."

"We'll wait," said the Ape.

"Fuck wait. Maybe we go in, find the fucker in the back and waste him. What the fuck we got to hang around for all night? I say we go in and look."

"Shut up, Joey," Cohen said, his eyes fixed on the storefront.

"Hey, fuck you too, you Jew bastard."

Cohen didn't respond, at least not verbally. He was thinking that he wanted to kill Joey Balls, break his arms and legs, puncture him a hundred times with a pick, burn him with a blowtorch a little at a time. Instead, he sat silently and waited. As he'd been told to do by Vincent.

Joey talked incessantly as they waited—about not minding balling Lucia himself; about baseball; about the racetrack; about his brother who was a homosexual in San Francisco; about a series of irritants to Jake Cohen.

"You know what I hate about these spic motherfucker drug dealers," Joey said. "They got no balls. I mean, you and me, we go up to a guy face-to-face, huh? We go up and put the fuckin' gun in his mouth and take him out. These cocksuckers, they stand in the middle a the fuckin' street with a machine gun and do everybody. Kids. Women. Whoever's there. Fuckin' cowards, man. You understand what I say, Ape? I mean, these fuckin'—"

"Shut up."

A man emerged from the store. He was short and squat, and wore a white suit, white topcoat, and white Panama hat. Light from the bare bulbs reflected off gold chains around his neck. He was accompanied by a big black man wearing a luminescent chartreuse sweat suit whose hair had been sculpted into a high bush, like a fancy hedge in an English country garden. They looked up and down the street, then walked in a direction that would take them to the corner where the nightlife was in full swing.

"Guy looks like the fuckin' Ajax cleaning man," Joey muttered.

"Let's go," Jake said, opening his door.

"How you want to do it?" Joey asked.

"I'll take the nigger. You do the spic."

"Yeah, yeah, okay, baby."

Joey and Jake walked quickly on the opposite side of the street. They were about to cross when the Hispanic man and his black friend stepped into another small store. "When they come out," the Ape said. They went to the store and stood on opposite sides of the doorway.

Minutes later, the black man in the sweat suit stepped out to the sidewalk, followed immediately by the white Panama hat. The Ape moved first. He wrapped his powerful right forearm around the black's neck and jerked hard. The sound of breaking bones punctuated the air. Joey Balls moved, too. He rammed the silencer on his revolver up under the Hispanic's chin and squeezed the trigger. His head exploded, sending bone, blood and brain everywhere. Joey was covered with it. "Shit, man," he muttered as the two victims fell to the sidewalk. "I got the cocksucker's brains all over me."

The Ape ran across the street to the Mustang, followed by an angry Joey Balls who continued to curse the slime that covered him. "Move," Cohen said. Joey started the car and whipped away from the curb. An hour later, after dumping the car in a parking lot at National Airport and checking into an airport motel, Joey Balls showered while the Ape did pushups on a stained yellow nylon carpet. In the morning, they would be first-class passengers on the first flight to Florida.

V

The Next Morning

Paul Dante woke to the sound of Julio banging around downstairs in Cuffs's kitchen. Julio—Dante's half-conscious brain fixed on his cook's name. "Me and Hooo-lee-oh down by the schoolyard." Once he started a day with that line from the Paul Simon song, he'd never get it out of his head.

He'd often awakened to the sounds of Julio rattling pots and pans and wondered if Salvadoreans were forced to learn to sleep through a lot of noise when they were growing up, resulting in a different response to clamor than people in the civilized world. Dante had an image of villages where the cocks crowed at dawn, the pigs squealed right after that, the children raised hell on the heels of the pigs, and mothers banged on pots around the campfire before the rest of the tribe opened its eyes.

He glanced at his watch. It was ten; Julio was getting his act together for lunch which, after all, was one of the things Dante paid him for. Monday *was* a workday, even for PI's with not much in the way of current paying assignments.

He dropped his legs over the side of the bed and pushed himself up to vertical. He stood motionless until his knees were locked and he was sure he'd remain upright, then headed into the bathroom.

He had a fleeting hope that the face in the mirror was not his. But facts were facts. He stuck out his tongue and wondered why it was so white. His mouth was as dry as sandpaper, and his brain played host to a revolving headache: now above his right eyebrow, then to his right temple, around to the base of his skull, then into his left eye-socket and around again. He decided he liked bourbon too much and needed to cut back. But that was a pledge he always made on mornings like this. It would be broken by lunchtime. Two buffered aspirins would help, and toothpaste added a momentary freshness to his mouth and color to his tongue.

Julia.

He reached into the shower stall and turned on the hot water, waited for it to come up and mixed in the cold. He kept it hotter than usual; hot water usually helped with the pain in his brain. He got in, drew the curtain, and made sure the bottom of it was inside the tub so there would be no rain on Julio's grill this morning.

Julia.

What was *that* all about? It was one of those wavelength things. You don't go to the wedding of someone who is almost family and expect to pick up a sensational-looking redheaded dancer with world-class gams. He grinned at the term. Good, old-fashioned word for legs. How had his former partner on MPD defined female legs? "Perfect legs, Paulie. Feet on the bottom, pussy on top." Gams were more fitting for Julia. How nice.

What he liked about the way they'd met was the spontaneity of it. They didn't have anything in common. This lady had college degrees. She was a classically trained ballerina. She taught college, ran a theater group. The last time he'd been to the theater was for *West Side Story*—summer stock in Pennsylvania. He'd never even seen a ballet. Ballet dancers were all fags, weren't they? All the women lesbians? He winced.

He hadn't been all that interested in finishing high school, except that the Marines insisted upon it. He'd ended up living over a bar—admittedly a bar he owned—where, as he soaped his body, an illegal alien was in the kitchen separating clumps of ground-up steak into raw material for today's bacon cheeseburgers. Julia probably had one of those neat-as-a-pin apartments with natural wood floors, Oriental throw rugs and prints from modern artists on every wall. He didn't even want to think about the record collection. This was ridiculous. But there was this stirring in his groin. I'm not completely dead, he thought, and let the hot water play on what had quickly blossomed into a full-fledged erection.

He stepped out of the shower and moved to the sink. He'd always considered his apartment to be large enough. But this morning he felt cramped. Like everything else in his life. A life stuffed into three rooms? This Julia Croce was not someone whose life would be cramped. What little he knew of her said "open," "wide vistas," "try things." Was that what yesterday had been all about? Was she looking to try him? A diary experience? Lots of laughs with her female professor friends?

He toweled a circle in the middle of the steamy mirror and looked at himself. He'd forgotten to shave. The brain wasn't working. His morning sequence was out of whack. Dry his hair now, or shave first? Do the hair first, Paulie, to keep it from drying on its own into an odd configuration. This confusion over simple things was what happened when he tried to break the rules and *think* in the morning. He dried his hair, then shaved. It was the right thing to do, as the Quaker Oats commercial preached.

Even though they were very different, their conversation had been easy. Even the word games had worked. He'd felt from the beginning that they'd clicked. At least that was his assessment. Human "reads" were his business. His instincts about people, male and female, were usually correct. Be honest, he told himself. He'd had his problems with some female reads, not on cases but when it got personal. Barbara had been a misread. Not that his ex-wife was a terrible person. To the contrary, she was a hell of a woman, maybe too good for him and, in the final analysis, *not* for him.

He pulled on a pair of tan wool slacks and slipped a teal cotton crewneck sweater over his head, repositioned hair he'd displaced in the process, then yanked on socks and got into his loafers. He'd call her today. Things hadn't been going all that great lately. What was one more shoot-down?

Shelly, who managed Cuffs for Dante, was sitting at the bar sipping a cup of coffee and reading the *Post* when Dante arrived downstairs. "Another hit on a dealer," she said, not looking up as Dante poured himself a cup from the twenty-four-cupper Julio had placed on the bar. He added a generous allotment of milk; Julio had that Latin American affection for coffee strong enough to strip metal.

"Another friendly neighborhood territorial chief?" Dante asked, sitting next to her.

"Looks like it," Shelly replied. "Spilled his brains all over the sidewalk."

Dante took the paper from her and read the article. "Interesting," he said.

"If you get off on that kind of thing."

"No, interesting the way it was done. Right out of a wiseguy movie. No ten thousand rounds from a semiautomatic and blood and guts everywhere, the way spic dealers like to do it. No Colombian neckties. This was no run-of-the-mill spic family squabble, Shelly. Somebody's delivering a message. What's with lunch reservations today?"

"Good. Sixteen people from the bank across the street. Somebody's birthday."

"Love them birthdays. That's it?"

"A few more. Paunchy executives taking their young daughters out to lunch. Touching."

"Profitable. They usually buy champagne—to toast their daughters. Right?"

"Of course. You ever consider running a brothel?"

"All the time. Excuse me, Shell. I have to make a call." He poured a second cup. Julio's black ooze was actually helping his head. "You do know, Shelly, that I appreciate the job you do here. I mean, you manage the place real good. I'm not here a lot and . . ."

"I appreciate the vote of confidence, Paulie." She kissed him on the cheek. A few years ago, it would have been a tongue in the mouth, but that phase of their relationship was over and gone. He considered the silver blonde with the voluptuous figure sitting next to him to be a good friend. Sometimes, he considered her his only friend. She put up with a lot, including a former husband doing serious time for beating her close to death, and for sexually abusing their three kids. Good people this Shelly was. He looked at her jutting breasts beneath a clinging black jersey dress and remembered. "I have to make this call," he said, heading for the office where he retrieved Julia Croce's calling card from the corner of the desk and picked up the phone. He flipped the card over and dialed the work number she'd written on the back. A young woman's voice answered: "Department of Drama and Dance."

"Miss Croce, please."

"Professor Croce is teaching her modern dance class, but I can leave a message in her box."

Professor Croce? "Sure," he said. "Paul Dante. Tell her Paul Dante called."

He started to spell his last name but the young woman finished it for him. "I read the *Inferno*," she said.

"You know my phone number, too?" he asked.

"Of course not."

He gave it to her and hung up. I'm in over my head, he thought.

He was nursing one of Julio's omelettes ("and hold back on the hot sauce") when Julia returned his call. "Sorry to disturb you at school," he said.

"No problem. I enjoy a break in the routine." It was the same easy, unaffected voice of the night before which put Dante at ease. He felt like a high school kid with terminal zits calling for his first date. "Look," he said, "I know this is sudden, but I find at my age that I don't like to wait for things unless there's a good reason."

"Paul," she said, "I've got to get to my next class. Are you asking me out for dinner? I accept."

"How about tonight?"

"Sure."

"Shall I pick you up?"

"I'm a big girl. I can find my way to Cuffs."

They agreed upon a time. He hung up and went into the kitchen. "Jesus," he growled at Julio, who was precooking burgers on the grill. "This menu is so fucking limited. Don't you ever try anything new?"

"How many things can you cook with chop meat, chief?" Julio answered, an infectious smile on his face.

Dante studied the menu. "How about some pasta?" he said. "Got anything you can add to a red sauce?"

"You got a bimbo coming in tonight. Right? You always want some fancy shit on the menu when you got a bimbo coming for dinner."

"So what?" Dante answered. "I'm sick of this menu anyway. Maybe if it had more variety we'd have more customers."

"Okay," Julio said, dropping more thick, juicy burgers on the grill. "I'll make you something special. Some kinda pasta. Okay? Now leave me alone. I got work to do."

Dante shuffled papers and inventoried the few phone messages he'd had hanging since Friday. All in all, there wasn't a lot going on. He had an ongoing surveillance job, but the client had asked him to back off for a few days because the target was getting nervous, which was okay with Dante because the client was not that good a payer. He tried to pick and choose his clients. He was a one-man agency. Take on a deadbeat and you spin lots of wheels without a brass ring.

It wasn't too long ago that Dante had built his agency into one of D.C.'s largest, with as many as two hundred men contracted out as uniformed security guards. He'd moved into a real office on K street and had a real secretary who called him Mr. Dante. But the bottom fell out when the D.C. city government reneged on a contract and failed to pay, citing a slew of nit-picking clauses that tied him up in court for months. It put him back into his one-man operation which, all things considered, was just as well. Handling payroll wasn't his thing and he knew it. Now, it was simpler. His PI work was paid out of the pockets of jealous husbands or wives, or businessmen convinced they were being ripped off by their partners.

Occasionally, he still served the D.C. bureaucracy, like the case of the Army captain who worked in a sensitive intelligence job. His superiors were convinced he was passing secrets to somebody. The brass figured the captain was too savvy for Army types to tail, so Dante got the assignment through a friend—of a friend—and it had gone pretty well. He documented the captain's erratic nighttime activities:

midnight meetings in sleazy hotels, an occasional rendezvous with a car outside the city, things like that. Those incidents didn't prove the guy was a traitor, but they weren't destined to support a call for a Medal of Honor, either.

Dante enjoyed that job. He was on it a month. The only problem was he was still waiting for a check—something to do with the funds to pay him not coming out of conventional channels. He didn't care what channels they came out of. "Give me a fucking break," he'd told his Army client the last time he'd called in search of a check. "You work for the fucking government. Tell 'em to print a few more bills."

He was at the bar nursing a seltzer with lime and talking early-season baseball with his bartender, Pete, when Julia arrived. She wore a long-sleeved kelly green cotton shirt that matched her eyes, a pair of form-fitting jeans, and plain black pumps. Her red hair had a wind-blown look to it that hadn't just happened. Her face was lighted with the warm smile of the previous night. She kissed him on the cheek. "Nice to see you again," she said as he assisted her onto a stool next to his.

It was seven o'clock, and slow. The Happy Hour crowd had emptied out, and it looked like the dinner crowd would be a late one. Shelly had grouped six couples at adjacent tables so Lucette and Sol wouldn't have to expend excess energy serving them.

Dante led Julia to a table in a corner of the room away from the others. Shelly tossed them a smirk when she saw how far away they were sitting.

"Ignore her," Dante said, noting Julia's raised eyebrows. "She was born with a smirk on her face."

Shelly trooped over with two menus, pulled napkins she'd turned into cloth tulips from the water glasses and placed them in their laps with exaggerated flourish. "Need a few minutes?" she asked.

"Yeah, sweetie, thanks." Dante knew she hated to be called by anything but her name.

"Julio has prepared a special pasta dish," he told Julia when

Shelly was gone. "It's not on the menu but it's one of his seafood-in-cream-sauce numbers. They're usually edible."

"Hoolio?" she said, exaggerating the H. "As in me and Hoolio down by the schoolyard?"

"Not you, too," Dante said. "I was just getting that goddamn line out of my head."

"Can Julio cook?" she asked.

"Of course not." He motioned Lucette to the table. "Two pasta specials," he said. "And tell Julio to wash his hands before he touches the fish."

Julia laughed.

"You said you wanted to slum it," Dante said. "Welcome to the slums."

As they waited for their food, two attractive young women took seats at the bar. They were regulars, secretaries from a neighborhood personnel placement firm. One, a stunning brunette wearing a sinfully short leather skirt, took the long route to the ladies' room in order to pass Dante and Julia. "Two-timing me again, Paulie?" she said, pausing at the table.

"Julia, this is Lisa."

"I don't give up without a fight," Lisa said.

"How admirable," Julia answered.

"Does this mean we're finished, Paulie?" Lisa asked.

"To be finished, you gotta have a beginning," he replied. He picked up his coffee spoon and pointed it at her. "Beat it," he said, "before I have to send you to your room."

"Oooh, I love it when you talk that way," she said, wiggling toward the restrooms.

"A perk of management?" Julia asked.

"Not in her case," he said.

"Other cases?"

"A few. Bogart set things up for all of us in *Casablanca*."

The pasta arrived and Dante insisted Julia taste it first in case Julio had spiked it with some Central American bitter-root. She pronounced it fit for human consumption, and he had to agree. He ate with that renewed vigor that comes when you've just gotten past a hangover. Or, as comic Joe E. Lewis had put it, "The problem with people who don't drink is that when they get up in the morning, it's as good as they're going to feel all day."

"I don't know how he does it," Dante said, mopping up the last of the fish sauce with a hunk of Italian bread. "If you went into the kitchen, you'd swear he had no idea what he was doing."

"I waitressed in a Chinese restaurant while I was in school," Julia said. "Since then, I make it a point *never* to go into a restaurant kitchen. Some things are better left unknown."

When Lucette brought their coffees, Dante asked Julia if she wanted an after-dinner drink.

"Small one," she said, gesturing with her thumb and index finger. "That much Amaretto over a lot of ice."

"Scotch, neat," Dante said.

"No bourbon?" Julia said, eyebrows raised. "This man is full of surprises."

As they nursed their drinks and coffee, Dante got Julia to talk about herself. He was good at that. You had to be as a PI.

"My father got my mother pregnant, then did the right thing by her," she said. "Actually, he did the right thing by me. My mother didn't have a good grip on what was right. She left my father when I was a baby, and he raised me. It was tough because he was a bartender fighting an alcohol problem. He'd bring home a new woman, somebody he picked up in the bar, every couple of months. I tried to recast the first few as my mother, but when that didn't work, I started to resent them. It created a lot of tension, but he was trying his best to take care of me and tend to his own needs, too. He sent me to ballet classes when I was nine because it sounded like a little-girl thing to do."

"It must have been tough for him, raising a girl," Dante offered. "My mother had the reverse problem when my father died. She was afraid that living in a house with two women—I have a sister—I'd have 'male orientation problems.'"

"You'd be gay."

"Yeah."

"My father was afraid I'd become a first baseman," Julia said. "That's why dance school. Actually, he had the right idea but his timing was off. When I was in my late teens, I came close to making several major ballet companies, but my strength and technique weren't there because I'd started too late."

"Nine years old?"

"In Europe, they start ballet when they start walking."

"So, what'd you do?"

"Those who can't, teach," she said. "I got my bachelor's, master's, and doctorate in drama and dance and landed the job at the U of Maryland. Met my husband there and started screwing up my own life, without any help from either of my parents."

"You ever meet your mother?"

"Actually, I did. I tracked her down through an aunt. Mommsy was living with a man in Pennsylvania and had populated the landscape with my half brothers and sisters. When I got her on the phone, she was reluctant to let me come up, but I told her I was prepared to let bygones be bygones. Face-to-face was friendly enough, if forced. We agreed to try to be friends, exchange birthday and Christmas cards, an occasional phone call, nice-sounding things like that. I called her twice, sent her cards, got nothing in return. I haven't spoken to her in five years."

"Sorry," he said.

"She has her needs, too. They just don't include me."

He asked if she'd like another Amaretto but she shook her head. She also declined more coffee.

"Feel like a tour?" he offered.

"Sure," she said. "Life is a learning curve."

He left ten bucks for Lucette and they stood. "Why don't we start with Julio?" Julia suggested. "I really should conquer my kitchen-phobia."

"Suit yourself." He led her into the kitchen where the cook was cleaning up.

"Compliments on the seafood pasta," Julia said.

"Seafood?" Julio said, taking her extended hand. "That wasn't seafood."

"See what I mean?" Dante said.

Julio smiled and looked Julia up and down. "Not bad, captain," he said. "Better than usual."

"Usual? You mean Lisa?" Julia said.

"Come on," Dante said, moving her toward the door. "You're fired," he said over his shoulder. He saw the concerned look on Julia's face and said, "I do it every night. He'll be here tomorrow."

Only because she insisted, he showed her his office which was its usual mess. He seldom had visitors. She pronounced it "authentic."

"Nice choice of words," he said. "Actually, it's embarrassing." Dante had been a neat person after the Marines, and after thirteen years on the MPD. But it had been downhill from there. He often wondered what had happened to all the organization he'd once had in his life. "It'll have to do until I get my next six-figure contract," he said.

"Paul," Julia said, "stop apologizing for who you are. My father has done that all his life. 'This is my daughter the PhD. She did it with no help from me.' Or, 'This is my daughter, Julia. She would have been a great ballerina if I hadn't screwed her up.'"

"Maybe something about you makes men try too hard," he said, about to usher her out. "Well, you've seen it."

She looked deep into his eyes.

"What?" he asked.

"Where do you live, Paul?"

"Upstairs." All he could think was that he hadn't changed the bed in two weeks. He let the silence that followed hold for a second to save her the discomfort of pressing. "Don't expect much," he said.

"Christ, this is more embarrassing than I expected," he said of the bedroom. "I was just here a couple hours ago."

"I didn't expect *Architectural Digest*," she said as she put her arms around his neck. She kissed him warmly.

"I hope you know what you're doing," he said.

"I think I do," she answered. "Like my mother, this girl has needs, too."

"Is that what this is, fulfilling your needs?"

"It'll help me justify it to myself in the morning," she said. "Besides, I just might fill some need of yours, too."

He closed the door.

He undressed first. Naked in bed, he watched her disrobe. It was an artistic performance, her slender but surprisingly full-breasted body arched like a dancer at the practice barre, proud, graceful, without false modesty. "You're beautiful," he said because she was. He'd been intimate with a few redheads, and remembered having enjoyed the delicate color of their pubic hair. The thought aroused him.

"Actually," she said, "I have an almost perfect body. Except for my feet. Ballet dancers abuse their feet."

"I heard," he said.

"Goes with the territory."

"Right."

"You won't mind?"

"About your feet? I wasn't thinking about feet."

"What were you thinking about?"

"Your—well, to be honest, I was thinking about your—your pussy."

"Why?"

"I've heard dumb questions before. Maybe I shouldn't have said pussy. Your vagina. Your private parts."

"Say it again."

"What?"

"Say you were thinking about my pussy."

"Say it again? Okay. I was thinking about your pussy."

She approached the bed and stood over him. "Here it is," she said.

His hand came up and his fingertips stroked her already lubricated sexual folds. Her hair was as bronze and soft as what was on her head. "We have positions in ballet," she said.

"Yeah?"

"The one I like best is when the male dancer puts his head between the female dancer's legs and performs."

"Performs. I think I just became a ballet dancer."

"And after that position, I like my partners to leap deep and hard."

"Nutcracker," he said, grinning.

"Nutcracker."

So much for art, he thought as she slipped in beside him and the ballet began, slow at first, then increasing in artistic intensity until he made his final leap into the wings. The crowd went wild.

VI

Two Weeks Later

One of the first orders of business for Genaro Orsini when he returned from his honeymoon in the Bahamas was to go to see Angelo Andreotti, the owner of Angelo's restaurant. Orsini didn't like to let a live one get away. He considered himself too shrewd a businessman to let that happen. He knew, as did most of Angelo's friends and patrons, that Carmela Andreotti, Angelo's wife, had terminal cervical cancer. Aside from the hopelessness of the disease, a succession of doctors had prodded, poked, scoped, and taken photographic slides of all the intimate areas of the old woman, who was from a generation uncomfortable with such personal exposure. These indignities heaped upon his wife only added to Angelo's pain.

When Orsini, a regular patron at Angelo's and now the husband of Santo Benedetti's daughter, had offered to help, Angelo viewed him as a concerned friend. The old man had been depressed for weeks over the imminent passing of the woman with whom he'd shared his life for fifty years. For all those years Angelo's days had been ordered by her, all his evenings shared with her. The prospect of the loneliness that lay ahead was frightening. He needed something positive to happen—anything. Orsini told the aching Angelo that he'd arrived to deliver just such a positive message.

They sat together at the tail end of lunch hour on a bright afternoon in May. Angelo pretended to eat a small plate of spaghetti Bolognese. Orsini enjoyed his full freebie—from antipasto to dessert cart.

"You shoulda bought more life insurance for you and Carmela *before* she got sick," Orsini said through a mouthful of rum cake. "You get sick like she is, it's too late to buy insurance."

"I never thought about it," Angelo said. "We were too busy living, making this restaurant, raising the kids."

"Yeah, well, there's always a reason. But you shoulda done it. Hey Corrado, another espresso, huh."

"I get some bad news from Angie today. Trouble, it just pile up."

"What's the matter with Angie Junior? Things goin' okay at his restaurant?"

Angelo shook his head. "He got money problems, bad money problems. I can't help him no more. Almost everything I got saved go to Carmela's doctors, and I need the little I got left to take care of her . . ." The word "funeral" stuck in his throat. He couldn't imagine Carmela laid out and lifeless.

"Your kid's joint not making it?"

The old man shook his head again. "He got so many expenses. He got to pay too many bills before he can bring home any money."

"That don't surprise me," Orsini said. "He's got too much fuckin' overhead down there on the river. His place is too big."

Angelo nodded.

Orsini wolfed down the last piece of cake. "A lotta things about that place never made sense to me. I always got a problem with an Italian restaurant that hires a 'chef.' You know what I mean?"

Angelo nodded again, this time disgust on his face. "I tell him you don't hire no cook from Chile. He say, 'Chef, Papa, *chef* from Chile.' And I say you don't put enough food on the plates. People don't care about how the mint leaf looks. They want a big piece of veal parmigiana, not one the size of a quarter with a drop a white sauce that comes from France."

"Nouvelle cuisine," Orsini groaned. "That's what they feed people in the high-rent districts. You charge 'em a lot for nothing so all of them can stay skinny and hate what they eat."

"I give him all the money I could for him to start up Angie's Too, but I don't have no more to give."

"That's why I'm here, Angelo," Orsini said. He motioned for Corrado to take away the dishes. After they'd been cleared, Orsini pulled papers from his briefcase. "Now pay attention," he said as he spread the papers on the table in front of Angelo. "I told you I had good news for you. I wouldn't do this for anybody, you understand, but you've been a good friend, huh? I come here all the time because you got good food, and because I like you."

"I have always been grateful."

"Yeah. You know my friend Tenaglia?"

"Sure," Angelo replied. "He eats here two, three times a week. Nice man."

"Okay. Now listen to me, Angelo. I can arrange through Tenaglia for a life insurance policy on Carmela. We can make it as much as three hundred grand."

"Dollars?" the old man exclaimed.

"No. Lira," Orsini said sarcastically. "Pay attention, Angelo. You listen to what I say."

"How you gonna do that? When the doctor, he examine Carmela, he's gonna say . . ."

"No doctor is going to examine Carmela. We'll fix that."

"Fix? How do you mean, 'fix'? She's dying, Genaro. Maybe a month, no more."

"That's not your problem, Angelo." How long has this old bastard lived in this country? Orsini thought. He still doesn't know how things work, how to get things done. No wonder his kid is going bust. He thinks like his old man.

"I been in this country forty-eight years," Angelo said, as though Orsini had verbalized his thought. "I never do nothing against the law."

"This is not against the law," Orsini said. "It's against the insurance company."

"Same thing, no?"

"No."

The old man sat silently, a puzzled expression on his lined, proud face.

Orsini's anger had begun to well up. The old bastard was about to screw up a good payday. "You're taking from the big guys," he growled. "The establishment. The guys who've been fuckin' you over since you opened this joint. The same for every other little guy like you."

He realized he was talking too loud and lowered his voice. "We're just getting something back for the little guy, in this case, *you*. That's all, huh?"

"How much?" Angelo asked. "Three hundred thousand?"

Orsini now spoke in a whisper. "Jesus, Angelo, I already told you. Three hundred big ones."

"I dunno," Angelo said, looking nervously around the now empty restaurant.

"Look, Angelo," Orsini said, "your end of the three hundred thousand can be used to bail out your kid's joint."

"If Carmela, she dies, I get three hundred thousand dollars?"

"Less my commission."

"How much that gonna be?"

"Only half."

"Half?"

Corrado brought another espresso. Orsini held the cup to his lips and looked at Angelo over it, a hard, questioning stare etched on his face. When the old man said nothing, Orsini said, "Without me you got all of zero, right? You got zip. Maybe your kid's joint goes bust, huh? You want that to happen? Believe me, it will."

The old man still didn't answer.

"Let me make it simple for you," Orsini said, his anger gaining on his ability to control it. He picked up the salt and pepper shakers, one in each hand. "The good guys," he said, raising the salt shaker. "The bad guys." He lifted the pepper higher.

He turned the salt shaker over and built a little mound of white crystals on the table in front of the restaurant owner. "This pile of diamonds is the hundred and fifty grand you're going to get to do right by Carmela and save Angie's Too. Otherwise . . ." He shook pepper onto the palm of his hand and blew it into Angelo's face. The pepper invaded his eyes and went up his nose. He fought back a sneeze but couldn't hold it. His eyes watered.

"Otherwise," Orsini said, "the bad guys win and you get fucked again, like they been fuckin' you all your life."

Orsini finished his espresso. "The hell with it, Angelo," Orsini said. "I come here to help an old friend and I end up gettin' sneezed at. Maybe next you spit in my face, huh?"

Angelo dipped a corner of his napkin into a water glass and wiped his running eyes. It occurred to him for the first time that he was dealing with someone to be feared. His relationship with the Benedetti family over the years had always been friendly. He'd never felt threatened by any members of the family, certainly not the high-ranking ones. The *soldati*, the family soldiers, never came near the place. Santo always treated him warmly, although he hadn't seen the younger Benedetti brother in a while. Lucia had had that bad period when you couldn't be sure what she was thinking, but that had passed with her marriage.

Now, this new member of the family, Lucia's husband, sat opposite him and said things that no longer sounded warm and friendly. It was nice of him to come with such a generous offer, but Angelo had the impression that to turn down Orsini would not be taken kindly, might even be viewed as an insult to the Benedetti family. Angelo rationalized. Orson, the newest member of that family, had gone out of his way to help a fellow Italian and to do it at the expense of the system. It wasn't illegal. Was it?

"A hun'erd fifty t'ousand?" Angelo asked again.

"Right. Less some expenses, of course." Orsini reached into his briefcase, pulled out an application from one of the nation's largest life insurance companies and started taking down information.

That night, Angelo Andreotti sat on the side of his wife's bed and spoke softly to her. "I have a pretty good day today, Carmela," he said.

"Good." She smiled. "I feel a little better, too. The pill the doctor give me is helping."

"Excellent," Angelo said. "You rest, you eat good, you get your strength back. We need you in the kitchen. The cook is good, but he don't have your touch."

She smiled bigger. "I showed him everything, Angelo. You know that."

"Yeah, I know. He stands there and puts in the same ingredients the way you do, but the gravy don't taste the same. Nobody can make it like you do."

"You just trying to make me feel better?"

"No. It's true."

Carmela repositioned herself in bed to give her husband more room. "You hear from Angie?" she asked.

"Yes. He's fine."

"How's business?"

"He's doin' good," Angelo said, not meeting her eyes. "He got some good news today."

"Good news?"

"Yeah. He got some more money coming in. Money he can use to help him over this rough time. He's gonna be okay."

"That is good news," Carmela said. She sighed and closed her eyes, her frail, waxy hand gently cradled by her husband, whose tears ran silently down his cheeks.

———

After leaving Angelo's with the signed insurance application, Orsini drove to a rest area off the Washington-Baltimore pike, dropped a quarter in a pay phone, and dialed seven digits that were fixed in his memory.

"Whelan," the voice at the other end answered.

"Orson."

"Hello, Gerry. Thought you'd forgotten about us."

"I'd like to."

"How's married life treating you?"

"Fuckin' great, just like you said it would."

"Don't give *me* all the credit, Gerry. The institution has been around for centuries. You're lucky. They say married men live longer than bachelors. We extended your life . . . in more ways than one."

"I'm really fucking grateful."

"How's business?"

"Not so hot, you'll be happy to hear. The big guys are feeling the pressure. I suppose you could say their problems are . . . taxing."

"Yeah. I heard something about that."

"I'm sure you did. I gotta go. You heard from me. I did my duty."

"What are you so pissed at, Gerry? You got yourself a sweet deal . . . and a belly-warmer every night as a bonus."

"Fuck off."

"No need to be unpleasant."

"Look. I called, okay. Now leave me alone a while. Things are just getting going. I need room to breathe."

"You got it, Partridge. Just don't be a stranger."

Orsini hung up and stared blankly at the phone, which immediately turned into a little TV screen on which he saw a rerun of events that had occurred the previous September, and that had created the situation in which he now found himself.

———————

He'd started the night with the black bitch, Fionia, who needed a hit but didn't have any coke in the house. He was empty that night, too. That would be resolved when he met with the nigger dealer at ten-thirty at the nigger's apartment. Even if he had some, he wouldn't carry it around with him. You get stopped for running a light, they find it on you, big trouble. Besides, he had other people who carried.

Fionia was wound like a watch that night and couldn't get loose. She had him hot and bothered, but wouldn't let him touch her unless he got her a hit. "Go see Carlos," she'd told him. "He's around and he's got a good stash. Just came in. Take us on a great ride."

"Take *you* on a fuckin' ride," he said. "You know I don't touch that shit. And I don't use Carlos. I use my own people."

"Baby," she said, "I gotta have my blow or I ain't worth shit tonight. Come on, pretty man. For Fionia." She ran her long, tapered brown fingers tipped with sparkling red over his crotch and played her pink tongue in his ear.

"Where do I find this Carlos?"

She told him. He went, bought a dime bag, and brought it to her. She got straight and they tangled up in each other for an hour.

"I gotta go," he said as he dressed. "Got to see a man about a big deal."

"Don't forget Fionia, baby. You buyin' shit tonight?"

"Yeah. Lots of it."

"Remember me, pretty baby. Ain't nobody does you better than Fionia."

"Yeah. Right."

He went to the address Diggs had given him that day and sat in the conversation area with the black man, the metal cat's red eyes recording every moment, every movement, the three microphones picking up every word.

After he was arrested and cuffed, he sat on the couch. With him was FBI special agent Tom Whelan. "Wrong place at the wrong time," Whelan said.

"Big fucking deal," Orsini said. "Whadaya gonna do, make a federal case out of me buying some shit?"

Whelan didn't answer.

"You entrapped me," Orsini said.

"Wrong," Whelan said. "You trapped yourself."

Orsini snarled at the agent. A spineless little punk, Orsini thought. A prissy little guy with glasses. He looked like a college boy.

"I'll get to the point, Mr. Orsini," Whelan said. "You're facing a long stretch away on the taxpayer. Trust me when I say that. We've got you where it hurts."

"Maybe."

"As I said, trust me. But if you don't buy that, let's talk about Santo Benedetti and his daughter."

Whelan now had Orsini's undivided attention. Why had this come up?

"You've been seeing Santo's daughter, Lucia, for some time now. Right?"

"So what?"

"So, let's say her father finds out that his daughter's boyfriend runs with black whores, and sells drugs in D.C."

The smug expression that had been on Orsini's large, hard face was gone now. His mind raced. What was this guy getting to?

"You know about the understanding, I assume."

"What understanding?"

"About not doing business in D.C."

"I don't know what the fuck you're talking about," Orsini snarled. Which was true.

"You know that the Benedettis don't deal drugs, and take a dim view of anybody in the family who does."

"I'm not in the family," Orsini said. "I do some work for 'em, that's all.

"But you'd like to be a real family member."

"Nah. It means nothin' to me."

"Let me explain, Mr. Orsini, why it should appeal to you. Let me explain why marrying Lucia Benedetti would not only provide you with a loving, caring wife, it might keep you from being butt-fucked every night in your cell."

The harsh words from the small, mild-mannered agent jolted Orsini. He hunched his shoulders in a final gesture of defiance, inhaled with gusto to clear his sinuses, and said, "Go ahead. I'm listening."

Early in May

A guard at the gate waved the steel-grey Mercedes through, then called the house to report it had arrived. It was midnight.

Ed Milstein, a tax attorney who headed the Benedetti family's team of accountants, was shown into Santo's study where a trio of men were at a table. Two had been familiar faces to Milstein over the years; he'd met the third man, Genaro Orsini, for the first time at Orsini's wedding to Lucia.

The soft sounds of one of Vivaldi's more doleful concerti flowed from a built-in Bang & Olufsen stereo system. The music was for Vincent's benefit. He had not had a good day. Earlier, Milstein had been the bearer of specific bad news. But things in general had not been going well for Vincent lately, and Santo knew the soothing effect Vivaldi had on his older brother.

The two-story walls of the room—oversized like everything else in the house—consisted mostly of floor-to-ceiling bookcases filled with leather-bound copies of the world's great literature, most in English, some in Italian. Although he had not read even a small portion of his library, Santo, like Vincent, appreciated books and what could be learned from them. He had managed to get through some of the more important works, and had a talking knowledge of many of the others. But the world's great books was not the topic of discussion this night.

"Sit," Santo said, motioning Milstein to a chair at the table.

"Just give it to me black, no sugar," Vincent told the lawyer-accountant. "If we're going to defend ourselves, I have to know what I'm up against."

"They've placed you on notice for a comprehensive audit," Milstein said, apology in his voice.

"You already told me that on the phone," Vincent said.

"Comprehensive," Milstein continued. "They'll be looking at everything, going way back."

"How far back can they go?" Vincent questioned. "Not that that matters. They'll find what they're looking for. They're good at that if they want to be."

"As far back as they want to go," said Milstein. He reached for a pitcher of ice water that was sweating on a silver tray near his end of the table and poured half a glass. He drank and cleared his throat in anticipation of the next question.

"I thought they could only go back so far," Orsini chimed in. He'd been waiting for any opening that would allow him to contribute.

"Not if they feel they can show evasion," Milstein answered. "You have to keep your support documents for . . ."

"Yeah, yeah." Vincent cut him off. "Let's get to the bottom line."

Milstein blew out a stream of air and cleared his throat again. "I'm a tax attorney, Vincent, not a criminal lawyer. I know you've been talking to Sal and Carl. They can probably provide you with better counsel. From what I can ascertain, it's evident they're determined to send you to prison. You know how Justice uses the IRS with you people—" He softened it to "people in your business."

The room waited for Vincent's response to Milstein's blunt statement. There wasn't any. Milstein heard the ice melting in his glass. Now he wanted to say something positive but had nothing positive to offer.

"You're paid a lotta money to make sure this doesn't happen," Vincent said, breaking the silence. His tone was deliberate, matter-of-fact. "Isn't that right?"

"And I'm working on it day and night, Vincent."

"How are they going to prove anything?" Santo asked.

"Evasion is the big thing," Milstein said. "They really don't give a damn what you write off. They'll fine you for that, make you pay penalties. But if they can show you're not reporting income, that's evasion. To do that, they'll impound the books of all the businesses, then match them against your tax returns."

"And how are our books?" Vincent asked.

"We had the examiners in from the state four years ago. They ended up refunding us for overpayments."

"So you're saying this is pro forma?" Orsini asked.

Milstein looked at Vincent; his expression asked, what is this guy here for?

"Why don't you answer the question?" Vincent said.

"Look," Milstein said after more throat-clearing, "who knows? You said it yourself. They find what they want to find. We've kept very tight books, both on you personally and the family businesses. Everything is accounted for, according to their own regulations. If they've already looked at your returns and the returns of the businesses—and I'm sure they've examined them closely—then they know everything is tight."

"Then why the fuck are they coming?" Santo asked.

"Exactly," Milstein replied. "Somebody tell *me*. Why are they coming?"

No one ventured an answer. Then Vincent said, "Thank you, Ed. Go home. Get some sleep."

Milstein did not welcome the dismissal. He was not being asked to stay and help plan strategy, which had always been the case. Given his long-term relationship of trust and respect from the Benedettis, that was not a good sign.

Santo and Vincent escorted him from the study and to the front door. "Vincent," the accountant said as he slipped into his coat, "I want you to know I have a half dozen of my best people on this. I get continuous reports of their progress, even hourly when they have anything important to tell me."

"I know," the Mafia don said. "Go home." He opened the door. "My best to your family." He smiled at Milstein.

"Thank you," Milstein said, studying the smile. He was relieved by it.

The Benedetti brothers returned to the study and took their places at the table. "Genaro has something he wants to say," said Santo.

Vincent's annoyance was written on his face. He didn't like to waste time, and time now seemed particularly important. Things needed to be done, decisions made.

"I've got this contact," Orsini said. "Charlie Pietrosanti. Used to work for the IRS. He left five years ago to start his own tax service. He was one of their top regional men when he left. He still knows the right people."

"What are you saying?" Vincent asked abruptly. The later it got and the more tired he was, the more surly he would become. Recognizing his brother's negative progression, Santo jumped in with, "This Pietrosanti may be able to do something for us."

"Do what?" Vincent replied.

"Fix it," Orsini said. "Get the feds off your back."

Vincent couldn't hold back a laugh. "What are you, Genaro, a little kid, a dreamer? This is nothing some freelance tax guy is going to fix. This is not something even an IRS insider can fix. It goes way beyond the IRS." He looked at Santo. "Does he know what we're dealing with here?" he asked.

It was a difficult question for Santo. Orsini was still not an accepted member of the inner circle. In fact, Vincent had been reluctant to include Orsini in the session, but Santo had insisted that Genaro was now family and might have a contribution to make.

"A little," Santo said. "I've filled him in on some family history."

Vincent nodded; Santo couldn't read if he was pleased or not.

"I'm just trying to help," said Orsini.

"Of course," Santo said.

"Look, I don't wanna butt in where I'm not wanted," Orsini said, "but I had Pietrosanti do some checking for me."

Vincent glared at him.

"He did it quiet, in confidence," Orsini quickly added. "As best he can determine, it's the new regional chief trying to make points by burning a coupla people with big money. The administration needs to show some action against the top one percent. It's only that. They're not taking direction from any other department, at least not in this case. Pietrosanti knows. Believe me, he's wired into the IRS real good."

"You buy this, Santo?" Vincent asked.

"Maybe yes, maybe no. But we can listen, right? There's no cost in hearing him out."

"All right," Vincent replied. "What is this gonna cost?"

"Hundred grand," Orsini said. "His standard fee." When Vincent said nothing, Orsini added, "Look, Vincent, I'm sorry I brought it up, all right? You're family to me. Santo was concerned about this problem. I thought I could help."

Vincent's face sagged from fatigue. "Okay, okay," he said. "It's been a rough day." He got up, walked to one of the bookcases and ran his fingers over the bindings as if searching for some reference source to help him out of his situation. He turned and said to Orsini, "Genaro, thank you for your suggestion. Now, if you don't mind."

"Sure," Orsini said, standing. "I'll show myself out."

"Give my love to Lucia," Santo said.

Santo poured himself a drink while Vincent played with the book bindings until they heard the sound of an engine catch and a car drive off. "I don't see this as a coincidence, Santo," Vincent said. "But maybe I'm getting old. Maybe when you get old, you think everybody's out to get you. We call it survival, huh?"

"I know you're upset, Vincent, but don't think you fight this alone. It doesn't only affect you. I mean, talk about survival, I gotta figure I'm next. Right? Whether Justice is pulling the strings here or not."

Vincent sat in a large leather chair and rubbed seventy-year-old eyes that looked as though they'd been set in putty. "I've always had good instincts about things like this, Santo. You know that. I don't need to have my nose too far in the air to smell Thornton and the Justice Department. But I'm thinking now, listening to you, to Genaro, and even Milstein, that I don't want to create devils where they don't exist. It could be just the IRS looking to break balls."

Santo faced his brother from a matching chair. "Do you think this guy Pietrosanti would try and beat you out of a hundred grand?" Santo asked. "Do you think he's going to be that ballsy, that fuckin' stupid? He's coming at us through a member of the family, Genaro, my own son-in-law."

Vincent let out a long sigh. "Maybe you're right, Santo. I just don't know."

"If he takes the money and can't pull this off, he's fucking with Genaro, a guy who knows him a long time. And he'd be fucking us. He's gotta know not to do that."

"I know all that, but how's he gonna pull this off, even if he does know somebody? How do you call off the hounds once they turned 'em loose."

"You are tired, Vincent. You want a drink? Some milk? Cake?"

Vincent shook his head.

"It doesn't seem so complicated to me," Santo said. "The auditors poke around, ask a lotta questions, have a couple of face-to-faces and then find the books in order. Case closed. A hundred grand can buy a lot of play-acting."

Vincent fought back a smile. "I wish it were that simple. And, I appreciate what your son-in-law is trying to do here. But he's new. He wants to make a good impression. Maybe he tries too hard."

"Vincent, he knows what's at risk here. He's not going to jeopardize something as serious as this just to say he gave it his best shot and failed. He knows the stakes."

"Does he?"

"Yeah. I'm sure of it."

Vincent pulled out a handkerchief and blew his nose. "Okay," he said, grimacing as he stood against the pain of arthritis. "It's an option. Maybe I don't have so many of them. Let's sleep on it. I need a clear head."

Vincent had decided to spend the night in a guarded guest cottage on the property. He raised a heavy eyebrow. "I don't know, Santo. I just don't like the sound of it."

"Get some sleep," Santo said as Vincent stepped out into the night air and was immediately flanked by two bodyguards who would lead him to the cottage and stand watch all night. He's getting old, Santo mused. The thought made him sad as he returned to the study for a nightcap and to read another chapter in a book about the Bill of Rights given him recently by his daughter, Lucia.

———

Weeks before the meeting in Santo's house, FBI special agent Tom Whelan had sat next to Charlie Pietrosanti at a lunch counter in Northeast Washington. Whelan had coffee and a piece of cherry pie. Pietrosanti ate a deluxe cheeseburger with fries. It was Whelan's check.

"Why do we have to meet in greasy joints like this?" Pietrosanti said through a mouthful of burger and ketchup. "All kinds of good restaurants and we meet in a grease hole."

"Budget," Whelan said. "You're eating taxpayer money."

Pietrosanti grinned and took another bite. "So?" he said. "I'm eating my money. I'm a taxpayer."

Whelan fixed on the large ring on Pietrosanti's pinky. Men who wore such rings, and suits with shiny threads running through them like the olive-green suit Pietrosanti wore, were anathema to Whelan. But the drapings said something important about the man, something to be used when applying the pressure. Pietrosanti considered himself a flash act, a high roller, a man-about-town and probably a real ladies' man. That told Whelan what buttons to push, what emotions to tap into.

"You don't have a hell of a lot of choice, you know," Whelan said.

"'Cause you say so?"

"Because you stepped into a deep pile of it, Charlie. You didn't cover your ass this time, but we have it covered. You don't go along, that naked ass of yours ends up an inviting target for serial killers and butt-fuckers in Attica." Pietrosanti started to say something but Whelan interrupted. "You won't do time in some country-club pen. We'll make sure there's a chain gang and bullwhips." The agent smiled. "Of course, you could always sell that godawful ring for some protection money. But in prison—well, nobody honors deals." He looked into Pietrosanti's sad brown eyes and smiled. "Trust me, Charlie. I'm your only game in town, and you'd better decide to play."

The dapper little man's face twisted into a look of displeasure, as though he'd suddenly ingested tainted beef. "You fuckin' guys are all the same. Whadaya care, huh, what happens to me? I pull somethin' like this on Vincent Benedetti, I buy a plot and a headstone. Right? Twenty-four hours later I'm part of the foundation of a new monument in this city. Right? Whadaya think I am, for christsake, crazy?"

Whelan looked around to insure they were still outside earshot of the few patrons of the luncheonette. He leaned close to Pietrosanti and said, "I've spent enough time explaining the facts of life to you, Charlie. Let me sum up. One, we have you by the nuts, and we're about to squeeze hard. Two, there is a way for you to stay out of the nutcracker. Three, that way is me and the program."

"And all I have to do is set up Benedetti, then disappear into your goddamn witness program. Beautiful. What do I get, a condo in Sun City and enough bread for the early-bird dinner once a week? That's a real incentive, Whelan."

"I'll sweeten it," Whelan said. "We'll find a used craps table and install it in your condo in Sun City. You still like to shoot craps?"

"Yeah, only the odds are better at the table. Hey, Whelan, let me ask you something."

"Go ahead. Talking to me is like going to college."

"Right. You tell me I'm supposed to set up Benedetti on a tax rap. He comes to a place, I got a guy who's supposed to be an IRS guy on the take, Benedetti hands over a hundred grand, and you cuff him? Right?"

"Right."

"Okay, Mr. College Professor, how the fuck do I get Vincent Benedetti to come to this place carrying a hundred big ones? Tell me that. I don't even know the guy."

"You know Gerry Orson."

A smile slowly spread over Pietrosanti's face. "You fuckers. You got him in your pocket, too?"

"It'll be a nice private little deal between the three of us. Gerry gets the don to the place, you do your number, the don goes to jail, and you get to live the high life with your own personal craps table in your kitchen. Sounds good, doesn't it?"

"It stinks."

Whelan stood. "You pick up this check, Charlie. Then, you pay again with long time in someplace not as nice as Sun City. Be at the office at noon. We'll be there with cuffs and the warrant. Have a nice night."

Whelan was halfway up the street when Pietrosanti came running out of the luncheonette. "Look, Whelan, give me a coupla days, huh? You know, to think about it."

"Noon tomorrow. And don't bother wearing your funny suits and shoes. Basic black with pearls will do just fine." He walked away knowing he'd left Pietrosanti staring after him, confusion written on his face. And fear. The agent's smile lasted all the way home.

viii

The First Day of June

Tommy Guardino, Vincent's driver of more than thirty years, considered himself the quintessential Marlboro man. Not that the term was in his vocabulary. It's just that he liked the image of a rugged man versus nature, a cigarette dangling from his lips as he surveyed the range and pondered life's mysteries.

He pulled one from the red and white box, lit it, leaned his bulky body against the side of the black Lincoln and stared up at the large building in front of him. Tommy always had time on his hands. He did a lot of waiting. While he waited, he did a lot of thinking. Always with a Marlboro dangling from his lips.

He didn't trust this building. It wasn't that he'd seen anything to make him suspicious—no wrong people coming or going. He just didn't trust it. The Benedetti family sometimes joked about Vincent's driver and his strange custom of assigning human traits to inanimate objects. He'd dumped his ex-wife because she liked to sew and seemed always to have scissors in her hand. Tommy saw those scissors as an extension of her vagina, poised to send him to eunuch land. He'd spent the last few months of their marriage sitting up in bed and cupping his genitals in anticipation of a scissor attack.

He once owned a green Chevy that eventually took on a life of its own. At least for him. He became convinced the Chevy had received orders to destroy him. It almost did the night he skidded on ice and wrapped the enemy around a pole.

Things. Nobody could tell him they didn't *live.* A stove could put a hit on you. So could a garden rake you'd treated badly. You had to be careful. It wasn't only people who could do you in.

The Benedetti family had decided that Tommy's obsessions answered some prehistoric need to indulge in superstition, born in the mountains of his boyhood Sicily. Tommy was glad they accepted it that way, but he knew it wasn't mumbo-jumbo. You sometimes got feelings from things and situations, not just from people. If you ignored them, they'd hurt you.

Tommy had never liked the Mayflower Hotel. Maybe it was its yellow facade; nothing good ever came from yellow. It was an evil color. Why they'd paint it yellow was beyond him. You could never trust anybody who painted things yellow.

Thirty years ago he'd sat outside this yellow building while his boss, Vincent Benedetti, reached his much-envied "arrangement" with the Federal Bureau of Investigation. J. Edgar Hoover himself. Memories of Vincent returning to the car after meeting with Hoover had remained vivid for Tommy. Vincent had climbed into the backseat and said, "It's done. The deal is sealed. He's like a member of the family now."

But despite the success of that meeting, Tommy still had negative feelings about the Mayflower. He'd never mentioned those feelings to the family, knowing what the hotel meant to them. But he didn't trust it. It had nothing to do with the cowardice others might read into the color yellow. It was less tangible than that. The building was a liar.

Now, on a night thirty years later, Tommy had wanted to warn his boss to stay away but knew he couldn't. Vincent had always had this need to personally shake on a deal, to lock eyes. He shouldn't be the one to personally hand over bribe money. Let a family flunky do it, run the risks. But that wasn't Vincent's style, never had been.

Tommy viewed Vincent as more than his boss and godfather. The man was, as far as Tommy was concerned, a saint, a god. He was smart and kind and took care of his people like they were his children. He should live forever, Tommy often said during silent prayers in church.

NICK VASILE

But Vincent was only human, Tommy would reluctantly admit to himself at times of extreme introspection. He had to be protected—so that he'd live forever. Tommy didn't trust any of the other Benedetti soldiers who were supposed to put their own lives on the line to protect Vincent. Fucking morons was the way Tommy viewed them. He was the one who knew how to shield Vincent Benedetti. He also knew what Vincent needed, like driving slow. Vincent hated going fast in a car, and Tommy always drove at a speed that pleased his passenger.

What could he say to this saint named Vincent Benedetti before he went inside for a "critical business negotiation"? "Don't go inside, Mr. Benedetti? I don't trust this building? It's yellow? This building is a liar?"

When they brought Vincent out in handcuffs, Tommy felt the building's smug satisfaction at its deception. He could almost hear a sinister laugh from it. What could he do then?

If he'd told the family of his feelings about the Mayflower *before* this had happened, they wouldn't be able to joke about his insane superstitions. But what could he say now? That he knew the building was lying, but couldn't bring himself to tell Vincent?

———

Charlie Pietrosanti's "IRS contact" had insisted that only the three of them be present at the meeting. "No muscle," Pietrosanti had told Orsini, who'd passed it along to Vincent. "Mr. Saunders must protect his position," Pietrosanti had told Orsini, who told Santo, who told Vincent. The fewer people involved, the better. The IRS guy can't be compromised. Otherwise, he might not be able to provide the same service again.

Vincent was inherently suspicious of people who gave you too many reasons for something when one would do. At the same time, he didn't delude himself about the kind of people with whom he was dealing.

"I don't understand," Vincent had told Santo. "Why would I need muscle?"

"You don't," Santo responded. "That's the point."

88

A MEMBER OF THE FAMILY

Vincent, Pietrosanti, and Saunders exchanged greetings in the suite at the Mayflower, then sat at a small table. Vincent was, as usual, impeccably dressed, this time in diplomat grey. Saunders was someone who wore clothes without distinction, a man who simply pulled out the next nondescript suit in line from his closet on any given morning. Pietrosanti was the natty dresser of the trio. He wore a shiny brown suit, a shiny tan silk shirt with French cuffs that extended too far beyond his jacket, and a shiny green silk tie secured to his shirt with a diamond stickpin. His shoes, of course, were alligator.

Given the nature of the meeting, Vincent would, as a matter of course, consider the men sitting with him to be adversaries. He understood business, however, and tried to keep the objectives, strategies, and tactics of the negotiation in perspective. While most aspects of the deal had been handled up front by other people, Vincent felt the true contest—and he viewed all business deals as a contest—was joined when the parties faced each other to determine the who-gets-what-and-for-how-much? That meant eye to eye. And a handshake to finalize the deal.

Trust was a key factor, of course, which spoke to the don's sense of honor. Much of his interfamily dealings were sealed as a matter of honor. But with outsiders, you had to look for assurances beyond trust. Whether he respected, or even liked the other parties was not relevant. He didn't like Saunders as soon as they met. He was not a man of honor, Vincent felt. He often made that determination by the way a man carried himself. The artificial stiffness of Saunders's carriage conveyed a lack of sincerity, a man Vincent would deal with only according to the strictest of rules. He would do or say nothing off the subject. He would deal with Saunders only because he had to.

His dislike of Pietrosanti was by definition. He had betrayed his profession, used his colleagues. There was nothing more to consider.

"Let's get started," Pietrosanti began. He fiddled with the gaudy, oversized gold ring on his left pinky, its center dominated by a large cluster of diamonds in the shape of a dollar sign. "You understand why we're here, Mr. Benedetti?" he asked.

"As it has been explained to me," Vincent answered.

"By Mr. Orsini. Right? He told you . . ."

Benedetti narrowed his eyes; a hint of color livened his ashen cheeks. "Why do you want to discuss this again?" he said. "I understand all the preliminaries have been taken care of. You know why I'm here. So do you, Mr. Saunders."

Saunders didn't respond, made no gesture of affirmation or dissent.

"Okay," Pietrosanti said. "But Mr. Saunders wants it clearly understood that his career, even his life outside the office, is at stake here if this isn't conducted under strict guidelines, and with a full understanding of what's involved."

"Mr. Saunders?" Vincent said.

Saunders nodded. "That's the way it's got to be," he said.

"I don't have a problem with that," Vincent said, "so why don't we get on with this?"

"I need to have you understand the consequences of what you're asking me to do," Saunders said, as if finally discovering that his voice worked for more than a few words. "I want to feel secure that no one in this room will underestimate the consequences we can all suffer if the wrong people find out about this."

"First of all, Mr. Saunders," Vincent replied, "what I am asking you to do is a result of your agent, Mr. Pietrosanti, approaching one of my representatives with the suggestion that he could supply the service I require. I accept that offer, in return for the agreed-upon services. I am paying Mr. Pietrosanti as a consultant for advice on a personal tax matter."

Pietrosanti, who played with his pinky ring, said, "Actually, Mr. Benedetti, I'm only the middleman who put you and Mr. Saunders together. You asked for this meeting. Right?"

"I usually meet personally with people I do business with. Am I, or am I not securing your services, Mr. Pietrosanti? If you cannot do what I require, I'll rethink the deal."

Pietrosanti looked at Saunders, who nodded.

"Do you have my fee, Mr. Benedetti?" Pietrosanti asked.

"Yes," Vincent replied. He lifted an attaché case from alongside his chair and placed it on the table.

"It's the one hundred thousand dollars we agreed upon?" Pietrosanti asked.

"You're free to count it," Vincent said.

"I won't bother," Pietrosanti said. "Let me make it clear for you what services this hundred thousand dollars buys from Mr. Saunders."

"No need for that," Vincent said. "We have an agreement. We understand what the terms of that agreement are. We are men of honor, are we not?"

Pietrosanti glanced at Saunders and fooled with his ring again. If you worked for me, Vincent thought, I'd have your finger cut off.

"I think we all understand," Saunders said. He leaned back in his chair and ran a hand over thinning hair that was combed into insufficient rows across a bald head. A door at the side of the room burst open and a half-dozen men entered. "Federal agents," the first man through said to Vincent. "You are under arrest for the attempted bribery of a federal official. You have a right to remain silent . . ."

Vincent barely listened. His mind was fixed on the irony of the scene. Thirty years earlier, he and J. Edgar Hoover had reached their understanding in this same hotel, and the director and his handpicked successors had abided by the terms. Vincent always respected Hoover for that. The day after Hoover died in May of 1972, Vincent had lunch in the Mayflower's restaurant and noted that the table where the director had sat each day for lunch had been covered with an American flag by the waiter who'd served him for years. The flag was not removed, nor was anyone allowed to sit at the table, until the director had been buried. Vincent had almost saluted as he passed the table that day . . . but that was another time, another generation.

———

While Vincent had waited upstairs in the Mayflower in November of 1961, Hoover spoke to a black-tie dinner downstairs in the main ballroom.

"He doesn't call himself a Communist—yet—but he has curious friends," Hoover said from the podium. "The day after your valiant brothers and fathers hit the beach last April at Bahía de los Cochinos, he was already receiving promises of assistance from Mr. Khrushchev. As the saying goes, if it walks like a duck and quacks like a duck . . ."

There was puzzlement on faces across the grand ballroom. The speaker let the sentence hang in the air before bringing it to what he'd thought would be an unnecessary conclusion. ". . . then it *is* a duck," he said in a shrill staccato familiar to every American who owned a radio or TV.

"*¿Castro es un pato?*" a man at the head table blurted out. "Castro is a *duck?*" He laughed, having missed the point.

America's top cop, J. Edgar Hoover, looked out over the second annual Thanksgiving dinner of Cuban-Americans for Freedom—CAFF to headline writers around the country. Anti-Castro Cuban-Americans did not have much to be thankful for as 1961 drew to a close, but this Thanksgiving event, started the year before, had been billed as an annual affair. Calling it off would be yet another defeat in a year filled with them. Besides, it was important to stick close and to circle the wagons in times of adversity, to find something—someone—to rally around.

They were disillusioned with President Kennedy and his close political advisors who'd abandoned their freedom fighters on that bloodstained beach known as the Bay of Pigs. Who better to turn to than America's legendary FBI director and strident anti-Communist, J. Edgar Hoover, who was viewed as loyalist Cubans' strongest supporter. That he was known to share their distrust of, and even scorn for, the Kennedys—never openly stated, of course—only sweetened his image with them. Those who carried the flame and dream of freedom for Cuba considered it a monumental coup to have Hoover address their second annual freedom dinner.

They'd selected the Mayflower because it was known to be Hoover's favorite: he lunched in its restaurant virtually every day. CAFF even paid for one of the hotel's most luxurious suites for the director to have at his disposal before and after his appearance.

A MEMBER OF THE FAMILY

Hoover had agreed without prompting to address the group. He viewed Castro as the Devil of the hemisphere and saw Cuba's operatives as a distinct threat to America's domestic tranquility and security. On this November night in 1961, Hoover was convinced that Cuba's incipient dictator would soon shed his sheep's clothing and come out into the open as the Soviet Union's fearless western wolf (a prophesy that soon proved correct when Castro declared himself a Marxist-Leninist, and announced the formation of a single-party government to bring Communism to Cuba).

He'd been incensed at the administration's bumbling in dealing with Castro, and considered CIA plans to employ Mafiosi to assassinate the Cuban dictator to be crazy at worst, silly at best. While he was constrained from publicly stating such beliefs, he was free to address groups such as CAFF and to make left-handed references to the world as he saw it.

"It is not enough to clear the streets of local hoodlums," Hoover continued before the packed CAFF dinner. "Today, the main streets of America too often stretch far from our shores. These same streets have become wide boulevards for a whole new breed of criminal. Because of years of dedicated work by special agents of the Federal Bureau of Investigation, we've been winning the war on crime and are poised to strike a definitive blow against the gangsters who have threatened the safety and sanctity of every American town and city.

"But today's international criminal takes his marching orders from foreign capitals, and recruits here among our own citizens. His hit list is not just another U.S. bank to rob. It is the U.S. banking *system* he covets. His goal is not one more block of real estate under the control of the mobster up the street. He wants the deed to the *country*. But then, I don't have to tell you people that. *You* know what I'm talking about. You've seen such evil at work in your own backyard."

Hoover paused for effect. "*Sí, sí,*" erupted from his rapt audience. He surveyed the room. At tables set lavishly with silver and linen, Cubans of substance hung on his words. Many of them had been the elite under Battista, a regime *friendly* to the U.S. Now, they sat in black ties and bright white shirts that shone, their women in sequined gowns too tight for their well-fed bodies. Jewels appointed both sexes: hanging from the necks and earlobes of the women; stuck through the collars, ties and shirt cuffs of the men.

They liked what they were hearing. The man who had made the streets of the United States safer than they had been in years was now a committed opponent of their own enemy, Fidel Castro. And they saw this man—J. Edgar Hoover—as a man who got things done.

They were, of course, right in their assessment. FDR knew it back in 1936 when he called Hoover in for secret talks and told him he wanted better information on subversive groups within the United States. Hoover suggested that the State Department make a formal request of the Bureau for such information. When it did, it opened the doors on a whole new landscape for the FBI director. He would use this opportunity to great advantage, cementing and enhancing his personal power and that of the Bureau by building massive sets of files on "undesirables," or extensive undesirable files on otherwise upstanding individuals, many in the Federal government.

"My friends," Hoover said in closing, "in this case the ant will not topple the elephant, even if he tries to borrow weapons from his big, bad friends. And that you *can* be thankful for."

The applause was loud and sustained; the crowd rose to its feet. Finally, a candle of hope to carry with them to light the gloom of the approaching holiday season.

A brass band struck up "God Bless America" as Hoover stepped from the podium and was quickly surrounded by a quartet of agents. They proceeded slowly along the center aisle toward the double doors at the rear of the huge banquet hall, Hoover acknowledging the response of the audience with controlled, jerky gestures of his short arms, or a curt nod of a head that seemed to rest squarely upon his cube of a body.

"Thank you for the encouraging words, Mr. Hoover," the master of ceremonies said into the microphone as Hoover navigated tables. Many tried to shake his hand but the director kept his arms close to his sides and looked straight ahead.

Hoover and his entourage left the room and went directly to a waiting elevator flanked by an additional brace of grey-suited agents. They entered and the doors silently closed behind them.

"Ready?" Hoover asked.

"Yes, sir."

"I don't want this to take any longer than it has to."

"Won't take but a minute, sir."

The elevator opened on the top floor and Hoover walked in the direction of his suite. But he didn't stop at its large double doors. Instead, he continued beyond to a single door at the far end of the hall where two more agents stood at attention. One of them knocked. The door was opened by a thick man with a square, deeply lined face and curly salt-and-pepper hair that hugged the contours of his head.

Hoover looked inside. Lighting in the suite's interior was deliberately dim, but he could see the shapes of other men standing on the perimeter of a large room. "Out of the way, please," Hoover said. He pushed past the man at the entrance and was inside, leaving concerned agents on the other side of a closed door.

Vincent sat on an eight-foot tan leather couch. He wore a conservative, painstakingly tailored black suit, white shirt, and a dense green silk tie. His black hair framed the sharp features of his sallow face, so finely etched it was almost effeminate. His deep brown eyes were riveted on the FBI director.

"Good evening, Mr. Benedetti," said Hoover. "We have an understanding, I assume." He moved closer to the couch, stopping two steps short of it.

"If we didn't, I wouldn't be here," Vincent said. There was no particular inflection to the tone of his answer, but the furrow it caused in Hoover's brow indicated the director had taken offense.

"I'm looking for a simple yes or no," Hoover said.

"And I," Vincent replied, "am looking for a handshake. To seal the agreement your people and mine have worked out."

Hoover glared at him.

Vincent's serene, yet steely face did not change. "Yes," he said, "we have an understanding." He pushed himself to his feet, closed the gap between them, smoothed the folds in his suit coat, and extended his hand. Hoover took it. Their eyes locked. Their hands dropped to their sides. Hoover's handshake had been as firm as was reputed. Agents entering the Bureau were warned to offer a firm handshake when welcomed by Hoover to duty with the FBI.

"Good night, Mr. Benedetti," Hoover said.

"Good night, sir. Thank you for the courtesy of your visit."

———

At the conclusion of the reading of his Miranda rights, Vincent was placed in cuffs. He looked at Pietrosanti as he was led from the room in a way that the dapper little man would never forget.

———

"We have it all on tape."

Thornton's pacing made Simonsen uncomfortable. "Have you seen it?" the attorney general asked.

"Of course."

"I don't want to hunt for this," Simonsen pressed. "Do we have what we need?"

Thornton leaned on the desk. "Come on, Stan. You know nothing is ironclad. We got some good footage and tape."

"But I *want* ironclad, Willard. I *need* ironclad. This bastard walks, he laughs in our faces. *He* ends up stronger—and *we* look like fools."

"Not necessarily true, Stan. Sure, he's out on bail in a few hours. In the meantime, he has to deal with this. He's gotten a message. While he and his guinzo friends fight this charge, we continue to build the RICO case through Partridge. Let's say he does walk away from this. While he thinks he's beaten the system again, his family erodes right out from under him. This is just the opening salvo of a war against Vincent Benedetti that will put him out of business for good."

Simonsen blew a sigh of exasperation. "He's a crafty old bastard, isn't he? Doesn't give anything away. He sensed he might have been set up?"

"Maybe." Thornton stretched a tired body. He'd been working day and night. "He's got a survival instinct," he said, plopping in a chair. "Benedetti protects himself wherever he goes, whoever he's with."

Simonsen shook his head. "Are you saying he's smarter than we are?"

"Not at all. Let's say this tax-bribery charge sticks, plays for a grand jury. Okay, he didn't mouth the words—at least not textbook—but it's clear from the video and tape what he's in the room for. We have him handing over the money."

"And our people. They didn't lead him? They didn't press it?"

"Not really."

"Yes or no?"

"Stan, I don't have to explain the law to you. I wouldn't insult you. It's open to interpretation."

"What about what's-his-name—Whelan? This Pietrosanti character. Saunders? They weren't coached?"

"Of course they were. It went well. I suggest we stop fixating on the worst-case scenario. Benedetti's in the room. He says he understands what he's there for. He hands over a hundred grand." Thornton lifted his right hand to slap on Simonsen's desk for emphasis, but brought it back into his lap. "I think we can get him on this, Stan. If not, we sure as hell will have him on RICO with Partridge feeding us the best goddamn insider information about the mob since Valachi. No matter how this sting goes down, Vincent Benedetti is history."

After Thornton left the office, Simonsen punched a button on his phone that rang directly in the office of FBI director Clark Mason. "Have you seen the Benedetti tapes?" he asked.

"Just got finished looking at them."

"What do you think?"

"Could go either way."

"Jesus!"

"Not as clear-cut as I'd like it to be. Then again, presented properly, it'll probably play to a jury."

Probably. A word Simonsen hated. "I'd like to see the tapes this morning," he said.

"We'll get them over to you."

"Good. I appreciate your cooperation, Clark. If this doesn't put Benedetti away, we always have Partridge."

"Exactly."

"That's proceeding smoothly?"

"As far as I know. It was well planned, well executed."

"It has to continue that way," Simonsen said. "Frankly, I don't think this tax thing will stick, not based upon what I've been told. But I don't care what gets the job done. This has to be resolved in a politically correct way. That's straight from the White House. I'll talk to you again after I see the tapes."

ix

The Next Day

Paul Dante rolled onto his side, but the mattress was softer than he was used to and urged him back to the middle. It wasn't that this mattress was too soft. It was more a matter of Dante's mattress being too hard. Here it was the first time he'd stayed the night at her place and already a conflict brewed. Maybe he'd buy her a bedboard as a gift.

In the semiconsciousness of awakening, he could still sense it was unfamiliar terrain. He cranked open his left eye but it was below the line of the pillow and revealed only a blur of white cotton. He forced open the right. This time he fixed on a swirl of color framed in a light-toned natural wood. He'd been right about the modern art, the hardwood floors, even the throw rugs. Oddly, however, the musical taste, which had concerned him the most, was not as intimidating as he'd expected. Although predominantly classical, it included strong representations of jazz—both traditional and modern—and an eclectic repertoire of popular and folk selections from all over the world, collected during Julia's trips abroad with college dance troupes.

Dante took a deep breath, swung his legs over the side of the bed, and picked up his wristwatch from a bedside table. Nine-thirty. As full consciousness returned, he remembered something to the effect of: "Eight o'clock class . . . there's a couple of cups of coffee in the Mr. Coffee . . . take what you like from the fridge . . . make sure the door latches behind you."

He went into the tidy, feminine bathroom; floral shower curtain, pink color scheme in towels and washcloths, antique cut-crystal potpourri holders with sterling silver caps. The faint smell of Julia lingered in the towels, which summoned a memory of the previous evening—a body only a dancer could own; skin softer than the bed linens covering taut muscles; the lithe contours of arms and legs outlining a torso that shaped to whatever pleasure struck their fancies. She was a beautiful lover. Adventurous, but also controlled. Giving, but understanding his need to give as well. A lovely person. She was lovely in bed. And she liked to talk dirty at the right times. Something nice happening here.

He didn't have fresh clothes so decided to shower back at his apartment. His mouth tasted bad; he squeezed toothpaste onto his right index finger and rubbed it along his teeth and gums, rinsed his mouth, then splashed water on his face.

Now half alive, he dressed in clothes that looked and felt as though he'd slept in them. A full-length view of himself in the hall mirror caused him to wonder when Julia would wake up to the reality of Paul Dante. Then again, they seemed to have reached a comfortable understanding. Despite differences in key cultural areas, their views of the world weren't all that different, and they appeared to enjoy each other's company. The sex? Terrific . . . and improving with practice.

The coffee was good. The woman knew how to make it strong. How could he not fall in love? He turned off the Mr. Coffee and pulled the plug to be sure the apartment wouldn't burn down while she was at the university. He double-checked the bedroom and kitchen to confirm that all the windows were closed and locked, then pulled the door to the apartment closed behind him and listened for the latch to catch. He tried the knob to make doubly sure. It occurred to him that each of these simple acts was, in its own way, protective of Julia. He grinned. Yeah, something nice *was* happening here.

———

He pushed open the door to his apartment and was greeted by the familiar musty smell of a room needing an airing out. The blinking red light on his answering machine drew him to it. He pushed the play button. The message was from Santo Benedetti: "Paul, I've got a big problem. I need your help. It's not something I can go into on the phone. Call me as soon as you get this message." The message had been left at three a.m.

He dialed Santo's private number.

"I expected you to call last night," Santo said. "Where were you?"

"I was on a surveillance assignment," Dante lied. "I was out of touch until I got back to my place just now. Sorry." There had never been a hint that Santo ever expected a payback for all he'd done for Dante and his family. Now, when Santo had needed his help, Dante hadn't been there. "What can I do?" he asked.

"You know about Vincent."

"What about him?"

It was a frustrated sigh on the other end. "Look, Paulie, could you come over to my place right now? I'm in the middle of a meeting."

"What about Vincent?" Dante persisted.

"Listen to the radio."

Dante took a two-minute shower—more of a rinse—put on a clean sport shirt and a fresh pair of slacks, and headed north to Baltimore.

He was angry with himself. He'd always wanted to do something for this man who had given so much to him, but Santo had never asked for anything. Dante knew the reason. Santo did not want to compromise Dante's position, first in government law enforcement, now as a PI. Not being there when Santo called made him feel bad. When he heard the news on the radio about Vincent, he *really* felt bad.

The guard at the gate waved Dante into the driveway, a long, lazy S-curve that wound to the front of the columned Benedetti mansion. A family soldier came to the car and told Dante to leave the engine running. Someone would park it for him. He was expected inside.

"Have a seat, Paul," Santo said when Dante entered the book-lined study. A half-dozen men sat around the mahogany table. Their faces said they weren't there to analyze the hidden meaning of obscure poets' words. Nor were they there to shoot pool at the billiards table, play poker at the elaborately inlaid card table, or to crank the arms of two antique slot machines from a long-gone casino. These were somber men whose deep creases and dark circles bespoke a sleepless night.

"You want coffee?" Santo asked. It was more a statement of what lay ahead than an amenity.

Dante nodded. An underling obliged his request.

Santo, settled in his customary seat at the head of the table, said to Dante, "You heard?"

"On the radio coming over. Sorry I was out of touch last night."

Santo shrugged. "No matter," he said. "You know everybody here?"

"Sure," Dante said, taking a quick inventory of the men at the table. He had only a passing acquaintance with most but knew they were heavy hitters in the Benedetti family—*caporegimes*, or *capos*, the family captains; the *consigliere*, whose counsel was respected; and, of course, Vincent's underboss, his brother, Santo.

"You notice who's *not* here?" Santo asked.

Others at the table shifted in their chairs, shuffled their feet, and avoided looking at Santo, whose face was an angry mask. His eyes were fixed on Dante, who wondered whether he was about to be blamed for what had happened. He gave Santo a palms-up and shrugged.

Santo ran a hand across his neck and pressed his fingers into the flesh, as though trying to knead a knot out of his muscles. "You guys have been at this for hours," he told the others. "I want to fill Paul in on the details. Go get some air outside. I'll call you when we're finished."

The room quickly emptied except for the Benedetti underboss and the investigator.

"My son-in-law." Santo said. "Genaro Orsini." The words stuck in his throat. "It's the reason I asked you to come here."

Dante was off balance. He'd raced there because Santo had summoned him. Now, there was a throw coming out of left field—a knuckle ball—maybe more a wiffle ball. "I'm at a loss here, Santo," he said. "My jigsaw's got a big hole in the middle."

"I'll fill it for you, Paulie. How does a man react when he finds out that his son-in-law, the husband of his only daughter, is a traitor? What does he do?"

Kill him, Dante thought. He furrowed his brow. Santo wasn't asking him to do *that*, was he?

Santo continued. "It looks like Genaro set up Vincent. He laid the trap my brother walked into last night. We don't know what else to think." He recounted the sting as he and his people had pieced it together. Orsini, his son-in-law—he added the title each time he used Orsini's name, but it was now a term of derision—had put Vincent in touch with someone named Charlie Pietrosanti, who claimed to have a rogue IRS director in his pocket. Vincent was to pay the director a hundred thousand dollars and his tax problems would go away. Instead, it was Hollywood, cameras and tape recorders rolling. The minute Vincent turned over the money, doors opened, the grey suits rushed in, and Vincent was arrested.

"Cuffs on his wrists, out through the lobby of the Mayflower with a crowd of businessmen watching, hands behind his back like some fucking street punk. That's the same fucking hotel where those bastards agreed thirty years ago with Vincent that nothing like this would ever happen. Ever!"

Were Dante capable of being totally honest at this point, he would have expressed satisfaction that Orsini was the villain. It wouldn't upset his next meal if Orsini got what was coming to him which, in this case, was bound to be unpleasant. But that fleeting moment of satisfaction was buried by the realization that Santo's brother, a man Dante did not know well but for whom he had respect, had been betrayed in this manner. Worse, it was obviously having a devastating impact upon Santo.

"I'm sorry," Dante said again. "Vincent doesn't deserve this treatment."

From the expression on Santo's face, pity was not what he sought.

"What do you want me to do?" Dante asked.

"Find the son of a bitch. He's gone. I talked to Lucia this morning. He never came home last night. He's skipped, the cocksucker."

"Oh, God, Lucia," Dante said in a muffled voice. He'd forgotten about her.

"She's stunned. The kid doesn't know what to think. After the tragedy with Marco, I don't know if she'll ever recover from this."

Kid? Dante thought.

"I'm not sure what this is going to do to her," Santo continued. "She's married just a few months to that bastard. Find him. Bring him to me. You can do it, Paulie, can't you? You're good at finding people. Am I right? I'm depending on you."

Dante said, "I'll do my best. You know that."

Santo told Big Dom Piaggio, his primary bodyguard who had taken up a position outside the study, to tell the others to return. As they filed in, Dante asked, "Do we have any leads where he might be?"

His question elicited only a prolonged silence. While Dante would have asked the same question of anyone when accepting this kind of assignment, he recognized the uncomfortable position it created for every man in the room. None wanted to play a role in the search for Santo's son-in-law. Knowing where to look would only raise questions among other members of the senior tribunal. On the other hand, there was nothing to be gained by finding him. It was now a policy matter. When someone, anyone, violated the family code, payback was required. But the return of Genaro Orsini, dead or alive, would be painful for Santo and his family, excruciating for his daughter. The person who achieved the distinction of finding Genaro Orsini would not be a hero.

Although Dante had a favored position with Santo despite not being a member of the family by blood or initiation, he was obviously not a favorite with Santo's closest advisors. Which relieved the others in the room. Let the outsider find Orsini. They were off the hook. They wouldn't offer much help. If he found Genaro, let him deliver the bad news to Santo and Vincent. If he didn't, it was his failure, not theirs.

"Try downtown where the *tootsoons* live." The words came from Dom Piaggio, a man who would do whatever the underboss asked. "He's always bullshitting about some hardware company he got a piece of."

"Anything else?" Dante asked.

More shuffles and shrugs but no words.

Dante broke the uncomfortable silence. "Santo, I can't do anything sitting here. I'll get on it and be in touch."

Santo walked Dante to the front door. "For some things, these guys in there are okay," he said when they were out of earshot. "For other things, they're not worth a shit. I can't depend on them for this. I'm depending on you, Paulie."

"I'll give it my best shot."

"Good."

"What about what Dominick said?" Dante asked.

"The company's called Victor and Armbruster," Santo answered. "I don't know where it is, but you'll find it." He shook his head. "Some things just don't make any sense, Paulie. You know what I'm saying? What the fuck is going on here? We had something that worked. It worked for years. Then, because a some fuckin' third party it starts to fall apart. Now this, by a member of my own family." For a moment, Dante wondered whether his friend was about to cry. But tears never came. Instead, Santo smacked his right fist into his left palm. "Find him, Paulie. As fast as you can."

"It might take time but I'll pull out all the stops."

"Don't think this is all on you, Paulie," Santo said. "I got everybody looking for him. If one a them finds him . . ."

"What are your plans for Orsini if *I* find him?"

"Don't ask a question you don't want to hear the answer to," Santo replied. "You got a license to protect. This is just a legit missing-person assignment. Keep it that way."

That Same Day

Finding a missing person is never easy. Finding one who knows that if he's found his brains become an abstract painting on the windshield of a Lincoln is a real challenge.

Dante left Santo's house determined to give the search for Orsini everything he had. Precious little had been asked of him by his friend over the years, and he'd always felt a keen sense of obligation to Santo for all the favors given his mother and sister—given to himself, for that matter.

He also knew that if he failed, others in the Benedetti family would tell Santo he shouldn't have wasted his time with somebody who "isn't one of us"—and they obviously wouldn't mean his ethnic heritage.

When looking for somebody like Genaro Orsini, the usual outlets utilized by private investigators to find a husband who's behind in support payments aren't much help. Finding those types was relatively easy. You explored conventional channels and, unless the missing person was a wizard at the disappearing act, you usually found your man.

But in this case, it meant seeking out the sort of people who hear things about men like Orsini, people who hang around the right bars and know the right street people; people who, like vampires, don't do business in the daylight. Nocturnal types whose actions play better in the dark.

And so Dante went through the motions for the rest of the day, driving the city he knew so well. It was still a beautiful place with its soaring and moving monuments, magnificent buildings and wide boulevards. But that beauty was on the surface. Over the years, the city had fallen victim to drugs and resulting crime. It was now the murder capital of the nation. Within spitting distance of the White House were crack houses, drug factories, and armies of desperate men better armed than the police.

It had become a city of unpleasant contrasts. He drove along Embassy Row on Massachusetts Avenue, one building more impressive than the next. Then, he was in Southeast D.C., where he eyed every battered car double-parked without a driver as the next potential car bomb. Saigon, he thought. Damn shame.

Dante got serious once the sun went down. He plied, prodded, and pressured every lowlife he could find to no avail. At midnight, he considered stopping by Orsini's house in fancy Georgetown but that would only further upset Lucia. There was something unsavory about a guy like Orsini living in Georgetown. Maybe that's why Orsini married Lucia, Dante mused as he drove past the house—to live in a fancy neighborhood. Too bad for the neighbors. Even having a savings-and-loan bloodsucker move in would do more to enhance property values.

The fact that Orsini now lived in Washington, rather than in Baltimore where the rest of the family resided, expanded the geography Dante had to cover, which stretched him thin. But he tried his best into the night and early morning hours, plugging into the network of contacts he'd built over the years, first as an MPD detective, now as a private investigator. Nothing. Not a lead. Not even a hint of where to look next.

Disgusted, he pulled up to a phone booth and called his former partner at MPD, Cal Williams.

Williams had special meaning in Dante's life. In the Baltimore neighborhood in which Dante had grown up, there wasn't much love for blacks. He'd carried that feeling with him to Vietnam where he suffered a sobering revelation—your color didn't mean a damn thing when you were trying to survive midnight raids on your mildewed tent by a bunch of fanatical gooks. Black, white, pink, or orange, you stood side by side;

everybody was the same color in the jungles of Vietnam, frightened-green.

When he'd come out of the service and joined Washington's MPD, lessons learned in Vietnam about racial harmony didn't seem to stick. Until he was teamed up as a rookie cop with Cal Williams, a smart, gutsy, and straight-thinking black man with a consuming passion for spicy Creole food, a Jamaican wife as beautiful as she was nice, and a liking for Paul Dante that Dante couldn't understand. Williams was no Uncle Jemima. Far from it. When Dante would let slip a slur against blacks, Williams was quick to pick him up on it, and they'd come close to blows on occasion. They also became friends, reluctant ones at first, but increasingly close as their dreary and dangerous tours of duty placed them in harm's way night after night. Eventually, Dante would tell Barbara, his wife, that there was no other man in the world with whom he'd rather stand back to back in a parking lot when a dozen hopped-up bikers were attacking than Cal Williams. Williams was no longer black to Paul Dante. He was just a man. A good man.

"What's the scuttlebutt about the Benedetti bust?" Dante asked Williams after they'd exchanged playful jabs.

"Strictly a federal case," Williams answered.

"What about Santo Benedetti's new son-in-law, Genaro Orsini, also known as Gerry Orson?"

"Never heard of him."

"Bullshit."

"A vaguely familiar name. No interest on this end."

"You wouldn't have heard any rumors about where Mr. Orsini might be these days?"

A familiar low, rumbling laugh from Williams. "Rumors? In the nation's capital? In this esteemed police department? Hey, my Italian friend, go home and go to bed. Or, meet me for a bowl of chili after tour. I'm off in an hour."

"I have too much respect for my stomach," Dante said. "Enjoying desk duty? Getting fat?"

"Check in the gym tomorrow and I'll show you what fat is. I'd love to bust that Roman beak of yours."

Dante laughed. "One shot to the gut and you're finished, champ.

You know what they say about you black guys. Can't hurt you to the head."

"Paulie?"

"What?"

"Walk easy. This Benedetti thing is big-time. Bigger than you and me."

"I figured. Got to go. Best to Cindy and the kids. Catch up with you soon."

Dante used the same booth to call a friend on the metro desk at the *Post,* a pasty-faced little guy named Jimmy Rooker who bled police blue, a cop junkie who'd do anything to be on the good side of a uniform. He wrote a regular column, "Crimes of Dispassion," which had been born of the wave of random, senseless violence that had gripped the city over the past few years.

"What you read, Paul, is what we got."

"No sidebar on Santo Benedetti's son-in-law, Genaro Orsini?"

"You see a sidebar in the paper? What's your interest in the case?"

"Just curious."

"And I'm Katherine Graham. You on Benedetti's payroll?"

"Right. I'm his personal astrologer."

"Give me a reading, baby. I'm a Pisces."

"You're a fish. Period. Come on, Jimmy, level with me. Nothing on Orsini?"

"Nothing. If there was, I'd give it to you. You know that. Right?"

"Right." Dante knew the little cop groupie with the pale cheeks would.

Exhausted, he stopped for coffee and eggs-over-easy in an all-night diner where he killed an hour and a half thinking, and nodding off in the booth. When he got back into the Riviera and headed off again, the presunrise had painted the eastern sky bloodred, and the first small clots of traffic for poor souls on the early shift had begun to appear on the roads. He circled the city for another hour with no real direction until ending up in the heart of the northeast black section where, as a cop, he used to bust drug dealers, pimps, and other contributors to society's baser needs. Policing districts like this was frustrating work. It was hopeless. The blacks in these neighborhoods seemed forever condemned to this sort of life with no hope of escape. It was one of the reasons Dante had left the MPD. After thirteen years, he knew there were no solutions, just problems, too many new ones every day. Even when someone from this hell-on-earth got something good going, it invariably turned sour.

He realized he was in the neighborhood where the company Big Dom had mentioned, Victor and Armbruster, was located. While he didn't see how checking into that sideline business of Orsini's would turn up anything, he wasn't exactly drawing aces anywhere else.

Victor and Armbruster was housed in a peeling, crumbling warehouse built during the postwar period, and sloppily renovated through some government grant to help the underclasses. A coat of cheap all-weather paint had been applied years before in a futile attempt to make the place look presentable, but it had just ended up an empty canvas for graffiti artists' spray cans. Piles of rusted metal curlicues and shavings littered a yard next to the building. A half-dozen vehicles, most of them pasted together by do-it-yourself mechanics, were parked haphazardly. An orange glow backlit each wire-reinforced window; the hum and thump of metal stamping machines, and the whine of metal against metal on the lathes testified to an early start. It wasn't even seven.

"We crank up at four," the thick-necked black man said as he ushered Dante into an office of secondhand steel furniture, a couple of dead manual typewriters, and a dial telephone. An out-of-place IBM personal computer was on the other side of a glass partition. A pretty young black woman sat at it.

"My daughter," Victor said. "Business grad student at Howard University. Redoing our inventory control and traffic programs."

"Impressive," Dante said. He accepted the offer of a cup of coffee and reluctantly spooned in artificial creamer. "Thanks," he said. "I needed this."

"You look tired, Mr. Dante," Victor of Victor and Armbruster said. "If you don't mind my saying so."

"And if I do?" Dante said.

"You look the same anyway, Mr. Dante."

"Call me Paul."

"What can I do for you, Paul? I'm a busy man. A company to run and too many bills to pay."

"Like I said at the door, I'm a private investigator. I've got some questions about your controller."

"Controller?" Victor seemed puzzled. Then, he sat back in a precarious chair that groaned with his movement and said, "You mean Gerry Orson. Our executive motherfucker."

"Genaro Orsini."

"A motherfucker by any other name." Victor laughed. It reminded Dante of Cal Williams. Did all black men laugh that way? All with the same genes as James Earl Jones? Why not? Weren't they all born with rhythm, too?

"Mr. Gerry Orson," Victor said, continuing to laugh, only Dante knew by his tone he didn't find it funny. "Friend of his?"

"No."

"Concerned relative?"

"No."

"I know. He's been left a million dollars and you've been hired to find him and hand him his prize."

"I'm looking for him because I want to kill him."

"Now we can talk. More coffee?"

"No. It tastes like it came out of a sewer."

Victor shrugged. "We make metal parts. You want good coffee, go to a fancy restaurant."

"As soon as I leave here. Tell me about your resident motherfucker."

"A saint. An angel of mercy. We needed money to keep going. We had military contracts but they slow-paid, like usual. Right?"

"I wouldn't know."

"Lucky man. A member of the privileged class. Anyway, somebody mentioned this guy Orson who had access to venture money. We looked him up, had a meeting, and he told us not to worry. Sure as hell, he comes up with what we need, only there's a hitch. He gets to play controller. At that point, he could have been anything he wanted to be, president, chairman. Money talks, bullshit walks."

Dante smiled. He liked this guy.

"That money saved our ass, at least until our new controller started siphoning it off for himself."

Dante sipped his coffee. He couldn't help the face he made. "Go on," he said.

"He just about run this place into the toilet," Victor continued, sounding like a man in need of a sympathetic audience. "Meanwhile, he runs his drug store outta one of my back rooms."

"Drug store?"

Victor gave Dante a hard look. "You don't come from the naive side a town, do you? I mean, you don't look like you do. Drug store, for christsake. Vials, needles, syringes, nickel-and-dime bags. Only he's a quantity supplier, no penny-ante shit."

File that, Dante told himself. "He come around any more?"

"Last Friday of every month, like clockwork. Hits me up for two grand. His walking-around money. Whether I get to feed me that month or not. Understood?"

"Yeah." Dante said. "Understood. Any idea where he might be?"

"It ain't the last Friday of the month. You don't think he hangs around here other days earning his keep, do you? I figure he's out chasin' white pussy the rest of the month."

"What pussy does he chase on the last Friday of the month?" Dante asked.

Victor, who'd exhibited an appealing relaxed sense of humor until now, leaned back. His face clouded. His eyes said he was feeling a sudden dose of sad. "He's got himself a piece of dark meat around the corner. Best piece of ass in the city, or so they tell me. *I* wouldn't know. I don't have that kind of disposable income."

"Where do I find her?"

"What you want to find her for? To get laid?"

"My business."

Victor sat up straight and leaned across the desk. "No, baby, *my* business. This particular lady is a relation a mine. A cousin. Distant. But blood. You hear me?"

"Yeah. Keep going."

Victor leaned back again. The sadness in his large, watery eyes remained.

"I'm not looking to party," Dante said.

"Connections," Victor said. "She works on appointment. You got to know her handlers."

"Who are?"

"The guys who run this neighborhood. The same guys who run it to hell."

"Introduce me."

Victor cocked his head and chewed on his cheek. "I always find dudes like you amazing," he said. "You start with the assumption that people like me are stupid. Dig?"

"Maybe. Maybe not."

"I grind out a living in this place," the black man said. "I point you to people who don't want outsiders asking questions and how long do you think I stay in business? How long do you think my voice keeps soundin' masculine?"

Dante's look hardened. "I fought with guys in Vietnam who came from the deepest part of the deep South," he said. "I never once looked over my shoulder, or saw them look over theirs."

"So I got across from me a white man with soul," Victor said. "But even if I know that's the case, the scum out on the street don't."

Dante drained the final dregs of the coffee, which had grown cold in the cup. "I drank your sludge," he said. "You owe me another answer."

"I'll have my daughter make it next time. Shoot."

"Do you have any idea where Orsini got the money for your loan?"

"He *said* it came from some big insurance company that likes to help small businesses, especially minority businesses, your garden-variety, nigger-loving insurance company. That's how he got our interest."

"You don't believe that?"

"Look, Mr. Dante, I'm going to tell you one more truth about your Mr. Orsini. Then you leave me alone. Right?"

"Right."

Victor hesitated, as though processing whether he'd already said too much. Then he said, "We had a problem with a guy in New York who owed us big. We told Orson about it and he says he'll take care of it.

He takes my partner, Armbruster, up to New York and they visit this deadbeat. I want the money, sure, but I always figure a little honey catches more than vinegar. My mother always said that. So Orson and Armbruster go up to New York and visit this dude in his office. It's in one a those office buildings built in the thirties and forties with windows that still open. Before they go in, they hook up with some guy named Tenaglia who, Orson claims, has a contact with a honcho in the lending department of one a the biggest insurance companies, which shall remain nameless. Anyway, the deadbeat balks at paying the money, so Orson throws open the window and hangs the fucker outside by his ankles—thirty-eight floors up." He stopped his tale.

Dante gestured for him to continue.

"People in the buildings on three sides see a guy hanging out the window. But when the cops come to investigate, the deadbeat tells them it never happened. So they return his wallet and his car keys, which a passerby picked up on the sidewalk and turned in to a doorman. He says he must have dropped them when he pulled out his handkerchief to blow his nose. Only I know, and you know, people don't keep their car keys, wallets, and handkerchiefs all in the same pocket. Anyway, this guy hands over every cent he owes in cash, Orsini pockets half, and my partner brings the rest back here."

"Thanks," Dante said, starting for the door.

"Wait," Victor said. "I got one for you."

"Go ahead."

"Why you lookin' for him?"

"A routine missing-spouse case."

"Routine, my ass," Victor retorted. "He just got married to the Benedetti broad, and her uncle just got taken down big-time. I don't have to be no Einstein to smell a connection."

Dante smiled. You guys always start with the assumption that people like me are stupid, he thought. Touché, Victor. "Let's just say that when his family reestablishes relations, he probably won't be coming around here the last Friday of every month anymore."

"In that case," Victor said, "good luck."

Dante took out his wallet and handed him his business card. "If you remember anything else that won't be bad for business, give me a call."

"Sure," Victor said. "But you'll never get to him."

"Why's that?"

"'Cause he's probably in the Bahamas."

"How do you know that?"

"Calculated guess."

"I'm still listening."

"Phone bills. Five, six hundred a month, all charged to the credit card that's part of our deal with him. I called it once out of curiosity, wanted to know who was costing me all that money. It's a bank. I gotta figure Orson stashed a good part of my profits in this bank in the islands so he can gamble it away. Nice way to gamble. Somebody else's money."

"Tough to lose," Dante said.

"Tell me about it."

"Give me one more?"

"Sure."

"How come your company's name is Victor and Armbruster? I mean, your first name and his last name."

"His first name is Armbruster."

"His mother had a sense of humor, huh?"

"His mother had a nigger slave uncle named Armbruster. You heard of slavery?"

"Sometimes I think I am one. Thanks for the time, Victor of Victor and Armbruster. If I find your controller, you'll be the second to know."

———

Back behind the wheel of the Buick, Dante chewed on what he'd just heard. If Orsini was involved in drug running on any level, it wouldn't make his new poppa-in-law happy. Not that that mattered if Orsini had, indeed, set up Vincent. You can only die once. It's the time it takes to die that counts. The Benedettis ran a lot of illegal activities, but drugs weren't on the list. It was an unwritten provision of the understanding. Violating that provision would put the family's favored position in serious jeopardy. Despite that, Young Turks were crossing the line because drugs were their ticket to big money, Vincent and Santo Benedetti be damned. For those who'd been caught, it had been a ticket to a big sleep in a deep swamp.

Dante fought to stay awake. I've got to get some sleep before I kill myself, he thought, and headed home.

But his mind continued to race. There was the matter of supply, he thought, licking his index fingers and rubbing his eyes in the hope it would keep him from conking out and embracing a light pole. Where was Orsini getting his drugs? It was unlikely it came from any of the families. It had to be from a major neighborhood supplier. Hispanic. Black. Victor had said Orsini had a thing going with a black hooker on Fridays. Dante had to give it to Orsini for guts, or stupidity. The bastard was literally sleeping with the enemy.

It had been a long, tiring day and, in the final analysis, fruitless, especially if Victor had been right about the Bahamas connection. If Orsini had skipped the country, how do you entice him back when he knows the Benedetti family is waiting with a lavish welcome-home replete with meat hooks, a piano-wire necklace, blowtorches, and probably worse?

———

Dante stretched out on his bed upstairs at Cuffs and nodded off for fifteen, twenty minutes at a stretch. But most of the time he lay awake chasing the ideas that raced through his brain. He didn't see this Orsini assignment as a small picture. This was a Cinemascope production that had become a blur, maybe because he was too close to the screen.

Orsini sets up his father-in-law's brother just a few months after marrying into the family, then splits for the Bahamas with money he'd been scamming from a small-time black business in the ghetto. Even if drug money had made the pot richer, it didn't make sense. Orsini stood to gain a lot more from being Santo Benedetti's son-in-law than he did from any of the other scenarios Dante envisioned. Was Orsini just a stupid, strong-arm guy who knew how to hang some white-collar guy out an office-building window, but didn't know how to deal with real success? While that was what Dante wanted to believe, it didn't play for him.

A MEMBER OF THE FAMILY

There were too many missing pieces, most having to do with blacks and the alleged drug connection. If Orsini was dealing, as Victor claimed, he was taking an incredible chance. Then again, any drug dealing would have predated his marriage into the Benedetti family. While it would have made sense for Orsini to sever such relationships after marrying Lucia, old habits can die hard, especially when they're still bringing in easy money. They said Spiro Agnew kept taking petty graft from Maryland after he became Vice President of the United States. Go figure.

The swagger to Orsini's step probably originated in that ill-conceived brain of his, Dante decided. Maybe he hung on to sources of good ghetto money just so he could keep beating up people who were ill-equipped to fight back. But to do that, he needed a godfather in the latino-black drug connection. For Dante, it kept coming up spades. He had to talk to someone, but the question was who? And then, how?

He finally fell into a deep sleep, awakening at four that afternoon. He had Julio brew him a pot of coffee before the after-work crowd sauntered in, and sipped it at the bar. Shelly was on break in the back. When she emerged, she tossed the *Times* in front of him. It was opened to the Metro section. A follow-up article about the Benedetti family, illustrated with the previous day's photograph of a cuffed Vincent Benedetti being led from the Mayflower, dominated the page.

"Your buddy," she said.

"I know the family," Dante answered, picking up the paper.

"Not a very dignified pose," Shelly said.

"Yeah," he said, staring at the picture.

The photograph was one of those freeze-frames that caught the subject midway between expressions. Vincent had an odd look on his face, equal part surprise and embarrassment. I don't know, Dante thought. I know I've taken sides here. I have a vested interest in this. Regardless, there's something rotten. On the surface, it seemed a triumph of good over evil. But he kept asking himself, what's wrong with this picture?

He took a quick inventory of his life. He'd gotten through combat

117

in Vietnam with one bum leg that acted up on cold, damp days. He'd grown up on proverbial mean streets, but came out of that okay, too. No advanced degrees from Harvard, but a pretty good life. He'd taken his lumps on Washington's MPD—a bullet in the thigh, a baseball bat over the head, plenty of anxious moments—but he was still here and breathing. The closest he'd come to dying was a botched gall bladder operation by one of the city's top surgeons. That one was touch and go for a few days, but he pulled through. Good times and bad times, like the rest of civilization.

Now, he was looking at the visual evidence of the Vincent Benedetti bust, and it spit in the face of what Dante believed the world was supposed to be. He'd been involved in plenty of stings when he was on the force. The setups were never as clean as the prosecutors would have liked them to be, but this setup was really amateur night. There was Vincent with a look on his face that seemed distorted. The press always did that, tried to pick a shot that made a mafioso look less human.

You may have done bad things in your life, Vincent, Dante thought. You may have broken the law, but you shouldn't go to jail because *they* trapped you into breaking the law. When he was in Nam, they called it burning the village to save it. He didn't like it then. He didn't like it any better now.

Dante called Cal Williams at MPD and told him he wanted a favor. "I need to talk to a hooker," he said.

"What do you want me to do, bring her in?" His tone was one of incredulity.

"No," Dante said. "I need to talk to her in an environment that's . . . well, less supervised."

"Then what do you want me to do?"

"Take me to visit her, get us in with your badge, then find an excuse to leave us alone."

Williams said, "Paulie, this ain't your way to get a free piece of ass, is it?"

"What time can you meet me?"

118

XI

The Next Day

While Dante tried unsuccessfully to get in touch with Julia to explain why he hadn't called and why he might be out of touch for a while, two FBI agents on the other side of the city were overseeing activities in a dilapidated, abandoned tenement, its front windows covered by a thick layer of white window wax.

They were in what had once been a living room. Against one wall was a rollaway bed in a disordered state. Beside it stood a small yellow plastic table that served as a stand for an ashtray overflowing with cigarette butts of various sizes bent at innumerable angles. A hanger holding a blue-grey sharkskin suit, as neat as its surroundings were slovenly, hung from the top of an open closet door. Beneath it, a pair of black wingtips polished to a metallic luster, and aligned as if ready for inspection, sat on a scarred footlocker.

Seated in a chair was Charlie Pietrosanti. He was wrapped in a striped barber's cloth. Two female agents in smocks worked on him; one brushed dye and highlights into his hair; the other applied a layer of theatrical makeup. A salt-and-pepper moustache was about to be positioned on his upper lip.

Pietrosanti was agitated; his legs bounced up and down in a disruptive staccato. An agent grabbed one of them. "Knock it off," he said. "You're making me crazy."

"You?" Pietrosanti said. "You can walk to the end of the block and know you'll make it with your balls still swinging where they're supposed to. Me, on the other hand . . ."

"You know something, Charlie, seeing you for the true coward you are is not a pretty sight."

"Hey, fuck you," Pietrosanti shouted, bolting forward in his chair and disrupting the work of the makeup girl and hairdresser.

"Get a grip on yourself," Agent Tom Whelan said. "What do you want us to do, push you out on the street naked, with your former face? The Benedettis have their own personal PI, Paul Dante, turning over stones trying to find your buddy, Gerry Orson. I'm sure he'd be happy to find you, too."

"Yeah, right," Pietrosanti replied. He scanned the room until fixing on Whelan's partner, Fred Wozinski, who puffed on a cigarette as he peered through a peephole rubbed in the window's wax. Wozinski was tall and heavy. His hair was like a wire brush; he had a closet filled with cheap suits that never quite fit right, like the one he wore that day. It was cut from shiny blue material. The collar of the jacket didn't lie on his neck, as though tiny wires held it out and away.

"Tell him to get away from that fuckin' window," Pietrosanti said. "*He's* making *me* nervous."

Both agents ignored him.

"Okay," Whelan said, "let's go through it one more time. You're going out West for a while. A couple of agents will be with you just in case."

"Just in case *what*?"

Whelan ignored the question. "Once there, you'll be settled in a nice place. Three squares a day, all your bills paid, TV, a deck of cards in case you feel like some recreation."

"For what? Solitaire?"

"If you're a good boy, Charlie, the agents who'll be with you in your new quarters might let you have some female companionship now and then. Not bad, Charlie. Could be worse."

"It's jail," Pietrosanti muttered.

"No it's not," Whelan said. "It's a nice, safe place for you until

Benedetti's trial begins. You come back here and testify, help put the old man away, and you go in the program. New name, a permanent new face, and plenty of walking-around money."

"It sounds thrilling."

"Of course," Whelan continued, "as far as the rest of the world is concerned, Charlie Pietrosanti is dead. That's a good thing, Charlie, especially where the Benedettis are concerned. Charlie Pietrosanti is dead and buried. They'll see proof of it. They'll believe it, which means they won't be out looking for you."

"Yeah, sure," Pietrosanti said.

"The surgery's already been done," Whelan said. "The corpse never felt a thing. Who counts limbs when they're headed for potter's field?"

The two women applied their finishing touches and stepped back. One held a large mirror in front of Piestrosanti so he could examine the result.

"Yeah, yeah, fine," he said, as though the face he surveyed was no different from the one he saw every morning when he shaved. He pushed the mirror aside, leaned forward, elbows on his knees, then rose from the chair and stretched.

"Okay," Whelan said. "Let's have it."

"What?"

The agent held out his hand, fingers beckoning.

Pietrosanti let loose a sigh of disgust. Then, with no small effort, he twisted the gaudy ring from his left hand and dropped it into the FBI man's open palm. "That was my good-luck charm," he said.

"It'll never bring you better luck than it will this time, Charlie."

––––––––

Cal Williams met Paul Dante in front of Victor and Armbruster. Only the lobster shift remained in the factory, playing to the thump of a lone stamping machine.

Williams sucked on a cigar and blew a cloud of white smoke at Dante. "I could do without this, Paulie," he said. "My ass is grass if this thing comes apart."

"Call it a citizen's arrest."

"Cute." He blew another smoke cloud. "*I* still got a career left, buddy."

"Come on, Cal," Dante said as they started up the block. "You wouldn't have an ass left if it wasn't for me. Besides, this chick's in an illegal business. Which side of the law are you on?"

They turned the corner and continued at a brisk pace.

"What's this all about anyway?" Williams asked.

"I need some info. What else?"

"Yeah, but for what? Who's your client?"

"Privileged information."

Williams stopped. Dante realized it two steps later, stopped and looked back. "What's the matter?" he asked.

"Don't ask me to trash regs and then tell me it's privileged information."

Dante came to him. "I'm doing a job for the Benedettis. Strictly legit. I'm trying to find Santo Benedetti's son-in-law, Genaro Orsini."

"Because the word is that Orsini set up Vincent on the tax bust. Right?"

Dante shrugged.

"And if you find him and deliver him to his father-in-law, what do you figure happens to Orsini?"

"Not my problem."

"Sure as hell ain't mine, either. But think twice about it, Paul."

"I've already thought about it ten times. Are you helping me or not?"

"What's this hooker got to do with it?"

"She does Orsini on a regular basis. I figure maybe she'll know where he is."

Williams shook his head. He took a final drag on what was left of his cigar, dropped it to the ground and flattened it with the heel of his shoe. "Okay," he said, jamming his hands into the pockets of his tan raincoat. "Okay. But I was never here."

"Of course not, Cal. What am I, stupid?"

"Maybe. Let's go."

Dante had gotten the building's location during a follow-up phone call to Victor of Victor and Armbruster. He had to squeeze the information out of him, succeeding when he convinced Victor that his hooker-relative's life could be in danger and that he, Dante, might be in a position to save it. "Just don't let her know where you got it," Victor had said. Dante assured him he wouldn't and, of course, would not.

The two men climbed stone steps leading to a heavy glass door with a decorative metal grate. The door, which was supposed to open when a resident of the building pushed a buzzer upstairs, was broken and open an inch. "Easy, huh?" Dante said as he led them into a foyer. A small, cramped elevator beckoned with open doors. Dante and Williams rode it to the fourth floor and went to apartment 4C. They stood on opposite sides of the door. Williams patted a nine-millimeter Beretta he carried under his left arm.

"Her name's Fionia Smith," Dante said in a whisper.

"I don't care what her name is."

"Talk to her by name. You're here on a complaint by a john. You're a bad cop, want to take her in. I'm the good cop. I talk you out of it and you get pissed off and leave. Simple."

Dante knocked. There was no answer. He knocked again, harder this time. Williams looked at him and shrugged.

"She's in there," Dante said, knocking still harder.

"You're early," came the high-pitched voice from the other side of the door. "Too early."

"Can't I sit somewhere?" Dante replied.

"Come back later."

"Come on, let me in."

"Later," the female voice insisted.

Dante nodded at Williams, who pulled out his police shield as Dante resumed knocking. "Police," Williams said in a loud, forceful voice. "Open the door."

Nothing.

"Police," he repeated. "Open up or we take it down."

Dante raised his fist to pound again but before he could, the door opened.

"Shit," a slinky black woman in a mint green teddy said. "What the fuck you want?"

"In," Williams said, flashing his badge in front of her face and leading Dante into the apartment.

"What the hell is this?" Fionia asked. "The captain short you on your vig this week?"

Dante took a quick tour of the apartment: living room, eat-in kitchen, bedroom, bathroom; typical.

"You got a warrant?" Fionia asked.

"We're not here to search the place," said Williams. "We're here on a complaint from one of your customers."

"Complaint?" She laughed. "Nobody complains about me, baby."

"You can tell us about it downtown," Williams said.

"What the fuck you doin', arresting me? For what? I done nothin' illegal."

"Get dressed," Williams said.

"Wait a minute," Dante said to Williams. "Maybe we can question her here. No need to take her out in the cold."

"It's not cold out," Williams said.

"Look, Jesse," Dante said, "we're making too big a deal outta this. The john says his wallet was emptied up here, but he's too chickenshit to file a formal complaint against her. Lemme just ask you a coupla questions, Miss Smith."

"Hey, you want to bullshit with her, go bullshit," Williams said in a loud voice. "You got the rank on me, so bullshit with her here. I'll see ya around."

"Don't get pissed, Jesse," Dante said.

"I'm not pissed, Richard. I'll see you back at the zoo."

Williams left, working hard to conceal a smile.

"Sit down," Dante told her, indicating the couch.

"Hey, what is this?"

"I said sit down," Dante repeated, taking her by the arm and leading her to the couch. "I just saved you a long night in a cell. Show some gratitude."

"What are you guys pulling?" Fionia plopped on the couch, her full breasts brushing his arm. He stepped back and she bounced up again. He put a hand on her shoulder to force her down but thought better of it. Getting physical wouldn't accomplish anything, just make her madder than she was. He couldn't push too far. She thought he was a cop. He wasn't. She could make trouble later if she wanted to, especially for Williams.

He sat. "Put something on the stereo," he said.

She studied him.

"Do it. Looks like you got a nice record collection."

She went to a vertical stack of albums on a shelf alongside a stereo rack system. As she bent over to scan her choices, Dante got an unobstructed view of her ass—polished steel sitting atop two perfectly turned, smooth coffee-colored legs. There was a gap at the top of her thighs through which Dante could see a wisp of black pubic hair. Nice view. He could see why she was popular.

Fionia put a Wilson Pickett album on the turntable, adjusted the volume, then turned to Dante. Her look was less ugly than before. "Look," she said, "I got guests coming in a half hour." She looked to the open bedroom door. "You want to party for a half hour? Come on."

"That's not what I want," Dante said. He was tempted, but reason prevailed. Safe sex be damned, he wasn't about to bang a pro in this day of AIDS and whatever else might be lurking in that pretty little wet package between her legs. "I just want to ask you a few questions." He smiled, patted the couch next to him. "Come on, Miss Smith, sit down. Only take a few minutes. You'll have plenty of time to get ready for your next guests."

She threw herself on the couch. "Let's get on with it," she said, crossing her legs powwow style under her. Little was left unexposed.

I have to stay focused, Dante thought. "It's about Gerry Orson," he said.

"Who's that?"

"Last Friday of every month."

"That some kind of code?"

"Enough with the cute, Fionia," Dante said. "You tell me about Orson or your business goes into Chapter Eleven."

"Never heard of him."

"I think you have."

"Think whatever the fuck you want, mister. I never hearda no Gerry Orson."

"How about Genaro Orsini?"

She guffawed. "I wouldn't do nobody with a name like that."

"Look," Dante said, "the last Friday of every month, you and Orson-Orsini get together. He picks up money from a client and spreads some of it on you. Regular. Like clockwork."

"I don't talk about my customers. Like a lawyer or doctor. It's privileged information." She gave him a smug smile as though she'd just won a major point in a trial.

"I'm your friend, Fionia," said Dante. "I have no beef with you. But I have to find Orson and hoped you'd help me. Will you?"

She cocked her head and narrowed her eyes. "You're no fuckin' cop."

"I was. I'm a private investigator now."

"Who was the other guy?"

"A friend."

"Carrying metal."

"No matter. Do you know where Orson, or Orsini, your regular Friday-night friend, is right now?"

Fionia stood. "Get out," she said, "before I call the real cops."

Dante slowly stood. He'd taken his shot and it hadn't worked. He could press but he knew it wouldn't loosen her tongue. He could get physical and maybe she'd tell him something. But people who tell you something to keep from getting knocked around say whatever you want to hear, true or not. He'd come up a cropper. Nothing ventured, nothing gained. He was tired, and frustrated.

The right spaghetti strap on the teddy had slipped off her shoulder, dropping that side of the garment and exposing her breast. She pulled the strap back up into place. "Get out," she said. "I'm in the middle of my business day."

Dante walked to where his car was parked in the lot next to the

Victor and Armbruster plant. He wasn't sure what he'd expected to happen with Fionia but whatever it was, it hadn't. It was time to give Santo an update, even if he didn't have anything worthwhile to tell him. What *would* he tell Santo, that some small-time black businessman said Genaro was beating his business for two grand a month? That Genaro went, once a month, to screw some knockout black broad who wouldn't admit that he'd ever been there? That the black man was sure Genaro was in the Bahamas? That he, Dante, didn't have a clue where Genaro really was?

"I can count on you for this, right, Paulie?" Santo had said. Dante had promised to give it his best, but his best had turned out not to be very good. He wished that wasn't the case.

———

The minute Dante was gone, a tall, rangy Hispanic man named Carlos, dressed only in tight black slacks, emerged from a closet in the bedroom and stood in the doorway. He slipped on a white linen shirt, casually buttoned the bottom two buttons, stuck his bare feet into a pair of tan loafers and sauntered toward her.

"You believe that shit?" Fionia asked, laughing nervously.

"Yeah. I believe it, and I don't like it."

"Wasn't nothin' I could do 'cept let them in, right?"

"You been talking to people behind Carlos's back?"

"What are you, crazy? You heard. I told them nothin'."

"They shouldn't have been here in the first place. No way. Just trouble."

She dropped the teddy to the floor. "Come on, baby, I got twenty minutes before the next one arrives. Time for Carlos and Fionia to have some blow and . . ."

He placed his hands on her shoulders and pushed her to her knees. He unzippered his pants and she pulled his semierect penis out and massaged it with her long, tapered brown fingers tipped with ruby-red. Then, as she took it in her mouth and slowly worked her tongue over it, it grew. His right hand rested on top of her head. She paused for a moment to look up at him. He yanked her hair, which caused her to gasp in pain. There was no expression of pleasure on his swarthy face, or in his coal-black eyes. She resumed sucking him until he came, his pelvis jerking forcefully into her face, a low moan from his lips. She scooted on her knees to a table, pulled Kleenex from a box and spit his semen into it, returned with more tissues and wiped his still erect cock.

He zippered his pants and went to the door. He turned. Fionia was still on her knees in the middle of the living room. "Walk easy, bitch," he said. "Don't cause Carlos no trouble."

———

Early the next morning, Dante had finally made it into a deep sleep when the jangle of the telephone on his night stand exploded in his left ear. He lifted the receiver from the cradle, dropped it onto the pillow and rolled his right ear into place on top of it. "Paul Dante," he mumbled.

"Paulie. Cal."

"Yeah, Cal. What is it?"

"That chick, Fionia Smith?"

"Yeah?"

"She's dead, Paulie. OD. Brought her in an hour ago. Client found her. The door was open. The body still warm. Hoss. Mainlined. Straight into the bloodstream."

"Shit," Dante said, swinging his legs over the side of the bed and keeping the phone pressed to his face. "That broad didn't have a mark on her. No tracks. She showed me most of her in the ten minutes I was with her. She was strictly a nose-shooter."

"Maybe, maybe not."

"Who else would have known we were there?"

"Nobody, far as I know, unless there was somebody up there all the time."

Dante knew that was a possibility. He'd busted lots of hookers while a cop. The first thing you did was to check the closets and under the bed for a john who might have picked the wrong time to be there. Or an open window if the place wasn't too high off the ground. He was getting careless. Too late to whip himself over that.

"Cut me some slack for a few weeks, Paulie, till I know this one is cold."

"Come on, Cal. You're talking about some hooker who ODs. It's cold already."

Williams hung up.

XÏÏ

Later That Day

Dante hadn't planned on telling Julia about the case. It wasn't that he
didn't trust her; he could tell that about a person in minutes. At least
that had been his experience. It was something you learned on the
streets. His street eyes had always been good. For a cop, that could be
the difference between life and death.

On the other hand, he had known her for only a few months. But
he needed someone—someone he could trust—to bounce ideas off. He
couldn't do it with Santo. Santo was the client and wouldn't be
interested in unsubstantiated theories, scurrilous accusations,
nonfacts.

His ex-wife, Barbara, had been a great foil when they were
married. She always *began* with the assumption that he was wrong about
any theory he placed before her. At first, he resented it. But over the
long haul, it had kept him sharp with clients, contacts, adversaries,
enemies. If he could get something past her, he knew he was on the
right track.

When he reached Julia, she told him he didn't have to explain why
he hadn't called. Yes, it had been a wonderful evening the last time
they'd been together, to which he wholeheartedly agreed. He apologized
for not having had a chance to tell her how much he'd enjoyed it. He was
wrapped up in a case and events had taken control of his life, the sort of

thing that happened a lot in his business. Now, he said, he needed to talk, and she was the one he wanted to talk to. Could he buy her dinner? Someplace other than Cuffs.

"Sure," she said without hesitation. "My place. It's on the house." She ended the conversation with a throaty laugh, the implied wickedness not lost on him.

———

"I don't have any hard evidence, nothing that leads anywhere. But I do have one dead body lying in my wake," he said as they sat on her soft leather couch and sipped black coffee laced with Nocello walnut liqueur. "Fionia, the dead hooker, didn't tell me a goddamn thing, but she's murdered hours after I leave her."

"Maybe she did OD, Paul. Maybe there isn't the cause and effect you see here."

"Based on what I've told you about her arms and legs, do you think she OD'd with a lethal dose of mainline boy?"

"Boy?"

"Street talk. They call heroin 'boy.' Coke is 'girl.'"

"Oh."

"So? What do you think?"

"Never having abused even aspirin, I wouldn't know."

"I'm not looking for an expert opinion. I already have that, and it's not worth much."

"No," she said. "I don't think she mainlined a lethal dose of—boy."

"Then why do you figure the police are treating it so routine?" he asked.

Julia shrugged. "She's a black prostitute from the ghetto. Maybe the police don't want to be bothered."

"Normally, I'd consider that a strong possibility, but my guts tell me different."

"It's because you're *involved* in this one."

"Sure, but that's not really important to what we're discussing. I just want to draw the most probable conclusions from what I know."

"Maybe she *did* tell you something."

"I thought about that," he said. "I've run it through my mind over and over. She wouldn't even admit to knowing Orsini. I was bluffing, and she knew it."

Julia sipped the flavorful coffee. She returned the cup to the table and wrinkled her face in a series of deep-thought expressions. The smallest of smiles curled her lips, then faded.

"What?" he asked.

"Just a thought."

"What? Try me."

"Okay. *You* know she didn't tell you anything, but whoever killed her was dealing only with appearances. Whoever killed her acted on what he *perceived* happened, not necessarily what *did* happen."

"Like maybe somebody hiding up there while we talked. But he'd *know* she didn't tell me anything."

"And maybe he told somebody else about it who didn't like the fact that a cop and a private investigator were there in the first place, and who saw it differently from what actually transpired."

Dante kissed her cheek. "You may be right," he said. "You're smart."

"College," she said. "Like you said at the wedding—big words."

"I know what 'perceived' means."

"Amazin'."

"So I'm asking around about Orsini-slash-Orson and there are people who don't want him found. I go to see Fionia the fox and they kill her. Why, after the fact—after I've already been there, already talked to her?"

"A message?"

"Could be."

"She's expendable. At least that's how they'd view it."

"But why do they care about Orsini?"

"I suppose that's for you to find out. One thing we do know about this Orsini creep. He's an anomaly. He's out of his zone, away from his people. The question is, what's he up to? How does he survive in this hostile environment? Why is someone killed at the mere suggestion she may have revealed something about him?"

He finished his coffee.

"Another?" she asked.

"No, thanks. I can barely keep my eyes open and I have to drive."

"No you don't."

He shook his head. "What are you trying to do, become habit-forming?" He tried to push to his feet but she took his arm and held him down. "No, really," he said. "I'm dead tired. A zombie. I won't be much company. Besides, I have to confront Santo tomorrow. That's the main thing on my mind."

She put her lips against his, held them there, would not let him get any other words out. Finally, she broke it off and put a finger over his mouth. "The bed's soft—and clean. You'll sleep like a baby. And the best part is, I'll be there to protect you all night."

He took her head in his hands and kissed her lightly on the lips. "Julia," he said, "why can't you be like all the other women in my life?"

"How's that?" she asked.

"Just hot for my body."

"But I am hot for your body. Come," she said, taking him by the hand and guiding him off the couch.

"Okay," he said, "but only because of that line about how soft and clean the bed is, not the one about my body."

"And you know the coffee's always good in the morning."

"Yeah, I do. You could become habit-forming," he repeated as she led him to the bedroom.

She unbuttoned his shirt and slipped it over his arms, loosened his belt, unzipped his fly and removed his pants. When he was standing in only his jockey shorts and socks, she put her arms over his naked shoulders and kissed him on the neck. Her right hand ran down the front of his chest and into his shorts.

His breaths began to shorten. "Julia," he said, "this is not what we agreed on."

"I know," she answered. "I'm such a liar."

She slid his shorts down to his ankles, pushed him back onto the bed and removed the shorts, then swung his legs toward the bottom of the bed and pulled off his socks. She slid a pillow beneath his head and ran her lips over his chest and belly, stopping just short of his penis. "Close your eyes," she said. "This is just a dream."

He was asleep in minutes, all the tension drained from him by this beautiful redheaded lady who was a dancer, who had great gams, and with whom he'd fallen madly in love.

The Following Day

It had been his first solid night's sleep in days, and he was up early and refreshed. The coffee was as good as he remembered it. As he sat breathing in the aromatic vapors, he tried to remember something about the previous evening. He'd been denying the effects of aging for the past few years, the inability to bounce back from nights with little or no sleep; the way liquor loosened his tongue when he was tired and turned him overly emotional; the way his mind too often seemed to be on vacation while his mouth worked overtime.

He'd told Julia she was different, not like the endless stream of women that passed through Cuffs, quick with a well-directed quip, a misdirected word, playful but never penetrating. As he got older, he needed a woman who could go one-on-one with him, take him on. He vaguely remembered he'd told Julia last night that she was that woman. Something about the cool length of a woman's flesh against yours when hers was the warmer of the two. Something about the exchange of heat between skins. Something about having a woman toy with your body when you're so beat you couldn't resist anything she wanted, didn't *want* to resist anything she wanted. Something about trusting someone to do whatever she liked and not expecting anything in return, at least at the moment.

Something about Julia.

He was alone again in her apartment on a second morning after, and felt comfortable there, almost at home. That was a good feeling, if not a little scary.

He tried to shunt Julia from his mind and to focus on his day, but that depressed him. He was not looking forward to the conversation he knew he must have with Santo. After three days, Santo would know there was no good news to report and would be aggravated, more likely angry, that Dante hadn't called. But ten minutes later, when Dante did make the call to his friend, Santo's ebullient voice threw him for a loop. "Paulie," Santo said over the sounds of background voices, "good to hear from you. But let's not talk on the phone. Come on over."

The background noises sounded festive. Something here wasn't computing for Dante. "Sounds like a party," he commented.

"Just get your ass over, Paulie," Santo said. "I've got good news to share with you."

Good news? Dante thought after he'd hung up. His mood was suddenly gloomier *after* the brief telephone conversation than it had been before. What could they be celebrating? Whatever it was, it was something *inside*, which only served to remind Dante how much of an outsider he was. While distance had always been best for the relationship, he didn't like the feeling of being left out. If that was a contradiction, so be it.

He drove with sullen resignation to Baltimore, arriving a little after ten. Santo's mood on the phone was mirrored by the unrestrained smile billboarded across his face when he opened the front door.

"I don't understand," Dante said.

Santo's smile erupted into a laugh, and he slapped Dante on the shoulder. It should have felt good, but it didn't. "Come in, Paul."

The atmosphere in Santo's study was markedly different from when Dante had visited a few days earlier. It *was* a party. A celebration. Boxes of rich Italian pastries were displayed across the center of the conference table. A small bar had been set up in a corner of the room and the group was helping itself to Bloody Marys, mimosas, and screwdrivers.

It didn't take Dante long to discover what had changed. Standing with a drink in his hand, dressed as though he were going to an opening at the Kennedy Center and accepting what appeared to be congratulations from everyone, was Genaro Orsini.

"What is this?" Dante muttered.

"Hey, why so glum?" Santo said. "We were wrong. Hell, *I* was wrong."

Dante had difficulty concealing his disbelief. Orsini, basking in any kind of favorable light, butted heads with everything he had discovered over the past several days. His expression wasn't lost on Santo.

"Look, I know what I said," Santo said. "I know what we discussed. But like I told you, I was wrong. Come on, I'll show you what I mean."

He led Dante into a smaller den, a private room Dante had never seen before. Santo closed the door and went to an antique rolltop desk. The top of the desk was down and locked.

Santo threw his friend a sly smile. "Sit," he said, motioning to a chair. Dante sat on its edge in anticipation.

"Ready?" Santo asked.

"Ready for what?" Dante didn't appreciate the dramatics.

Slowly and deliberately, Santo unlocked the rolltop and slid it open. Sitting on the horizontal desk surface was a leather case, its lid closed. It looked like an expensive commemorative box in which fancy liquors are packaged.

"So?" Dante said.

Santo turned his back to obscure what he was doing. "I know about that precious PI license of yours," he said over his shoulder. "You've told me lots of times what you can and can't see." He opened the box with the loving care of a salesman at Cartier about to display a rare jewel to a wealthy matron. When he'd retrieved what was inside, he closed the lid and turned. "Here," he said, tossing an object to Dante.

Dante plucked it from the air; it felt like a small, weighty stone. It was, in fact, a heavy gold ring. Dante examined it. In its center was a gaudy dollar sign created of diamonds and rubies. The stones were encrusted with dried blood. Dante frowned and looked to Santo for an explanation.

"Let's just say that Mr. Charlie Pietrosanti, the go-between in Vincent's setup, won't be shaking hands with any more of his buddies."

"I don't know what to say," Dante said, shaking his head. "Congratulations, I guess." As he stood and handed the ring to Santo, he couldn't help but see what was in the box. A human male hand that had been severed at the wrist.

Santo replaced the ring in the box and closed everything up.

"I think I get the picture," Dante said. "No need to explain any more." Part of him wanted to know more, part of him didn't. And a third part of him was disgusted by the whole affair. None of him wanted to hear anything good about Orsini.

His attention was distracted by loud laughter outside the room. Orsini's laugh was loudest.

"Paul," Santo said, "I should have known better all along." Dante knew Santo couldn't let this go. He was feeling very much the traitor, was doing his mea culpa.

"I don't know," Dante said. "You say the ring came off this Pietrosanti character. How do you know it did?"

"It's his ring, Paulie. Genaro and Vincent verify it."

"It's circumstantial, Santo."

"He's family, Paulie, married to my daughter. I should have trusted more."

"You had reason to think what you did. Things came together at the same time. The setup, his disappearance. It looked like what it looked like at the time."

Santo placed his hand on Dante's shoulder. "Thank you for understanding, Paulie. I'm sorry I ever involved you in this."

"Don't let that bother you."

They paused at the door. "You know what Genaro did, Paul?" Dante shook his head.

"He was so embarrassed," Santo said, "so upset that he led Vincent into trouble, the first time he ever did anything important for the family, he went out, found this little prick Pietrosanti on his own and made sure he'd never sell anybody out again."

"Yeah," Dante said. "I saw."

"He came to me with the ring and begged my forgiveness. He admitted he'd made a mistake, a big one in trusting this Pietrosanti, and went out to make amends. He's okay, Paul, a stand-up guy like I thought all along. Lucia did good. Sometimes you get lucky. I feel a hell of a lot better about things now, I can tell you. Come on. Have a coffee, a drink, some pastries."

Don't you want to hear what I found out? Dante wanted to say, but didn't. He would be reporting only hearsay. Santo had shown him what he considered hard evidence; he'd held it in his hand, a bloody ring. But he wasn't buying it.

"Hey, Paulie, wipe that gloomy look off your face. Cheer up. This is cause for celebration. The lawyers say there's no way in hell that Vincent will be convicted on the bribery charge. Pure entrapment. The feds really fucked up on this one."

"How'd he know where to look, Santo?" Dante asked. "I'm confused about that."

Santo gave his friend a quizzical look. "Somebody dropped a dime on Pietrosanti, that's all. Somebody made a call. One of Genaro's contacts. Hey, what's the matter?"

"Tired."

Santo slapped hands on Dante's arms. "You didn't fail me, Paulie. I know I can call on you when I'm in a jam. For that I'm grateful. I know you worked hard on this. Believe me, I'll make it worthwhile. But enough. There's been justice here, huh?"

Dante drew a deep breath and slowly followed Santo to where people congregated around Orsini. Sure, he'd have a cup of coffee, maybe even a drink, because it was expected of him. But he wasn't about to congratulate Orsini. For openers, he wasn't a fan of cutting off anybody's hand. That's the way *they* did it. That's the way *they* dispensed justice. It wasn't *his* justice, and he wished he didn't know about it.

Orsini beamed in the middle of his well-wishers, and Dante still wondered how he'd found Pietrosanti so quickly, did him in so fast, and then proudly delivered proof of his allegiance to Santo and the family. Even if someone *had* dropped a dime, tipped him off, who was it? Why? How did he get to Pietrosanti? And wouldn't there be an investigation of Pietrosanti's disappearance? Wouldn't Orsini be a suspect? Or was this part of another setup? Was someone now trying to pin a murder charge on Vincent? Or even Santo? It was too neat. Too orchestrated. A package all wrapped up with bows on it. And, given the present circumstances, there wasn't a thing he could do or say about it.

He resigned himself to joining the crowd for a fast cup of coffee and a pastry or two. He was still a sucker for Italian creams and spices. Call it ancestry. Call it an incurable sweet tooth. And these looked like good ones. Santo always bought good.

He would have liked to avoid contact with Orsini but knew that would be impossible. As he stood sinking his teeth into rum-soaked sweet dough, Orsini came to him and said loudly, "Hey, Dante, whatcha been up to lately?" Dante peered into Orsini's ever-present piano-keys smile. Does this guy ever do anything but shout? he thought.

"Just digging around in dirt," Dante replied, his voice muffled by the mouthful of dough.

"Turn up anything?" Orsini asked.

"Sure. It's not a pretty world out there." Dante swallowed the rest of his pastry. "What have you been up to?" he asked.

"Business. Strictly business. I just made a score. Didn't Santo tell you? Aren't you going to congratulate me?"

"Congratulations." Dante walked away.

"You don't like him much, do you?"

"Huh?" Dante turned. The voice belonged to Big Dom Piaggio, Santo's bodyguard, whose plate was heaped with pastries.

"Does it matter?" Dante answered.

"Sure," Big Dominick said. "Your guts is all that matters."

Dante studied the big man for a moment. His look was deadly serious.

"You're right, Dominick," Dante replied. "You gotta go with your instincts."

"Yes," Dominick said. "Somethin' stinks here." He wandered away.

At least somebody isn't buying this crap, Dante thought. Sometimes you find believers in the most unlikely places.

Dante finished his coffee, took leave of the group, and said good-bye to Santo.

"There'll be a little something in your mailbox," Santo said.

"No need," Dante said.

Santo only smiled. Years of association with Santo had taught Dante that there was no point in arguing with his friend about such things. Besides, he could use an infusion of cash. It also meant he was off the case officially. Which bothered him. He had turned up things about Orsini that could hurt Santo and his family in the long run. He'd been hired to perform an investigation but never got a chance to discuss with his client what he'd found.

Which, he realized, was enough incentive to really get himself in trouble. He was off the case—but maybe he'd take it upon himself to stay on it a little longer. Just long enough to satisfy his soul.

XiV

Three Days Later

Dante fell in behind the white '81 Cadillac Seville and followed it
through a crisscrossing pattern of small streets. He'd been waiting two
hours for Victor of Victor and Armbruster to leave work. During that
time, the night had gone from cool and starlit to damp and drizzly—as
if the weather itself were trying to keep pace with Dante's deteriorating
frame of mind. Except for Julia, not a lot had gone well for him lately.

He set his wipers to intermittent and they did their groaning
stutter-step across his windshield. He'd meant to have them replaced
for months, a promise to himself he knew he wouldn't keep until the
world through the windshield became an opaque smear.

Victor headed east around the city, then took 95 north in the
direction of Baltimore. Dante kept a comfortable distance from the
Caddy until it exited at Monroe Street on the southern fringe of
Baltimore, snaked its way north through a depressing grid of black
neighborhoods and finally pulled into a tight space in front of a block of
row houses in the Franklin Square section.

Dante watched Victor exit his car and enter a building, whose
address Dante jotted down. He found a parking space three blocks
away and returned to the building. The short walk in the spritzing rain
made his clothes feel like they'd been prepared for a steam-ironing; a
musty odor encircled him. Paul Dante had a thing for odors, was
sensitive to them. Even though he knew he wouldn't smell to others

the way he did to himself, he felt as though he'd become permanent-
ly mildewed.

He climbed two stone steps to a weathered red door and knocked.
Victor of Victor and Armbruster was not happy to see him.

"Ask me in," Dante said.

"Wrong," Victor said. "Stay the fuck *out*."

Dante started to push past him into the modest house. Victor
grabbed Dante's arm. Dante pushed him against the foyer wall and
pressed his right forearm against Victor's throat. "Okay, okay," Victor
gurgled, struggling to suck in air.

Dante eased the pressure. "We need to talk again," he said.

"Shit," Victor wheezed. "I got nothin' more to say to you." He
jerked loose and walked down a hallway to a small kitchen at the rear of
the house. A pervasive grey-white haze and putrid smell hung over the
room, the result of burning butter in a frying pan. "Damn," Victor said,
moving the pan to a cold burner.

"Don't let me disturb your dinner," Dante said, taking a seat at a
brown, vinyl-topped card table with folding legs that served as the
kitchen table.

"You already have," Victor said. He cut off another block of butter,
dropped it into the pan and replaced it on the live burner. He cracked a
half-dozen eggs into a bowl, whipped them into a frenzy with a fork, and
poured them into the pan where they immediately hissed and crackled
in the too-hot grease. He took a potato from a brown wicker basket
beneath the sink, washed it, poked a couple of holes in it with a fork
and placed it into the microwave. He set the timer. Dante waited
patiently as his host went through his food-prep ablutions. "Forgive my
manners," Victor said, making a point not to offer Dante anything. "I
wasn't expecting guests."

"Look," Dante said, "I'm sorry. I didn't mean to push you out
there. I'm a little uptight."

"Yeah," Victor said, stirring the eggs. "Tell me about it." He took
a bottle of malt liquor from the refrigerator, popped the cap, took a
swallow and placed it on the counter alongside the stove. Then he
pulled another bottle from the refrigerator and placed it in front of
Dante.

143

"Thanks," Dante said.

"One beer," Victor replied, assembling the elements of his dinner on a plate. "That's all the time you got, my friend. One beer's worth."

"I want to talk about Fionia," Dante said.

"Look," Victor said, a forkful of eggs poised at his lips, "the only reason I spoke to you last time was you were handing me this crock of shit about Orson being in trouble." He shoveled food into his mouth. "I told you where she lived and worked because you said her life might be in danger, and that you were the man who might save her. I bought your shit, Mr. Dante. Looks like you were right about the first part. The second part? You sure were wrong."

Dante thought back to his initial visit with Victor. He hadn't been reluctant to talk then because he was looking for a sympathetic ear about Orsini before Dante had even told him why he'd come.

"He *was* in trouble," Dante said.

"Right." Victor sliced off a piece of potato and popped it into his mouth. "Shit!" he said, quickly swallowing beer to quench the fire. "Fuckin' microwave." He blew onto the plate. "I got a call from Orson today. He said he just wanted to see how business was going. Orson never calls to see how business is. He just shows up for his monthly 'dividend.'"

"The point being?"

"He asked if I'd heard about Fionia. Said it was a shame she got careless, but that carelessness was dangerous when you played around the way she did. He said bein' careless wasn't good in my business, either. Said all it took was one bad decision and the whole fuckin' roof can fall in. He repeated that, Mr. Dante: 'The whole fuckin' roof can fall in.'"

"What does that mean?"

"I don't want to find out, you dig? Accidents, even when nobody gets hurt, can do a number on a business like mine. Contractors don't like subs who can't deliver on deadline. I been down that road. It's bad for the health of the principals. Shit, my partner, Armbruster, he's living in a clapboard house in the desert near Tucson. Massive heart attack the last time we got in financial trouble. Needed to get outta things altogether. Go where the air is clear, the humidity is low, and the pressure ain't nowhere. I send him a little each month, whatever's left over after—expenses." He went back to his meal, the potato now cool enough to chew.

"Why should Orsini give a damn about Fionia?" Dante asked, trying to get the conversation back on track.

"Good piece of ass," Victor said.

"Bullshit. Orsini doesn't strike me as a connoisseur. One ass is as good as the next to a guy like him."

Victor finished his dinner, wiped the plate with a piece of bread, drained the remaining beer from the bottle and got another. Dante hadn't touched his. "Are you gonna leave me alone?" Victor asked, sitting again.

Dante didn't answer.

"Look, Dante, why do you think I live here, in this building, on this block, in Baltimore when my business is in D.C.? It's 'cause I got to get away, change the scenery at night. I'm in the middle of those bastards every day, the whole rotten bunch of them. I saw what happened to Armbruster even when they don't get rough with you. Man, he was a worrier. Worried about the broken windows, the looted cash boxes, the graffiti on the walls, every fuckin' thing. Now he's sweating his worried balls off looking out a window at orange dirt in his front yard and hoping the mailman brings a check from me."

"What happened to Fionia?" Dante asked.

"*You* happened to Fionia," Victor answered, disgusted that Dante was not about to leave. "She let you in."

"I let myself in."

"Tell me about it."

"I still don't get it. We spoke maybe ten, fifteen minutes. She told me nothing about nothing."

"What can I say? Silence is golden with that crowd."

"How does Orsini fit in?"

Victor let out a sarcastic laugh. "She owed him. He always gets what he's got comin'."

"Owed him what? What did he have coming?"

Victor furrowed his brow, examined Dante's face for any kind of reaction. "Shit, you don't know about the bust?"

"Bust?"

Victor leaned back in his chair, sorting out what to say next. "I'll make a deal with you," he finally said.

"Go ahead."

"After this, you leave me alone. Forever."

Dante didn't say yes, didn't say no.

"I'm going to tell you something that will help you. I want to see that bastard Orsini fall more than you do. But after this, you got to forget you ever knew me. Orsini don't come down, my ass is grass."

Dante pondered what Victor had said, then said, "Okay. We got a deal."

Victor took a swig of beer. "He was sitting in my office fuming about Fionia," he said. "When he saw her later that night he was going to beat the shit outta her. Said he was going to rearrange her pretty face, reposition her pretty ass. Only he wasn't going to do shit—and he knew it—'cause she works for Diaz's people, and Orsini can't mess with Diaz."

"Why was he pissed at her?" Dante asked.

"That's what I asked him. He wouldn't say. But then a couple of days later, I'm in a conversation with a friend who knows a lot about what goes down in D.C., especially street action. He tells me he's heard that Orson got himself set up."

"Set up how?"

"Some kinda drug bust. My friend says he heard that Fionia had something to do with it."

"Fionia set Orson up for a drug bust?"

"Can't prove it by me, man. I'm just passin' on what I was told. Ask Diaz."

Riccardo Diaz and his brothers and uncles and cousins were at the top of the drug empire in the District. Ruthless, cold-blooded killers in the best Colombian tradition. They brought in most of the narcotics in D.C. Their mules—local runners and sellers—were almost exclusively black. There were rival gangs, of course, but Diaz was king of the hill, at least for now, provided the war recently waged against them by the Benedetti family didn't put them out of business.

"So here's what I figure," Victor said. "One of Diaz's people sees you at her apartment that night and everything changes. They find out that you were there looking for Orson. Orson's off-limits as far as Diaz is concerned. Hell, Orson's Italian, a soldier in the Benedetti family married to Santo Benedetti's daughter. Diaz and his scumbags get nervous having guys like you asking questions of their whore. So they kill her. That's the simple way to do it."

Victor's eyes glistened; Dante averted them to spare the black man embarrassment. He looked down at the table and said in a low voice, "I wasn't gone a couple of hours when they brought her in."

"It doesn't matter shit, does it?" Victor said, blowing his nose. "But it happened."

"When did this happen?" Dante asked.

"When?" Victor replied, a questioning look on his face. "Shit, man, you know."

"No, not Fionia's death. The Orsini bust."

"No idea. Not even sure it ever did happen."

"Maybe I'm dense," Dante said, "but something doesn't play for me. You told me Orson is in the drug business, does business out of your back room."

"Used to."

"No matter. As far as I know, there's only one source of drugs in this city, and that's through people like Diaz. The blacks push the shit, but they get it from the South Americans. Right?"

"So I'm told."

"So where does Orson get his? How does he do business on Diaz's turf without getting his balls blown off?"

"Good point, Dante. Maybe he hasn't heard about the war with the Benedettis."

"Or doesn't give a damn. You don't know any more about this so-called drug bust of Orson?"

"Nope."

"Well, thanks, Victor. Sorry to barge in on you."

"It's all right, Dante. You want to talk again, come see me."

Dante's eyebrows went up. "Why the change?" he asked.

"Maybe I'm stupid," Victor replied. "Hell, I know I am. But I decided a minute ago back in the kitchen that you're as dumb a fuck as I am. White skin, black skin, a coupla fuckups. That means we're pretty much on the same side, only not out to fuck each other. That don't mean I look forward to ever seeing your ugly face again, but if I have to talk to somebody, I could do worse. Drive careful. Roads are slick."

Dante walked out into the night and heard Victor close the door behind him. The clunk of a deadbolt being twisted into place was loud.

The drizzle persisted but the drive back to D.C. was easy. Dante watched the road slip by and thought of other roads. They all lead to Orsini, he thought. The road from Victor and Armbruster. The road from Fionia. The road from Diaz and his people. Orsini was nothing if not busy. He was playing every angle, and was relentless in getting his way. And from Dante's perspective, that was the problem. If every lead he followed dead-ended in Orsini, then what? Orsini was the one person he couldn't approach, couldn't question, couldn't even attempt to pin down. He wasn't on the case anymore, at least not officially. Santo would not be pleased if he knew Dante was still chasing the ghost.

And, he had to admit to himself, he was also out of ideas.

He thought of the kitchen conversation he'd just had with Victor. What was Victor's last name? A good man trying to get through this life he'd been given, like everybody else. Vietnam again. Would he ever shake those memories, be able to divorce it from his everyday existance?

It was hard enough getting through life with all its downturns and boobytraps and acts of nature without having to deal with the likes of Genaro Orsini. He didn't want to see Victor hurt; the poor guy had enough problems trying to keep his business going with an incapacitated partner vegetating in the Arizona desert, being squeezed from too many directions and trying not to burn his mouth on hot potatoes.

I *am* a fuckup, Dante decided. Why should he care about Orsini, or anything else having to do with the Benedetti family? He had Julia. He had his investigation agency and Cuffs, neither of which were making him rich but provided enough to keep him from following the rest of the country into Chapter Eleven. With Julia—he'd now come to project them into the future as a couple—he might be able to inject new order into his life and turn the agency and the bar into something bigger than they currently were. He knew he'd never pull it off by himself. The energy just wasn't there anymore.

Which wasn't exactly true, and Dante knew it. He had plenty of energy. The problem was he squandered it, a luxury that costs more the older you get. Here he was digging further into Orsini even though he was off the case. Stupid. A waste.

"Hardheaded," his ex-wife always said.

"Excessively driven," his MPD superior had often written on his performance reports.

"*Loco,*" Julio, his cook, was fond of saying.

"*Me,*" Dante told himself. Take it or leave it.

So immersed was he in this introspection that he never noticed he was being followed by a car that had tailed him from D.C. to Victor's house.

———

Dante had a friend at the FBI, who had a contact, who had another friend in records. The friend of a contact of a friend said give him a day, two max. Dante called back the next day.

"Nothing, Paul. Never happened."

"About a year ago, maybe more, maybe less, but not a lot less."

"I know. You told me that."

"Maybe my dates are a little off."

"We ran the name. Nothing. Someone's blowin' smoke up your ass."

"I don't think so."

"There's nothing, Paul. You figure it out."

"Could the record be someplace else, classified, pulled from the main computer, squirreled away?"

"Nah. Somebody's bullshitting you."

Dante thanked him for his efforts and hung up.

If Orsini had been busted on a drug setup, there'd be a record of it someplace. Unless it had been pulled for security reasons.

Victor wasn't a liar but maybe he had his facts screwed up. Maybe he'd made an honest mistake. Possible, Dante reasoned, but he didn't think so. If he couldn't get corroboration from the files, he'd have to get it from other sources. He knew he was pissing in the wind but he couldn't stop, no matter how many times the wind shifted.

XV

A Week Later

It had not been a good dying.

Carmela Andreotti was in severe pain until the end when even the morphine stopped helping. Now, after the undertaker's art had been practiced, the body of the once-robust woman, withered away to less than eighty pounds, was somehow made to look snug and contented in the silks of her coffin. It was a bitterly ironic end for the woman who had helped attract hundreds of devoted guests to her husband's restaurant over the years, both with her delectable Northern Italian white sauces and her pink-faced smile. When the lid was thumped closed the final time, Angelo's face quivered but did not break. The final sleep would be better than the agony she'd endured. The struggle of loneliness now belonged to the living.

Angelo's eyes finally grew wet as his wife was lowered into the great clay hole that would be her final resting place. His son, Angie, moved to steady him when it appeared his father's knees would buckle.

"Vai bene, con Dio"—Go well with God. Angelo had arranged for that to be cut into her marble headstone. He had no doubt that it would be Carmela's truth in heaven.

Among those attending the burial, and who remembered what Angelo's had once been, were Paul Dante and his companion, Julia Croce. Genaro and Lucia Orsini were there, too. Santo Benedetti was out of town on business but sent his regrets, along with one hundred bloodred roses, Carmela's favorite flower. The accompanying note said that his daughter and son-in-law would represent him and his family: "On this somber occasion, the hearts of the Benedetti and Orsini families are with you."

One by one, mourners passed the yawning, rectangular hole in the green hillside and dropped single rosebuds into it.

Eventually, with Angelo and Angie Jr. bringing up the rear, the group turned from the gravesite. Only Orsini lingered at the hole. He had handled all the funeral arrangements for Angelo, telling him it was part of the service he performed for holders of large life insurance policies. Angelo had been overwhelmed by the extent to which Orsini had gone to create a lavish sendoff for Carmela. The flower arrangements were spectacular, the casket expensive and luxurious. The funeral home, owned by a man Orsini told Angelo was Washington's best, and whom he claimed was a close personal friend, had been a study in dignity and concern.

"My Carmela, she sleeps on the bed of a saint," Angelo had told Orsini as tears streamed down his cheeks.

"Without a doubt," Orsini had replied. "Don't worry. I'll take care of everything."

Which he did.

Now, as Orsini stood at the gravesite and looked down on the polished metal cover of Carmela's coffin, he wasn't thinking of her sleeping on the bed of any saint. Your Carmela, he thought, sleeps on the upper floor of an apartment house.

———

Donnie Tenaglia had outgrown his usefulness. He'd become dangerous, harping at Orsini about receiving a bigger cut of the insurance policies they were scamming. "It's getting riskier," he kept insisting. "That thing with the old lady was really pushing it. They're asking a lot of questions. I may have to beat it. I'll need money to take with me."

"If you beat it, why should I give you more money?" Orsini had said, his anger growing. "What fuckin' good are you to me if you can't provide what I need?"

"Call it payment for services already rendered, Gerry."

"I don't dwell on the past," Orsini said, his muscles tightening. "I'm a forward-looking kind of guy."

"Then consider this future," Tenaglia offered, fear for his own position obscuring the signs he should have been reading in Orsini. "If I'm not outta here, they may corner me. And Gerry, I gotta tell ya something. I go down, you go down."

The rage welling inside Orsini had given him a pulsating headache. Tenaglia *was* going to get caught. He was accepting it as inevitable. He didn't have the stomach for it and hadn't from the beginning. Orsini was the one who had shown him the possibilities, the profit potentials. Now, at the first sign of pressure, Tenaglia was about to cave in.

"And you know how it is in business, Gerry," Tenaglia continued. "Bigger risks, bigger rewards."

"Sure," Orsini remembered saying as he lurched for Tenaglia's throat. "Here's your bigger fucking reward." He experienced a rush of excitement as he stared down into the bulging face of the insurance salesman, watched it turn beet-red, then purple as he struggled for air. Orsini squeezed harder until he could feel the windpipe crunch under his oversized fingers and continued to tighten his grip until Tenaglia went limp.

"Do him with a hard-on sticking through his fly in case the old lady gets horny," Orsini had told the undertaker when he delivered Tenaglia's lifeless body to him. The undertaker, whose funeral parlor was one of many silently owned by the Benedetti family, was in the process of embalming Carmela Andreotti when Orsini arrived.

"Jesus, Gerry, that's sick," the undertaker told him. "You're kidding. Right?"

Orsini's icy stare answered the question. "You got the double-decker casket like I told you?"

"Yeah," the undertaker replied.

"Good. This is my own little private joke, huh? You tell anybody—*anybody*—I put you in with the next stiff. Got it?"

"Yeah, sure. I forgot it already."

———

"So long, Donnie," Orsini said to himself as he stood over Carmela's open grave. "You go down, I don't, you asshole." A quartet of grave-diggers leaned on their shovels and waited for him to finish with what they assumed were his final respects for the deceased old lady. Must have been really close to her, they thought. Maybe a son.

Orsini had known that the added weight of the portly insurance salesman would not be that noticeable under the all-but-weightless body of Carmela Andreotti. His final thought before he left the gravesite to join Lucia at the limousine was whether the old lady would get any sleep with fat Tenaglia and his stiff dick just below her.

As Angelo Andreotti stood near the long black Cadillac that would take the family back to the restaurant, Orsini came up to him and wordlessly handed the old man a white business-size envelope, plumped to several inches in thickness. Angelo stood motionless and stared ahead, an empty expression on his face, the envelope in his limp hand. Then, comprehending what it meant, his face began to quiver, and broke. He let out a loud whine as tears rolled down his cheeks. Orsini rested a hand on his shoulder and said, "She's at rest now, Angelo. Her pain is over."

Angie Jr., who'd watched the exchange, came to his father's side. "What's goin' on?" he asked.

"Angie," the old man said, "if there is any good to come of this *tragedia,* it is this. This would have made your momma happy." He patted the envelope, now safely nestled in the inside pocket of his suitcoat.

"What is it, pop?"

"*Salvaggio* for your restaurant, Angie. Even in death, your mother arranged to help you through the bad times."

"What was that all about?" Julia Croce asked Paul Dante as they waited for the Andreottis to lead the procession back to Angelo's restaurant. They'd observed the dramatics of Orsini's final vigil at the gravesite, and the exchange with Angelo.

"I don't know," Dante said, his eyes still narrowed from focusing on the scene. "But if Orson-Orsini is involved, I don't trust it." He hadn't told her of the celebratory scene at Santo's the morning Orsini returned with the bloody ring and the hand in the box. You don't share things like that with your lady. You keep them to yourself because that's where they belong. But he was no longer reticent about voicing to her his open dislike of Orsini.

She'd questioned him that morning as they drove to the funeral parlor if he might not have become obsessed with "this Orsini thing."

"No!" he'd snapped. "Forget it."

Dante pulled on the lights of the Buick and they fell into the long line of vehicles. Julia touched his arm. "Funny," she said.

"What?"

"Oh, I don't know. I'd like to tell you to get off this Orsini kick, but now I don't know. There's something about that man's face."

"What about it?"

She shook her head. "I said I don't know, Paul. I guess we should skip it. I'm sorry I brought it up."

"No, tell me."

She sighed. "He's a liar, Paul. His face, his body language, the way he holds his hands. I don't have to hear a thing he says. You know what I mean?"

"Yeah. I sure do."

They exited the cemetery through large black iron gates and turned onto the perimeter road.

"Have you talked to Santo about your feelings?" Julia asked.

"No. I almost did a couple of times but before I get it out, Santo starts in on his member-of-the-family routine and I back off. Member of the family, my ass."

They were quiet for most of the trip back to Angelo's, but as the procession turned down Constitution Avenue, it was clear that Dante's train of thought had been consistent. "I'm more a member of that family than Orsini is," he said. "Lucia is like a sister to me. We grew up together. Now this guy marries her and Santo suddenly develops an unquestioning blood tie." He found a parking space in a municipal lot down the street from Angelo's. "Family's great," he said as he came around and opened the door for Julia. "I honor it. But it never turned slime into whipped cream." He took her arm and they walked to the restaurant. "Hungry?" he asked.

"Not after that analogy." She smiled. "Starved, actually."

When Dante and Julia walked into Angelo's, the old man's mood had grown increasingly black. At first, Dante attributed it to Angelo finally realizing that Carmela would no longer be with him. But the gloom seemed rooted more in anger than sorrow.

Orsini entered with his usual flourish. "Somebody going to watch the cars, Angelo?" he asked in a loud voice as he came through the front door. "I don't want to lose my hubcaps." He laughed loudly.

The restaurant owner did not laugh. Instead, his jaw tightened. "Signor Orsini," he said. "Can I see you in my office?"

"Sure," Orsini said. "Grab a seat, Lucy. I'll only be a minute."

"Expenses," Orson said the moment Angelo closed the door behind them.

"Expenses?"

"Yeah. You know what they are, don't you? Overhead, people you got to grease, transportation, phones, faxes, not to mention the cost of that funeral. Expenses."

"You say the funeral was included."

"Funeral included? Where did you get that idea? You said you wanted the best for Carmela. That's what I gave her. The best."

"But you say I gonna receive half. One hun'erd fifty t'ousand dollars."

"Right. *After* expenses."

"I got here in this envelope, maybe twenty-five t'ousand."

"Twenty-four, five," Orson corrected.

"The policy, it was for t'ree hun'erd."

"Right. Less my end and the expenses."

"Two hun'erd seventy-five t'ousand for you and the expenses?"

"Two hundred seventy-five thousand, five hundred. A lot of overhead, Angelo."

The old man slumped in a swivel chair whose stuffing protruded through three holes. He covered his eyes and shook his head. Was he about to cry? Orsini wondered. He didn't need that.

Finally, Angelo leaned forward and slapped his hands on the desk. "No," he said.

"No?"

"Please, there has to be more, Signor Orsini."

"It's Orson," he corrected. "Gerry Orson."

"Orson, Orsini, what the hell I care about that? You gotta gi'me more. Angie, he need more to keep his place going."

"Listen, old man," Orsini said, "your son has made his own problems. It's time he grew up, learned how to fix things himself."

"You gi'me more," Angelo said. "I gotta help Angie. I promise him. This money, she come from Carmela. She's resting in her grave. Please, don't do this to me. I promise him."

"This money," Orsini aped, "she come from *me*. Without me, you don't get shit." He got up and straightened his tie, buttoned his jacket.

"No!" Angelo said, moving as quickly as he could to block the door.

A smile twisted Orsini's face as he grabbed the old man by his jacket collar with one hand, and tightened the other about his throat. "You old guinea fuck," he growled. "Be happy with the twenty-four grand or I take *it* back. Un'erstand? *Capice?*" He pushed Angelo down into a chair and left the office.

As Orsini blew by Dante's table, Dante stopped what Julia was saying with a raised hand. "Look at that smug son of a bitch," he said. "Probably getting the old man to eat his house account on the day he buries his wife."

"I don't know, Paul," Julia replied. "That sounds a little irrational."

"Sorry," he said. "You were saying?"

Before she could answer, the door to the office opened and a scarlet-faced Angelo Andreotti slunk out. Dante stopped him as he passed the table and asked what was wrong.

"What's wrong?" the old man repeated. "I just lose my wife. My restaurant, she goin' down the sewer, and now, Angie's . . ."

"Angie's what?" Dante asked.

The old man's eyes were red, and his lips trembled. "I thought— the insurance—Mr. Orsini, he tell me . . ." He sadly shook his head.

"He told you what?"

The old man started to answer, then, "No, Paolo, not your problem." He managed a smile at Julia. "Excuse me, signorina. I don't mean to upset you." He took a breath and steadied himself on the table. "I got guests to see to. I was gonna close the restaurant for a few days out of respect, but Carmela, she always say that you do that, people don't want to come no more. Eat. Carmela may be gone, but her hand, she's still in the kitchen. We got to celebrate her life."

"That bastard's up to something," Dante said to Julia as Angelo headed across the room. "Somehow, he's managed to upset the old man more than the funeral did."

"I don't know what to say."

"I'll talk to Angelo when he's had a few days to deal with his grief."

Dante didn't enjoy his dinner much, even discounting the solemn reason for the occasion. Orsini seemed too pleased with himself as he wolfed down his food and greeted other mourners with a big smile, as if this were a wedding reception instead of a funeral dinner. The sour feeling in the pit of Dante's stomach didn't leave him much company for Julia, and she asked after coffee that he take her home. She had an early class the next morning and was tired.

He said he understood, didn't blame her, and would try to be better company next time. He drove her home.

"I'll call you in a day or two," he said. "Okay?"

"Of course." He came around and opened the door for her, escorted her to her building's door. "Paul," she said.

"What?"

"Drop it."

"I can't."

"I don't like you this way. Your face. It . . . frightens me."

"You know I don't want to do that," he said. "Maybe I can. I mean, drop it. I'll try."

"Good." She kissed him again and disappeared inside.

He pulled the Buick into the alley behind Cuffs, turned off ignition and lights and sat quietly. After what seemed an eternity, he got out of the car and went directly to his upstairs apartment, looked in the mirror. "Sorry, baby," he said aloud to his reflected image, "but I'm gonna nail that son of a bitch."

XVI

Early Summer

Santo Benedetti met with his son-in-law to discuss his future with the family business. He told him he would like to see him become more involved in activities that generated the major portion of the family's income.

"Exactly what I been thinking," Orsini said as he and his father-in-law faced each other in red-leather chairs next to the rolltop desk in Santo's inner sanctum. "Like I told you when I first started working for you . . ." He laughed. "That was before I fell in love with Lucia, huh?" Santo nodded. "Anyway, back then, Santo, I told you everything I had going at the time would come under the family once I joined up. You told me that was the way it had to be, and that's the way it's been. Am I right?"

"Yes," Santo replied. "You've generated good money since you came to work for us. It has been noticed and appreciated."

"It's as though you read my mind, Santo. I still have my own businesses to work—our businesses actually—and I will do that. But I want to phase them out and work my way into more important family businesses, Santo, the businesses that are of most interest to you and Vincent. With your permission, of course—and your blessing. I'm glad I now have that blessing."

They were words Santo had wanted to hear. With no son, he hoped to leave his legacy and fortune to whomever his daughter married. That eventuality had been the cause of considerable concern for him. It was an unknown, something over which he could not exercise the near-absolute control with which he felt most comfortable. The future of his son-in-law and, by extension, the future of his daughter, was the most important thing in his life, along with the future of the family itself. Deep in his heart, he knew he had the priorities wrong. The family—La Cosa Nostra—was to reign supreme. It was to be placed above all else—wife, child, life itself. But he saw both families as indelibly wedded together.

He'd barely begun to establish a career path for Marco when his former son-in-law died in the car crash. And he had started to ponder what the future would hold for Genaro when the unfortunate situation with Vincent developed.

Now, with Pietrosanti dead, Genaro in the role of avenger, and Vincent's lawyers talking more confidently about making a strong case for entrapment, events in the family had regained a proper footing and were moving in the right direction. It was time to get back on course concerning the future of the family—both families.

But Santo was also aware that succession in rank in the family involved a great deal more than familial relationships. He made that point with Orsini. "You don't know the fine points of the way we do business," he said. "There is much to learn, and trust to be gained. Starting at the bottom is always the best way. It is the way Vincent and I started."

"I know that, Santo, and I agree. But haven't I earned respect? Haven't I been working at a low level? I don't say promote me to capo. All I say is that it might be time—if you see it this way, of course—that I learn more about, like you put it, the fine points. I was thinking that gambling—"

Santo smiled, said, "Now it seems you're reading *my* mind, Genaro. We are talking of setting up a casino on Southern Avenue, across the line into Maryland. We have the necessary people in our pockets. It will need management. Atlantic City would help prepare you for such responsibility."

Orsini nodded. "Yes," he said, "that would be good experience for me. I have been to Atlantic City a few times recently. Things are good there. So busy. There is obviously need for trusted people to work there to protect family interests. I would like the opportunity to do that. Maybe not full-time." He laughed. "I couldn't do that anyway, not with my other businesses that got to be run. But if I could work a few nights a week in a casino where we have an interest, do something that would help the family and, at the same time, give me a feel for the organization, it would be good. Exactly like you said. To start at the bottom, and to learn."

Santo sat back and rested his chin on fingers he'd pressed into a tent. He scrutinized Orsini. Everything Genaro had said was what he'd wanted to hear. But nothing good was ever gained by going too fast—with any decision. As much as he personally wanted to elevate Genaro to a position of leadership for Lucia's sake—to give her husband a sense of status and, by extension, give her that status, too—there were time-honored traditions to be observed. He could do virtually anything he wanted because of his position as underboss; Vincent seldom denied him such decision-making powers. But it was prudent to minimize the chances of making mistakes in judgment. Genaro's role in Vincent's setup, as innocent as it had obviously been, testified to that.

Orsini beamed. "You know how much I would appreciate it, Santo," he said. "Only a few nights a week."

"That'll be a tough schedule, Genaro. Atlantic City is hours away."

"I know, but I'm a workaholic." He grinned, shrugged. "I thrive on hard work."

"You're also newly married."

"Yeah. But I got to think about the future for Lucia and me, and the kids we'll have. If I don't start moving now, it'll be harder later on."

Santo let a small, discreet smile escape the corners of his mouth. "You'll discuss it with Lucia before making this decision?"

"Sure," Orsini answered, diverting his eyes down to his shoetops. "I wouldn't make a move like this without first talking it over with her."

Santo slapped his hands on his knees and stood. "I'll make a few calls," he said, "put you in touch with the right people. It'll take a few days. You just can't go on the payroll. We have to get you a casino employee's license."

"Don't worry about that," Orsini said. "I got a contact who has a guy on the New Jersey Gambling Commission in his pocket. He can get me the license in twenty-four hours. Can do it for anybody else you need it for, too. Something to keep in mind."

Santo's eyes narrowed. "We have our own contacts on the commission, Genaro. Our partnership in the casinos is silent, and is to remain that way. We'll handle it through our own channels."

"Of course," Orsini said. The change in Santo's expression had tempered his braggadocio. "Of course you will. I guess I'm just excited, that's all." He smiled and extended his hand. "You won't regret this, Santo."

"No," Santo said, his face warming, "I'm sure I won't."

———

"It'll only be a couple nights a week until I get established. Until I get rid of my other commitments."

"I don't like it when you're away at night," Lucia said. "I want you here with me."

"Hey, you're not some little girl, are you? You afraid of the dark? I work for your father. He tells me to do this, I do it. Be a good wife."

Lucia knew what "being a good wife" meant. There were rules for women married to men in organized crime:

POLICE: "What does your husband do?"

WIFE: "He never discusses business with me. He's a good provider."

And, there was the understanding that the businesses in which their husbands were engaged demanded strange hours, night hours, often extended periods away from home. Other women? Probably. But no love involved. Better not to ask. Her mother had never asked. But she was of a different generation. Her father was reputed to be a gangster, like her uncle Vincent. Despite knowing that it was true, she'd developed a defense against it, a denial system that allowed her to remain aloof of the Mafia wife's code.

They sat at the kitchen table in their Georgetown home, a scotch-rocks in front of him; she sipped an iced tea. It was ten at night. A meat loaf and baked potato heated in the microwave.

"When you didn't come home for those three nights after what happened to Uncle Vincent, I was very upset. My father didn't like it, either."

Orsini shrugged, drank. "That was different," he said. "I had to do something and couldn't involve nobody. It was a touchy job, a dangerous coupla days."

"But why do you have to work nights now?" she persisted. "The casino is open days."

"I do my other business in the daytime. Hey, get off my case, okay? I work hard for us. Show a little thanks, huh?"

A timer bell sounded. Lucia opened the glass door to the microwave and placed a plate of baked beans and a small cup of brown gravy inside, next to the meat and potato.

"I know, Genaro," she said, returning to her chair, "but I keep house all day in anticipation of you coming home in the evenings. With you gone nights now . . ."

"It's tough when you start something new, huh? You know that." He drained his glass. "No," he said, "I guess you don't know that. You never had to struggle. You wouldn't know a struggle if it slapped you in the face. Daddy's always been there to take care of you."

The timer bell rang again, which diverted her from the direction the conversation had taken. She removed the food from the microwave, arranged it on the plate for her husband and placed it before him. "Can I get you anything else?" she asked.

He ignored her. "You got any idea what it takes to keep money coming in?" he asked. "You ever had to worry about where your next buck comes from?"

She did not reclaim her seat at the table, opting to lean against the counter. "Genaro," she said, "what are you talking about? I just want you to understand that I don't like you to be away nights. Why is that hard to understand?"

"Because I got things to do," he said, cutting a piece of meat loaf with his fork and dipping it into the gravy. He put it in his mouth, then spit it back onto the plate. "What the fuck?" he snarled. "This is lukewarm."

"Let me see," she said, touching the meat with her finger.

"Get your fingers outta my food," he said.

She jerked her hand away and turned to the microwave. "I'm sorry," she said. "I had the setting too low. I thawed out some butter before and forgot." She reached for his plate. "Let me have it. I'll . . ."

"No!" he snapped. "I don't want it. This is no meal anyway. What kind of shit is this for a man to come home to? Cold meat loaf."

"Genaro, don't talk like that. You like my meat loaf. It wasn't cold. It's ten o'clock. You didn't call and tell me you were going to be this late, I had no way of knowing . . ."

"Forget it," he said. "I'm going out and get something." He slid the plate across the table to where it teetered on the edge. Lucia rushed to steady it but her jerking hand knocked it to the floor. "Oh," she said, "look what you . . ."

He pushed away from the table and stormed toward the door.

"Genaro," Lucia said, "let me make you something else. What do you want?"

"Out!" he said. He slammed the door behind him.

She stared at the closed door for a long, painful minute. Then, weeping, she went to her knees and cleaned the mess off the kitchen floor.

———

Later that night, Orsini sat in Too Tight Titone's office at the rear of the topless club. Titone was at the bar resolving a customer dispute, which left Orsini alone. He picked up the phone and dialed a number in Atlantic City. "Hello?" a sleepy female voice answered.

"It's me. Gerry. I wake you?"

"Yes."

"I think things are gonna work out, Doris. You won't believe this, but my father-in-law wants me to work in Atlantic City. He said he'd set something up for me there. That is, if my wife doesn't screw things up."

"Your wife? What happened?"

"She's a goddamn whiner, that's all."

"When?"

"I don't know. A coupla weeks maybe."

"Can't you do it sooner?"

He flinched with anger. He hated it when someone—anyone—questioned him, put pressure on him. If he had any sense he'd . . .

"Don't get mad at me, Gerry. It's just that I miss you so much when I don't see you. You said last time we were together that it would be quick. Weeks?

"I dunno. As quick as I can. Okay, Doris?"

Her voice rang with rejection. "I suppose I don't have any choice. Did you tell your wife about us?"

"Christ, no. Too soon. I told you I'd have to work things out with her father first. Get off my case, Doris. Get off my fucking case!"

Titone opened the door; the loud canned rock music filled the tiny office. "What's that music?" Doris asked.

"I'm in a joint with a frienda mine who owns it. I gotta go, I'll call you again."

A deep, sustained sigh filled his ear. "Hey, cool it, baby. Everything's gonna work out. I just gotta do it right."

"I know," she said, injecting pleasantness into her tone. "I love you, Gerry. You do know that, right?"

"Yeah, I know that." He laughed. He did not want the conversation to end on a sour note.

"And you know how much I miss you," she said, her voice now exuding sex.

"You only miss me 'cause I come attached to something you can't get enough of."

"How can you say such things?" She giggled.

"Baby, I been there."

"Don't you miss *me*?"

"You know I do, baby. Gotta go."

Titone remained standing in the doorway. "You mind?" he said when Orsini hung up.

"What? You want your chair back so you can sleep? Here." Orsini got up and spun the chair. "Sit all you want, you fat fuck." Orsini pulled a glassine envelope from his pocket, poured its contents on Titone's desk and used a straw he'd grabbed on the way through the club to snort the white powder into both nostrils.

"Not in here," Titone whined from his chair.

Orsini left the office and sat in a dark corner of the club where he nursed a beer. Off-duty dancers who approached him were waved away. The conversation with Doris had upset him. They'd been seeing each other on and off over the past few months. At first, she was just another woman to sleep with. Plenty of those in Washington, D.C., where women outnumber men. But then it got special. Too much talk along with the sex. What was she? Just a cocktail waitress at a casino in Atlantic City. But she'd gotten to him. The good, strong feelings had spread from his groin to other parts of the body. Mistake, he reminded himself every time he left her. Get smart. Dump her. She'd been pressing him lately, wanted him to dump Lucia and marry her. How stupid can she be? But he hadn't said no because he didn't want the relationship to end. It was too good. He didn't want to lose her. What am I, falling in love? he asked himself as he tossed bills on the table and went to the street where he got in his car, had a fleeting urge to head for Atlantic City but drove home.

———

"Genaro. It's my father."

He had bought Lucia two dozen roses and taken her for dinner to the Jean-Louis restaurant in the Watergate. For the past three days he'd been home early and spent quiet time with her. He hadn't heard from his father-in-law and hadn't expected to.

"We got your license," Santo said. "I've arranged for you to work with the night manager at the casino. I told him to put you to work, but to give you some time to wander around, talk to people, shmooze with some of the high rollers, get the general lay of things."

"Sounds great, Santo."

"His name's Paddy Provenzano. He's expecting your call." Santo read him the number and rung off.

Orsini turned to his wife, who had been busying herself in the kitchen. "Look," he said, "just for a couple of months until I get the hang of things. Then I'll ask for something during the day." He took her arms, pulled her head onto his shoulder and kissed the top of her head. "Okay?" he murmured.

"Okay," she said. "But just for a couple of months."

"You got it, Lucy," he said. "A coupla months. That's all it should take."

XVİİ

That Same Day—Three Thousand Miles Away

Charlie Pietrosanti stood naked at the window of a room that was his on the second floor and in the back of the Oasis Motel on the outskirts of Barstow, California. The two FBI agents guarding him on the night shift sat in the small coffee shop off the lobby where they watched an Angels baseball game on TV.

Charlie turned and looked at his bed, where Millie had dozed off. It was the sixth time she'd been there, and he welcomed her company.

The irony of ending up again with Millie McGuire had not been lost on him. When he was told he'd be kept in a safe house in Barstow, he immediately thought of her. They'd had an affair years ago when she worked as a cocktail waitress in Los Angeles. He'd heard she'd moved to Barstow. When he was told by the agents in charge of his protection that he could have a wife or girlfriend spend occasional nights with him, he called Millie.

Naturally, she was never allowed to visit the house in which he was confined. Their sessions together always had to be at the Oasis.

Millie hadn't worn well. Her belly was big, and her breasts drooped. But she was nice enough. A loser in life, beat up by men, used, kicked around. He knew she had a kid, a son named George living in San Francisco. She hadn't seen him in a long time.

He also knew she turned tricks part-time, and was pleased to see that she still did. When he first called and asked if she'd spend the night with him in the motel, she turned him down. But he offered three hundred a night, and there she was at the appointed time. As far as the FBI agents were concerned, she was just an old girlfriend. Hookers were off-limits to guys in Charlie's situation.

Besides asking for Millie's occasional company, Pietrosanti had made another request that had been granted. He'd used the plane trip to California to sketch, in minute detail, what the ring taken from him by the FBI had looked like. He missed that ring, felt naked and vulnerable without it.

The first day in the rented house, he gave the sketch to one of the agents and asked him to find a local jeweler who'd re-create it. The original stones had been real; diamonds and rubies. "Just phony stones," he told the agent. "Just so long as it looks like this sketch." He measured his finger with string and gave that too to the agent, along with five hundred dollars from the large amount of cash he'd been allowed to bring with him. "Keep the change," he'd said, which, of course, the agent did not. A week, and four hundred and fifty dollars later, Charlie had his bogus ring.

He sat on the bed and stroked one of Millie's breasts. She opened her eyes and smiled. "Again?" she asked.

"Nah," he said. He leaned close and asked, "Does that car of yours run good?"

"Sure. Yeah, it does. I just had a tune-up the other day. A friend of mine has a garage. We sort of trade services."

Pietrosanti went to the window again and looked down. No more than a twelve-foot drop. "Good, good," he mumbled.

"What's good?" Millie asked.

He rejoined her on the bed. "How would you like an all-expense-paid trip to Frisco?"

"San Francisco?"

"Yeah. Not only that, there's a grand in it for you."

"I don't understand."

"I'll explain everything on the trip. Whadaya say? I'll make it fifteen hundred. Best hotel. Fancy restaurants. You'll get to see George. Maybe you'll end up living there."

Millie sat up. "Sure. Why not? You always were a class act, Charlie."

"Lemme ask you something else, Millie." Pietrosanti smiled and ran the back of his hand over her cheek. "You are still a very pretty lady," he said. "Very, very pretty."

"Thank you."

"You own a gun?"

"A gun?"

"Yeah. Some kinda gun? Rifle. Handgun?"

"I have a little pistol. I carry it in the car in case I meet a weirdo."

"Very smart for a lady to do in this day and age. You with me?"

She shrugged. "I guess so," she said. "But why the gun? I don't like that."

"Lemme level with you, Millie. Downstairs are two guys suckin' coffee."

"So?"

"So, they are there because 'a me. They're bad dudes, Millie. Real bad. I got to get away from them."

"Wait a minute, Charlie. If you're in some kind of trouble, I don't want to get in the middle of it."

"You won't be. Trust me. Forget about the gun. All I need is a ride the next time we get together."

"Just a ride?"

"Yeah. To Frisco. The two of us."

She frowned and bit her lip.

"I'll make it three grand," he said.

"San Francisco is expensive, Charlie. How long will three thousand dollars last me there?"

"Not long, baby, but it won't have to. I got half a mil stashed in Frisco. For us. We find a fancy apartment together and it'll be like old times."

Her expression said that her concerns were dissipating.

"The good life, Millie," he cooed. "Lots of dough. Besides, I don't go around beating up on women like some of your other men do. Am I right?"

She smiled, touched his cheek. "You're right, Charlie. You never hurt me. I'm with you, just as long as I don't get into any trouble."

"Okay, Lady Millie. Here's what we do."

XVIii

Later That Week

In an office at FBI headquarters on Pennsylvania Avenue, in Washington, D.C., Tom Whelan and Fred Wozinski, the two special agents from the organized-crime task force assigned full-time to the Vincent Benedetti case, sat at a small conference table. It was Whelan and Wozinski who'd put together the specifics of the Benedetti sting, reshuffled Charlie Pietrosanti's life, and made a hero of Genaro Orsini with the Benedetti family by providing "proof" that he'd killed Pietrosanti.

They'd been handpicked for the job by Assistant Attorney General Willard Thornton, and were on loan from the Bureau to a special unit established under Thornton's direct supervision, with overall responsibility resting with his boss, Stanley Simonsen.

Thornton had meant what he'd said following the Virginia meeting—if Vincent Benedetti crossed the line, he would no longer operate with impunity. With the disappearance and murder of several members of the Riccardo Diaz organization, and the potential for further violence as the Diaz gang pushed deeper into Benedetti territory, there was also the potential for damaging political fallout. The Justice Department's failure to rid the capital's streets of increasing drug traffic, and the resulting violence—America's murder capital year after year—were not lost on the administration's political opposition. It had become a highly visible failure; the media reported daily on it. Editorials were stinging. Citizen groups demanded action, most led by a vocal white middle class who came each morning to the city to work, and then hightailed it to their suburban homes before the sun went down, their children happily esconced in private or parochial schools, their tree-lined streets as gentle as the city's streets were mean, their homes protected by alarms and fences and barking dogs. Given those circumstances, the added downside of a full-scale Benedetti-Diaz street war was not something Simonsen and his White House leadership coveted. No. An understatement. It drove a stake of fear into their collective hearts.

When Vincent Benedetti had come to Camp Rappahannock with his ultimatum to Thornton, he'd made the decision for them. They'd choose sides. It would be the Benedetti side of the equation that would be their target. They'd determined that the Benedettis were an easier target than Diaz and his organization. Thornton had decided, with the approval of Simonsen, that the best way to move was to put an end to Vincent's reign as the majordomo of the powerful Benedetti crime family, watch the power vacuum develop nationally, and bask in the resulting positive public relations fallout.

They'd accomplished their immediate objective: Vincent Benedetti had been charged with tax evasion, and attempting to bribe a federal officer.

But problems had developed. Unknown to anyone on the task force, the judge at Vincent's arraignment had long and serious ties to the family. Bail was set at a minimum, and Vincent was free within hours.

Worse, evaluation of the audio and video tapes was less than positive. The popular consensus was that it would take a jury of twelve men and women on the payroll of the Justice Department to find him guilty. It had been a blatant case of entrapment, and an amateur one at that. Vincent Benedetti would walk, and would continue to stand at the head of the family, even more ready to heat up the battle against Diaz.

This day, Agents Whelan and Wozinski discussed how to make

greater use of their productive secret weapon within the family, Genaro Orsini, aka Gerry Orson, aka the Partridge, as a means of building a RICO case against Vincent.

Orsini represented the most important "plant" within a major criminal organization in the history of law enforcement. But while he provided a constant stream of information to the FBI and its sister agencies, most of it trivial, some of it of major importance, he proved to be a troublesome, nettling presence in the lives of those charged with working him.

"Have you ever seen his wife?" Wozinski asked.

"A couple of times. From a distance," Whelan replied. "Why?"

"Why? I don't know. She doesn't look like she deserves this. She sure as hell doesn't deserve *him*."

Whelan laughed. "*We* don't deserve him," he said.

But they had him. He was their ward because it had been their idea.

When routine surveillance uncovered the fact that Orsini was dating the daughter of Santo Benedetti, the family's powerful underboss and the godfather's brother, they started exploring "what-if" scenarios, and presented them to their boss at the Bureau who, in turn, passed them on to Thornton. Until that time, law-enforcement agencies had shown little interest in Orsini. They considered him a low-level street hustler, unworthy of any special effort. But Thornton became intrigued that Orsini was dating Lucia. He particularly liked the what-if scenario that went this way: What if they could make a strong case against Orsini for his drug dealing, and then offer him a way to get off the hook? Marry into the Benedetti family, keep the Bureau informed of activity within it, and then disappear into the witness-protection program when things got hot. It seemed an outrageous suggestion, but worth a try.

A special DEA unit had worked closely with Justice to nail Orsini on the narcotics buy. Then, while talking a good game about how long they could put him away, their real trump card was the threat of exposing his freelancing to unsympathetic members of his Mafia power base. Orsini knew the penalty for dealing in the District and violating the understanding. He was told that enough noise about his arrest would be made to ensure that the Benedettis would hear about it. "A wedding bouquet or funeral flowers," they told him.

He opted for the former without much additional persuasion.

But while those involved from Justice congratulated themselves on the brilliance of their coup, Orsini had some ideas of his own.

"The guy's a real loose cannon," Whelan said to his partner. "But we need him."

"Loose cannon. You got that right," Wozinski said, playing with papers on the table.

"You've worked with enough informers," Whelan said. "You know what they're like. Not the cream at the top of the bottle."

"The bastard's still dealing, you know," Wozinski said. "Laughing up his sleeve at us. Like that fuckin' attitude he always cops when we talk to him, bullshit about greasing his casino employee's license when it was unnecessary. It's going too slow," he mumbled.

"Why do you say that?"

"How long can Orsini pull this off, for christsake? How long can he make his wife believe he married her for love? *Nobody* inside is suspicious of him? Can't be. The Pietrosanti thing worked out okay, but I hear some of the lower-level goons in the family don't trust him. Tommy, that whack-job who drives Vincent. Big Dominick, Santo's bodyguard. I'm getting a bad feeling about it, Tom. The slower it goes, the more chance of a foul-up."

Whelan quietly digested what his partner of long standing had said.

Wozinski had been doodling on a piece of paper. He dropped it to the table said, "Let's tighten the noose a little around the old man's neck. Maybe we can help push this thing along."

"Meaning?"

"Gerry Boy pressures them to become a 'made man.' He burrows even deeper into the inner circle. We get what we need, then pull the plug."

"Made man? Sure, if he can get the family to do it. They've got all those rules about making a guy. Orsini's relatively new."

"He's Santo's son-in-law, Tom. A member of the family in a real sense. Santo loves his daughter. Right? Lots of talk about that. The sun rises and sets on her. I bet Orsini can make it work. Let's at least lay it on him."

"After we run it by Thornton."

"He'll like the idea, believe me. So will Orsini. His ego's the size of The Mall, for christsake."

"Okay," said Whelan. "We'll see Thornton tomorrow." The studious-looking Whelan smiled. "Yeah. I think you're right, Fred. I think you're right."

As Wozinski drove his partner home later that evening, he couldn't get Orsini out of his craw. "Sometimes I wonder about getting in bed with scum like Orsini," he said. "I mean, this guy is really bad."

"Since when did you get religion?" Whelan asked.

"It's religion that bothers me," Wozinski replied. "*Our* religion."

Whelan understood what his partner was getting at. Working with someone like Orsini bothered him, too. Yes, informers *were* part of the game. You needed them if you were going to have any chance of taking the worst criminals off the streets. You never liked informers; you weren't supposed to like them, and the feeling was mutual. But there were informers, and then there were people like Genaro Orsini, evil to the quick and with no redeeming values.

Was putting away a Vincent Benedetti justification for dignifying somebody like Orsini, for saving his hide, for having to put up with his swagger and boasting and the expense of keeping him in the witness-protection program for the rest of his life? What would he do after entering the program? Probably continue to inflict pain on innocent people. Nothing would change except his face, name, and Social Security number.

Sometimes, as Whelan, Wozinski, and every other agent knew, you had to question it, maybe not officially but inside yourself, or with your wife before falling asleep. While Stan Simonsen had been fond of referring to the arrangement Hoover had made with Vincent Benedetti as "a pact with the Devil," now, as far as the two agents were concerned, they'd entered into a new pact, with a new and worse Devil.

"You know what I think?" Wozinski said as they pulled up in front of Whelan's house.

"What?"

"I think that when the Benedetti thing is over, and after Mr. Orsini is sitting comfortably someplace with his new name and identity, I think—I think maybe *we* drop a dime on him. One call, man. Just one call to anybody in the Benedetti family."

Whelan laughed, slapped his partner on the shoulder, and opened the door. "You need a vacation, Fred." Then, as he stepped outside and was about to close the door, he looked back, grinned and said, "Maybe we'll take a vacation together . . . *after* we make the call. See you in the morning."

XIX

Sunday Morning

According to initial reports Santo Benedetti had received, Genaro Orsini was doing well in his new part-time job at the Atlantic City casino in which the family had a sizable stake. Santo had asked Paddy Provenzano, the operations manager, to "let me know how he's doing, but don't let him get in the way. I don't want him to become a burden on you."

Paddy understood the underlying message: Give Santo an occasional informal report on how his son-in-law was doing, and make sure it was positive. Paddy knew the potential political problems in providing negative feedback. He didn't like Orsini, who'd started throwing his weight around the first night he was there. As far as Paddy was concerned, Orsini's attention span was as limited as his interest in the day-to-day drudgery of casino business. The only thing that seemed to capture his attention was the action at the tables, and the busty cocktail waitresses, one in particular. Were it Paddy's call, he would have tossed Genaro Orsini out on his ear. But it wasn't his call, and he knew it. One day, Orsini would probably end up running the place. His survival instincts intact, Provenzano's reports to Santo always indicated that things were going well, and that Orsini had quickly fit in. "A real asset to the place," he'd told Santo.

Santo hadn't spoken directly with Genaro since he'd started

commuting to Atlantic City two or three nights a week. But then he received a phone call from Orsini early one Sunday morning. "I would really appreciate being able to sit down and talk with you today about a serious matter," he told Santo. Santo readily agreed to see him. He assumed his son-in-law wanted to personally report on his experiences in Atlantic City, and he looked forward to hearing it. They met at noon in Santo's small personal study.

"Well, how goes it up there?" Santo asked.

"Fine, fine," Orsini replied. "I'm grateful for the chance you gave me."

"You were right. It is a good way for you to begin learning more about family business. Plans for the gambling club on Southern are coming along faster than we anticipated. Paddy Provenzano says you're a real asset to the casino."

Orsini was relieved to hear that. He sensed that Provenzano didn't like him. If Provenzano had bad-mouthed him to Santo, he was prepared to tell his father-in-law that he believed the casino manager was skimming from the casino take. No need for that now.

Santo coughed. "Too many cigars last night," he said, taking one from an inlaid humidor, clipping its end and lighting it without allowing the flame to touch the tobacco. He noticed that Orsini was eyeing the cigar. "Excuse me," he said. "Want one?"

"Yes, thank you."

After a moment of mutual puffing, their smoke melding to create a blue haze in the small room's confines, Santo said, "Anything else, Genaro?"

"Yes." Orsini expressed his desire to become a made man.

It caught Santo off guard. "You want to be made? These things take time, Genaro. To become a made man, you must have demonstrated certain attributes. It's not that you don't have what it takes. It's just that these things must come slowly. In their own good time."

"I apologize if I appear, like, forward," Orsini said. "I understand how important it is to the family. I don't take it lightly."

Orsini moved to the edge of his chair. "But at the same time, Santo, I deal from a deck that misses some important cards. To become one of the family's inner circle, and to have the trust of people at the center, you got to be a made man. In my case, as your son-in-law, the question those around me ask with their eyes is why I am not made. How could I be married to Lucia and not be part of the inner circle? What is it I've done or didn't do that has delayed it for me? They don't say it, but they think it. They wonder about it."

"I wouldn't call it delayed, Genaro. Those closest to me understand that such a thing must run its course. They should not be asking such questions of you—with their eyes or with their mouths."

"Again, I apologize if I seem to be pushing," Orsini said, trying to tiptoe through delicate terrain, "but I think I bring some good things to the family. I will always use what abilities I have to the benefit of the family, but I know I can use them better if I'm a full member. If I'm made into the family."

"I am working you into those things now," Santo replied. "It's important for you to play an increasing role with this family but . . ."

"I know you feel that way, Santo, and I am grateful. I feel like I am putting you on the spot and I don't want to do that. I raised the question. It's important to me to be a full part of this family. Let's leave it at that. You know how I feel, and now I know how you feel. It's good we have this on the table."

"I'm not sure you fully understand how I feel, Genaro," Santo replied, his brow furrowed.

"I know you have your rules, Santo, rules that have been written over a thousand years. They must never be broken."

Orsini was pleased with himself. His careful choice of words had been the right ones, he was certain. His father-in-law was on the defensive.

Santo said, "I would have to—"

Orsini interrupted. "No," he said. "I understand. I don't want you to explain further. It makes you uncomfortable, and that makes me uncomfortable. I won't mention it again until you feel it's the right time."

Santo let out a prolonged sigh. "You're right," he said. "That's best. I will think about what you have asked."

Orsini felt he'd sold Santo on the concept, which was enough for the moment. A good salesman makes the sale and gets out, he thought as he extended his hand to his father-in-law. Santo rose tentatively from his chair. He did not like ending a meeting on another person's terms, even someone close to him. His new son-in-law's desire to be made was understandable, but not so easy to achieve. Others in the inner council would have to agree, which posed some diplomatic problems. He'd first have to work this out in his own mind, then finesse it with family leaders. He would give it serious thought; he did not want Genaro to feel there was a layer of distrust of him within the family. Genaro had redeemed himself with the Pietrosanti matter, something Santo could not forget. At the same time, he'd fulfilled an important condition for being made; he'd killed someone on the family's behalf.

"How's my baby girl?" Santo asked.

"Oh, fine," Orsini answered. "She is a wonderful wife. I count my blessings every day."

Santo coughed again and placed the cigar in an ashtray. "Give her a kiss for me."

"With pleasure," Orsini said. "I'll add it to all the kisses I give her from me each day."

———

Eleven o'clock that same Sunday night.

Victor of Victor and Armbruster had grown restless at home in Baltimore and decided to drive to the plant to work on a government proposal that would generate considerable income for the company. He sat alone in his office, the light from his desk lamp casting a warm pool of yellow illumination on the desktop.

It had been a good weekend. Orsini hadn't shown up Friday night for his two thousand dollars, which prompted a number of pleasant fantasies for Victor. Maybe some misfortune had befallen him. Maybe something he'd told Dante had made a difference. Wishful thinking. Concentrate on the proposal. If the firm won the bid, it would turn things around, relieve the crushing financial pressure that had sent his partner, Armbruster, to an early retirement.

At midnight, Victor was immersed in spreadsheets strewn all over his desk. There was a knock on the metal door that led directly from the office to outside. It was Orsini. He was accompanied by a brute of a man he introduced as Jorge Belmondo. "He's a guinea from Argentina," Orsini said after Victor had let them in. "His old man was one of those Fascist refugees."

Jorge said nothing as Victor mumbled a greeting.

"Sorry I didn't show up Friday," Orsini said. "I got tied up. Family business."

"The envelope's on the table," Victor said, pointing to a small metal table against the wall. The envelope was always there, but Orsini seemed to draw a perverse pleasure from having Victor point it out to him each month.

"That's it?" Orsini said. "No 'How are you?' 'How's business, partner?' 'What can I get you and your friend?'"

"I'm sorry," Victor said. "It's late. I'm working on this bid. It has to be ready early. I'm meeting a government rep at nine. I just wanna get out of here and go home."

"You gonna bullshit again with Paul Dante when you get home?"

Victor's spine stiffened. "What are you talking about?" he asked.

Orsini smiled, then shook his head. "You know," he said, "I really hate it when I'm being called a dumb fuck right to my face."

"What are—"

"Ssssh," Orsini said, placing a finger over his lips as if asking for quiet in church. "I'm a member of the family. You seem to forget that. I know everything that goes on with the Benedettis. I know who's talking to them. I know who's talking about them. I know who's talking about me."

"I—"

"Ssssh, ssssh, ssssh," he said, moving closer to the black man whose face reflected the fear he felt.

Victor looked at Orsini's giant companion, who'd positioned himself between Victor and the door.

"I don't know, Jorge," Orsini said. "What should we do to somebody who can't stop flapping his lips?" He twisted his face against an irritation in his nose. He'd been snorting coke since leaving Santo's house that morning.

Victor saw that the heavy metal door leading to the outside was slightly ajar. He made a desperate lunge for it but Jorge grabbed him and threw him into the wall. Victor grabbed the edge of the door to steady himself. Jorge slammed the door closed on Victor's fingers and continued to apply pressure until the latch caught. Victor's scream was shrill and high, an animal caught in a legtrap. Inhuman. He sucked in air in a useless attempt to alleviate the excruciating pain. Four fingers on his left hand were crushed. Blood ran down the crevice between the door and wall. He was pinned in place, totally defenseless.

"Here it is," Orsini said. He'd gone to Victor's desk and picked up a heavy-duty industrial stapler. Victor's eyes widened in terror as Orsini approached, a twisted smile on his face. Orsini nodded. Jorge held the black man's head in a viselike grip as Orsini fitted Victor's lips between the jaws of the stapler. "Nice lips, Victor, only they move too fuckin' much." He squeezed off a staple that sliced through the flesh of Victor's upper and lower lips. Blood ran from the staple's two entry points; Victor's sounds were more a whimper now. Orsini stepped back and examined his work. "I don't know, Jorge," he said, shaking his head. "You think one's gonna hold? I don't think so. Those are some big lips." Orsini laughed as he ejected a second staple into Victor's lips, and then a third.

Victor groaned and his stiffened body went limp. Jorge opened the door and Victor slumped to the floor. Orsini stepped over him, picked up the envelope from the table, and said, "Good night, Victor. Good luck with your bid. We need the money."

XX

The Following Week

"Partridge says Vincent Benedetti ordered the Tierranueva hit," Thornton told Simonsen at a late-afternoon meeting. "And others."

"Maybe he did, but there's two dozen layers of insulation between Benedetti and his hit men," Simonsen responded. He paced behind his desk, his hands on his hips, then went to the window and crossed his hands on top of his head. "There's no way he'd allow himself to be tied in to such a thing directly. Besides, I understand that this Genaro Orsini, our so-called man inside, doesn't have all his wires connected. A certifiable head case is what I hear."

"But Orsini can corroborate the charges," Thornton said.

"Not enough," Simonsen said tersely. "The word of an informant and nothing else." He returned to his desk and poured himself a glass of water. "And a particularly sleazy one at that. Hell, I wouldn't give him credibility if *I* were on the jury. Besides, we don't want to play the Orsini card until the pot on the table is big enough. We stand a much better chance under RICO. Partridge tells us they're about to open a gambling joint over the D.C. line in Maryland. He also claims to have documentation that links the Benedettis directly to part ownership of Atlantic City casinos."

Thornton smiled. He liked the card-game analogy. "I was thinking more on the order of a bluff," he said.

"A bluff?"

"Right. Charge Benedetti on the Tierranueva hit. Bring him back in again. Hell, we can do it. Let him know that a revolving door makes full circles. Every time *he* walks out, *we* walk him right back in. Keep him busy. Make him squirm. The guy's never had to deal with real trouble because he's always been immune, thanks to that stupid deal Hoover cut with him. Now, we get him twice, in quick succession. Keep up the pressure until he does something desperate."

Simonsen slid easily into his leather chair. "Will," he said, "I've given you a lot of latitude with this. So far, all I've gotten in return is grief. It's starting to make me uncomfortable—very uncomfortable. I'm going to need tangible results for the President, and I assure you he won't consider a mafioso who makes bail, then walks out our front door two hours later with a big smile on his face, as tangible results."

"What can I say?" Thornton said. "I've got a legal system to contend with, and an ancient understanding that was none of our doing. When you're sliding around on ice, Stan, you grab anything that's nailed down."

"If we're on ice, maybe we should stop skating."

"And lose Benedetti?"

"If we're destined to lose him anyway, I'd rather do it without fanfare."

"We won't lose him, Stan. I guarantee that. Okay, maybe I was wrong in suggesting we bring him in on every little charge. But there's nothing wrong in leaking that we're considering going after him on the Tierranueva murder. Just to make him sweat a little. But you're right. We'll get him under RICO. We've already built quite a case in that direction, thanks to Partridge. It may take a while, but I guarantee we'll nail him."

Simonsen's laugh was sardonic. "Somehow, Will, guarantees in things like this make me nervous."

"Will you trust me on this?"

"If I have reason to. Maybe Hoover was right. Let them ply their trade as long as they stay out of our hair."

"Impossible," Thornton said. He didn't like the negative direction the conversation had taken, and wiped a thin layer of perspiration from his brow. "Benedetti will only honor the deal he cut with Hoover thirty years ago as long as we get rid of Diaz and his type in the District. And you know damn well we don't have the resources to do that."

"I also know that putting Vincent Benedetti away isn't easy. A lot of ice between him and us. He's spent thirty years building a network of contacts within the government. I got a call from Senator Walling this morning. He wanted to know why we were trying to railroad Benedetti. That's the word he used. 'Railroad.' Benedetti's done Walling lots of favors over the years, and he's not the only one who's enjoyed Benedetti's generosity. There's a new wing on the city hospital thanks to Vincent Benedetti. A children's wing. He'd have to blow up Chesapeake Bay before anybody in law enforcement in Maryland would indict him. He's connected, like no mafioso has ever been before in this country. So don't guarantee me anything where Vincent Benedetti is concerned."

Thornton had to control a festering anger. He'd deny to anyone that putting Vincent Benedetti and his family away for good was an obsession with him. Yet it was, and the urgency of it had grown in recent days in proportion to his frustration. That the leader of a Mafia family had been able to shake hands with the legendary head of the world's finest law enforcement agency, the FBI, and reach an agreement that would give him relative impunity to prosper through criminal acts was too bitter to swallow.

"Stan," he said, "I will see to it that Vincent Benedetti, and maybe others from his family, are put away. What I need from you is your faith, your confidence, and your clout."

"My clout?"

"That's right. You have the power to keep the snipers out of our foxhole while we put the pieces in place and get the job done. Will you do it?"

"How much time?"

"As quickly as possible. We're pushing Partridge to get deeper inside. I think it'll happen fairly soon. He'll be made, which puts him smack-dab in the middle of the inner circle where he'll know every decision made. And that means we will, too." Thornton rested his case.

He'd been a prosecutor before joining the Justice Department and had been a good one, with a high conviction rate.

"Okay," Simonsen said. "But one condition."

"Name it."

"That the next time I see a photograph of Vincent Benedetti, he's not smiling. The next photograph I see of him shows cuffs on his wrists, and pissed-off written all over his face."

"A murder indictment? Are these fucking guys out of their minds?"

Vincent Benedetti was in his office in downtown Baltimore. The phone was pressed to his ear. "What murder?" he bellowed. "What murder are they talking about?"

He paused to listen to Burton Carter, a former Justice Department lawyer who now represented him, and who'd related what he had heard from a former colleague in the department. When the lawyer stopped talking, Vincent shouted, "When?" He listened again before saying, "Find out! Get back to me! Do something!" He slammed down the phone, gave it barely enough time to stop vibrating, then picked it up again and dialed. "Santo," he said, "please come here right away. We need to talk."

"I'm not going back in," Vincent told his brother before Santo could even remove his coat. "They're fucking with me. They're playing some kind of game and laughing at me. I'm not going to let them do it. This is bullshit. What kind of country is this?"

Santo hung his coat on an antique rack and joined his brother on a couch. The office was on the top floor of a new glass-and-steel skyscraper that looked down over Baltimore's rehabilitated Inner Harbor complex, on the Northwest Branch of the Patapsco River. The office was furnished in chrome and soft beige leather. A huge desk of light hardwood was imposing in front of floor-to-ceiling windows. Built into it was an electronic communications console that would have been at home on the flight deck of the starship *Enterprise*. Vincent and Santo both loved electronic gadgets.

The modern look of the room was interrupted by two paintings from minor Renaissance artists that hung on the wall opposite Vincent's desk. Though the artists may have been minor, even lesser Renaissance artists commanded a price. The two had been bought at auction in Italy, by Vincent himself, for more than eighty thousand dollars.

But the room was more than a showcase for Vincent's taste in art. Another wall housed business books and reference materials. His in-box contained reports on the movement of goods through ports in Europe and the Pacific Rim. Vincent was convinced there was great growth opportunity in a Europe that had recently been unified. He saw the family's future bound up in it.

Import-export manuals and tariff directories were all neatly arranged each morning by his secretary, Angela Rinaldi, an older woman whose blue hair and conservative clothing was as neat as the way she kept the offices. She'd been Vincent's loyal employee for more than twenty years. As far as she was concerned, he was a saint, a man who treated her as family, and whose ongoing generosity had enriched her life.

The soft strains of an eighteenth-century violin piece provided a soothing background.

"What do you propose to do?" Santo asked.

"I don't know. That's why I called you. I don't think waiting around for their next move is the answer. They've taken the initiative, and they don't seem to be long on patience. Burt Carter's calling his contacts now to see what he can pick up."

"We're in a war here," Santo replied. "For the first time in decades we're fighting the big enemy, and we haven't planned well enough. We've been too busy fighting disconnected skirmishes." He got up and went to the windows. Below, the U.S.S. *Constellation* rested at its berth in the basin, and dozens of tourists milled about the nautical exhibits, and drifted in and out of many fashionable stores that filled the minimalls, or that lined the streets of the harbor. A street minstrel played songs on a guitar, his music soundless outside the barrier of glass that separated Santo from the world below. It was a bright and breezy day; white clouds raced across the sky as if in a hurry to be somewhere. "They're working from a battle plan," he repeated over his shoulder. "And we fight small battles."

"Another page from one of your military history books?" Vincent asked. Santo enjoyed reading about past military battles, and possessed a sizable library on the subject.

Santo turned. "I haven't had time for heavy reading these days," he said. "Besides, I don't recall you as being someone who ignores important lessons of history."

"No," Vincent said, "you're right. But we're dealing with current events, Santo, the here-and-now." He held down a button on his intercom and told Angela to send out for two cappuccinos from a gourmet shop on the pier. He turned to Santo. "Actually," he said, "I agree with you. They've got some broad-based strategy. They want to redraw the maps around here. We've been lulled into a false sense of security by the sweetheart deal we had all these years. But nothing lasts forever. We should have planned for that. Now we have to look ahead."

"And?"

"And, I'm not going to do it from behind bars. You understand, don't you? I'm too old to go to prison, Santo."

"Of course, but I'm not the one you have to convince."

Over the years, other heads of crime families had expressed quiet but pointed criticism at Vincent for never having served any significant jail time. Jail toughened a man, it was thought. Doing your time showed that you weren't afraid of it, and wouldn't bend to pressure when offered a deal to avoid it.

"Fuck 'em."

"Who?" Santo had been thinking about those veiled criticisms of his brother and thought he was referring to other crime families.

"The feds. They won't do this to me, Santo. I won't let them."

"And if they hand up an indictment?"

"I'll disappear. Go visit the relatives in Sicily. I'm not going back. I wouldn't survive prison because they won't let me survive it."

"Survive it? You sound paranoid."

The intercom rang. "I'm coming in," Angela said. "And Mr. Carter is on line one."

Vincent picked up the phone. "Yeah, Burt," he said. "What did you find out?"

The secretary entered, placed a tray with the coffee on a glass-and-chrome table in front of the couch, and left.

Vincent, who'd been listening to his lead counsel, said, "Burt, this is ridiculous. You've got to do something. Press them. Make them produce their evidence. Do what you've got to do to stop this, or at least to slow it down. Call me later."

He hung up and said in answer to his brother's questioning look, "By the end of the week. Could be as early as the day after tomorrow. I've got to get out of here, Santo. I need some space, some time to think."

"There's no way they can bag you on any spic drug hit. You know that, Vincent."

"Yeah? So what? They're after me. Next comes some fucking RICO Act charge. No, Santo, I have to get away for a while."

The coffees remained untouched on the table.

"I don't know what to say," Santo replied.

"Find me a place to hole up."

"You're going to skip bail?"

"If I have to. Tell them I'm away. You don't know where. Tell them anything. Buy me some time."

Vincent was rattled; Santo had not seen him like this before and it concerned him. "I'll take care of it," he said, not sure that he could, or should.

XXI

That Night

"He can stay with Lucia and me."

It was a calculated offer. Orsini didn't want to let Vincent slip away on the chance it would erode his position with the feds. He was angry that his FBI "keepers" had not alerted him to this change in their strategy regarding Vincent, and felt he had to do something, say something on the spur of the moment until he could wrangle an explanation of what was happening.

"Family is the first place they'll look," Santo said. He sat with Orsini and Lucia in their kitchen.

"They can look, but they won't find him," Orsini answered. "We have a room set up in the basement, a wine cellar from the previous owner, a guy who was a real connoisseur."

"You've seen it," Lucia added.

Orsini said, "It's perfect, got lots of space, temperature-control equipment, good lighting, the works. We just had it converted into sort of a study for me, a place to go to in case the Indians ever attack." He laughed at what he'd said. "Hey, sure, if they decide to rip the house apart, they'll find him, but they'd need a reason to do that. Am I right? I mean, they just can't force their way in and start rearranging the architecture, can they?"

"I'll check with the lawyers."

"We could move some stuff in front of the door and you'd never know the room was there. Meantime, Lucia's home and can take care of him. It would work in the short run till you have time to figure out how to get him out altogether."

"I don't know," Santo said. "I'm not sure I want to involve you in this, Lucia. But it's a generous offer."

"I don't want to be the reason Uncle Vincent doesn't come here," Lucia said. "I love him. If he needs help, I want to be the one who gives it to him."

"I'll talk it over with Vincent," Santo said.

―――――

Vincent Benedetti had serious reservations.

"We discussed the possibility of the feds coming after family first," Santo explained to his brother. "While it's a factor, we think they'll figure you'll put distance between yourself and family. Besides, Genaro's clean. They'd have no reason to harass him."

"May I remind you, Santo, that it was Genaro who got me into this situation in the first place? Remember?" Vincent's usual calm demeanor had been replaced by overt nervousness and agitation.

"That was a completely different matter," Santo said. "Anyway, Paul Dante checked him out for three days after the Pietrosanti thing. Genaro's clean."

"Santo, *I'm* not clean, *you're* not clean. Nobody's clean."

"Well, Paulie didn't find anything."

"He told you that?"

"Not in so many words."

"Did you ask? In so many words?"

"Vincent, Genaro brought me Charlie Pietrosanti's hand in a cognac gift box."

"I'd have preferred his head."

"That would have been too messy. Besides, his ring was significant. A trademark."

Vincent thought a moment before asking, "Do you still have the hand?"

"Are you crazy? Of course not."

"I'd feel better if you had run a print check on it."

Santo shook his head. "This thing is making you crazy, brother," he said. "I can appreciate what you're going through, but I think it's fogging your perception. You're seeing villains everywhere."

"Just being careful," Vincent answered, his look growing distant. "I got a lot of things to think about. They *are* coming at me from too many directions. I have to think better and move faster than they do."

———

"What the fuck are you guys up to?" Orsini spit into the phone. He was at a booth on a street corner in Foggy Bottom, near the Kennedy Center. A passing couple heard him and did a double-take.

"Came down from up top, Gerry," Whelan replied in his matter-of-fact, bureaucratic tone.

"I gotta know about this shit before I get it from my father-in-law."

"Sorry. We were busy."

"That really fills me with fuckin' confidence."

"What is this, Gerry, one of your beat-up-on-the-feds calls?"

"No, numbnuts. I got some of that hard news you're always looking for."

"Which is?"

"The big man's going to stay with me."

"What?"

"I had to do something when I found out he was gonna run. It was the first thing that popped into my head. I went with it."

"Where are you going to put him?"

"I got a room in the basement."

"I don't know what my bosses are going to think about that."

"I don't give a shit what your bosses think about it. He's moving in. That's all. I'll call you later in the day."

"Do that. It's important."

Whelan hung up and turned to Wozinski. "What was that all about?" Wozinski asked.

"Our good friend Orsini is about to become an innkeeper for Vincent Benedetti himself. The old man's planning to skip."

"And he's going to *Orsini's* house?"

"That's right."

"He thinks it's a safe house?"

"Evidently."

"Holy shit."

"Fun, huh?"

———

"Actually, it buys us some time," Thornton said. "We can assemble more evidence against him, find more people to testify. The fact that he's run on the tax thing will support our request for no bail on the next charge we bring."

"You're right," Simonsen replied. "Knowing he's down in Orsini's basement with his wings clipped will help us keep tabs on him."

Thornton fell silent.

"What's the matter, Will?"

"This guy's no dummy, Stan. He'll expect us to look for him with family."

"And?"

"We need to search Orsini's house, but not find him."

"Isn't that a little melodramatic?"

"Sure. But in a mind game like this, *we* have to structure the game. Make the rules."

"It could blow up."

"We'll set it up to minimize that possibility. It's beautiful, Stan. The old guinea will be living with Partridge. What could be better? We do a sham search of Orsini's house and move on. We don't know where Vincent Benedetti has gone. All we know is that he's skipped bail, and we're searching for him. At least that's what everybody will be told. It'll play, believe me."

Simonsen looked at his watch. "I have to go, Will. Dinner date. Run with it."

"I sure will."

"With the usual covenant. Cover your ass. Cover mine."

"Count on it."

XXii

The Next Day—Monday

Vincent and Santo decided that before moving in with Genaro and Lucia, Vincent would hole up elsewhere until the authorities had made a search of the Orsini house. That occurred on the following Tuesday. With that behind them, Vincent left the small Annapolis hotel in which he'd been staying and came to the house in Georgetown. He was driven by Tommy and arrived at three **A.M.** "Thank you," he told his driver and bodyguard of many years.

"You'll be okay here, Vincent?" Tommy asked.

"Yes. Fine. Santo will be in touch with me every day. It is his daughter's house. No one will wonder why he visits each day. Things will go on as before. Family business will not be interrupted. Santo will meet with me every day and deliver my decisions."

Although the front of Orsini's house wasn't yellow, Tommy didn't trust it. "Maybe you should get outta the country," he offered, something he seldom did. He wasn't paid for his opinions.

"This will be fine for a while," Vincent responded. "Good night, Tommy. Don't worry. Everything will be good again."

Vincent found the room claustrophobic. There were no windows. Even cells had a window. Here, all the walls were whitewashed stone. He felt like the Prisoner of Zenda, the Count of Monte Cristo.

Of course, he wasn't confined to the room. During most of the day he was free to wander the house. The blinds and drapes were kept

196

closed. When someone came to the house, he would retreat to his basement quarters and wait quietly until Lucia or Genaro gave him the all clear.

Vincent gravitated to the kitchen most days where he nibbled on a constant array of snacks provided by Lucia. He enjoyed talking to her in the kitchen, took comfort from her unfailing pleasantness. He seldom complained about his situation to her; in fact, he often expressed his gratitude for "putting up with this foolish old man." To which Lucia would reply, her voice always buoyed by a light laugh, "You aren't a foolish old man, Uncle Vincent, and I don't consider myself putting up with you. Have another cookie. Wine?"

Santo came by every day, and the brothers would huddle in the basement room. There was much family business to consider, decisions to be made, actions to be taken—all Vincent's responsibility. Santo had made it clear to other family members that although Vincent would be away for a period of time, he was still very much in charge of the family. They didn't need some ambitious underling looking to step in and take control.

At night, it was decided that Vincent was to sleep in his basement room. There were other vacant bedrooms in more amenable parts of the house, but the consensus was—more accurately, Santo's reading was—that it was always possible for the police to conduct a surprise raid at night, warrants in hand. Too much time would be spent spiriting Vincent from where he slept to the basement. "Let's be cautious," Santo had said. "Let's not take any chances. It won't be for long."

Orsini wasn't home much. Between his daytime business activities, and his forays to Atlantic City, he was absent most of the time. When he was in the house, Vincent considered his overt friendliness to be gratingly condescending. He perceived an uneasy glitch in Orsini's voice, a kind of vocal camouflage that always troubled the elder Benedetti. Blatant insincerity was always easier to identify. It was a billboard. Vincent preferred that, and found it easier to accommodate to that kind of person. You got what you saw.

Not true with Genaro. He was too slick for Vincent's taste, too skilled at being whatever the moment called for. Like most politicians with whom Vincent had dealt over the years. Chameleons. Snakes.

Changing their colors, shedding their skins to suit the seasons. There was, of course, the added complication of Genaro being Santo's son-in-law, Lucia's husband, who would sire Santo's grandchildren and provide for Lucia and her family.

There was also Vincent's self-acknowledgment that his judgment might be clouded by his own personal prejudices. No matter how Genaro had redeemed himself in the Pietrosanti mess, Vincent had gone through with the meeting because of Orsini's assurances. He couldn't help harboring lingering suspicions about Orsini. It was like a car that often breaks down; even when it's fixed, you never quite believe it will start.

And so Vincent withheld final judgment about Genaro Orsini. It was better that way. There was enough family tension without adding unnecessarily to it.

But that didn't mean he stopped thinking about Orsini. He had a lot of time to think, especially when in the basement. Having time to think was the reason he was there. There were many other things to ponder and many decisions to be made, but no matter how hard he tried to focus on these other matters, the setup by Charlie Pietrosanti invariably intruded. He would be in the middle of a book and the setup would replace words on the page. The most passionate movements of a symphony played on his compact-disc player would suddenly fade, leaving Vincent in that room in the Mayflower Hotel, the feds bursting through doors, the handcuffs, the shame of being led through the lobby like a common criminal.

When he would say to Lucia that he was a foolish old man, it reflected those moments of doubt about the Pietrosanti sting. At those times, he came at it from the perspective that perhaps Orsini had been duped by Pietrosanti, that everything had been laid out as neatly as it had been portrayed, and that reality had simply interrupted the script Genaro had written. If that were so, his reservations about Genaro were more the result of his own bad luck than anything Orsini had or hadn't done. In that case, Vincent was honest enough with himself to consider the possibility that he was looking for a scapegoat to avoid having to admit his own carelessness. He forced himself to give that scenario credibility, to try to make it work, to see himself as the fool. If a man was not hard on himself, especially a leader, he presented to his enemies a weaker opponent.

But there were other moments during Vincent's confinement and resulting reverie when he did not consider himself a fool.

Pietrosanti had been Orsini's man. He had worked with him in the past. There was, of course, the possibility that something could have intervened to turn Pietrosanti. Genaro might have been unaware of that and become a victim of it, too. If that was what had happened, Orsini had allowed Vincent to proceed into a deal that he had not examined closely enough. At best, he'd been careless, and Vincent was intolerant of careless people. They usually got other people killed.

At the opposite extreme was the unthinkable—that Orsini had been an active participant in the setup. That had been everyone's immediate gut reaction, and was the only reaction that made sense to Vincent at the time. Orsini had disappeared right after the sting. Orsini-as-villain had been the assumption upon which everyone had proceeded in the early hours.

What turned them from that belief was Orsini's alleged hit on Pietrosanti. Vincent had bought it initially, but was now suspicious of the evidence. He'd never been enamored of the ancient Mafia sense of symbolism, at least not when it substituted for fact. Orsini could have gotten the hand anywhere. It could be a distraction, a dramatic statement to counter hard evidence. The moment Orsini delivered the hand, everyone stopped asking questions.

And what of Paul Dante? Santo had sent him rummaging around the fringes of Genaro's life but, according to his brother, hadn't listened to what Dante had found. That was not like the Santo of old, the Santo Vincent knew best. He understood his brother's actions, or lack of them. They were dealing with family; the hand and its garish ring had eliminated a great embarrassment to Santo, a deep hurt. It provided the answer Santo needed to hear, whether true or not.

Was he himself doing something similar? Vincent wondered. Had he made a determination about Orsini and now was collecting, in his own mind, evidence to support that preconceived notion? Granted, his own feelings about Genaro were based more on instinct than fact. But his instincts had always been his most trusted ally. They had made him a reliable judge of character, which had helped build the family and to place it in the enviable position it had occupied for years. His instincts, along with his accurate evaluation of the political climate at the time and the men with whom he was dealing, had given him the confidence to propose the Hoover deal, a deal that had served the Benedettis well for years.

Until now.

He decided he wanted to talk to Paul Dante. He'd have to finesse it with Santo, but would do it. It was a matter of survival. Diplomacy was generally important; survival always took precedence.

———

"Why do you want the house searched again?" Special Agent Tom Whelan asked Orsini.

"Because the old man keeps asking me about when you guys hit it before he moved in. Like he doesn't believe me. Give me a fuckin' break, huh. My ass is on the line. I'm tellin' you, come in again. I'll have him in his basement room. Make a lot a noise, then go away. That way, they're likely to let him keep stayin' there. Otherwise . . ."

"All right," Whelan said.

"Santo's been talking about moving him. I tell him I think Vincent's safest with me and Lucia but——"

"Stop telling them anything," Whelan said. "Butt out. Let them decide. Don't blow your cover."

"What if they do move him someplace else permanent?"

"That's when you speak up. After the fact. Tell them it doesn't make sense now that your home has been swept twice. The room is secure? Well hidden?"

"Sure. The room used to be a wine cellar. I've got a couple of those floor-to-ceiling wine racks we moved out of the room when we made a bedroom in there. The racks are real elaborate, like hardwood wall units. We'll cover the door with them. You come in, don't find him, and he'll really feel secure. Makes sense. Am I right?"

"Okay."

"When?" Orsini asked.

"Unless you hear otherwise from me, tomorrow."

———

Orsini was right. Vincent was uneasy about staying at Orsini's house. Armed with a search warrant, the feds could tear it apart. But Vincent had been told that their search of his office and home had been perfunctory. The visit to Santo's house had been an in-and-out affair, and Santo was convinced the feds believed that his brother was now far away, maybe even out of the country.

When the knock on the door came, Vincent was all but sealed behind the stone wall to his basement room. He'd been listening to *Cavalleria Rusticana,* which was up to the stunning intermezzo when the disturbance came. He had been reading one of the new books that reexamined Hoover and the FBI he'd headed for so many years. If the information in the book was correct, it confirmed certain reservations Vincent had had about Hoover. But one thing was certain. For whatever his reasons, Hoover had been a man of his word. The innuendos about Hoover's sexual preferences bored and angered Vincent. He was always suspicious of cheap shots against someone unable to defend himself. Hoover's compilation of evidence to use against important people if they crossed him was simply good business as far as Vincent was concerned.

He turned off the CD player and curled up on his bed.

He heard them banging around upstairs, opening doors and sliding furniture across the floor. Within minutes, they came to the basement, accompanied by loud protestations from Genaro about the sanctity of his home, and how his family was being violated by the intrusion. What did they intend to do, he asked, keep searching the home and business of every person who had even the slightest family tie to the fugitive?

Vincent winced. Orsini's protests rang hollow. He protested too much. Vincent lay motionless and controlled his breathing.

They were gone in twenty minutes. A few minutes later, Vincent heard Genaro and Lucia slide the wine racks away from his door. He wanted to shout "Wait. Make sure they don't double back." But the door opened and he was met by Orsini's smiling face.

"They were pushovers," Orsini said. "I shouted them out of here."

"Don't be so sure," Vincent said. "I think I should stay in here for a few hours in case they come back."

"Nah," Orsini replied. "They seemed late for something when they drove off. They won't be back."

"Besides," Lucia chimed in, "I have a chicken in the oven. Let's have a nice lunch." A smile lit her face. She was enjoying playing host to her uncle. "It'll be done soon," she added. "You come upstairs, Uncle Vincent, and enjoy your meal like a human being. Have a glass of wine. You're safe here now."

The following day, Vincent was added to the FBI's "Most Wanted" list, and a fifty-thousand-dollar reward was offered for information leading to his arrest and conviction.

———

The next night, at the casino in Atlantic City, Orsini received a call from Santo. He took it in Paddy Provenzano's office. "Call me at this number," Santo said. "Call from a booth outside the casino." He gave the number to his son-in-law; he was in a booth in Baltimore.

Orsini ran from the casino and found a booth on the boardwalk. Santo answered on the first ring. "It's arranged," Santo said. "Members of the other families will attend. We'll do it at my house. I'll let you know the date."

"I'm deeply honored," Orsini said. "I will always do the family honor."

"Yes, Genaro," Santo said. "I know you will."

Then, almost as an afterthought, Orsini added, "Will Vincent preside?"

"We don't know," Santo answered. "It will depend upon his situation."

"Will he be there?"

"Again, it depends."

"I see."

"We'll hope for the best," Santo said.

XXiii

At the Same Time—Three Thousand Miles Away

Originally, Charlie Pietrosanti had intended to head for Los Angeles, eighty miles due west of Barstow. But once he realized he might actually be able to escape from the motel, he reconsidered. The FBI would assume he'd head for L.A. because it was close, or to Las Vegas where he was known to have spent considerable time before being sandbagged by the Bureau. San Francisco made more sense. Besides, that's where Millie's son, George, lived.

As he lay awake in bed at the house the night before leaving, he had fantasies of dressing in drag and losing himself in San Francisco's gay community, or buying a wig with a pigtail and settling in Chinatown. Silly, he decided. I won't be there that long. Not if things work out the way they should.

Now, the next night, he opened the door to his motel room for Millie. She'd done what he'd told her to do. She'd parked at the rear of the motel instead of in front, and had lingered in the lobby to ensure being seen by the two agents, who watched another Angels game. This one was with the Texas Rangers. It was in the sixth inning. Nolan Ryan was going for yet another no-hitter. The agents were riveted to the screen.

"Ready?" Charlie asked Millie.

She nodded.

He opened the window. A hot desert breeze fluttered lacy white curtains. "Smells good," he said. "Here I go."

Millie watched as he climbed over the sash, poised as though to jump, then grabbed the sash with both hands and lowered himself until he dangled above the ground. Millie came to the window and looked down at him. "You all right?" she asked.

He released his hands and fell. Even at that short distance, his landing shot pain up his legs and back. He looked up at Millie. "Come on," he said. "Don't worry. I'll catch you."

"I'm—I'm afraid, Charlie."

"For christsake, come on. We ain't got all night."

She climbed onto the windowsill and allowed her legs to hang outside. "Turn around," Pietrosanti said. "Use your hands like I did. It ain't so far to fall then."

Ignoring his advice, she pushed herself out the window and fell ass-first. Charlie raised his arms to grab her but she hit him broadside, knocking him to the ground and landing on top of him. Every ounce of his breath was knocked out of him. "Get off me," he managed.

She stood and straightened her blue denim skirt. He continued to lie on the ground. "Charlie, did I—?"

He slowly pulled himself to his feet. His ribs felt broken. His head pounded with pain.

"Charlie, I'm sorry," Millie said.

"Yeah, yeah," he said, taking her hand and leading her to the waiting red Honda. "You're more dangerous than them guys inside."

Charlie drove. He took back roads to the highway that ran north up the center of California. It was hot, and he turned on the Civic's air-conditioning. It didn't work.

"It's broke," Millie said.

"I noticed," he said, rolling down his window.

Millie said little for the first hour, which was fine with Charlie. He felt like a bird freed from its cage. He knew he'd set into motion the potential for big trouble but it didn't matter, at least not at that moment. He was free to operate again, to cut a deal that would be the most important of his life—that would *save* his life if it worked.

Millie said, "I think it's awful what those men did to you, keeping you there that way."

"My fault," Charlie said. "I got in with the wrong crowd, borrowed money from the wrong people. They're Mafia."

"I hate the Mafia," she said. "They hurt innocent people like you."

"Yeah. That's right. Thanks for rescuing me. No telling what they might have done to me. They're animals, Millie. Scum. They know your name? Know your license plate?"

"I don't think so."

"That's good." He squeezed her thigh. "You're okay, Millie. It was my lucky day when I met you."

"The feeling is entirely likewise."

When they reached Bakersfield, Charlie pulled into a small used-car lot that was obviously not a threat to the Japanese auto industry. The only person there was the manager, a scrawny little guy with bad acne and a big tick in his left eye.

"What are you doing?" Millie asked.

"Treating this beautiful lady next to me to a bonus. A new car. One with air-conditioning."

"But I like this car. It's paid for."

"So will this one be," he said.

Fifteen minutes later, they drove off in a 1989 black Mustang. Its plates had been provided by the used-car lot's manager, who said he'd take care of registering it personally for Mr. Peters, an extra three hundred dollars in his hand.

The air-conditioning worked.

"This is for *me?*" Millie asked giddily.

"For you, babe. A token of my appreciation."

"You're a classy guy."

"I'm a guy who appreciates his friends," Charlie answered. "I always take care a my friends."

They arrived in San Francisco as the sun was setting over the Golden Gate Bridge.

"I never saw anything so beautiful," Millie said.

"Spectacular," Charlie said. "Mother Nature. You can't top her."

He pulled up in front of Sabella's Restaurant on Fisherman's Wharf. "Okay, Lady Millie," he said. "Here's where we part."

"What?"

"I got things to do, and you'll just be in the way. Here." He peeled off two thousand dollars and gave it to her.

"I don't understand," she said.

He handed her the keys to the car. "Yours. Go see George. Be good to him. He's your son. I gotta split. Nice knowin' you."

"I thought—"

"Yeah, I know. You're okay, Millie. Get out of the business. Go straight. Better for you." He kissed her on the cheek, got out and disappeared into the milling crowd of tourists.

———

"Charlie? I don't believe it."

"Yeah, it's me. How's the kid?"

"Fine. He's ten."

"Ten? How'd he get so old so fast?"

"He grew. That's all."

"Boy, oh boy, oh boy. Ten, huh? He still look like me?"

"Spitting image, unfortunately." She added a laugh.

"Give him my best. Hey, Carla, I need a big favor."

"What kind of favor?"

"I need you to make contact with somebody for me. I need you to call somebody, pass on a message."

"Are you in trouble, Charlie?"

"Me? Nah. How's things in my favorite city?"

"Are you here in Vegas?"

"No. I got another check for you and the kid. A big one."

"I'll say that for you, Charlie. You always come through with the money."

"'Cause I owe you and him. Do me the favor?"

"Sure. What do you need?"

"I want you to call a guy in Washington, D.C., named Paul Dante. I hear maybe he's got some connections I need to get out of a jam. He's a private investigator, and owns a bar called Cuffs. I don't have the number. Get it from Information. Tell him this . . ."

He completed his instructions. "Got it?" he asked.

"I think so."

"Remember, Carla, if he agrees to meet you, you make the decision whether he can be trusted or not. You tell him the story. If he comes off okay, send him here."

"Where's *here*?"

"I'll be in touch. Love you, baby. Give the kid a big hug from daddy."

XXIV

Later That Week

Dante's Buick was an hour up the turnpike from Washington, and Julia Croce still didn't understand why they were taking this trip. Maybe if it hadn't been so last-minute. He'd called that morning: "You don't have any classes, right?"

"Right."

"You have the week off, right?"

"Right."

"You can be ready in an hour, right?"

"Wrong."

"Why not?"

"Give me a reason to be."

"A coupla nights away. Just the two of us."

"Where?"

"Atlantic City. Best suite in the house."

"I don't like Atlantic City."

"You've never been there with me. Whadaya say? Be adventurous. Hour and a half?"

"Two hours. Can I play the slots?"

"You can play with anything you want."

"An hour and a half."

"You told me you're not a gambler, Paul," she said early in the ride.

"I'm not, but I have my moments. I like to shoot craps once in a while." He turned his attention from the road to smile at her. "But I'm conservative," he added. "No middle-of-the-table bets, just pass-line, odds, and a few bets on the come."

"I haven't the slightest idea what you're talking about."

"Just as well. Stick to the slots. All you gotta do is put in the quarter and pull the handle."

"I intend to, but I can only do that for so long. What will I do the rest of the time?"

"The same thing I'll be doing, eating bonbons in bed. We've been looking for some time away alone, just you and me. Besides, Santo insisted. He doesn't think he's paid me back enough for the wild-goose chase he sent me on with his son-in-law. He'd be insulted if I didn't take him up on it, and he specifically suggested I take you. Just consider yourself kidnapped for a couple of days."

"How exciting," she said. "I love playing the victim. What about that other case you told me about—the guy you've been following?"

"I've taken it as far as I can go." He dropped his hand into her lap. "And, I can use a break in the action."

"A break? Who you kidding?"

"Yes. A break. From the routine of my life—of our life. A plush hotel suite in Atlantic City means we can lock the door and stay in there all week if we want."

"Don't count your chickens, Paulie Boy. I'm not always that easy."

"Neither am I."

"That'll be the day."

"You're okay, babe." He patted her thigh and suggestively raised an eyebrow.

"Yeah, you too, *babe*," she mimicked.

He'd neglected to tell her that he'd just learned that Orsini was now working in the casino, and decided he'd pretend to be surprised. If she knew that the primary reason he wanted to make this trip was to watch Orsini in action, learn more about him, maybe finally discover some hard facts to pass on to Santo, she wouldn't be happy.

He'd also decided that he would keep Orsini low on his list of things to do. Her needs would come first, and he'd try to live up to his promises. A week? Nice fantasy, but the way he'd been falling asleep on her lately, their bacchanal wasn't likely to last more than a couple of days. Even that was wishful thinking. He wasn't a kid anymore, a reality that hadn't thrilled him lately.

By the second evening of their stay in Atlantic City, Julia admitted she was having a good time, enjoying breaking even at the slot machines (all gamblers claim they break even when they lose, Dante thought when she recounted to him her gambling finances). He'd done all right at the craps table. He was ahead about four hundred (sure, she'd thought when he bragged about his winnings. All gamblers claim to win when they lose).

They'd enjoyed a couple of shows, and particularly liked a jazz quartet in one of the lounges. The food had been typical casino food, rich and fattening and hardly deserving of the term "cuisine" that accompanied all the printed hype about the restaurants. The high-caloric menus hadn't deterred Julia, who'd obviously spent her adult life watching her diet. "The hell with calories," she'd said while eating a dessert that was capable of sending a healthy person into sugar shock. They were having a good time together. He was glad they'd come.

By early the third night, there hadn't been a sign of Orsini. When he did show up, Dante felt a rush of excitement. Julia gave him her best jaundiced eye when she saw the swaggering Orsini strut into the casino. Dante threw her a palms-up.

"Coincidence?" she asked.

"Yeah."

"You lie."

His expression was one of abject offense. "My mother would turn over in her grave if she heard you say that."

"You might join her faster than you think." Her voice softened, and she placed her hand on his arm. "Please, don't start anything." He promised he wouldn't.

Orsini didn't notice them, and they left to have dinner at another casino a short walk up the boardwalk. When they returned, Julia said she was tired and wanted to curl up in their suite with a Stephanie Blake historical romantic novel she'd started that afternoon. The book was a welcome relief from her usual fare of academic reading. "I love the bodice-ripping scenes," she told Dante.

Her claim to be tired, and wanting to go to the suite to read, was only partially true. She'd been initially disappointed that Dante had an ulterior motive for taking her to Atlantic City. But his constant attention and affection, along with some vigorous and altogether satisfying hours in the king-sized bed, sans bonbons, had mitigated her feelings. She'd closely observed him once Orsini entered the scene. His whole posture had changed. He was alert, on his toes, eyes taking in everything, senses attuned to his surroundings. He was a cop on a surveillance detail. A professional. She liked what she saw. It was one of the dimensions that attracted her to him. Paul Dante had many sides. So far, she hadn't bumped into any of them that raised a red flag and told her to bail out. Let him play his cat-and-mouse game with Orsini. Besides, the suite really was luxurious. She was enjoying her book. A good movie was on TV that night. Give him his space. Don't cling, Julia. It wouldn't be politic.

As Julia read in the suite, Dante nursed a scotch-rocks while playing roulette with decided disinterest. He chose the roulette table because it gave him an unrestricted view of Orsini, who kibitzed with a busty strawberry-blond cocktail waitress serving high rollers at a fifty-dollar-minimum craps table. Dante knew Orsini had seen him, although Orsini pretended not to have. Dante considered going over and saying hello, but decided not to. He was a customer. Let Orsini come to him.

Dante knew from Orsini's posture that he was now less comfortable than he had been earlier in the evening. After years as a cop and private investigator, Dante knew that when someone was uncomfortable, there was always a reason. Initially, he thought it was his presence, but he changed his mind once he saw the statuesque strawberry-blond waitress with melon breasts, sultry hips, and ruby-red lips polished to a jewellike gloss. The shooters at the table couldn't keep their eyes off her as she jiggled through their midst, free drinks spilling over on a small round tray she balanced with aplomb.

Orsini lingered at the craps table served by her, casting frequent nervous glances in Dante's direction. He obviously knew her well. Whenever she whispered something in his ear, or rubbed against him, it pumped up the pronounced swagger in his shoulders.

At the same time, there appeared to be a tension between them that Dante didn't read as sexual. Maybe it was just Orsini's personality. He seemed to create tense relationships wherever he went. It was obvious to Dante that the staff didn't like him. As son-in-law of one of the property's principal owners, Orsini threw his weight around with an authority that went far beyond his official position at the hotel which, as far as Dante could determine, was to glad-hand heavy-hitters.

Orsini made another circuit of the area of the room in which the craps tables were situated, apparently found nothing to hold his interest, and drifted away.

"Screw him," Dante said under his breath. There wasn't much he could do in the casino to build a case against Orsini. Santo had placed his son-in-law there, and he was doing his job. The hell with it, Dante decided, thinking of Julia reclined on the big bed in the sheer lavender nightie she'd brought on the trip. Maybe she'd just finished a section of the book in which the heroine was ravaged, and was identifying with her. Great time to make his entrance and put out her fires. Fool around a little with her, then rip her bodice and ravage her. No. Julia Croce wasn't the sort of woman who would appreciate having her bodice ripped. He wasn't even sure what a bodice was. A bra? Something in the chest area. He was tired. That was the problem with vacations. You got tired from doing nothing, sleeping late and taking naps.

He drained his glass, dropped a buck on his waitress's tray, and left the casino.

As he headed for the elevators, he heard the strains of the jazz combo from the lobby lounge. Even at a distance, the music had an invigorating effect on him. Duke Ellington's "Satin Doll." One of his favorites. A cognac in the lounge was appealing.

He entered and walked along the bar. There weren't many people there, a couple of guys hitting on a young woman with frizzy hair, a large table of revelers from some convention who wore badges and laughed too loudly. True music lovers.

As he reached the end of the bar, his peripheral vision caught a flash of white in a liquor pantry behind it. A sleeve. A white dinner jacket. Orsini had been wearing a white dinner jacket. Should he take a quick look? Why not? If he upset anyone, he'd pretend to have blundered in a little drunk. It always worked for him, or at least got him off the hook when rushing in where fools feared to tread.

Orsini had the strawberry blonde pressed up against the wall.

"Excuse me," Dante said. "I was looking for the bartender."

Molten lava flowed from Orsini's eyes. "The bartender is behind the fuckin' bar, Dante," he growled.

"That's right," Dante said pleasantly. "So he is. My mistake." He couldn't resist a smile as he did an about-face and ordered a Rémy from a waitress on his way to a banquette against the wall.

Orsini arrived at the table before the drink and sat heavily. "What's your act, Dante?" he asked. "What's your beef?"

Dante smiled. "Act? I'm no actor, Genaro. Beef? Too much beef is bad for the cholesterol. At least that's what my doctors tell me."

"Funny, Dante. You're a real fuckin' comic."

"You think so? You want to book me here?"

Orsini twisted his large frame in the booth and looked out over the lounge. Dante took in his profile. He knew Orsini was considered handsome, but it was in a crude way, a tank fighter's face, every feature a little oversized, heavy eyelids, a nose that could have resulted from a break—or maybe family genes—thick, cruel lips. His perpetual expression was one of arrogance, but like so many arrogant people you sensed he didn't have much to back it up. A wise guy out of an Elmore Leonard novel; maybe more a character from *The Gang That Couldn't Shoot Straight.*

Orsini turned and peered into Dante's eyes. "Get off my case, Dante. You hear me?"

"You're not my case, Orsini. You're not even my type."

Orsini leaned closer. "You are some dumb guinea," he said.

"Yeah? You read my school records? You know my IQ?"

"I'll tell you what I know, Dante. You have eggs under your feet every step you take with Santo, Vincent, and the others. Nobody trusts you except my father-in-law, and I'll make sure that changes."

"It was generous of your father-in-law to send my friend and me up here, Orsini. Santo and I go back a long way. Got the best room in the house."

"Big fucking deal. So you and Santo happened to grow up on the same block in the same slum. Whadaya think that gives you, certain fuckin' privileges?"

Dante leaned back and draped his arms over the banquette's bench. "You know, Orsini, that's the trouble with guys like you. You think everybody's out to get something. Like you, for instance. You can't deal with people like me who aren't looking for anything from a friend. You got any friends, Orsini?"

Orsini looked as though he'd been stung by the question. He said, "Yeah. I got a lot of friends."

"Good. You'll need 'em. Charlie Pietrosanti a friend of yours?"

"What the fuck are you getting at?"

"I just find it interesting that you set up the IRS deal that started all this trouble for Vincent. Then, you go out and haul back Pietrosanti's ring, or finger, or whatever, and you're a big hero."

Orsini, who seldom laughed, guffawed. "You are some piece of shit, Dante. Yeah, I went out and found him because it was the right thing to do. You fell on your ass on that one, and Santo knows it."

"Right. I felt bad not finding you." Dante noticed that others in the lounge were taking in their conversation. He wasn't unhappy about it.

"Nice class of people at this place, Gerry. Bet you get lots of insurance men."

"Insurance men?"

"Yeah. Scumbags who write phony policies on nice dying people and renege on the payoff."

Orsini reddened. It looked to Dante as if his mercury had shot through the top of his thermometer. For an instant, Dante thought Orsini was about to strike him. When he didn't, Dante added, "I talked to Angelo. Not a long talk, not many details, but he told me what you did to him. Now, I have to ask myself why anybody would take advantage of a nice old man like Angelo whose wife just died from cancer, and who's having trouble paying his bills. I have to wonder why somebody would do that."

"I don't know what you're talking about."

"Maybe you don't. Then again, maybe you do. We should talk about it again someday."

The waitress brought Dante his cognac. He tossed some bills on her tray as Orsini stood. "Buy you a drink, Orsini?"

"Shove your drink, and watch your ass. Don't say I didn't warn you."

"I appreciate your concern."

"Why don't you and your old lady just get the fuck out of here?"

Dante laughed. "I would, except I like the scenery." He swept his arm around the room at the bevy of cocktail waitresses in skimpy, skintight outfits. Now, even more aware that attention in the lounge was focused upon them, Dante said in a deliberately louder voice, "I'm on to you, Orsini. I know what you're all about. And your father-in-law will, too. Trust me."

Maybe it was Dante's broad smile that caused Orsini to stiffen, to thrust his fist at him. But Dante was on his feet before Orsini's hands ever reached him. He grabbed Orsini's wrists, snapped them down into his crotch, and shoved him into the seat. "That's the first time, Orsini. The second time, you don't get up."

A waitress, transfixed by the scene, widened her eyes at what

Dante had done. He threw more money on the table and said, "Buy Mr. Orsini a drink. He looks like he needs one."

As Dante slowly walked from the lounge, the bartender nodded and smiled. He was obviously pleased with what he'd seen. Dante winked. "Just a minor squabble," he said. "All in the family."

Now awake, he returned to the casino where he found space at a ten-dollar craps table. The table and the shooters around it were cold. Down a hundred dollars, he decided to call it a night and snuggle in bed with Julia.

He stood at the elevators and watched the panel of tiny illuminated numerals flicker. Slow, he thought. Eventually, the elevator at the far right arrived and its passengers exited. Dante looked around; no women to allow to enter first. He went through the open doors, pushed the button for his floor and leaned against the back wall. He was alone until two men wearing suits suddenly joined him. The doors slid closed and the elevator began its ascent.

Dante didn't know the men, but he was suddenly jolted by an animal instinct of fear. Suits? Virtually every guest at the hotel was dressed casual, as he was. He stiffened into a defensive posture but he was too late. The men had positioned themselves to either side of him. Dante spun around to face the one on his right, who drove his knee into Dante's groin. At the same time, the other man, who was now behind him, brought a short piece of lead pipe down onto the back of Dante's neck. A deadly, heavy pain joined the pain in his groin. He slumped to the elevator's floor. Both men kicked him, one focusing on his back, the other on his face. He felt his nose collapse; a searing pain radiated from his kidney.

The door opened at Dante's floor. The men stepped out and ran down the hall to a stairwell. As the doors started to close, Dante managed to extend his leg to keep them from shutting tight. They opened again. He crawled through and reached the carpeted hallway. The doors closed behind him.

It took him a couple of minutes to summon the strength to sit up against the various pains that wracked his body. Another elevator arrived at the floor and a man and woman exited. "Jesus, mister," the man said to Dante. "Can we . . . ?"

Dante waved them away. "No, I'm okay, thanks. Took a nasty fall."

He waited until they disappeared into a room, then hauled himself up using the wall for support, and made his way to his suite. He knocked; it was too painful to reach for his key in his pants pocket. Julia opened the door. "Oh, my God," she gasped as he leaned on her. She led him to the bed and he fell across it. "What happened?" she asked.

"Guess," he said.

"Not Orsini."

"Not personally. His *babbos*."

"Oh, Paul, what can I do?"

"Cold water, huh? I think my nose is broken."

"I'll call a doctor."

"No. Just some water. It's been broken before. It fixes itself so you'd never notice."

She tended to his wounds, helped him undress, and lay beside him on the bed. "What do you need?" she asked.

"A good hug, babe."

"Anything you say, babe."

Their thoughts while falling asleep differed. He thought of Orsini. She thought of the man next to her and, for the first time since meeting him, was afraid—for him, for her.

XXV

The Next Morning

Orsini drove back to Washington the next morning. His sustained anger over the previous evening with Dante threatened to send him careening off the highway. He pulled a twenty-two revolver from beneath the driver's seat and fingered it. "I'll blow your fuckin' brains out, you fuck," he said, seeing Dante in his sights.

He'd calmed down by the time he reached his house in Georgetown.

"Daddy called," Lucia said as he walked past her.

"What's he want?"

"He wants you to be at his house at seven."

"How come?"

"I don't know. Are you hungry? I have a—"

"No, I'm not hungry. I got to call him back?"

"If you want."

He called from his private office in the house.

"It's set for tonight," Santo said. "Seven. Be here."

Orsini was now in a considerably better mood than when he'd entered the house. He had lunch with Lucia and Vincent. Would Vincent be at Santo's house, too? He was afraid to ask, and didn't. The old man looked at him strangely, Orsini thought. Fuck you, he thought. I'll be at your funeral.

When he arrived at Santo's house at seven sharp, he was surprised at the unusually large number of vehicles parked near the mansion. "This is it," he said to himself.

Tommy Guardino met Orsini at the door and told him to go to the basement. A cold chill raced up Orsini's spine as he descended the steps.

In the stark stone surroundings of a small room behind a larger storage room, they waited for him, two dozen men from the Benedetti family and from other major families from adjacent territories.

"Vincent couldn't make it," Santo said. "It would have been unwise for him to come."

"Of course," Orsini said.

The family's *consigliere* conducted the brief ceremony. Next to him was Orsini's sponsor, Santo Benedetti. A gun and a knife were on a table around which the men gathered. The weapons were covered with Kleenex.

The *consigliere* pointed to the weapons and said in somber tones, "Genaro, this is the gun you live by, and this is the knife you die by."

Orsini nodded.

"Your hand."

Orsini extended his hand to the *consigliere*, who pricked his index finger with a needle. The family's chief counselor wiped the blood with the tissue that had covered the weapons, crushed it, placed it in Orsini's outstretched palm and lit it. While Orsini endured the pain, the *consigliere* said, "Repeat after me. If I should betray La Cosa Nostra, my soul will burn in hell like this paper." Orsini was made to say it twice.

Everyone around the table joined hands and said, "Now you are born over again. You are a new man from now on."

The ceremony was concluded with the *consigliere* stating the family's rules, which included not having sexual relations with the wife of another family member, or doing physical harm to another made man without permission from the highest levels.

"Congratulations, Genaro," each man said, shaking his hand.

Genaro Orsini was now a made man in the Benedetti family.

XXVI

Thursday

In the days immediately following the FBI's second "search" of Orsini's house, Vincent increasingly took to his basement room where he read and listened to music. There was the daily meeting with Santo at which family business was discussed, but Vincent seemed to have folded inside himself when alone.

Lucia tried to coax him upstairs for more than cursory meals, but he was immersed in retrospection. He said little, smiled even less.

She was concerned about her uncle, but there was more than altruism involved. Her husband was now spending virtually all his time out of the house, and she was lonely. She would have monopolized all of Vincent's time had he let her. When he was not in his shell, he was good company, an interesting and provocative conversationalist. When inspired, he would weave stories from his childhood, his poor beginnings, and the events that had lifted him and his brother out of poverty and to the lifestyle they now enjoyed. He could talk of political names with whom he'd been involved, his comments peppered with historical references and political insight.

Lucia respected his need for privacy. She knew he needed time to think, and to indulge his love of reading and music. He particularly loved history, especially American history, and politics. With his present troubles, he felt he needed a better understanding of how today's American political mind worked. He had his own opinions, of course, but wanted other, more independent analyses. He sent Lucia to the library on an almost daily basis with a list of books, magazines, and newspapers he wanted to read. She was happy to be of help, and told him so each time he asked her to run such an errand for him. In a sense, he was as concerned about her solitary life as she was about his. Genaro's absence bothered him. It was not necessary to be away that much, especially from a new bride. Every wife of a Mafia leader knew, and accepted, her husband's lifestyle. It was not nine-to-five. Moreover, it was never to be discussed. But there were ways to appease. An intelligent man knew these ways and practiced them.

Before Vincent's wife had died six years ago of a sudden and totally unexpected heart attack, he'd always tried to balance family business demands with her needs. He'd honored his wife; Genaro Orsini was not honoring his, and it gnawed at Vincent. She was, after all, his niece and goddaughter.

Vincent read books on law enforcement, and pored over analyses of the FBI, both positive and negative, written by former agents. He read exposés about the workings of the Justice Department, and political dissections of elections—how they were won, lost, and stolen. He devoured tales of the fall of political figures. He wanted desperately to understand his adversaries. Great generals, he knew, had been masters at that, their battles won or lost because one side understood its enemies better than the other. Santo often talked about such battles; he was steeped in their lore through the books he enjoyed most. In both cases—for generals and their men on the field of battle, or for Vincent Benedetti and his soldiers—a correct evaluation of the motives, strengths, and weaknesses of the enemy would determine the outcome of the fray. For him, it could determine where and how he would spend the rest of his life.

He saw himself as part of a much larger picture, as a player in the history of his day. And he now understood that what was at stake was not simply the breakup of a thirty-year marriage of convenience between the family and J. Edgar Hoover's FBI. Careers were at stake on the other side too, perhaps even a presidential election.

He came to the conclusion that his enemies had made some dramatic mistakes. Their incompetence had allowed the international drug cartel to take over the streets of major American cities, including the nation's capital. They'd infested the streets of Washington. The line Hoover had painted across the pavement had been crossed by an army.

When the director had shaken Vincent's hand thirty years ago, Hoover had done so because he knew what was at stake. Washington needed to be a holy ground, a home base cleared of criminal intrusion. With Washington secure, Hoover was free to pursue the rest of his agenda. Without the confidence that his home territory was secure, the director would have been weakened. The handshake had strengthened his hand.

Hoover knew the deal with the Benedettis represented the classic definition of "a good deal." Both sides stood to gain. The family would not foster the growth of drug traffic. And, it would stay clear of Hoover's home territory out of respect for the director, and because it would be lucrative. As a fringe benefit, the crime family would actually help law enforcement keep the city clean.

Hoover had little concern about the Benedettis ever revealing the agreement to outsiders. It would not be in their interest. Nor would Hoover speak of it outside his inner circle. Again, a good deal for both sides. The agreement made economic sense to the family, and political sense to the government.

But now, the new breed in law enforcement didn't understand. They were not sophisticated enough, nor did they possess the understanding of their esteemed predecessor, J. Edgar Hoover. Hoover was aware that in order to garner and sustain power, one often had to give away lesser pieces of it to others. He'd been a master at it. Those now in charge were not only incapable of understanding the principle, they were inept at carrying it out. They'd allowed the situation to get out of hand and were not competent to regain control. The flank Hoover had secured for them three decades earlier was now threatened. If that flank collapsed, the battle would surely be lost, and with it the political war.

If Vincent's analysis proved correct—and after days of intense evaluation, he was certain that it was—then they would never let up on him. They had to hold him in check, which meant the entire family was in jeopardy. The family's position would be weaker than it had ever been before, even before the arrangement with Hoover. Those in government who had profited for so many years from their connections with the family would now begin to circle at the scent of blood.

But they weren't the only sharks who would infest the murky, bloody waters. Other crime families from around the country, who had also profited from Vincent's thirty-year arrangement, would closely evaluate the situation. The Benedetti territory, from Atlantic City to Atlanta, was prized. Some leaders of the other families were enemies, perhaps not overt in their animosity, but always poised to take advantage of weakness. It had happened with Castellano and the Gambino family. It had happened with Carmine Persico and the Columbo family. The annals of organized crime in America were rife with such stories. History. To ignore history was to repeat it.

And there was still another enemy to fend off—the powerful drug cartel that had staked out Washington and Baltimore as theirs to hold and defend.

There was much to be concerned about.

———

"What's with all the books?" Orsini asked Lucia. It was a rare at-home for Orsini. He sat at the kitchen table reading the sports section of the *Post*.

"What else does he have to do?" Lucia answered. "You don't expect him to watch the afternoon soaps. Or Geraldo, Oprah."

"Why not?"

"It's not what Uncle Vincent would do."

"He's too bound up with all this historical and political shit."

Early in the marriage, Orsini had made a concerted effort to not swear in front of his wife. When he had, she'd asked him nicely not to. But as the weeks and months passed, he'd increasingly ignored her wishes.

"Uncle Vincent is a complex man," she said. "He's always loved history."

"Yeah. Well all that ancient history never made anybody a buck."

"Uncle Vincent knows what he's doing," she said, continuing to cut cloves of garlic and dropping them into a shallow pan already coated with olive oil. She was pleased Genaro would be home for dinner and decided to cook a true peasant dish, ziti with broccoli rabe and sun-dried tomatoes. Macaroni with rabe had always been a family favorite; the sun-dried tomatoes added a modern touch. She'd already cut the stalks of rabe with their tiny, broccolilike heads, and had brought them to a slow boil on a back burner. The vegetable's strong smell filled the kitchen and drifted throughout the house. She smiled. Hopefully, the pleasant smell would entice Uncle Vincent upstairs for a leisurely family dinner.

"How's the job going?" she asked.

"A lotta work. Very time-consuming." His answers came from behind the barrier of the newspaper.

"Will they find a permanent spot for you soon? A day job at the casino?"

He let out a sigh of exasperation. "They're talking about maybe me managing the little joint on Southern Avenue, over the D.C. line in Maryland."

The family, with the cooperation of the Washington and Maryland police and some highly placed politicians, was about to open an after-hours gambling house in Maryland. Other such operations had attracted a large crowd each night, including off-duty cops who went there with the understanding that they walked out with winnings, but that their losses would be reimbursed by management.

"If I managed that joint, it'd make you happy. Right?" he asked his wife. "I'd be close to home. But that's weeks, maybe months away."

"Months?"

"These things take time," he said. "That's why I haul my ass to Atlantic City damn near every night. To learn. You gotta learn things before they give you a joint of your own."

"It's just that I hardly see you anymore."

"You got Uncle Vincent here. Maybe we should put another chair in his room. You could read about ancient Rome together."

Vincent had been standing in the doorway. He crossed the threshold into the kitchen and said, "You can learn a lot from the Caesars." To Lucia: "You want help with the dishes?"

Orsini put down his newspaper. "Hello, Vincent," he said. "I didn't hear you come up."

"For an old man, I'm still pretty light on my feet," Vincent said, taking a trio of bowls from his niece and placing them on the table.

Orsini folded the sports section and dropped it on a chair. He separated the bowls and positioned them in front of three remaining chairs around the butcher-block table.

"I know you're not so happy having me here," Vincent said to Orsini. "I don't like it either, but it'll have to do for now."

"What are you talking about?" Orsini said. "Stay as long as you want." Lucia chimed in, "I love having you here, Uncle Vincent. I never saw enough of you before. Now—and I know you're here for the wrong reasons—but now I get to see you every day. I like that." Her voice was light and sincere.

"I'll stay only as long as I *must*," Vincent said. "An uncle in the basement is not good for the domestic tranquility. A household doesn't work with two men—even if one of them is gone too much."

Orsini looked away.

"I'll make more permanent arrangements soon," Vincent added.

"It's no problem," Orsini said, forcing sincerity into his voice. "I feel privileged to have you in my home and to make a contribution to my family."

Lucia had gone to the refrigerator to get grated cheese, and a pitcher of ice water to be on the table with the white zinfandel. The wall phone rang. She was closest to it and answered. "It's a woman," she said, her hand over the mouthpiece. "She wants you, Gerry."

A quizzical look swept Orsini's face. He took the phone from his wife and walked into the hallway, stretching the cord to its full length. He cupped his hand over the mouthpiece and spoke softly, barely above a whisper; his words weren't understandable to those in the kitchen, but the strain in his voice was.

Vincent set the table with napkins and silverware. He pulled the cork on the wine, filled three tulip glasses, then took his seat. Lucia had combined the ziti, broccoli rabe, sun-dried tomatoes, olive oil, and garlic into one large, aromatic bowl and placed it in the center of the table. They said nothing to each other as both tried to hear the conversation from the hall.

"Yeah, yeah," Orsini muttered, his voice rising. "Okay, okay, right away." He returned to the kitchen to face the questioning expressions he knew would be there.

Lucia verbalized it. "Who was that?" she asked.

"A manager," Orsini answered. "Got to go. Trouble at the casino."

"Trouble?" Vincent questioned, a concerned look on his face. "In Atlantic City?"

"Nothing to concern yourself about, Vincent," Orsini replied. "We're light on staff up there. They need more bodies tonight."

"Tonight is your night off," Lucia protested.

"It's a crazy business," Orsini said, adding a smile for effect. "Got to do what you got to do. Right, Vincent? Business comes first. Am I right?"

Vincent said nothing.

"Ask them to get someone else," Lucia said.

"No can do. I'm low man on the totem pole. This is the kind of thing low men do."

"No," Lucia said, her voice a mixture of anger and sorrow. "Call them, Genaro. Tell them to get someone else. I made a beautiful dinner. Vincent is with us and—"

"Lucy, this is *my* business. Keep out of it."

Lucia turned to Vincent. "Could you call someone?" she asked her uncle. "Why would this woman have the authority to call here and—?"

"Lucy!" Orsini snapped. "Don't ever question my business decisions again." His jaw clenched; his teeth ground against themselves. "And I don't need Vincent to make any calls for me." He looked to where Vincent sat at the table. The old man's face was hard, unforgiving. His gaze pinned Orsini in his place.

Orsini's posture quickly relaxed and a smile appeared. "Forgive me, Lucy," he said. "My nerves are frazzled. I don't mean to get mad at you. You're my wife. I love you. It's these long hours. I'm working too hard. But I'm just trying to get someplace and that means being there when they need me. Try to understand, huh?" He kissed her on the cheek, then said to Vincent, "Sorry you got to see a little domestic spat, huh? My apologies."

The anger left Lucia's face. "Can't you at least have supper?" she asked.

"No, I can't. You two enjoy the meal. I'll make do with something at the casino. The food's not so good but what the hell." He said to Vincent, "Again, my apologies, Vincent. Have a second helping, on me. Nobody cooks better than my Lucia."

"Do what you have to do," Vincent said matter-of-factly, his face still stone.

Orsini kissed Lucia again.

"Don't drive like a maniac," she said. "They'll just have to wait."

When Genaro was gone, Lucia ladled out a bowl for her uncle, then one for herself. "He's very dedicated," she said, as though trying to explain his actions and treatment of her. "He's working such long hours. I hope this job doesn't kill him."

Vincent's answer was to spear a forkful of ziti, rabe, and a tomato. He was unimpressed by Orsini's charmer routine that had closed the act in the kitchen. It had been blatantly transparent. He'd seen it too many times before with men who'd been brought before him, men who had something to hide. He wondered how the scene would have ended if he hadn't been there.

It was apparent that his niece was being treated badly by her husband, but he was not sure what he could do about it. That both saddened and angered him. He shared none of his feelings with Lucia. There were no women in management positions at the casino. If there had been an urgent need for a family member to leave his home in the midst of dinner, the call would have been made by a man, a manager, most likely Paddy Provenzano or one of his male assistants. Vincent made a mental note to bring it up with Santo. It could not be left unresolved.

XXVii

That Same Night

There was the usual pile of mail, most of it junk, under Dante's door when he limped home from Atlantic City. The country was drowning in junk mail, he thought as he skipped through the envelopes, many of them with gaudy writing on the outside announcing he was a sure winner in some million-dollar sweepstakes. So much unwanted mail. Paper-company stock must be a great investment, he thought.

There were, of course, the usual downers: gas and electric bills, phone bills—now he got two, one from the local company and the other from the long-distance carrier (he missed Ma Bell and rotary phones). Bills from his meat and dry-goods suppliers. The Benedetti family did a lot of business with restaurants but left Dante alone. A perk of Santo's friendship that was not lost on him.

There was one pleasant surprise, a check for forty-five hundred dollars as partial payment for the government-surveillance job. It was only four months late.

He checked his answering machine. A lot of hang-ups, a few business calls, a solicitor with a stock offering guaranteed to make him rich, and one last call that captured his immediate and total attention.

"Mr. Dante, I'm calling from Las Vegas on behalf of a special friend, Mr. Charles Pietrosanti."

Charles Pietrosanti? The guy who set up Vincent on the tax and bribery sting? He was dead.

228

The woman continued: "Mr. Pietrosanti wishes to resolve his differences with Mr. Vincent Benedetti." She sounded as though she read from a script. "I'm sorry I missed you. I'll try again."

Click!

Dante sat at his desk, swung his legs up onto a corner of it, and pondered what he'd heard. Who was the caller? The next question was, why me? Dante was not a Benedetti family intimate. Only those who knew the family well would know anything about his unique relationship with Santo. Why wouldn't the caller contact a family insider?

The answer to that question became obvious to him: "Resolve differences with Vincent Benedetti." The caller was seeking a go-between, an ambassador, someone outside the immediate family.

By mid-afternoon, Dante had exhausted all the thoughts he was willing to waste on the mysterious phone call. He had things to tend to at Cuffs because he'd been away, and he wanted to get the check to the bank before it closed. The mystery would just have to sit there until the woman called again.

———

"Hello?"

There was no response.

"Don't hang up. This is Paul Dante."

"Hello," the same female voice said. "You got my message?"

"Yes."

"Can you help me?"

"I don't know. Tell me more. Maybe I'm not the best person for what you need."

"You're the *only* person who can help. Mr. Pietrosanti said so."

"Mr. Pietrosanti. Charlie Pietrosanti?"

"That's right."

"You're sure this person you're calling for is really Charlie Pietrosanti?"

Her laugh was more a snort. "Of course."

"Go on. I'm listening."

"Mr. Pietrosanti can help Mr. Vincent Benedetti with the legal problems he's having."

"Yeah? How?"

His question obviously did not have a scripted answer. Dante said, "I don't represent Vincent Benedetti, never have. So why call me?"

"Because Mr. Pietrosanti feels he can trust you to intervene in this matter."

"Do I know you?" Dante asked.

There was silence on the other end. Then, "No."

"Then why trust me?"

"Mr. Pietrosanti knows you have a special relationship with Santo and Vincent Benedetti. Very close friends."

"I don't know Vincent Benedetti."

"But you know his brother. Am I correct?"

"Yes, you are."

"According to Mr. Pietrosanti, Mr. Santo Benedetti would like to do something good to get his brother, Vincent, out of the legal problem he faces. Correct?"

"Probably."

"And you would like to do something good for Mr. Santo Benedetti to help him do that for his brother."

"I'm getting bored," Dante said. "Get to the point. What do you want from me?"

"Not on the phone," the caller said.

"Why not?"

"Phones are not to be trusted. Would you come here to meet me in Las Vegas?"

"No."

"Mr. Pietrosanti has authorized me to send you airline tickets and a hotel confirmation."

"Why?"

"I'll tell you more when you get here."

"I need more than that before I commit to this."

"I told you, Mr. Dante. Mr. Pietrosanti wishes to offer Mr. Vincent Benedetti something valuable. He wants to correct a wrong he feels he's done to Mr. Benedetti."

"Look," Dante said. "I can't speak for Vincent Benedetti."

"If you agree to come, the tickets and hotel confirmation will arrive by Federal Express tomorrow morning. If you agree, I'll meet you in Vegas Saturday night."

"Who are you? How would I know you?"

"Will you come?"

"Send the tickets."

"Thank you, Mr. Dante."

The line went dead.

XXViii

Two Days Later—Saturday

Dante had a lot of time to think on the America West flight to Las Vegas. Despite the mystery caller's refusal to provide anything tangible, Dante kept connecting the call to his own involvement in what he now began to call the Orsini case. Julia—and Barbara, his ex-wife too for that matter—would tell him that what he was doing was reaching a conclusion, and then searching for facts to support it.

He, on the other hand, considered it simple instinct, a reaction based on years of exposure to the lower species of the human animal.

He'd told Julia about the woman's call, and that he was going to Las Vegas to meet with her. "This is strictly between us," he added. "As far as you know, you *don't* know where I am. Agreed?"

"Sure."

"I'll be gone just a couple of days. If you need to reach me, I'll be at the Mirage, on the Strip."

"You're chasing the Orsini butterfly again, aren't you?" she'd said.

"Butterfly?"

"Sorry, but I worry about you. I know there's something sleazy going on with Orsini and his involvement with the Benedettis, but I just don't understand your obsession with it."

They'd been over the ground before, so he didn't argue the point. "I'll call you when I get back," he said. "Be good. Miss me."

She drove him to the airport and kissed him passionately before he got out of the car. "Come back," she said. "I want you back with me." Her sentimental comment flustered him; he managed an awkward good-bye. "And stay out of elevators with strangers," she yelled after him.

The note that had accompanied the tickets and hotel confirmation instructed him to be at the hundred-dollar craps table in the Mirage at ten that night. The writer of the note, presumably the same woman who'd called, indicated she would be wearing a black turtleneck, black slacks, and a cream-colored cashmere cardigan sweater.

It was six-thirty when the cab driver dropped Dante at the Mirage, one of the newest and gaudiest hotel-casinos in Las Vegas. His arrival coincided with the eruption of a fifty-foot-high volcano in front of the hotel that is set off at regular intervals. "What the hell is that?" Dante asked the driver as he fished in his pocket for money.

"A volcano."

"A volcano?"

"Yeah," the driver said. He'd told Dante during the drive that he'd come to Las Vegas fifteen years ago on a gambling junket, had lost every cent he had and never went home. "They got white tigers and dolphins inside."

"Loose?" Dante said. All he could think of was Julia being notified that he'd become a meal for a white tiger.

He checked in, dropped his carry-on bag on the bed, received instructions from the bellhop—palm up and extended—about how to work the air-conditioner controls, tipped him and flopped on the bed.

He hadn't been to Vegas since the Marines conducted a joint night-attack exercise with F-4 Phantoms of the 832nd Tactical Air Division headquartered at Nellis Air Force Base, northeast of the city. On the last day of the exercise, F-100s from the 27th TAC Fighter Wing out of Cannon Air Force Base in New Mexico, flying close air support for the exercise, had dropped dozens of rolls of toilet paper out their speed brakes during a final pass. The Marines responsible for clean-up got their CO to order the pilots and crew chiefs of the 27th to help.

"You're going to the asshole of the earth," one of them told Dante when he learned that Dante's unit was headed for Vietnam. "We figured dropping toilet paper would get you in the mood."

What Dante had dropped before heading out was most of his paycheck at the Sands' craps tables. He'd felt guilty for wasting money while people struggled to get by back home, but rationalized it as a final fling. He knew he was about to die. Broke, he'd joined his unit for its journey to Subic Bay in the Philippines via San Francisco, and then directly to Nam.

His mind and muscles told him to take a nap. His body still ached from the beating he'd received in Atlantic City. His nose was swollen and had taken on an ugly blue-green cast. He'd had trouble sleeping since Atlantic City, and hadn't been able to sleep on the flight. A long nap and hot shower was appealing. But he was restless. In a few hours he would meet with his mystery lady. Thinking about it pumped a fresh dose of adrenaline into him. He got up, showered, and headed downstairs.

The Mirage was a bustling hub of activity. Shoulder-to-shoulder people surrounded the gaming tables and slot machines. Dante wandered away from the main gambling areas and found himself face-to-face with six magnificent white tigers that peered at him from their large, artificial sanctuary behind a glass curtainwall. The tigers were part of the illusionists' Siegfried and Roy's act that had been Las Vegas's premiere attraction for years. "Pretty pussy," Dante said to the closest tiger as he headed for the outside.

Next door was Caesars Palace, its giant, floodlighted fountains spewing sheets of water into the black desert sky. It was a warm, still night in Vegas. Lots of casino-hopping people on the streets. Dante jumped as the volcano went off behind him. "Jesus," he muttered, returning to the Mirage where he had dinner in one of its eight restaurants, a coffee shop where the prices were low and the food pretty good.

Belly full, he strolled the main gambling room. Las Vegas had changed since he'd been there as a Marine twenty-five years ago. Somehow, it hadn't seemed as glittery back then, but maybe that had to do with his frame of mind and reason for being there.

He'd noticed the greatly expanded circumference of the city on his plane's approach to the airport, and the immensity of the new resort hotels during the cab ride. The amount of money generated by the human obsession to gamble, the chance to get something big for something small, the sheer pleasure of making a killing through luck rather than toil was amazing to Dante. The big reward only came to the very few which, of course, made the prospect of it all the more inviting.

You had to hand it to Bugsy Siegel, Lucky Luciano, and Meyer Lansky for vision and guts, Dante thought. Almost fifty years ago they pooled six million and opened the Flamingo, named after the long legs of Siegel's girlfriend, Virginia Hill. The rest was history, as the saying goes. If anyone had told Dante that you could build a hotel in the middle of a desert, and that millions of people would flock there to throw money at it, he would have called for the men in white coats. So much for his business vision.

Dante got to the hundred-dollar craps table at nine-thirty, tossed five hundred dollars on the table, was given chips by the dealer at his end, and started to play. The dice came quickly to him, and he rolled two sevens in a row, winners. His next roll was an eight, which became his point. Now, a seven was a loser if it came up before he rolled another eight. Another player "bought" the ten, his five-hundred-dollar chips placed on that number by the dealer. The stickman pushed the dice to Dante. He rearranged them with his fingers so that each presented a four to him—a superstition—picked them up and tossed them against the ribbed rubber wall at the far end. Ten. The man who'd bought the number whooped: "Way to go, baby. Do it again."

Dante rolled an eight. Another winner. People who'd been observing the action now bellied up to the table, bought chips, and joined the play. The guy was on a roll. Go with him until he cooled down.

Dante was arranging his dice again in preparation for another roll when a female hand to his left plopped a hundred dollars in small bills on the table. "Change," she said to the dealer. As her money was exchanged for chips, Dante picked up the dice and held them. He glanced at the woman, who appeared to be in her early forties. About five-two. Attractive. Close-cropped brunette hair. Fair complexion, with makeup nicely applied to enhance her features. Black turtleneck and slacks, cream-colored sweater.

"Let's go," the boxman said from where he sat between the two dealers as the man in overall charge of the table.

Dante threw the dice. A five. His point. He rolled again. Seven. A loser. There were moans from the other players.

The dice went to the woman on Dante's left. She placed two chips on the Don't-Pass line, betting with the house and against the other players. Dante didn't bet.

She rolled a three. A winner for her.

Dante leaned close to her. "Where's Pietrosanti?" he asked.

"Not too loud," she said, picking up the dice and rolling again. She won some more betting with the house, much to the chagrin of others at the table who were betting "the right way."

"You wanna go talk somewhere else?" Dante asked.

"In a minute." She quickly lost what little she'd won, along with her original hundred. "Come on," she said.

Dante's senses were on full alert when she led him into an elevator, which they rode to the thirtieth floor. She opened the door to a room and Dante followed her inside. It was a typical hotel room. Dante could see a small balcony through sheer white curtains that covered sliding glass doors.

"Would you like a drink, Mr. Dante?" she asked. "It's over there." She pointed to a minibar. Dante filled a glass with ice and poured three miniature bottles of Teachers scotch over it. Might as well take advantage of the offer. She parted the curtains, opened the sliding glass doors, and stepped out onto the balcony, motioning for him to join her. As he did, the volcano went off, causing him to flinch.

"Sure are a lot of lights," Dante said, looking down at the Strip and its firestorm of neon.

"I know," she said. "It always amazes me, and I've been here for twenty years."

"I didn't know anybody lived in Vegas," he said.

"Fastest-growing city in America," she said. "A nice place, actually, to bring up kids."

"You have kids?"

"A boy. Ten."

"I have two daughters."

"Uh-huh."

"What do you say we even up? You know my name. What's yours?"

"Carla."

"Just Carla?"

"Charlie told me not to give you my last name."

"Speaking of Charlie," Dante said. "If this is the same Charlie Pietrosanti, he's a miracle man. He's supposed to be dead."

She sighed and looked out over the city and the black scrim of the desert and mountains beyond it. "Well," she said lightly, "he isn't. Dead. He'd like to speak with you."

"About what?"

"About acting on his behalf with Mr. Vincent Benedetti."

"Yeah, you said that on the phone. And I told you I don't know Vincent well enough to do that."

"But his brother, Santo."

"That's another story. Tell me, Carla, what is it that Pietrosanti wants? Provided he really is Charlie Pietrosanti."

She ignored his skepticism. "I have to ask you, Mr. Dante, are you wired?"

"Wired? With the Benedetti family?"

"No. Charlie told me to make sure you aren't carrying a tape recorder."

Dante laughed and held open his sport jacket. "No recorder," he said.

"Don't take offense. I promised Charlie I'd do everything he asked me to do."

"No offense taken. Look, why you? I mean, how come if Charlie Pietrosanti wanted to talk to me, he didn't just show up here in Vegas?"

"Because he's afraid. He's too well-known here to risk coming."

"Who's he afraid of?"

"Everyone. Mr. Dante, although he didn't tell me why, I just know he did something to Vincent Benedetti."

"That's an understatement. Who else is he afraid of?"

"He had to escape from where he was being held."

"Held. Held by who?"

"The government." Dante started to ask another question, but Carla held up her hands. "That's all I know, Mr. Dante. He said he escaped and is hiding out until he has a chance to speak with Mr. Benedetti. Through you."

"What's he want from Vincent?"

"He'll discuss that with you if—I'll be straight with you. I'm supposed to decide whether you can be trusted. If I feel that you can, I'll tell you where he is."

"Not here in Vegas?"

She slowly shook her head.

"What's your connection with Pietrosanti?" Dante asked.

"He's the father of my son. We were close ten years ago."

"Married?"

"No. But he's been very good to us. He's always sent enough money so that I wouldn't have to work and could stay home and bring up our son. He's a good man."

Dante stifled the urge to debate it with her. "Okay," he said, "what do I have to do to get you to trust me?"

"Excuse me," she said. She returned from the room carrying a small piece of paper. "I wrote down the questions he wanted me to ask you."

"And if I give the correct answers, I get to advance to Go."

They both laughed.

"I feel like I'm on Jeopardy," he said. "Shoot."

Ten minutes and six questions later, Carla put the slip of paper into the pocket of her sweater.

"How'd I do?" Dante asked.

"As far as I'm concerned, fine. Will you go see him?"

"Where?"

"San Francisco."

"San Francisco?"

"I have a ticket on a flight that leaves here Monday morning."

Dante pondered it for a minute. Then he said, "Okay, I'll go. But you have to understand that I can't guarantee you or Pietrosanti a thing. Nothing. I can talk to Santo Benedetti—*if* I think I should after meeting with Pietrosanti—but I can't predict what happens after that. What your friend Charlie did to Vincent Benedetti has left what might be called a bitter taste in his mouth. I'm sure you know about the family, what it does, that it's part of the Cosa Nostra. They have their own rules, their own code of justice. Understand?"

"Yes. Mr. Dante, I don't want to see Charlie hurt."

"Sure. I promise you one thing."

"What's that?"

"That after I talk to Pietrosanti, I'll decide whether to speak with Vincent based on whether I think it's in the Benedettis' best interests—and Charlie's, too."

"I suppose I can't ask more than that. Another drink?"

"No, thanks."

"Come in. I'll give you the information on how to contact him in San Francisco, and the ticket. You'll have to take care of your hotel yourself, but Charlie said he'd reimburse you."

They rode the elevator together down to the casino.

"Buy you a drink?" Dante asked.

"No. I have to get home. I promised the sitter."

"You must really think a lot of the guy," Dante said.

"And no one would understand that, Mr. Dante. Charlie is a funny-looking little man. He gambles like a drunken sailor and usually loses. He runs with the wrong people and always seems to be in some kind of trouble. But . . ."

"But he's been good to you. No explanations needed, Carla. Take it easy."

"You, too. Give Charlie my love."

He watched her disappear through the lobby and out into the night.

Dante hadn't planned to stay an extra day in Las Vegas, but the ticket to San Francisco changed things. It was like a replay of his soldiering days—Vegas, and then the City by the Bay. If he found a note in San Francisco instructing him to look for Pietrosanti in Saigon, he'd start believing in the supernatural.

He dwelled on the situation in which he found himself, and the potential ramifications for everyone involved. This little creep named Charlie Pietrosanti could substantiate everything Dante believed about Genaro Orsini. Santo would know that his son-in-law was scum, a traitor to the family, and Dante could put his "Orsini case" behind him.

But he also knew that there was much to be lost. Santo would be devastated to learn that his only child, Lucia, had married someone like Orsini. He might blame Dante for having gone ahead on his own and exposing such dishonor in a family that prided itself on its sense of honor. Too, what would happen to Orsini once the family knew about him? It was a grizzly contemplation.

Pietrosanti might not survive. No matter how many assurances Vincent and Santo would give—if they would give any—they still might act on the family code. Pietrosanti might not last a day in their hands.

Tough decisions. But too late to back out now. One of these days, he'd start listening to others in his life who had more brains.

Another resolution to be broken.

XXIX

Monday—San Francisco

"The Sam Wong Hotel," Dante told the taxi driver at the San Francisco airport.

"Where's that?" the driver asked.

Dante consulted the paper given him by Carla. "On Broadway. In Chinatown."

"Figures."

Dante hadn't been in San Francisco since embarking from there for Vietnam, but he knew it had some fancy hotels—the Mark Hopkins, Fairmont, famous names. Sam Wong? He hoped he wouldn't end up in the middle of a Tong war.

The small hotel was situated on the border of Chinatown and North Beach. Dante, the soldier, remembered North Beach. He'd dropped what was left of his money after gambling in Vegas at a couple of North Beach's topless-bottomless clubs. Coming of age, they called it. He remembered it as just plain fun.

He entered a lobby whose walls were covered with faded photographs of Chinatown-of-old, and Chinese prints of dragons and women in gold and red dresses. A wizened old Chinese man was behind the desk.

"Mr. Charles Pietrosanti, please," Dante said. "He's expecting me."

The man reached into a message box for room eight and handed a pink slip to Dante: *Meet me at a restaurant called Swish on Castro Street. I'll be at the bar. I'll be wearing an American flag in my lapel. Charlie P.*

Dante swore under his breath and went to the sidewalk where Chinatown was in full blossom. Pungent food odors hung in the air; the drone of sibilant Chinese voices filled his ears.

"Enough hide-and-seek," he told himself. "You'd better be there."

This cab took him through downtown, Union Square, an area known as South of Market, and finally to Castro Street and the restaurant. Dante paid the driver and stood in front of Swish. Two young men holding hands strolled past him. Dante went inside.

Although it was now after three in the afternoon, the place was almost full. Long lunches, Dante figured. He surveyed the bar. Seated at the end was a man who looked distinctly out of place. Others at the bar, and most people at the tables, were overtly homosexual.

Dante approached the man, saw a little red, white, and blue American flag in the lapel of his black and white checkered sport jacket. "Pietrosanti?" Dante asked.

"Dante?"

"How come here?" Dante asked as a masculine-looking girl moved to another bar stool, freeing up the one next to Pietrosanti. Dante sat.

"Trying to keep a low profile," was Pietrosanti's answer. "I figure nobody'll be lookin' for me in a gay joint."

"Or a Chinese hotel."

"You got it. They ain't my style, but neither is dead. Drink?"

Dante ordered a beer. "Skip the glass," he told the young black bartender, whose right ear was weighted by four gold earrings.

Beer in front of him, he looked Pietrosanti in the eye and said, "So, here I am. Your girlfriend, Carla, says you want me to propose a deal to Vincent Benedetti. Tell me about it."

Pietrosanti took a deep breath, started to reply, then ordered another Bloody Mary. "Okay, Dante. Here it is. You know about the tax setup."

"Sure."

"They had you out lookin' for Orsini. Am I right?"

"Yup."

"But you never found him. Am I right again?"

Dante nodded.

"You didn't find him because you didn't have to? Right?"

Ask me one more time if I'm right, Dante thought, and you're going off that stool.

"You didn't have to find him because he delivered me to them."

"Right," Dante said before he could be asked.

"Orsini delivers to the Benedettis my hand with my ring on it."

Dante looked at the large, ornate ring on Pietrosanti's finger. "What's that?" he asked.

"A copy of the ring. For good luck."

Maybe you are Charlie Pietrosanti, Dante thought. He'd been reserving judgment.

"Obviously, it wasn't your hand," Dante said.

"Now you're in the game, Dante," Pietrosanti said enthusiastically. "But it was my ring. The real one. Those federal fuckers took it from me. They got that hand offa some poor cocksucker out of a morgue."

"How'd the feds suck you in, Charlie?"

"Nailed me on extortion and laundering. I had no choice 'cept some prime time in a federal brig. Not for me. I get itchy when I'm cooped up." He saw that Dante's bottle was empty. "Another beer?"

"No. Get to the point. What are you asking me to do?"

Pietrosanti chewed his cheek as he thought. "Okay. Here's what I want. The way it falls now, I got no place to go. The Benedettis would like to kill me, and the feds want to do the same."

"How come the feds?" Dante asked.

"'Cause I split on them."

Dante whistled. "What are you, some whack job?" he said. "All your wires not connected?"

Pietrosanti smiled. "I always live on the edge, Dante. Just the way I am. Anyway, what I want is simple. You go to Vincent, his brother, whoever, and tell them if they let me off the hook with the family, I come back and testify how the old man was set up."

Dante shrugged, ordered another beer. "That's no deal to offer, Charlie. Vincent's going to walk away from that charge without anybody's help. It was amateur night, a bald setup, entrapment defined. You'll have to do better."

"All right. Genaro Orsini."

"I'm listening." Dante didn't indicate how closely he was listening, how interested he was personally in what the strange little man was about to say next. "What was Orsini's role in the setup?" Dante asked when Pietrosanti didn't say anything. "Was he in on it from the beginning, or was he set up, too? By the feds? Or by you? Did you drag him in?"

Dante hadn't been successful in concealing his interest in Orsini. Pietrosanti grinned, placed his hand on Dante's arm. "You want Orsini? You want the Benedetti family to know what a scumbag married into it? I can give you that, Dante. I can hand you Orsini on a big fuckin' silver platter." He laughed. "For the feast, like a pig. Vincent Benedetti would like that. Am I right?"

"And in return, you get to be forgiven for setting up Vincent?"

"Whatta you, crazy? Sure, that's part of the deal. Along with it, I get a million bucks in cash, protection, and a trip to a warm, sunny country where they don't know from extradition."

It was Dante's turn to laugh. "Your elevator doesn't go all the way to the top, Charlie. You set up the head of the Benedetti family and you want a fucking reward." He laughed louder, not so much out of scorn but because he found Pietrosanti and his "deal" to be funny.

"Take it or leave it," Pietrosanti said. He was obviously offended at Dante's response.

"I'll think about it," Dante said.

"How long?"

"A couple of days. I'll call you."

"Bullshit. I'll call you at that bar you run."

"Cuffs."

"Yeah, right. Cuffs. Whadaya got to think about? You tell Vincent, his brother, whoever you decide. They make the decision. Right?"

"Wrong. Look, Pietrosanti, lemme level with you. I don't like you. But I liked your lady friend in Vegas, Carla. She told me about the kid you two had, and how you always come through with money for them. That's a plus for you, the only one I can come up with at the moment. I promised Carla I wouldn't approach the Benedettis if I thought it might hurt you. In other words, if I think they'll agree to the deal, and then cut off your balls the minute you show up, I won't bring you to them."

"I thought they were men of their word. Whadaya call it? *Un'uomo d'onore?*"

"They are. But maybe not where you're concerned. You did a bad thing to them, Pietrosanti."

"Big deal. You say he'll walk anyway."

"Tell me more about Orsini."

He guffawed. "For a lousy coupla drinks?"

"I thought this was your treat."

"I changed my mind. Make the deal, I tell everything. Hey, no offense, but what happened to your face?"

Dante stood. "An elevator accident," he replied. "I need some time. Call me at Cuffs next Saturday night at nine."

An older man at the other end of the bar openly flirted with Dante.

"That's a whole fuckin' week," Pietrosanti mumbled. "I won't be at that Chink hotel no more, Dante, in case you decide to send somebody lookin' for me. Understand?"

"Sure," Dante said, tossing money on the bar. "You'll call Saturday. *Am I right?*"

"Yeah, yeah."

Dante could have taken the red-eye back to New York but decided to stay over. He checked into the Mark Hopkins Hotel on Nob Hill and enjoyed a couple of leisurely drinks in the Top of the Mark, with its spectacular views of the Golden Gate Bridge under which Dante had sailed on his way to war. The sunset was magnificent, setting fog that rolled in across the bay on fire. The bridge was swallowed by it.

He called Julia from his room, told her he'd be back the next evening, and took a long walk, found a nice restaurant called Alfred's where he treated himself to a steak dinner that was first-class, and priced like it, then fought his way back uphill, his legs turning to jelly, to the hotel and a good night's sleep.

XXX

Wednesday Morning

Santo Benedetti was not his usual gracious self when Dante arrived. He told Dante that Johnny Morelli, one of the family's *capos*, had been murdered the night before. "Those Colombian fucks did it," Santo snarled. "Their fucking Colombian necktie. Johnny's wife just had a kid a week ago."

"I'm sorry, Santo."

Santo peered into Dante's face. "You don't look so good yourself."

"I fell down," Dante said. He couldn't prove Orsini had arranged for the beating.

"Since when did you get clumsy, Paulie?"

Dante forced a smile. He wasn't much of a liar.

The atmosphere in the room was charged enough for openers. But now, after Dante briefly recounted for Santo his trip to Las Vegas and San Francisco, it became overbearingly tense. In all the years Dante had known Santo, he'd never before seen him this angry. He paced the floor of his study, his face red, his breath coming in short, hard bursts. He stopped walking, spun around and shouted, "Jesus Christ, Paul. What the fuck did you think you were doing?"

"I was contacted anonymously, Santo," Dante said. "I was told Pietrosanti could help Vincent. His girlfriend sent me the tickets. I didn't even know who she was until I got to Vegas, and I didn't have a clue why she, or Pietrosanti, wanted to see me. I knew nothing. But now I do, and I have to share it with you."

Santo's body coiled into a tight spring ready to unwind. His face was even more flushed, if that was possible; his hands wrapped into fists.

Dante felt intimidated, wondered if his friend was about to physically attack him. It was as though he were being blamed for Pietrosanti's very existence.

Dante knew, of course, after returning from California the night before that it wouldn't be a pleasant confrontation. Too much was at stake for too many people. He'd acted strictly on his own, which meant there was no corner in which to hide, no other person upon whom to lay some of the blame.

Dante's primary motive in following up on Carla's phone call had proved out, at least to his satisfaction. He'd become convinced that Genaro Orsini posed a distinct threat to Santo, Vincent, and the entire Benedetti family, and had gone to Vegas in search of corroboration. He felt he now had it. Although Pietrosanti hadn't confirmed it in words, Dante had left San Francisco without any further doubt that Orsini had acted in concert with Pietrosanti to set up Vincent.

Why?

Why else? The only plausible reason was that Orsini had also been working with the government. Dante wanted Santo to act upon Pietrosanti's request to return. Pietrosanti could plaster Orsini to the Benedetti wall, which would vindicate Dante at the same time.

The problem was, at least from Dante's perspective, that he couldn't gauge which way Santo would turn.

In the Mafia, Dante knew, family came first—the Family. The Benedetti crime family. Sure, personal family was precious, and it would take a major breach of faith on the part of an immediate family member to cause harm to that person.

Under La Cosa Nostra's code of honor, a family member who betrayed the trust was to be dealt with harshly and in the same manner reserved for those outside the family. It was Santo's obligation to take swift and definitive action should Orsini—no matter that he was married to Lucia—be revealed as a traitor. Dante knew Santo, and Vincent too, had acted out of that obligation in the past.

But Dante couldn't be sure that would be the case because of Lucia's involvement, and the resulting blow it would deal her. Santo was a proud man and loving father. It was possible—and Dante had reminded himself of it with regularity since his trip—that Santo might actually prefer to overlook even the potential that his own son-in-law had betrayed the family. If his allegiance to Lucia's happiness was that strong, he would be leading the larger family into treacherous waters. If Santo's pride was that great, he would be furious at Dante for acting on his own and raising an issue Santo would as soon ignore.

Dante didn't want to deliver this message to his friend. He kept going over what he'd learned about Orsini, not only while in Vegas and San Francisco, but from his snooping around in Washington. Could he be wrong? Was there the possibility that Pietrosanti had suckered Orsini, had sandbagged him? Dante couldn't accept that. Orsini had plotted with Pietrosanti to sell Vincent down the river. But Dante had to prove it, and Charlie Pietrosanti was his star witness.

Santo seemed to have calmed down. His voice was now low-pitched and matter-of-fact. Dante knew, however, that the change in voice was an affectation. It told him that Santo's mood had become even darker and more menacing. "You say this is Pietrosanti, the guy Genaro killed?" Santo said. "Genaro delivered the guy's hand and ring, for christsake."

"It *was* Charlie Pietrosanti," Dante said.

"That's who he *says* he is, Paul. That's what he tells you. You didn't consider the possibility that this guy might be lying?"

He wasn't lying, Dante thought. "Why would he?" he asked.

"Why? Paulie, did it ever occur to you that it might be a scheme to get Vincent to show himself? Some federal ploy? There could be a lot of reasons."

"Possible," Dante conceded. "But what if he's telling the truth? Which, by the way, I believe."

Santo stared at Dante. The Benedetti underboss wore a white cable-knit sweater over a black and brown checkered button-down shirt.

His pants were baggy chinos, the kind you wear when you plan a leisurely day around the house catching up on chores. But Santo's broad, square face was not that of a man puttering around his home. His expression was hard. His heavy brows seemed to have swelled above his dark eyes. All the Benedetti formidability was on display. The possibility that Charlie Pietrosanti was alive and well weighed heavily.

"Look, Santo," Dante said, "I'm not drawing any conclusions."

"Sounds to me like you have."

Dante shook his head. "I just gathered info, Santo. Let me lay it out for you again. Then you can decide what we've got."

Santo leaned back in his high-backed chair. "All right," he said. "I'll listen."

Dante went over everything—how the anonymous phone call had come; the airline tickets and hotel reservation; and his trip west. He detailed his encounter with Carla; with "this guy who claims to be Charlie Pietrosanti"; Pietrosanti's offer to provide a sworn affidavit that Vincent Benedetti had been entraped into the bribery attempt or, if that wasn't enough, testimony before a grand jury to that effect. In return, he wanted a flight out of the country and a million in cash.

"You should have clipped him while you had him, Paul."

"I don't whack people, Santo. I'm a PI. Remember?" Santo obviously would have been happy had Dante taken it upon himself to get rid of Pietrosanti. End of conflict.

"And if he's not who he says he is?" Santo questioned.

I don't think he's heard a word I've said, Dante thought. "Why wouldn't he be?" he asked.

Santo shook his head. "You know, Paulie, I'm trying to figure out why you're so ready to believe this guy."

"I'm not believing, or disbelieving. I'm just trying to understand what his motivation would be to lie."

"How's a million bucks for starters?"

"He won't get that until he delivers."

"And if he's a federal plant working to lure Vincent out of hiding?"

"Possible. But even if that were the case, Vincent won't show himself until Pietrosanti delivers."

"Vincent's facing a worse rap than tax evasion and bribery. You know that. What good can this so-called Pietrosanti do for him where RICO is concerned?"

"Nothing."

Santo said in the same lowered voice, "Maybe this guy's got some vendetta against the family. Even if he really is Pietrosanti, maybe *he's* got a bitch against us, against some individual in the family. Maybe he's out to get Genaro. If he's alive, where did Genaro get the hand? Answer me that."

At last, Dante thought. Now we get to deal with the big question, the one he couldn't raise before with Santo. "That's possible," he said. "We should look into that real close." He was sorry he'd said "we." He wasn't family. Any decisions would be made by Vincent and Santo.

Santo leaned forward and looked at Dante with eyes that seemed to plead for something. He extended his hands to enhance the plea. "I just don't understand, Paulie. Pietrosanti's dead. Genaro brought me evidence of that. Dead men don't show up at some fag bar in San Francisco."

"No," Dante agreed. "They don't."

"So what are you saying, Paulie?"

It was time. Santo had asked a direct question. Dante, despite reservations, would answer it with the same directness.

But he wanted to choose the right words. He stood, went to the fireplace and looked at family photos—Santo and Gina with Lucia when she was a child, a teenager, and a picture taken at her wedding to Orsini. He turned to his friend and said in a somber voice, "You never asked anything about what I found out about Genaro when you sent me looking for him. Everything stopped cold when you got—your evidence."

Santo looked at him quizzically. "What *did* you find?"

Dante returned to his seat. "Santo, you know how I feel about you and all that you've done for me and my family. I don't—"

"Yeah, yeah, I know all that. Cut to the chase, Paulie."

"Okay. I'll tell you straight-out what I found."

Dante laid it all out for Santo—Orsini's drug dealing in the District; his association with members of the Latin American and black drug cartels; his shakedown of Victor and Armbruster; his long-running insurance scam and the painful result for Angelo Andreotti; his visits to Fionia, the black hooker, and her sudden death; and what Pietrosanti had intimated. He concluded with, "I believe Genaro, your son-in-law, wasn't duped by Charlie Pietrosanti. I believe he was working with him. Pietrosanti's alive. He busted loose from the feds. If he hadn't, he would have been brought in to testify against Vincent and ended up in the program. Maybe that's what Genaro will end up doing, too."

"No." It was a verdict. "You don't like Genaro, do you, Paulie? It's like a jealous thing with you."

Dante's posture went slack. "Santo, you insult me with that question. The last thing I would ever want to do is bring down hurt upon you, or Lucia, or Vincent. I would never do that because of some petty dislike or jealousy. I've only told you what I learned. I was out there trying to find him at your request. I had to ask questions, dig out people who might know where he went. I learned a lot. That's what I do for a living, and I used everything I had because you asked me to. I went to Vegas and Frisco for the same reason."

"Go on," Santo said.

"I couldn't decide what was worse," Dante said, "giving you information I knew would hurt you personally, or holding out on information I knew could hurt the family."

"Okay. So you asked questions when you were looking for Genaro. Why did you keep after it once I took you off it?"

"Because I found things out that I didn't like. Because—because I care about you, Santo. That's why."

"But you wait until now."

"Before, what I had was weak. You didn't seem to want to hear anything negative about Genaro."

"You think I want to hear such things now? You think what you've told me now isn't weak?"

"No, Santo, I don't. I think it's very strong. Very damaging. Maybe even deadly for you and Vincent and the family."

"Why do you believe a total stranger, someone you admit you never met before? Why do you believe that person instead of a member of my family?"

Dante heaved a heavy sigh. "I'm sorry to have to say this, Santo, but in my business, you develop instincts. You pick up a sixth sense about who's being straight with you, and who's bullshitting."

"In *my* business it's called survival," Santo said.

"That's exactly what we're talking about," Dante said.

"I don't like what I'm hearing here, Paulie."

"What are you hearing? What don't you like?"

"I'm hearing I tell you to get off my son-in-law's case and you keep investigating him. I'm hearing some scumbag crawls out of a sewer and you buy the sewage he dishes out."

"Sewage? Santo. The guy can help your family, maybe in more ways than one. Can I talk with Vincent?"

"Come on, Paulie. What do you want, a sit-down with Vincent? You don't think the feds are watching you right now?"

"I don't know," Dante said. "I hope not, and I'm not suggesting you tell me where to find Vincent. Do it yourself, Santo. Tell Vincent what I told you about Pietrosanti's offer. Okay?"

Santo stood. The conversation was over. He walked Dante to the door. "Consider the message delivered," Santo said. "I'll take it from here."

"Fair enough," Dante said. "But Pietrosanti will only accept an answer through me. He's supposed to call me Saturday night."

"Yeah."

"I'm sorry I get to be the one to bring this kind of news to you, Santo."

"In the meantime, stay off Genaro's back, Paulie. Give me time to sort things out."

———

Vincent was livid when Santo told him about the Morelli hit. "The drug scum think they have taken away our power," he said. "We have to teach them they're wrong. They want an eye-for-an-eye, so be it. Deliver this message from me to Joey and The Ape."

————

Raphael Tierranueva rode the elevator to the garage level of a luxury condominium in Crystal City, Virginia, just across the Potomac from D.C. The sensual smell of Isabel still clung to him. She'd been snorting coke all day, and was high as a kite when he'd arrived. He'd come three times, once in her mouth, once between her breasts, and the third time in his own hand while she masturbated in the shower using one of those hand-held shower-massage gizmos. She'd told him she didn't want to do that, but he told her that if she didn't, he'd use his knife where his cock had been to make sure she never sucked anybody off again. "Who pays for this fucking apartment?" he'd screamed at her. "I talk, you do, bitch." Whore! There were plenty of them, all as pretty as Isabel but none with breasts that big. *Gigante* tits.

The elevator reached the parking level, and Tierranueva decided he was through with her. This particular *chiquita* had begun to wear on him. Variety. It was the spice of life, they said. His life.

Life *was* good. It had been a long journey from his village near Medellín, Colombia, where he'd begun by harvesting poppy plants for a local grower. But the future, he'd quickly realized, was with a gun. Power and respect. That's what he wanted, and he got it by demonstrating fierce allegiance to a succession of local lords until they gave him the territory he wanted. In America. A piece of Washington, D.C. The nation's capital.

The doors opened at G-level and Raphael walked toward his tan Mercedes where the Macho Man would be waiting. As he approached, he saw his driver motionless in the front passenger seat. He appeared to be asleep.

"*El hijo de la puta madre*," Raphael mumbled. "Son of a bitch. You spend every nonworking hour sniffing pussy, and then you sleep on my time."

Raphael pulled open the door and Macho Man's head snapped toward him, each eye as round and wide as a satellite dish. He tried to speak through two wide pieces of white tape across his mouth, but only squeals came out. Raphael heard the clink of metal on metal as the driver jerked his right arm against handcuffs that chained it to the seat rail.

"¿*Como*—?" Raphael exclaimed. Then he felt the cold, unfriendly circle of a gun barrel pressed against his temple, and heard the sickening click of the hammer cocking.

"Let's go, asshole," a voice said from behind. "Or should I say Señor Asshole. We're holding a midnight picnic in the park."

"I'm not hungry," Raphael said defiantly.

"Then you'll just have to force yourself to eat, or daddy will feed you."

"Go fuck yourself," Raphael snarled.

"Don't make me end this too fast," the voice growled. "I've been lookin' forward to a moonlight dinner with you."

A second man emerged from the shadows of the garage, reached inside Raphael's jacket and removed a nine-millimeter Beretta from its shoulder holster. He slid his hands down the Colombian's leg until he found a snub-nosed thirty-two in an ankle holster and removed that, too.

Raphael's hands were yanked behind his back and handcuffs were clamped on his wrists. One of the men pushed Raphael onto the back seat of the Mercedes and climbed in alongside him.

The other man got into the driver's seat, started the engine, dropped the car into gear, and drove from the garage, tires screeching.

That Same Night

"He's asking for you."

"Who?" Dante asked through a ballpoint pen clenched in his teeth. He looked up from a stack of bills he was juggling in his office at Cuffs.

"Didn't say," Shelly said, standing in the doorway. "A big guy, a monster, boxy build, eyes that bounce around like he's looking for shooters in every shadow."

"Tell him I'll be right out," Dante said. "I got a couple more bills to pay."

"And impatient," Shelly said. "Did I mention that?"

"All right. I'm coming."

Tommy Guardino, Vincent's personal driver for thirty years, stood at the far end of the bar, his hands folded in front of him. He surveyed the room like a health inspector. "Tommy," Dante said, extending his hand. "How are you? How is Vincent? I hope he's well."

Tommy shook Dante's hand and continued to examine his surroundings. They were alone. "He wants to see you," he said.

"Who? Who wants to see me?"

"Vincent."

"Why? What's this all about?"

"He told me to tell you he needs to get out into *l'aria fresca*, into

255

the fresh air. He wants to go for a ride. He doesn't want anybody from the family to take him. He wants you to drive him."

"Jesus, I don't know, Tommy. I mean, I'm a PI. Got a license."

As a licensed private investigator, consorting with a fugitive, in any capacity could cost him that license. He was prepared to go through with the Pietrosanti thing because it was important—to him—and would involve only a brief, in-and-out meeting. But taking the head of the Benedetti family, a fugitive, a bail-jumper, for a ride was something else. Besides, he had told Santo everything he had to say about the Pietrosanti offer. If Vincent needed clarification, he had none to offer. Pietrosanti considered the arrangement a quid pro quo. There was no negotiating.

"Vincent said to tell you it would mean a lot to him, and that he would be grateful."

Dante recognized the family-speak: I ask you to do this for me, and therefore you will.

"Won't that be dangerous?" Dante said. "Him coming out into the open?"

Tommy shrugged. "We'll meet you at the Gulf station just this side of the Chesapeake Bay Bridge tomorrow night at eight sharp. I'll bring him there. Then he gets in your car and you go for a ride."

"For some *l'aria fresca*," Dante said.

"Right. You got everything?"

"Yeah. I got everything."

"You'll be there. Right?"

"Yeah, Tommy. I'll be there."

Guardino refused Dante's offer of a drink and left the bar. Dante returned to his office and chewed on what had just transpired. He didn't like the sound of it, the logistics, the idea of the ride, or the thought of conferring at close quarters with a fugitive, especially one as celebrated as Vincent Benedetti.

Why did Vincent want to see *him*? He'd never had a close rapport with the don and, frankly, never felt completely comfortable in his company. Maybe never felt completely *safe* was more accurate. But Dante knew there was nothing to be gained by discussing it with Tommy

Guardino. The driver hadn't come there to debate the pros and cons of Vincent's request. No, call it Vincent's demand. Tommy had simply delivered a message.

Dante wondered whether to call Santo and see if he'd arranged this. He decided against it. He'd stirred Santo's pot of troubles enough that day.

Shelly returned to the doorway. "So?" she said.

"Nothing," Dante said. "An old friend reminding me of a poker game tomorrow night."

Shelly studied him. "You stopped playing poker years ago."

"I miss it. Nice to get together with friends, drink some beers, play nickle-dime."

"I hope you win," she said.

He looked up from his desk. "Me, too," he said.

"You going to be all right?" she asked.

"You're too smart to work in a dump like this," he said, smiling. "Yeah, I'll be fine." The words trailed off like the burnt-out entrails of a Roman candle. "As long as I get the right cards."

XXXïi

The Next Night—Thursday

Dante arrived at the Gulf station early and sat with his motor running and parking lights on while waiting for Vincent. Night had taken firm hold. The bay spanned by the bridge had gone inky black in the distance except for an incandescent fringe along its near edge created by waterfront buildings. The gas station was quiet. A teenage attendant pumped gas into a pickup truck. The station sat on a large plot of land, which allowed Dante to park in a far, dark corner. The only sound was from cars speeding on the parkway.

At precisely eight o'clock, a light grey Mercedes driven by Tommy Guardino entered the station. The Mercedes pulled up next to Dante's Buick, passenger door to passenger door. The back door of the Mercedes opened. Vincent Benedetti emerged, immediately climbed into the front seat of Dante's car and closed the door.

"'Evening, Vincent," Dante said. The old man nodded. "Where to?" Dante asked.

"Easton," Vincent said. "On the Maryland shore. You know it?"

"Yes," Dante answered, smiling. "As a matter of fact I do."

"Good."

"Any special route you'd like me to take?"

Vincent, his face an ashen mask in dim light coming through the windshield, shook his head. "It doesn't matter. Just don't drive fast. I don't like to drive fast."

Dante pulled away. Tommy followed in the Mercedes. "Tommy's coming with us?" Dante asked. Benedetti nodded. The Buick cautiously joined the speeding traffic on the highway. A driver who had closed the distance too rapidly leaned on his horn. Not *too* slow, Dante told himself. You can get killed going too slow.

The impatient driver seemed to have had no effect on Vincent. He was lost in reverie. "Maybe we go for soft-shell crabs," he said after a minute's silence. "Little place I like over there. Enrico's. You know it?"

"I've been there," Dante replied. "It's been years, but I have good memories of the place."

Dante remembered Easton as a quaint village dating back to the early 1700s and settled primarily by Quakers, including no less a personage than William Penn. The small crabhouse Vincent mentioned was on the Tread Avon River. Dante had been to it years before when he and his ex-wife, Barbara, took a weekend drive to the Eastern Shore. Enrico's was small, comfortable, and secluded. Even romantic. That had been early in the marriage when they were still discovering each other—when they were still in love. He'd been back a few times since but Enrico's was never the same for him. The crabs might have been as good but they fed the belly, not the heart.

They started across the bridge. Dante drove slowly and deliberately in the right lane. Vincent stared out the window at the moonglow on the water. "Beautiful," he said.

Dante looked down at the shimmering natural beauty of the bay. "Sure is."

Dante tried to make small talk, but beyond the initial banter, Vincent had settled into a series of grunts or, at best, one-word responses. Moody bastard, Dante thought. But then again, he's got a lot on his mind.

"Want the radio on?" Dante asked.

"I wouldn't mind," Vincent answered. "Maybe you can find some classical music. You got a tape machine?"

"No."

"I brought a coupla tapes."

Dante played with the dial until he found a classical station. A

259

violin piece filled the car. He adjusted the fade control until most of the sound came from the rear speakers.

As they proceeded in the direction of Easton, Dante found himself increasingly annoyed at the family leader's sullen behavior. After all, Vincent had asked for this little outing. But he held his annoyance in check. It wasn't his place to complain. And, he reminded himself that Vincent Benedetti, as old as he'd become, and facing mounting legal problems that could effectively end his reign—if not his life—was still an imposing figure.

Dante stopped trying to compete with the music, leaving the violins the only sound. Then, Vincent abruptly straightened up and said in a loud, vital voice, "I've always liked studying the world around me. Too many people walk around wearing blinders. They live in their own goddamn tunnel they create for themselves. I always look for the big picture, the broader landscape. That's why I don't like what's happened to me. I'm too confined where I am now. I read a lot because there's nothing to see from where I am. I don't see much of the world with my own eyes these days so I read about it. I hear about it from Santo and Lucia. That's okay, but too confining. It's not the way I want to spend the rest of my life. You understand what I say?"

"I think so," Dante said, grateful for any conversation. "What kind of books do you read?"

Benedetti adjusted himself in the seat so he looked at Dante. "History books mostly," he replied. "I read about presidents and kings, dictators, generals, how they won or lost. Who fucked them up and who they fucked over."

"That's pretty heavy stuff," Dante said. "I never much got into history. It always seemed too complicated. Besides, I figure history doesn't have much to do with my life today. That was then. This is now. At least for me."

His passenger shook his head. "You fought in Vietnam, didn't you?"

"Yes."

"History created that war."

"I thought politicians did."

"The same drama."

"Like I said, it's too complicated for me."

"Today is more complicated than history," Vincent said in the measured tones of a patient teacher. "Times were simpler back then. A handshake was all you needed to be comfortable with a deal. You shook hands, the deal was done. If it wasn't, if somebody fucked it up, you did what you had to do. Much simpler, Paul."

They reached a division in the highway, Route 301 branching north, 50 continuing south. "We're almost there," Dante said.

"Maybe we could just drive around a little," Vincent suggested.

"Any place in particular?" Dante asked, glancing in his rearview mirror to confirm that Tommy was still with them. At the speed he was driving, there was little chance of losing him.

"Drive near the water. I like the water."

Dante meandered along small roads that skirted Chesapeake Bay. Vincent lapsed into deep thought again.

They passed through Easton and took a road leading to a peninsula that jutted into the bay, then reached the village of St. Michael's. "Stop here," Vincent said, pointing to a small Protestant church. Dante pulled up in front. "Turn off the engine and the lights," Vincent said. Dante obliged. Tommy parked thirty yards behind.

Dante waited for Vincent's next instruction. He thought of Julia and silently wished he was home with her. "Where to next?" he asked pleasantly.

"You know what they did in this town, Paul, in the War of 1812?" was Benedetti's reply.

"No."

"The British raided this town, but they were beaten off. The people in the village fooled the British by putting out all the lights in the town. Then they hung lanterns in a bunch of trees somewhere outside the town. The British thought that was where the town was and aimed their cannons at the wrong place."

"Smart," Dante said.

"Yeah, smarter than sometimes we are."

"We?"

"Some of the people who work for me. They're loyal, most of them. They have no choice; they have to be. But that doesn't make them smart. Some of them are stupid. Santo always says you're smart, Paul, smarter than most people he knows."

"That's nice to hear," Dante said. "Coming from Santo, I take it as a real compliment."

"Santo always liked you. You know that?"

The direction of the conversation was puzzling, considering Dante's last conversation with Santo. "I hope he knows how much I like and respect him," Dante said. "I would do almost anything for Santo."

"He knows that."

Dante gazed out the window at the church, a shadowed facade against the moonlit sky.

"Too bad you didn't come work for me, Paul. You would be something if you had."

Dante started to say that he already "was something," but held back. The men regarded each other for a moment before Vincent said, "Excuse me. I'll only be a few minutes." As he started to get out of the car, Dante asked if he wanted company. Vincent shook his head. "No. Stay here."

Dante watched the elder Benedetti walk slowly toward the entrance to the church, his gait a shuffle, his head down as though searching for something on the sidewalk. An old man's walk, wanting to be sure each step would provide solid footing. Tommy came from the Mercedes, sauntered to the church and stood next to Vincent, who tried the door, opened it, and disappeared inside. Churches didn't leave their doors open back in D.C., Dante thought.

What had prompted the old man to want to go into that particular church? he wondered. Like virtually everyone in the family, Vincent Benedetti was Catholic. But maybe when you're facing the kinds of problems he was, any church in a storm. Maybe you went into any building that God was supposed to have built. Maybe you said prayers in temples, mosques, or cathedrals, and the prayers all went to the same place, caught the same ear.

A few minutes later, Vincent exited the church, stood by the door and waved for Dante to join him. Dante headed in the old don's direction. What was it that Vincent wanted to show him? What historical tidbit had he discovered inside?

The church was empty and dark, the only illumination provided by the moon whose shaft of light came and went as clouds covered it, then allowed its searchlight to shine again.

They went to a pew on the right side, halfway to the altar, and sat next to each other on the hard wood.

"You go to church, Paul?" Vincent whispered.

Dante stared at him. It was the sort of question the priests always asked when he was a kid, making sure he was doing his part to extend the flock. Making sure his coins would be there to join others in the collection plate.

"Sometimes," he answered. "Not as much as I should. I was brought up Catholic but other things got in the way. Sometimes you get distracted—by life." Dante's quiet laugh was forced, nervous. It *was* as though he were talking to a parish priest.

Vincent said in the same hoarse whisper, "We've let religion get away from us. We're ruled now by the marketplace and the politicians. Politicians. No honor with them any more. They're without honor, without souls."

"You're right," Dante said, lamely unsure of where this conversation was heading. He added, "I guess we traded morals for dollars, power, women, anything."

"Without God, we don't have guidelines, Paul. We're unable to measure. We can't tell those who love us from those who are our enemies. We look at a man in terms of whether he has anything of tangible worth to bring to us, not whether he is a man of morality and respect—*un'uomo di rispetto*."

Dante grunted. Maybe Vincent had been spending too much time cooped up. Too much time to think.

"You know Sicily, Paul?"

"I never been there."

"A beautiful place where honor and respect are valued. In the *mezzogiorno*, the part of Italy south of Rome, people are poor, but only with money. Their souls are rich. I promise myself often that I will visit there again, but life becomes too complicated for vacations, huh? It is so beautiful there. In Sicily we call it the eternal spring. Very beautiful."

Dante knew one thing as he sat in the pew next to Vincent Benedetti. The man was complex. What subject would he raise next? He didn't have to wait long to find out.

"What do you think of Genaro?" Vincent asked, looking straight ahead.

The question caught Dante by surprise. He assumed that if Vincent had intended to discuss the Pietrosanti offer with him, he'd slide into it, preface it with other questions. And he certainly didn't expect the dialogue to take place in a Protestant church on the Maryland shore.

"I really don't know him," Dante replied. He hoped Vincent wouldn't see through the transparency of the answer.

But he did. His whisper now had an angry edge to it. "You know him better than you tell me you do, Paul. Santo says you don't like Genaro, that you don't trust him. Is my brother right?"

"Vincent, I really don't think it's up to me to—"

"Nobody thinks it's right to question Genaro. He's family, Santo says. He tells me to trust him because he's family. But I *don't* trust him. I watch him in the house and I don't *like* him. But I also know I don't like many who work for me, so I think maybe I'm becoming an old man who doesn't like anybody, doesn't trust anybody. I don't know what to think anymore."

He *doesn't* know, Dante thought. He doesn't fucking know. All Santo has told him is that I don't like Orsini. It suddenly dawned on Dante why they were in the church having this conversation and not in the car. Vincent wanted to be sure the discussion wouldn't be taped. He didn't trust anybody, including Dante.

Dante drew a deep breath and focused on the altar as he collected his thoughts. Vincent was playing cat-and-mouse with him. The old man obviously had formed an opinion of Orsini and it was negative. As far as Dante was concerned, Vincent was right about that.

But Vincent had reached the conclusion without benefit of information Dante had provided Santo about Pietrosanti. It was outrageous. Sufficient time had passed since Dante had told Santo of his trip, but Vincent still didn't have the information. What was Santo doing?

"Santo asked you to look for Genaro the day after I was arrested," Vincent continued.

"That's right," Dante answered, thankful for an easy question.

"And what did you find out about him?"

Dante stalled. "I didn't turn up Genaro," he said.

"That I know. What did you turn up *about* him?" Vincent pressed.

"A lot of circumstantial stuff, third-party accusations."

"You're dancing around me," Vincent said.

Dante turned to the head of the family and looked directly into his eyes. "You're right, Vincent. I'm dancing around you. No, I don't think much of Genaro Orsini, but he is married to a woman I love like a sister, and she is the daughter of a man I love and respect like a father. It isn't easy for me to deal with this, Vincent. Grilling me doesn't make it any easier."

"I need someone to be honest with me, Paul. I want you to be honest with me. My life—the family's existence—may depend upon such honesty."

"I understand, but there is much I can't tell you." He glanced in the direction of the altar. "As God is my witness, I cannot tell any more than I already have."

"Why?"

Dante shook his head. "I can't even tell you that."

Vincent leaned forward in the pew. He rested his forearms on the back of the bench in front of him and folded his hands as if about to start praying. "It's my brother, isn't it?" he said into his hands. He raised one of them and said, "You don't have to respond."

Dante didn't.

"Santo is blinded by this thing, isn't he? He is so worried about the effect a second disastrous marriage will have on Lucia that he lets it determine how he thinks. It is a terrible situation." Vincent dropped his chin onto the backs of his folded hands. "It is turning into a nightmare for my brother, for Lucia, and for me. If it continues, it will destroy our family."

Dante let the words sit in the church's silence. He started to say something but Vincent cut him off. "Don't say anything, Paul. I'm sorry I put you through this. You're a good man. I wish I had an army of men like you."

Vincent stood. "I appreciate your loyalty to my brother," he said. "He should know what a good friend he has in you."

"I owe him a lot," Dante said.

"He owes you much, too. You have the courage to tell him the truth."

At the door to the church, Vincent turned to Dante and said, "I don't think it would be a good idea to eat in a public place. Not good for me, not good for you. Thank you for bringing me here. Tommy will take me back."

"Whatever you say."

Dante's thoughts were a confused jumble during his solo drive back to D.C. The picture he saw was blurred.

Vincent was a general of sorts, but his command was keeping things from him. Emotions now seemed to be making command decisions. Even Vincent's own brother. Business and family were in conflict.

As the leader of the Benedetti crime family—as its general— Vincent wasn't getting what every general needs: good intelligence. Honest reporting and analysis. Generals depended upon their close advisors for good information. In this case, Santo was second-in-command and a brother to boot. Dante knew Orsini was no good, but Santo didn't want to know that. And that placed the general, and all his troops, in jeopardy.

There was obviously a climax building over Orsini, and he, Dante, had been a major contributor to it. Vincent had complimented him on being honest with Santo, which meant Santo must have told his brother at least something Dante had reported about Orsini. But chances were he'd also dismissed much of it as untrue. Which, Dante reasoned, had prompted Vincent to seek him out.

But Dante hadn't been any better than Santo had been where Vincent was concerned. He hadn't been honest with the general, either. Then again, he reminded himself as he pulled into the alley behind Cuffs, Vincent wasn't *his* general. It wasn't *his* army.

XXXiii

That Same Night

The phone call caught him off guard. "I can't talk now, Doris," he whispered. Lucia was upstairs.

"Fine. Then I'll talk to your wife."

"Don't start this shit with me, Doris. We'll talk when I get to Atlantic City."

"Put your wife on."

Orsini shuddered with rage. He needed a minute to collect his thoughts. "Okay," he said. "You're right. We need to talk. Gimme ten minutes, I'll call you right back."

"You won't call me back, you bastard."

"I'll call you back. If I don't call you back in a half hour, call the house again."

"How long?"

"A half hour."

———

She replaced the phone in its cradle and checked her watch. At first, the relationship had worked. Orsini's new position at the casino meant they were able to spend more time together. Then, he'd made an effort to be reliable and to do everything he said he would for her. The gifts were expensive, the promises for the future expansive.

She pleased him sexually. She was good at sex. She enjoyed it. There was never a need for her to fake pleasure with any man. It erupted fast and powerful, and there were times she wondered if she were a nymphomaniac, although she wasn't quite sure what that was. She liked sex. No need for big words to describe it.

Orson—she knew his real name was Orsini but deferred to his wish to not use it—wasn't the best lover she'd ever had. Far from it. He came too fast most times and seemed uncomfortable going down on her, something she especially enjoyed. She tried to encourage him to do it by trimming her strawberry-blond pubic hair into the approximate shape of a heart, and using expensive perfumes there. He did it a few times but the unpleasant look on his face was enough to temper any pleasure she received.

But that didn't matter. There had been many skillful, obliging lovers in her young life. While some had taken her to heights of sexual ecstasy, none offered the sort of future Gerry Orson could. At first, she understood why he couldn't divorce his wife, not with her father a powerful leader of a major Mafia family. But he promised it would happen one day.

Once, he'd laughed and said, "Maybe she'll die a premature death, huh?"

His comment had frightened her, but she didn't dwell upon it. He was a man on the way up, someone who could lift her out of the casino and her skimpy little costume, whisk her away from the cheap gamblers who never dropped a toke on her tray for delivering free drinks and who made sure their hands brushed her thighs, their eyes always boring down into her cleavage. Slobs. She hated it there, hated her dingy little studio apartment on the wrong side of Atlantic City. She checked her watch again. Ten minutes had passed.

———

He called her from a phone booth in the lobby of the Four Seasons hotel.

"Gerry," she said, sarcastically. "It's good to hear your voice. Twenty-four minutes. You're even better than your word."

He let it go.

"I've had it, Gerry. It's time to make your move."

She was wired. She was out of control. She'd obviously been snorting coke all night. Her voice gave it away. She *would* call Lucia. His grip tightened on the receiver, his knuckles turned white. If she were standing here, he'd kill her, or at least beat sense into her.

But she wasn't here. As long as she could pick up a phone she could destroy him.

"You're right, Doris. I been putting off what I have to do. Look, baby, I've been doing a lot of serious thinking about you. About us."

Her heart raced. "Yes?"

"Things have really changed here. It won't be long before I dump my old lady. I've met a lot of good-looking women in my life but you are the most gorgeous creature on this earth."

She giggled. Her heart pounded even faster.

"I mean it. Look, here's what I think. I think Doris Sawyer deserves more than a cocktail-waitress job and a rathole to live in. I see those slobs drool over you at work and I want to kill every fuckin' one of them. That's how I feel, and I finally decided I have to do something about it."

"Gerry, I don't know what to say. I'm sorry I got angry with you."

"You don't have to say nothin'. Here's what I want to do. I want you and me to talk. Really talk. In nice surroundings, the right atmosphere. I want us to talk about your future. *Our* future."

"You do?"

"I'll try to get up there in the next couple of days."

"No," she snapped. Her voice was cold and ugly again. "I'm coming to D.C. tomorrow."

"Okay, okay. We'll do it up right. Lemme show you I know how to treat you the way you should be treated. When I hang up, you call the Watergate Hotel here in D.C. and reserve us a suite for tomorrow night."

"All right, but—"

"But what?"

"What will I use for money?"

"You got a credit card, huh? Visa? MasterCard?"

"*My* credit card? I can't pay off what's on it now."

"Baby, will you please hear me out."

"Go ahead."

"I'll pay the bill in cash on the way out. They like reservations made with a card. Nails down the room in case of a no-show. I don't use no cards. Strictly cash with me. Just do it. Okay?"

"I will."

"You go to the suite and wait for me. I can't get there until later, ten, maybe ten-thirty. Have dinner. Order up your favorites and charge it to the room. Have some good champagne for when I get there. And caviar, stuff like that. We'll make it a real special night for the two of us."

"I'm a little confused, Gerry. What's come over you?"

"Like I told you, I've been doing a lot of thinking about us, Doris. I decided life's too short to be stuck married to a woman I hate. I had a talk with my father-in-law, and he understands. He wouldn't with just anybody, but I'm important to him and the business. Indispensable, I guess. He knows the business has to be more important than his daughter, or anybody else. I'm ready to make some big changes in my life, and they start with you."

"You mean it, Gerry? I don't want to be let down."

"And I won't let you down. I got to run. A meeting. See you tomorrow night at the Watergate. Oh, and why don't you buy yourself some new perfume from the gift shop at the hotel? Soak in a hot tub and rub it all over you, especially down in that pretty blond pussy of yours. I'll be visiting it all night." He laughed and hung up.

She replaced the phone in its cradle and began to cry. At last, she thought, rummaging through her closet for clothes to take with her for the big night.

Finally.

271

XXXiv

The Following Night—Friday

"Again?" Julia said as Dante prepared to leave her apartment after an early dinner.

"Just one more night," he said, securing his revolver beneath his left armpit. "Pietrosanti is supposed to call tomorrow. I just want one more look at Orsini before he does."

"I kind of thought we might hunker in here tonight, watch a little TV, get to bed early."

"Don't tempt me," Dante said. "I'm sorry. As soon as this thing is over, we'll hunker in every night and go to bed early." It occurred to him that what he'd just said sounded like a marriage proposal. Go to bed early? As a private detective and restaurant owner? Fat chance. Don't lead her on, Dante. Choose your words carefully. No lies to this woman. She's too good for that.

"Paul," Julia said as he put on his suit jacket and straightened his tie in a hall mirror.

"Huh?"

"You've got to drop this thing. You say Vincent indicated he'd take it from here. Santo *told* you to get off it. This obsession is going to hurt you."

"Just one more shot at it," he said, going to the door.

"It's almost sexual," Julia said.

"Sexual?"

"You're getting a strange thrill out of playing where you're not supposed to."

"Sexual?"

"It's like playing around with somebody else's wife. You know the husband is going to catch you dipping in the honey pot and probably shoot you, but your hormones are in charge."

"Sexual?"

"I wish it were."

"Julia, stick to modern dance."

He kissed her and left. She was right, of course. It *was* a-moth-drawn-to-a-flame affair and he couldn't stay away, no matter how searing the heat.

He'd started staking out Orsini's house in Georgetown right after his trip to the Eastern Shore with Vincent. He hadn't seen much.

On this night, Dante found a parking spot up the street from the home Orsini and Lucia shared, maneuvered the Buick into its tight confines, sat back and waited. He wondered what it was like inside, just the two of them together. Did they get along or fight a lot? Maybe Orsini turned into the perfect husband once he came in off the street. Dante shook his head at that notion. He doubted whether Orsini was good at anything except talking big and strong-arming the weak.

He knew his hatred of Orsini was overblown, considering how little he had to do with him. It shouldn't have developed into a mission, a cause. Dante never trusted anyone who had a cause that went beyond the reasonable. Like antismoking zealots, the "health Nazis" as Cal Williams had once described them. All of a sudden there were millions of people coming into restaurants and other people's homes like bounty hunters, their noses perpetually sniffing the air, all suffering from a sudden, life-threatening allergy to smoke. Causes. Even the best of them got out of hand, like this one with Orsini had.

But that was always the trouble when you were on a stakeout. Too much time to dwell upon things that weren't worth thinking about.

He didn't know whether Orsini was home, or had already struck out on his nocturnal prowl. But he felt lucky. There was that rush you get when you know something worthwhile is going to happen. At a craps table. Meeting the right woman. It was almost—sexual.

273

At 9:45, a beam of light shafted through the front door. Someone was leaving. Orsini. Dante waited until Orsini climbed into his new silver Lexus sedan, then started the Buick's engine and fell in behind as the Lexus passed the busy boutiques along M Street to the edge of a newly rebuilt fashionable district on the Potomac, just shy of the beginning of Rock Creek Park.

Orsini took Rock Creek Parkway to the river and turned into the entrance to the underground parking garage beneath the Watergate complex, scene of the famous hotel break-in that toppled Richard Nixon. Dante waited a few minutes before entering the garage. He found Orsini's car and chose a space for himself from which he could see the Lexus, but wouldn't be noticed. He got out and debated whether to go inside the hotel. He didn't want to run the risk of being spotted by Orsini but decided it was worth the chance. If Orsini saw him, he'd pretend to have blundered into him again, the way he'd done in Atlantic City. Maybe he wouldn't even bother pretending. Hell, the Watergate Hotel was a public place.

Dante wandered the lobby with the practiced nonchalance he'd developed while a cop. No Orsini. Nor was he in any of the restaurants or shops.

He's meeting a bimbo upstairs, Dante decided, leaving him little choice but to return to his car and wait. He wasn't about to peep into rooms, if that were possible.

Ballsy on Orsini's part, Dante thought as he retraced his steps to the garage, playing this close to home. Granted, Santo didn't come into D.C. much. Vincent was holed up someplace. And Lucia wasn't the type to go out searching for her husband.

He reached for a cigarette that hadn't been there since he quit two years ago, sat back and did what he'd done so often as a cop and PI—waited—and thought of causes and the collapse of the Soviet Union, his ex-wife and kids and other women he'd had, cases he'd broken—and of a night lost with Julia.

Orsini had barely time to take off his jacket before Doris slipped her arms seductively around his neck. He looked past her to a table set with everything he'd suggested—champagne and strawberries with cream, caviar, and smoked salmon. And the residue from a line of cocaine.

"Did I get everything?" she asked into his ear.

"Looks like it, babe. Everything's the way I wanted it to be."

"Mmmmmm," she murmured as she nibbled at his earlobe.

"Hold on a second, baby," he said, freeing himself. He slipped out of his jacket and draped it over a chair.

Doris resumed her embrace. "I could get used to this," she purred.

"Well, *get* used to it," Orsini said. "You're going to be living this way for the rest of your life."

She wore a satiny white robe with a white fur collar, the kind she had seen in all those black-and-white movies of the thirties and forties that she liked to watch on the classic movie channel. "New?" Orsini asked, running his hands over the silky smooth shoulders of the robe and down to the contours of her hips.

"Yeah," she said. "I bought it in a boutique downstairs. Charged it to the room like you said."

"Nice," he said. Must have cost a fortune, he thought.

She read his ambivalent expression. "I hope you don't mind, Gerry. It felt so good buying it. I knew you'd like it. I thought it would turn you on."

"Yeah, it does," he said, smiling. "Just money, baby. Plenty a that."

She smiled and pecked him on the cheek. "In that case, there's more," she said. She lifted her leg onto a chair, which caused the robe to fall open revealing sexy white undergarments: a lacy, see-through bra, which somehow made her already-large breasts appear enormous, and a garter belt attached to sheer white stockings.

"Phew," he said. "You got whips and chains somewhere?"

"No," she said, "but maybe cream will do." She reached behind him, snared one of the large strawberries, swiped it through the heavy cream and brought it up to his lips. "Open," she said, placing the berry on his tongue.

He bit off the cream-coated tip. She took the remaining half from his mouth, dipped it in the cream and sucked it seductively into her mouth, bit it off up to the leafy stem and dropped the stem to the carpet. "That's so nice to suck on," she said.

"Yeah. You look like you enjoy it."

"Champagne?" she asked. He moved away from her and reached for the bottle but she tugged his shirtsleeve. "I'll pour it, Gerry. There's a nice fluffy robe in the bedroom. I couldn't believe they give robes when you stay here. I never saw that before."

There's a lotta things you've never seen, he thought.

"Go on. Get undressed and into a robe. I'll have champagne for you when you come back. It'll get us in the right mood. Not that we need anything." She patted the back of her hand, which she'd had manicured that afternoon in the hotel's beauty shop, against the bulge in his pants.

With Orsini in the bedroom, Doris reached into the silver champagne bucket, removed the bottle of Dom Pérignon, wrapped it in the white hand towel that had been left alongside the bucket, and unraveled the retaining wires from the cork. She popped the cork; the champagne gushed over the neck. She hurriedly grabbed one of the crystal fluted glasses and caught the overflow, then filled both glasses.

Orsini returned. He was naked under the white robe with the Watergate's emblem on its breast pocket. She handed him his glass. He raised it and said, "To one glorious night, baby."

"To the rest of our lives together," she said, touching her glass to his.

They moved the food to a coffee table in front of the leather couch and nibbled on strawberries and sipped champagne. Doris enjoyed the caviar, which she spread on toast points and garnished with finely chopped onions and capers. She insisted he have a bite: "No fair I'm the only one with onions on my breath," she said. He didn't like caviar but went along, swallowed a piece of toast on which he'd heaped onions and a little sturgeon roe.

"Do you want to talk now?" she asked.

He looked at her quizzically.

"About us. I mean, do you want to talk about us and the future now, or make love first?" She slid her hand into the folds of his robe and fondled his flaccid penis, which quickly hardened in her hand. He took one of her large breasts in his hand and squeezed.

"Oooh, too hard, Gerry," she said, pulling back.

"You asked," he said.

"I want you so much," she said, exaggerating her urgency. But she didn't reach for him again. Instead, she sat back and said in a dreamy voice, "You'll never know how wonderful it was to get your phone call yesterday. I mean, I didn't know what our situation was, you and me. Not that it mattered. It really didn't. But I'd be some liar if I said I didn't want it to be permanent. I knew about your problems with your wife and her family. I understood. I really did. It must be terrible being married to a woman like that and not being able to end it because of her father. She must be a bitch, a real bitch."

"Yeah, she is."

"I don't understand, Gerry, how you can resolve it with her father. I mean, everybody knows the Benedetti family and what they're like. You must be scared out of your wits."

"Look, Doris, I told you on the phone I got it worked out. It'll take a little more time but there's no sweat. I'm taking care of it."

"Have you talked to your wife about it? She must be—"

"If you're trying to find a way to fuck up this evening, Doris, talking about my wife is heading in the right direction."

"Oh no, Gerry. You're right. I don't want anything to ruin this night. I'm sorry. I guess I'm nervous about it, that's all. It's so right."

"What is?"

"You and me. We make a good team, Gerry. We've both had hard knocks. We're survivors. I can make you happy, Gerry. So happy." She drained her glass, put it down, took his from his hand and placed it alongside hers on the table. She pushed him back on the couch, scrambled up his body and kissed him, her tongue still tingling from the chilled bubbly. With her lips pressed tightly to his, she reached down and grasped his erection. He ran his hands inside her robe and up over her back where he fingered her bra strap. She realized he was having trouble, released her lock on his lips and said, "Wait. Let me." She straddled him on her knees, reached around with both hands and released the bra's catch. It fell from her freckled shoulders and her breasts dangled free like large, tempting melons over his face. His hands immediately went to them and kneaded the soft, supple flesh of the rounded white globes, the nipples decorative cherries on mounds of vanilla ice cream. He leaned forward and took the right one in his mouth. She moaned and threw her head back, then tossed it forward, her loose strawberry-blond hair cascading over his face. She ran her fingers through his hair as the sensation of his sucking sent a message to her sexual core. "Wait," she said.

She pushed herself to her feet and untied the white satin belt around her waist. The robe slipped over her shoulders and became a swirl of white satin at feet that had been pampered that afternoon too, each toe tipped with crimson polish. Dressed in only the white garter belt and stockings, she fell to her knees in front of the couch. Orsini's eyes widened and a contented smile crossed his lips as she took him in her mouth. He ran a hand under the elastic band of her panties and played with her buttocks. He stretched to reach between her legs but couldn't get there. She had him pinned to the couch and he was not about to have her stop what she was doing. Her warm, wet mouth felt exquisite as it moved easily up and down his shaft.

His breath now came in short bursts, and his heart pounded. She felt in her mouth the beginning tremors of an orgasm and slid her mouth off him, her tongue leaving a trail of saliva along the underside of his penis. "Time for act one, scene two," she said.

She stood and removed her panties. Naked, she pulled a cushion from the couch and lowered herself to the deep pile carpeting. She placed the cushion beneath her buttocks and spread her legs. "I bought new perfume like you told me to and put it on when you were getting undressed. Come here." Her hands reached up to him. "Please."

He rolled off the couch and kissed her breasts and belly. She placed her hands on his head and urged him lower to where most of the perfume had been applied. He resisted, but she continued to guide him to her pubic patch. She arched her back and brought herself up to his lips. "Lick it, Gerry, lick it," she gasped, feeling his hot breath on her.

His explorations of her were tentative and cursory. He saw her hands on her belly and thought that her fingers were too short and ugly. The combination of the perfume and the natural smell of her was making him sick. He sat up, got onto his back, and said, "Get on top."

She masked her disappointment; she'd been close to a climax despite his disinterest in what he'd been doing. She straddled him, her wet sex swallowing his penis without friction. She rode him wildly, his hands groping along her back, grabbing her buttocks, then her breasts, as if he were lost in this embarrassment of fleshy riches.

She felt him begin to tense and slowed to a measured, seductive grind. "Feel good?" she said.

"Yeah, perfect. Keep it like this, nice and slow." His face twisted into a pleasure-pain mask. He stiffened. "Yeah, yeah," he groaned as his body went into the tremor of release and he shot into her. He pushed his pelvis hard against her vagina, as if trying to stuff all that he could up into her. Then, he fell back on the carpet.

She'd felt climactic quivers inside but hadn't come. She wanted him to use his tongue again to bring her over the edge but was afraid to ask. She bent down and kissed his face, ran her lips over his mouth, cheeks, eyes, and forehead. "Oh, God, you're great, Gerry," she said. "You make me soooo happy. It's going to be great all the time for us. Forever. I love you so much."

"Yeah," he said, lifting himself up on his elbows. She was still sitting on him and he felt himself going limp inside her. "Let's have a nightcap," he said. "Lift up, huh."

She smiled, kissed him one more time, then dismounted. Some of his semen ran out of her and formed a small puddle on his stomach.

"First," she said, "I need to drain out."

"Sure," he said, his eyes following her ample naked form as she headed toward the bathroom.

He reached for the hand towel by the champagne bottle and wiped the come from his stomach. He put on his shorts, pants, and shirt.

"Gerry," she called from the bathroom.

"Yeah?"

"Come here."

He went to the bathroom door which she'd left partially open.

"What?" he said.

"Come in."

He pushed the door fully open. She sat on the toilet, legs spread, her head bowed as she examined her crotch. Revulsion shot through him.

"Would you bring me some champagne?" she asked, not looking up.

He said nothing as he returned to the living room where he filled the two glasses halfway. He took them out to the balcony and placed them on a glass table that was surrounded by four wrought-iron chairs. He rested his arms on the railing and gazed out into the black evening. Below, the Potomac River slid slowly by. A lone small powerboat moved against the current, its red and green lights the river's only illumination. He looked straight down. Just shrubs and bushes, a sidewalk and the road separating the hotel from the river.

He heard the faint sound of the toilet flushing and then her voice from the living room. "Gerry," she called out. "Gerry, where are you?"

"Out here," he said.

She joined him. "Why did you get dressed?" she asked. She wore a hotel robe.

"You think I should be out here naked?" he replied.

"There's only the river to see."

"I feel more comfortable. Okay?"

"Sure. Do you want me to get dressed, too? I thought the robe was—"

"You're fine. Nice out here, huh?" He picked up the two glasses and handed one to her. She raised it. "To a beautiful night, and it's just started," she said, her voice that of a giddy little girl.

"Cheers," he said.

She kissed him. "It's so black out tonight," she said. "Spooky. Let's go inside. We still have to talk."

"About what?"

"Gerry, come on, about you and me. I know you don't want it to ruin the evening, but we need to talk about that bitch you're married to."

"Yeah. Later."

"Now!" It was the voice on the phone again. "I won't wait until tomorrow, Gerry. I'll go to the house. I swear to Christ I'll go to the house."

He placed the champagne glass on the table. "There ain't gonna be any tomorrow for you, Doris." He went to his knees and grabbed her by her ankles. The surprise of his move caused the glass to fly from her hand and go over the railing, shattering on the concrete pavement eleven stories below.

He heaved his shoulders, pushed her back against the railing, and then, her ankles in his beefy hands, lifted her up and over the rail. She fought to avoid going all the way over but it was in vain. She was suspended headfirst from the balcony, her only anchor his hands that sustained their viselike grip.

"Please," she said in a barely controlled voice. "I'll do anything you want. I'll go away and—"

"So long, baby," he said, letting go. "Have a nice trip."

He was inside the suite before her body hit the ground. He collected his belongings, picked up the semen-stained towel to wipe away his fingerprints, laughed, said, "Fuck it," and exited the room.

———

Dante saw Orsini walk across the concrete floor toward his car. He slipped down in his seat and watched the Lexus through his right sideview mirror. Orsini had that arrogant, thought-laden expression on his face as he dropped down behind the steering wheel. Somehow, he didn't look like a man who'd just enjoyed a roll in the sack.

Orsini started his engine and pulled away. Dante trailed, keeping a safe distance. The Lexus followed the parkway south along the Potomac past the Kennedy Center, across the Key Bridge into Virginia, then headed north up the George Washington Memorial Parkway past the flowery esplanades that had been Lady Bird Johnson's pet projects. Eventually, he pulled off into a wooded cutout where a navy blue Chevy sedan sat idling.

Dante had no choice but to keep going and hope they stayed for more than a few minutes. At the first chance for a U-turn Dante took it, doubled back, passed the cutout heading in the opposite direction, did a second U-turn and pulled off the highway just short of the rest area. He turned off his lights and watched. Orsini had joined another man in the blue car. But because of the night and the distance, Dante was unable to see faces.

Five minutes later, Orsini got out of the blue sedan, made some animated gestures at the other driver, climbed into his Lexus and pulled away.

Dante had to make a choice. I know where Orsini lives, he thought. Let me see what this other guy is all about. He followed him to Falls Church where, eventually, he turned down a street lined with old maples and pulled into the driveway of a post–World War II Dutch colonial. The man who got out was tall and skinny, and was dressed in a business suit. He disappeared into the house. Dante quickly left his car, went to the head of the driveway, and jotted down the house address and automobile plate number.

Twenty minutes later he was back at Cuffs where he brushed his teeth, stripped to his shorts, and fell into bed. I'm getting too old for these hours, he thought as blessed sleep slowly took over. His last thought was of Julia sleeping soundly in her neat and clean apartment, coffee already prepared for the morning, a blissful smile on her lovely face. He called himself a jerk out loud and was gone.

———

He awoke at ten and heard Julio waging World War III downstairs. "Good morning," he told his cook as he came into the kitchen, pulled a quart of orange juice from the refrigerator and gulped from the carton.

"Bad night, huh, amigo?" Julio said, a gold tooth highlighting his smile.

"No. A gourmet dinner, a game of bridge, and early to bed."

"Bullsheet."

Dante collected the newspaper from in front of the restaurant, went to the bar and picked up the telephone. He was in luck. Cal Williams was pulling a Saturday shift. Williams answered on the first ring. "Cal. Dante. How are you?"

"Fine. You?"

"I'm good. A favor."

"Forget it."

"Come on, Cal. This is an easy one. No hookers. Just run a plate for me."

"Whose plate?"

"I'll know that after you run it."

"Where are you?" Williams asked.

"Cuffs."

"A half hour." Dante gave Williams the number as Julio delivered a cup of his coffee-flavored pudding to the bar.

Dante opened the *Post* to the Metro section. A late story in a small box immediately caught his eye: "**WOMAN PLUNGES TO DEATH AT WATERGATE.** In her early thirties, registered under the name of Doris Sawyer, home address Atlantic City . . . the redheaded woman had checked in that afternoon using a credit card . . . apparent suicide . . . no note . . . autopsy to be performed."

Dante's mind raced. Redheaded woman? Strawberry blonde? Atlantic City? Orsini in the hotel when it happened? Slow down, he told himself. Don't go chasing demons again, inventing foul deeds where they might not exist.

The phone disturbed his thoughts. "Not registered, Paulie," Cal Williams said.

"Not registered?"

"I gotta draw you a picture? Government vee-hickle. FBI, DEA, a federal agency. Thousands of them on the street. Hey, weren't you a cop once?"

"In my better days. Not thinking this morning, Cal. Sure. No registration. Translation: government car. Sure. By the way, this woman I'm reading about who took a header at the Watergate last night. Anything on it?"

"No my yob, Paulie."

"Yeah. Well, thanks for running the plate. I owe you."

Williams laughed that rumble of his. "Go to bed."

Which he did, for a few hours. But he didn't sleep. He'd been right. Orsini *was* in bed with the feds. Son of a bitch, Dante thought. How about that?

And what do I do with it?

Two o'clock. Seven hours until Pietrosanti was to call—*if* he called.

Somehow, a fleeting memory of being in combat in the jungles of Vietnam was strangely appealing.

XXXV

Two Days Later—Monday

"It's Santo Benedetti," Shelly said as she stood in the doorway to Dante's office. Standing in the doorway was Cuffs's version of an intercom.

"I didn't hear the phone ring."

"He's here. At the bar."

"Thanks. Do me a favor, Shell. Put him in nine." Nine was the most secluded booth in the restaurant. "And tell him I'll be out in a minute. Give him whatever he wants."

"He has some friends with him."

"Friends? Who?"

She laughed and pressed against the side of her nose with a finger.

"Get lost. I mean that. Get them what they want and go play checkers with Julio in the kitchen. Got it?"

"Oh, I certainly do, Mr. Dante. The last thing I need is to be in the middle of a mob hit." She gave him another nose-press as a parting gesture and left.

Dante drew a couple of breaths before heading for the bar. Santo seldom came to Cuffs, at least in the past few years. He used to come in often with friends, but his appearances had tailed off. There'd been some private parties thrown by Santo for which Dante had closed the place, and he'd used it a few times for a meeting, again necessitating

285

shutting the doors for the night. But this had to be a different visit. Different reasons. Dante didn't like it.

Santo was in booth nine when Dante arrived. Two Benedetti soldiers whom Dante recognized as Tommy Balls and Jake "The Ape" Cohen sat at a corner of the bar from where they could keep their eyes on Santo. Their boss wore a dark brown leather jacket over a black V-neck sweater, no shirt. A club soda with lime sat in front of him; he tapped a swizzle stick against the glass. This was serious. Santo was fond of quality alcoholic beverages, but never drank the hard stuff when what he was about to discuss had meaning.

Dante slid onto the booth opposite his friend. "You should have called," he said. "I would have had Julio whip up something special."

"I'm not here to eat, Paulie." He was stone-faced, his jaw an anvil.

"Lay it out for me," Dante replied. They'd known each other too long to waste time on polite preliminaries.

"You went to see my brother," he said. "After I asked you to back off."

"Time out," Dante said, making the T-sign of a referee at a football game. "Vincent sent Tommy around for me. He didn't act like I had a choice."

Santo visually probed Dante's face. Dante had the impression that his friend was trying to determine if he was lying.

"I just assumed Vincent had discussed it with you," Dante said. He obviously hadn't. The communications gap continued. Tommy must have told him.

Santo sipped from his drink. "My brother's confidence in Genaro isn't what it used to be."

And in *you*, Dante thought. He frowned. "You think it's because of me?" he asked.

"You haven't helped."

"That hurts, Santo."

"Don't start with the hurt-feelings crap, Paulie. I'm not interested in emotions. I've got a crisis situation building here and I have to deal with it before it gets out of hand."

"And you shut out everybody who wants to help, Santo, anybody who gives a shit about what happens to you."

"Meaning who?"

"Your brother. Me."

"You're telling me how to conduct myself with my brother?"

Dante sighed. "I don't want to get into word games like the last time, Santo." He shook his head. "You're more concerned about taking me on, beating me down because I kept after Genaro than you are with what I have to say, what I know about him. I can't win that one, Santo. I don't want to win that one." Dante ran a hand through his hair. "What do you want me to say, Santo? What do you want me to do? What the fuck do you want from me?"

"I want you to back off, like I asked you to last time."

"All right, so I didn't listen. But Santo, you've got to listen to *me*. I just found out that—" He stopped. Santo's eyes had suddenly focused on something over Dante's shoulder. Dante turned. A trio of female bikers had come through the front door and sat at the middle of the bar. They wore the torn jeans and high jackboots of their breed. Black leather jackets bore the insignia of their club: *"Diablos Negros"*—Black Devils. They were well known to Washington's MPD. The Black Devils patterned themselves after New York's infamous "Westies," an Irish gang whose penchant for violence rivaled the most vicious members of New York's five crime families.

"Nice crowd you get in here these days," Santo said.

"Never saw them before," Dante replied. "Must have seen the Cuffs sign and figured it was an S-and-M joint."

Pete, the bartender, had just come on duty. He placed six Budweisers on the bar in front of them. Two apiece. Trouble, Dante thought. Bad timing, ladies. Tommy Balls and the Ape looked distinctly unsure about what their next move should be.

Santo continued to stare at the women in black. One of them glared back at him, then made mocking impressions of how he looked to her companions.

"You let that kind of garbage hang out in your place, Paulie?"

"It's a public establishment," Dante answered. "I don't have much choice unless they make trouble. Right now, all they're doing is sucking beers."

The door opened and three male companions dressed in the same uniforms entered and joined the women at the bar. The one who'd been making faces at Santo said something into the ear of one of the men and pointed in the direction of the booth.

"Forget them, Santo," Dante said. "Let's get back to what we were discussing."

"What did my brother ask you to do?"

Dante shook his head.

"You won't tell me?"

"It's not that I don't want to, Santo. It's just that I don't know why you have to ask me about a meeting with your brother. I've never gotten between you and Vincent before."

"Exactly."

"Talk to *him*, Santo. Ask *him* why he wanted me to drive him around. Ask *him* what we talked about."

"I'm talking to you," Santo said. Then he yelled to the bar, "What the fuck are you looking at?"

"Not too fuckin' much," one of the male bikers replied.

"Whoa," Dante said, standing. "Let's everybody calm down here. Pete, buy them a round. I don't want any trouble from nobody in my place," he said to Santo.

"You don't get rid of trouble by wishing it away, Paulie," Santo said. "Once you start something—"

"I started *this*?" Dante said, sitting again.

"You miss my point."

"I guess I do."

Santo sipped his club soda, looked at the bikers, then said to Dante, "You started something with my son-in-law, and now it's getting away from you. Like it's got a mind of its own. It's fucking up too many relationships, yours and mine, yours and my brother's, me and my brother's."

"And you want me to make it right again?"

"Right. By getting off Genaro's fuckin' back, Paulie." He grabbed Dante's forearm. "Listen to me. Get out of Genaro's life, out of Lucia's life. You hear me? You get out and I'll make it right again for everybody."

"And you won't even consider that your son-in-law may be into something that could hurt you, hurt your brother, hurt the whole family?"

"That's the point, Paulie. It is family. We'll take care of it like family."

Dante knew his frustration was spilling over but he couldn't contain it. "Santo," he said, "Vincent sent Tommy to me. Vincent said he wanted me to drive him. That's how it happened. It wasn't me poking my nose into something."

Santo sat back and sent a stream of breath into the air. "I know," he said softly. "Look, I got no quarrel with you, Paulie. You understand what all this crap about Genaro does to me?"

Santo had now put the conversation onto more human, personal grounds. Dante felt for his friend. He said, "Of course I do. There's Lucia."

In a gesture of helplessness, Santo extended his hands to Dante. "You understand, Paulie? It's my family. My close family. My daughter."

"Shit," Dante muttered, angry at his inability to offer anything of usefulness to his friend, a condition he'd experienced too many times over the years. Genaro Orsini was Santo's cross to bear. No one could help him carry it.

"You want a drink?" Dante asked. "I have some good cognac in the office." He grinned. "I can't leave it out. Pete will water it down and sell it. I got a bottle of single-barrel bourbon, too. The best. I got it after I tasted some at Lucia's wedding. Rock Hill."

"No, but thanks. Look, I'm sorry I barged in on you like this, bent your ear." A small smile came to his face as he cuffed Dante on the side of his head. "It doesn't matter much anymore."

"Why do you say that?"

"Vincent didn't tell you?"

"Vincent didn't tell me nothing except how the British blew it at Easton." Santo cocked his head. "Some piece of history your brother laid on me. What do you mean it doesn't matter anymore?"

"Things are going to be okay for Vincent. Real soon. It's worked out."

Dante's blank face said he didn't know what Santo was talking about. He searched his friend's face for clues but none were there.

"I gotta go, Paulie."

Then, it hit Dante as though he'd been slapped. Vincent was leaving, probably leaving the country. For Sicily. For his "eternal spring."

"He's leaving?"

Before Santo could respond, Dante added, "Does Genaro know about this?" The mention of the name returned hurt and anger to Santo's eyes.

Christ, Dante thought. Orsini probably knows about whatever plans have been made for Vincent, which means the feds would know too.

"Santo, listen to me," Dante said. "Listen close to me. Last night, I—"

"Fuck you, you gutter scum," Santo yelled over Dante's shoulder.

Dante spun around. One of the male bikers had left the bar and was approaching the booth. Santo's bodyguards sat ramrod straight, their hands on weapons beneath their jackets, eyes on Santo in search of guidance.

The biker didn't have the angry look Dante expected in response to Santo's verbal challenge. His face was eerily calm, and bore a faint smile. Santo reached inside his jacket, but the biker turned and headed for the door.

Dante got up and intercepted him as he was about to leave Cuffs. "Don't bring any iron into my place," he said. His voice was no-nonsense, matter-of-fact.

"What the fuck you talking about?" the biker said.

"Go back and join your friends," Dante said. "Have another round on me. Forget about whatever's in your saddlebag outside. It's got no place in here. Understand?"

"You gotta be shitting me. You hear the way that motherfucker talked to me?"

"He's had a tough day, son, but he and his friends will be leaving soon."

"I don't give a shit about his tough day," the biker said.

"Lemme lay a little advice on you, fuckface," Dante said. "You go out and grab whatever it is that gives you a cock and you and your friends are dead. The man is important. The man doesn't take lightly to having pimple-faced young broads making fun of him. The man would like to see you and your friends dead. The important thing, asshole, is that he can make it happen. Understand? I run a nice place here. I treat all my customers the same. I bought you a coupla rounds, didn't I? This is a civilized eating establishment. Fine cuisine. Go on, get back to the bar and enjoy my hospitality."

"Nobody says what that fuck said to me."

"I've been nice to you, kid. I'm tired of being nice. You got a choice, only now it's different. You and your moron friends get up and leave, or the man and his friends at the bar, which includes me, turns these pretty black leather jackets of yours into red. We stuff the pockets with your eyes and balls, and the garbage men pick you outta the Dumpster in the morning." Dante smiled. "Your choice, Marlon. But make it fast."

The biker studied Dante's face. He saw ice. "Then tell the fucker to knock it off," he said.

"No. *You* knock it off. Pack it up. You give the place a bad image."

Dante returned to the booth. He and Santo watched the bikers leave, their muffled growls of protest trailing behind them.

"What the fuck was that all about?" Santo asked.

"Customer service," Dante said. "I suggested they look for service elsewhere. Let me get back to what I was saying. Last night, I found out that your son-in-law is—"

Santo stood abruptly. He waved to his men at the bar, who quickly came to him. "So long, Paulie," Santo said, dropping a twenty on the table.

"On the house," Dante said.

"A buyback on the first round is bad business," Santo said.

"Not for a very good and old friend," Dante answered.

"That's right," Santo said. "A very *old* friend." He left the restaurant, followed closely by his protectors.

Dante slumped in the booth. Pete came to him and said, "Punks, huh? You want a drink?"

"He won't listen," Dante said.

"Who?"

"It doesn't matter. There's a half-bottle of good cognac in my desk drawer in the office. Go get it and fill a snifter for me."

"You okay, Paulie?"

"One thing I'm not is okay. He won't listen. But I can't do anymore. Get the cognac, Pete. If we had a piano player, I'd tell him to play the blues."

Later, as Dante sat in his apartment finishing the last of the cognac, he thought of Victor of Victor and Armbruster. He called the office. An answering machine.

He dug out Victor's home number and dialed it. The man who answered didn't sound like the same Victor Dante was used to hearing. "What's the matter?" Dante asked. "You sound drunk."

"Hard to talk, Dante. My controller paid me a visit with a gorilla a few weeks ago. They knew you were here at my house, didn't like it, thought we might be talking about them."

Dante's stomach tightened. "What did they do to you, Victor?"

"Not much. Four busted fingers and my lips stapled shut. Sorry I don't sound so good. I got a mouth full of sores and scabs."

"I'll make this up to you," Dante said. "I'm sorry. I know I dragged you in."

"Yeah. Well, it's over. Take care, man. He's crazy. He gets off on hurt, you know?"

"You take care too, Victor. I'll be back to you."

———

Special Agent Tom Whelan had told Thornton it was an emergency. Whelan was livid, and Thornton had said to come right over.

"He pushed the woman off an eleventh-floor balcony at the Watergate Friday night and he acts as though we can fix it, like the judges his father-in-law has in his pocket to fix parking tickets."

"Does MPD have anything yet?" Thornton asked.

"They're running the latents. It's just a matter of time." Whelan drew a deep breath, rubbed his eyes, and said, "Orsini laughed when he told me what he did. He actually laughed. He's fuckin' crazy. He's killed a woman. We're dealing with a crazy here."

"Get a grip on yourself, Agent Whelan. There are larger issues at stake here. Slow the MPD down. Tell them it's out of their jurisdiction, that it involves one of our people. A witness. A damned important witness."

"And when they find out she worked at the casino the Benedettis have a piece of? That she and Gerry-boy have been seen around together? That someone, anyone who had seen him in the hotel that night . . . ?"

"We need to buy time," Thornton said. "Think this through. And whatever you do, keep his name out of the papers. Pull rank on MPD. This is federal. Do whatever you have to."

"Okay," Whelan said, "but this guy's running amuck. He thinks he can do whatever he wants, and we come in and mop up. I mean the son of a bitch admits to murdering a woman, laughs about it, and we end up taking his side."

"A psychopath."

"Yes, sir, he is."

"And our best witness against Benedetti."

"Yes, sir. He's fed us a lot of good information. We've got Benedetti under RICO now. Frankly, I hate Orsini. If it was my decision, I—"

"I'll square this up top," Thornton said. "I think we'd better square this away all the way around, the quicker the better. You say you have enough for RICO?"

"Yes, sir. That's our opinion."

"Then we'd better start thinking about moving Orsini."

"Moving him?"

"Into the program. Bring the case against Vincent Benedetti to the grand jury and get this crazy son of a bitch out of circulation before he screws us." Thornton pursed his lips and grunted. "You trust him?" he asked.

"As an informer? Yes."

"No possibility he might start feeding us bad info about Benedetti?"

"I don't think so, sir. He's scum in the best sense of the word, but he won't backstab us. We have too much on him."

"Okay. But until we're ready to move on Benedetti, keep a damn close eye on him. Maybe you trust him, but I sure as hell don't."

The Next Day—Tuesday

Santo called a sitdown of the inner circle on short notice. He sat rigid at the head of the table, his stern look never breaking, dark shadow lines striping his face from the intentionally low lighting. The room was as somber as a prayer chapel. His announcement was brief:

"Vincent will be leaving us for a while."

Confusion swept around the table.

Santo continued: "He has decided it will serve the best interests of our family if he departs from the scene until we can straighten out the legal problems he's having. The lawyers and accountants who, as you know, are the best that money can buy, are working on the situation and report steady progress. Vincent, however, has decided that things cannot proceed smoothly if he has to be constantly worried about his own security. He'll go to a safe place, outside the country where we'll have freer access to him. He'll be leaving soon. The destination will be revealed to you after he's gone. I have nothing more to add, and I won't answer questions. I expect you to be available twenty-four hours a day until Vincent's departure. Genaro, I need a word with you. Everybody else can go."

Tommy Guardino escorted the group to the door. When they were gone, Santo turned to his son-in-law. "I have an especially important assignment for you," he said.

"However I can be of help, Santo."

295

"Vincent will need a large sum of money to take with him. You will be the one to deliver it to him."

———

The thought of the suitcases—and their contents—had his thoughts spinning. In the trunk of Orsini's Lexus the next day were four brand-new American Touristers, each with a quarter million dollars in bills of different denominations, old bills, out-of-sequence bills. The cash had been laundered through the Atlantic City casino, and Paddy Provenzano and a team of people there had worked all night to get it together.

As he drove back to Washington from Atlantic City, his heart palpitated. He was short of breath as he thought of the bounty in the trunk. Only a father-in-law would send him on a mission like this. Only a father-in-law who wanted to believe in him, *had* to believe in him because of his pathetic daughter, would do it. Not even his own father would have trusted him on such a mission. His own father knew him better than Santo Benedetti. The thought caused Orsini to laugh.

The don would be spirited away on a freighter out of the cargo terminal in Baltimore Harbor. The money Orsini was to deliver was to help him get set up in his new life. A million bucks just to get set up? And then what? Hang around with other old Sicilians whose teeth had turned yellow and play *bocce*, or Sicilian card games like *bris-cola* or *trisette?* And at night? Sit in his marble bathroom with gold fixtures and jerk off to Italian skin books?

A waste of money. He, Orsini, could get some real use out of it. He rolled down the window and lit up a cigarette. He had to think this through, had to clear his mind.

It was time to get out. How long, he wondered, could his role as a paid informer for the FBI be kept secret from the family? The walls were closing in; the enemy was circling. Paul Dante was obsessed with showing him up to Santo and Vincent. That was evident in Atlantic City. He should have told his men to kill Dante, not just rough him up in an elevator. He'd had Dante followed all over Washington, and a good thing he had. You couldn't trust a nigger like Victor to keep his mouth shut. Orsini smiled as he recalled the scene in Victor's office. That was one nigger who wouldn't talk again.

Orsini knew that Vincent didn't like him, only tolerated him out of respect for his brother, and compassion for his goddaughter.

No, it was time to fold, to testify for the government, as the agreement called for and to disappear into the witness-protection program. Whelan had told him only the other day that Orsini's information from inside the family had put together a solid RICO case against Vincent. It was time.

Until now, the contemplation of losing his identity and spending the rest of his life in hiding had not been a pleasant one. He'd considered not letting Whelan know that Vincent would be on the move, pretending that it had taken him by surprise because it had been kept even from the made members of the inner circle. But that would have been hard to sell. He'd have to tell Whelan, just as he now had to get out of the family while he still could. A healthy piece of the million dollars earmarked for Vincent would ease the pain.

Although Santo hadn't said as much, he'd intimated that Vincent would be going somewhere in Sicily. Orsini had checked the cargo-ship departures in the business section of the Baltimore *Sun*. There was only one ship scheduled to leave Baltimore for Italy that week, the *Quattro Stagioni*. It was due to sail in the early-morning hours of Friday, less than forty-eight hours away. That had to be it.

He arrived at the Georgetown house and dragged the four suitcases into the living room where Vincent sat reading a magazine. Santo had just left.

"Here it is, Vincent," Orsini said. "All of it."

Vincent slowly opened each case and made a cursory check of the contents.

Aren't you even going to count it? Orsini almost quipped. But this was no time to get cute. The possibility that anyone in the Benedetti family would try to short Vincent would never enter the old man's mind. Stupid!

"Put these upstairs in a closet somewhere," Vincent said. "And then leave me alone. I need time to myself for the next few hours."

"You got it, Vincent," Orsini said. "I'll take care of it. You don't have to worry about a thing with the money. I won't let it out of my sight."

Orsini took the suitcases to a small office he maintained on the third floor of the house. He was winded from carrying them up and sat motionless, staring at a blank wall for the next few minutes. Finally, he went to the landing and called down to Lucia, who came to the foot of the stairs. "Listen, baby," he said, "I got some serious paperwork to deal with up here. I don't want to be disturbed until dinner. Okay?"

"Sure," she answered. "I'll call you when it's ready."

Orsini closed the door to his office and locked it. He went to a closet where he kept supplies and removed several reams of paper and cut it into stacks the length and width of paper currency. Next, he opened the suitcases and systematically went through the stacks of bills, removing their rubber bands, taking them from the bottom stacks and replacing the missing money with cut paper which he sandwiched between the real bills. In all, he removed more than a quarter-million dollars and shoved it into his own large leather briefcase. He put the briefcase underneath his desk, came downstairs, and went to the kitchen. "I'm out of cigarettes," he told Lucia. "Be back in a minute."

"I wish you'd quit," she said pleasantly.

"I think I will." He kissed her on the cheek, left the house, and went to a tobacco shop on Wisconsin Avenue where he stepped into a phone booth.

FBI Special Agent Tom Whelan answered.

"The family's on to me," was his opener. "I gotta get out."

"Whoa, wait a minute," Whelan said. "What do you mean they're on to you?"

"They're on to me. What do you think I mean? They know about you guys, my relationship with you."

"How did they find out? What happened?"

"How the fuck do I know? They just know."

"How do you know they know?"

"I'm a member of the family. Remember? I know what goes on inside."

Whelan didn't respond immediately. Then, he said, "Sounds like you're getting cold feet, Gerry-boy. That's all it is. No one's confronted you, have they?"

"Confronted me? Confronted me? Do you think I'd be talking to you now if they'd confronted me? It's instincts. I know what I know."

"Hang on a little longer. We don't have the exit plan in place yet."

"The exit plan? Hey, I don't need any of your fed bullshit. *They* have an exit plan ready for me and it ain't the one you're talking about."

"We're not ready yet. We're close, but I need another couple of days."

"You don't have a couple of days."

"Why?"

Orsini hesitated before saying, "Vincent's leaving. He's getting out."

"What!"

"He's getting out. Leaving for Italy. The cargo terminal, Baltimore Harbor. Two A.M. Friday morning. A ship called the *Quattro Stagioni*."

"And I had to pry that out of you? What do we pay you for?"

"You don't pay me shit."

"How long have you known this?"

"Today."

"I have to move on this, Gerry. Now."

"That's what I said, didn't I?"

Whelan was silent.

"Well," Orsini said impatiently, "what do you say?"

"I'll get back to you. We have to set up an intercept."

"Just don't forget about me."

"Call me again," Whelan said. "Give me—three hours. Then call me."

"You better be there."

"I'll be here."

———

Orsini's mood at dinner was upbeat and pleasant. Vincent had asked Lucia to bring his food down to him, which meant Orsini didn't have to deal with the old man's penetrating looks on this, the last night he would have to endure the don's company.

The conversation at the table was light and playful, which pleased Lucia. She hadn't seen that side of her husband for months. It was as though a weight had been lifted from his shoulders. They talked of starting a family: "Time we had a little Orsini," he said. Their future was discussed: "I told Paddy that I was through working nights at the casino. No way to live, Lucy. From now on, I'll be home here for you and the kid. I want to change the way we live. Hey, we live in a great city, huh? The Kennedy Center's right around the corner. So's the museums. We should start takin' those things in, living a little. How's that sound?"

Lucia: "I love the sound of it. I'm so pleased."

The prospects of upcoming tense moments didn't concern Orsini. The mechanisms were in place. He had everybody under his control and he liked the feeling. It was as though someone had injected him with a megadose of steroids. He was king of the hill. Always had been.

The feds had no choice but to go along with him. They had forced him into this mess and now, as always, he held all the picture cards; the pot was big.

He'd never looked forward to the moment when his true identity would be revealed and he would have his final confrontation with the Benedettis. But that was before he had gotten to know them better; before he had had to endure the demeaning looks of Vincent; the demands of having to suffer through a life with Lucia; before he'd had to worry about going head to head with Santo.

Now, as the confrontation was about to take place, he savored it. He relished being part of the final act, the ultimate takedown. The contemplation energized him.

He would enjoy watching them squirm when the feds moved in. Knowing that the government wouldn't be able to conclude it without his testimony, he'd be center-stage. It was where he belonged.

He told Lucia after dinner that he needed a walk to digest the wonderful meal she'd prepared. He frequently checked his watch as he strolled Georgetown. When it was precisely three hours since he last talked to Whelan, he entered a phone booth and made his second call.

"Okay," Whelan said. "Vincent will be arrested at the ship. You'll be busted too to make you look legit."

"Thanks for seeing the light," Orsini said.

"Look," Whelan said, "I don't need any of your crap right about now. I've got a lot to do, so I'll be saying good-bye."

"Just one more thing," Orsini said.

"What's that?"

"The reward."

"What reward?"

"The fifty grand for turning in Vincent."

Whelan laughed. "There's no reward and you know it."

"Bullshit. I get the fifty or I testify to nothing. I don't testify, you got zip on Vincent except that stupid tax setup and jumping bail. I testify, you got your fucking RICO case."

"Jesus, Gerry," Whelan moaned. "I don't need this. That reward was phony. A sham. There is no fifty grand."

"You don't have a bigger problem than this one, *Tommy-boy*. I get the bread, or none of this comes down like you planned."

"We'll take it under advisement."

"No good. I got to know what I'm coming out of this with."

"We'll talk tomorrow."

"I gotta know now."

"I can't make that decision myself."

"Tough."

"Okay," Whelan said. "Okay. Fifty grand to you—you slimy cocksucker."

Orsini grinned. "The feeling is entirely mutual." He said as he hung up.

XXXVii

The Next Night—Thursday

Julia had suggested a quiet dinner at her place.

Dante had found it impossible to relax since the previous weekend when he learned that Orsini was having clandestine meetings with federal agents, and undoubtedly had pushed his strawberry blonde off a balcony at the Watergate. He had a tightness in his chest that felt as though he were growing a fist beneath his breastbone and between his lungs. He had no idea what the resolution would be of the Vincent-Santo-Orsini-Pietrosanti affair. He was sure of only one thing—it was going to be messy.

As he sat at the table with Julia, his overriding concern was being on the outs with Santo for the first time in his life. That certainly hadn't been his intention. But as his mother had often said, the road to hell is paved with good intentions. He declined Julia's offer of another helping of mashed potatoes kissed with garlic.

She was determined to talk about anything but Orsini and the Benedettis. After dinner, they sat in the living room watching a TV "investigative reporting" show and sipped cognac. Julia had hoped that the subjects being investigated would involve a series of bizarre sexual practices that would get Dante's mind off his work and in the mood for some post-dinner frolicking. Her plans were dashed, however, by the lead-in to the show. The host, whose hairpiece was as obvious as the fact he read from a TelePrompTer, said they would be interviewing Attorney General Stanley Simonsen.

"Let me find something else," Julia said, reaching for the remote control.

"No, leave it on," Dante said.

Simonsen talked about major steps his department was taking to alleviate the menace of organized crime across the nation; how successful they had been using the RICO laws to put away underworld kingpins for long stretches; how that was breaking up the mob and pushing organized crime into permanent disarray.

"And there are more dramatic moves coming," Simonsen told the interviewer.

Dante started to make a comment but Julia cut him off. "Can we watch something else?" she asked. "I'm really tired of hearing about organized crime. If it's not from you, it's coming at me from the TV."

"Suit yourself," Dante said. "Simonsen's a whore, like the rest of the Justice Department. Go ahead. Click."

"How about turning off the TV and putting on some music?" she suggested.

"Sure," he said. "Mind if I use the phone?"

"Of course not."

He called his answering machine for messages. There was one from Cal Williams. Dante dialed the number Williams had left.

"Your friend, Orsini," Williams said, "is about to make a big change in his life."

"What are you talking about?"

"He's calling in accounts around the neighborhood, more frantic than usual, and talking like somebody who won't be back. He's demanding settlement on all his outstanding accounts."

"Where did you get this, Cal?"

"We put people on him after that woman took a dive at the Watergate. His prints were all over the place. They told us to lay off, so we did it quiet."

"Who told you to lay off?"

"Big Brother. Hey, my friend, I just work here. And I figured you'd want to know what was happening. Was I wrong?"

"No. You were right. Lay it out for me."

"Not that hard to figure. Orsini must have something else going. Considering his sense of urgency, I got to figure he's going with it."

"Thanks, Cal," Dante said. "Hey, I thought you were staying clear of me for a while."

"What can I say? I got this sense of obligation to a dumb wop who saved this black ass more than once. See ya."

"What is it?" Julia asked when Dante hung up on Williams. She'd put on an album of the Count Basie Orchestra playing Broadway show tunes.

"There are more big moves coming," Dante said, repeating what the attorney general had said. "The bastard's leaving. Orsini's going into the program and the feds are going to make their move on Vincent. Orsini was involved in the sting that set up Vincent. He talks to the feds. He grabs money wherever he can swindle it, and now he's calling in his chips. Why? It's a setup, Julia. The big bust is coming down. They know Vincent's planning to leave and they're going to nail him."

"You're assuming a lot, Paul."

"Yeah, I know. But my assumptions have kept me alive for a lot of years. I always assumed there was a Vietcong in a tree, and there sure as hell was. I always assumed there had to be somebody else in a tenement we busted for drugs and there he was, semiautomatic and all. Yeah, Julia, I'm assuming a lot, and I have to go with my assumptions. Besides, I got a little more than just assumptions this time."

"Forgive me for asking this," she said, "but what is it you can *do* about any of this?"

"I've got to get to Santo."

"And tell him what?"

"I've got to warn him about Vincent. He's in danger."

"Based on your gut reaction to what Simonsen said on one of those dreadful TV shows, and the fact that his son-in-law has decided to press the lowlifes into paying what they owe him? I'm beginning to see why Santo wonders about you."

Dante threw her a hard look. "I'll pretend you didn't say that," he said.

She immediately softened. "I'm sorry, Paul, but I don't want to see you hurt."

He kissed her without emotion. "I've got to go," he said. "Got to pick somebody up and get over to Santo's. I'll call you tomorrow."

"Paul," she said.

"Yeah?"

"Be careful." He started to move away but she grabbed his arm. "I'm frightened," she said. "For you. For me. It's a life I don't understand."

He kissed her again, this time with feeling. "Don't worry, baby," he said. "I'm a big boy. I can take care of myself. And I'll take care of you."

———

They announced Dante from the gate. The Benedetti soldier eyed Dante's passenger. "He'll wait in the car," Dante said.

Dom Piaggio let Dante in the front door. "Wait in the big study. Okay?"

"Sure."

"Santo's on the phone. He knows you're here."

As Dante waited, he thought the time might make him less confident about what he had to say, might shake his composure the way a long time-out rattles a placekicker before attempting a game-winning field goal. But the more he thought about it, the more convinced he became that he had to confront Santo.

No matter what the ramifications.

The door opened and Santo stood in the threshold. "What is it, Paul?" he said. "I'm busy."

"Santo," Dante said, standing and taking a step toward his friend. "We have to talk."

XXXViii

Friday Night

Tommy Guardino arrived at Orsini's Georgetown house at precisely midnight. The four suitcases of money were lined neatly abreast in the foyer. Vincent made a last-minute adjustment to the knot in his tie. "Let's go," he said.

Orsini kissed Lucia on the cheek and the three men headed for the black Mercury. The suitcases were stacked in the trunk. "Up front with me," Tommy told Orsini. "Vincent likes to stretch out."

Vincent settled into his customary silence and Tommy concentrated on the road. There was little traffic.

"Well," Orsini said, turning to Vincent. "I bet you're happy to get out of here."

"This is not what I would have preferred," Vincent replied.

"Of course," Orsini said. "But you'll be safer in Italy. And you'll still run the family. I thank God for that."

Vincent closed his eyes. Orsini squared himself in his seat and looked ahead.

Tommy took the off-ramp at the Route Forty-six exit and pointed the Mercury in the direction of Baltimore-Washington International Airport.

"The harbor's straight ahead, isn't it?" Orsini asked.

"I know where I'm going," Tommy said.

"What are we taking, the long way around?" Orsini asked.

When Tommy didn't reply, Orsini turned to Vincent.

"There's been a change in plans," the don said. "I'm leaving by air. But first we meet with Santo at a company we own near the airport."

"Why the last-minute change?" Orsini asked, his voice betraying his anxiety.

"Because it makes sense," Vincent said.

"How so?" Orsini pressed.

"I don't need to explain," Vincent said. The subject was closed.

I've got to get to a phone, Orsini thought.

At Camp Meade Road, Tommy took the cloverleaf exit, then headed southwest until he brought the car to a stop in front of a building that housed a light-manufacturing company. It was modern stone-and-glass design and was situated in a small industrial park on the airport's perimeter. A burnished metal sign above the door read: LIFE-SAVER POOL COVERS. A blue Lincoln Continental sat alone in a parking space in front of the entrance.

Tommy pulled alongside the Lincoln and turned off the engine. He got out and opened the rear door for Vincent. Orsini, carrying his brown leather briefcase filled with what he'd skimmed from Vincent's money, warily exited through the front passenger door.

Vincent led the way to the front door where Big Dom Piaggio ushered them inside. Piaggio stayed outside with Tommy Guardino.

Vincent strode at a brisk pace down the corridor, Orsini a few steps behind. They passed business offices with computer stations and a large engineering/drafting room with drawing tables and oversized computer monitors. The don opened a door at the end of the corridor that brought them into a testing area and warehouse. Piles of dark green plastic sheets the texture of body bags, from which the company's pool covers were fashioned, occupied much of the floor space.

Santo emerged from a small supervisor's office that jutted out from a wall in the testing area. He greeted them and told Vincent there would be a delay while the aircraft's two-man crew went through its preflight checks.

"Not ready?" Orsini questioned.

Vincent did not seem concerned.

"Anything I can do for anybody?" Orsini asked, exhibiting a wide friendly grin. "Want me to get the suitcases?"

The door behind them opened and Tommy and Dom entered, each carrying two of the cases. Santo pointed to the supervisor's office. "In there," he said.

"I saw a water fountain on the way in," Orsini said, not adding that he'd seen telephones, too. "I'm thirsty as a dog. Anybody want some water?"

Santo pointed to a water cooler next to the supervisor's office.

"Right, right," Orsini said. "Didn't see it." He pulled a paper cup from a cylinder attached to the cooler, and filled it.

"Feeling okay, Vincent?" Santo asked his brother.

"I feel good," Vincent said. "Very good."

"What's holdin' up those fuckin' pilots?" Orsini asked.

"You don't rush pilots, Genaro," Santo said. "It can be bad for your health." The crew of the sleek Cessna Citation V business jet were pilots-for-hire and had been used by the Benedettis before. Most of their work, however, came from drug smugglers, something Santo and Vincent chose to ignore.

"So far, so good," Santo said to Vincent. "In a few minutes you'll be out of here and safe."

Orsini paced nervously.

Tommy emerged from the office and whispered something to Santo. Both men entered the office and closed the door. Minutes later, Santo reemerged. "There's a problem," he said.

"Problem?" Vincent replied.

"Your money. It's light." He removed a stack of bills from his jacket and fanned it, revealing the cut pieces of blank paper. "There are a lot of these." He turned to Orsini. "You got any theories about this, Genaro?"

"Shit!" Orsini said. "Those bastards at the casino fucked you."

"At the casino?"

"Sure. Where I picked up the money. What else?"

"Interesting. Why do you say that?"

"They were the only ones to handle the money. Them . . . and me."

"Yes."

"Santo, you don't think I'd . . . ?"

Santo stared at his son-in-law. "Everything at the casino is recorded on videotape, Genaro. The cameras taped Paddy and his people pulling the money together. That was my instruction to them. Want to take a look at the tapes?"

"Here? You have them here?"

"Yeah. I have them here. But we won't have to waste time looking at them." He called toward the supervisor's office, "Bring him out."

Stepping into the bright fluorescent light, escorted by Dom Piaggio, was a man in a dark blue sharkskin suit. "Hello, Gerry," he said.

Orsini's eyes widened, then relaxed. He grinned at Santo and hunched his shoulders. "Who is this guy anyway?" he asked. "I don't know him."

"I do." The answer came from Vincent. "I wish I could say I was happy to see you, Mr. Pietrosanti, but that would be a lie."

"I guess it would be," Pietrosanti said. "But we're gonna fix all that."

The smile was gone from Orsini's face. His head jerked back and forth in search of an escape, and he reached inside his jacket. But the iron grip of Tommy Guardino's left forearm was around his neck before he could free his Beretta from its shoulder holster. "Drop it," Tommy said. Orsini brought the weapon into the light and dropped it to the cement floor. Orsini gasped in pain as Tommy wrenched his right arm behind his back.

Defenseless in the crunching grip, Orsini faced his father-in-law. "Santo, I was trapped," he blurted out. "They didn't give me any choice."

"They told you to bring in my brother?" Santo said.

"Yes," Orsini said in a voice mirroring the pain in his arm and shoulder. "It was all their idea, Santo. Believe me. They made me go along."

"They made you steal from us?"

"You don't understand," was all Orsini could manage before Tommy tightened his grip and forced him to his knees.

Santo stepped forward. "Vincent predicted what you would do if left alone with the money. I'm sorry he was right."

Orsini started to sob and lowered his head as though to kiss Santo's shoes.

"You dishonored my daughter. Did you ever think of that?"

Orsini looked up; tears rolled down his cheeks. "They made me do that, too."

"To marry her?" Santo was now shouting.

"That's right. But I love her, Santo. You gotta believe that. I would do anything for her. Ask her. Tell her to talk to you about how much we love and respect each other. Think about her, Santo. Think about what it will do to her."

Santo spit into Orsini's raised face. "Don't you mention my daughter's name again. Don't ever say anything again." He turned toward the exit. "Let's go," he told Vincent. "You've got a long trip ahead of you."

"Please," Orsini called after them. "I can help you. I can help you with the case against Vincent."

Santo spun around. "The way you planned to help him tonight?"

"No," Orsini cried out. "Not like that. Not like tonight."

Orsini struggled against Tommy's grip but the bodyguard's hold showed no sign of weakening. Then, from the corner of his eye, Orsini saw Joey Balls and Jake "The Ape" Cohen emerge from the office. They stood next to Santo and looked down at Orsini. "You fuckin' scumbag," Joey Balls said. "I knew all along what you were, you piece a shit." The Ape, his shaved head gleaming in the fluorescent lights, said nothing. His small black eyes said more to Orsini than any words could.

"So long, Genaro," Santo said. He said to Joey and the Ape, "Give my daughter a divorce."

"Nooo," Orsini cried as Dom Piaggio gripped his head and the

Ape pried open his mouth. Joey Balls removed a small, six-inch folding knife from his pocket and carefully unfolded the blade. Then, with his left hand, he removed a pair of pliers from another pocket. The Ape stretched Orsini's mouth open to its breaking point. Joey thrust the open pliers into his mouth and squeezed the jaws closed on Orsini's tongue. "You fuck," he said, raising the knife.

Charlie Pietrosanti was relieved he didn't have to stick around for the ending. He knew from the moment Dante brought him into Santo Benedetti's house and had him tell his story about Orsini that it was over for that member of the Benedetti family. As much as he hated Orsini, being there for his execution was not the kind of thing he relished. Violence sickened him.

He breathed easier now that he was aboard the sleek twin-engine business jet heading out over the Atlantic, Brazil his ultimate destination. It was part of what he'd asked for—a trip out of the country. The money, he was told, would be there for him when they arrived in Rio.

He would have preferred to travel alone; being in the plane with Vincent was unsettling, especially since the old don had said virtually nothing from the moment they'd boarded. But maybe that was okay. Leave well enough alone.

He had to say one thing about Vincent Benedetti. He was a man of honor, a man of his word. So was Paul Dante. Sometimes you get lucky. Pietrosanti found a more comfortable position in his leather seat and glanced through a copy of *Time* magazine.

He looked back to where Orsini's body, wrapped in dark-green plastic, rested on the floor at the rear of the passenger compartment. You asked for it, Pietrosanti thought. Dumb bastard. You had it made being married to Santo Benedetti's daughter. Couldn't really blame him, I guess. The feds had struck a tough deal with him. They must have really squeezed Orsini's balls to put him in that situation.

Pietrosanti had heard Vincent's bodyguard, Tommy Guardino, and the guy they called Big Dom discussing how Orsini's body would be disposed of once they were out to sea. He was anxious for them to get

that over with so he could really relax. He reminded himself to keep his
seat belt fastened to keep from being sucked out when they opened the
jet's door.

Tommy, after conferring with Vincent, went to the cockpit and
instructed the pilots to bring the aircraft down to an altitude of a
hundred feet over the water and to slow airspeed to just above stalling.
Pietrosanti sensed the change in altitude. It was time. He decided not to
look when they did it. He thought of Carla and their son in Las Vegas.
They deserved a bonus. He'd send it as soon as possible. A hundred
grand. Maybe two hundred.

Tommy Guardino and Big Dom removed their seat belts and
headed toward the rear of the plane. The co-pilot came from the cockpit
and joined them. The aircraft had slowed considerably and had begun
to circle. Come on, get it over with, Charlie said silently. Let's go. Get
up high again where it's safe.

The co-pilot released a latch, swung the door handle through a
complete three-sixty degrees, and pulled the door inward, then up and
out of the way. There was a rush of cold air, and the loud sound of the
backdraft whistling along the fuselage.

"Ready?" Tommy asked Big Dom.

"Yeah."

They lifted the green plastic bag, swung it back and forth a few
times and with one final heave tossed it out of the aircraft and into the
choppy sea below.

"Fucker didn't make much of a splash," Tommy shouted.

"In that chop?" Piaggio said. "Who the fuck would notice?"

"Good meal for the sharks, huh?" Tommy said.

The co-pilot started to close the door but Big Dom stopped him.
"We got one more thing to do," he whispered.

Pietrosanti had avoided watching the scene at the door. But then
two sets of large hands yanked him from his seat, their efforts impeded
by his seat belt.

"What the fuck?" Pietrosanti said.

Tommy threw a grip around his neck and Piaggio released the belt.
"Oh, no, man. Nooooo!"

He was lifted from the seat and dragged to the open door, his feet desperately trying to dig into the carpeting. When they reached the door, Tommy pulled the replica of Charlie's gaudy good-luck ring from his finger.

"Mr. Benedetti!—Vincent!" Pietrosanti cried. The old don never turned as his two soldiers pushed the ex-financier out into the night air.

"Didn't make much of a splash, either," Tommy said.

"Small men," Piaggio said, "big ocean."

"Shut the door," Vincent said. "It's cold."

The co-pilot pulled the door down, secured it and returned to the cockpit. As the aircraft climbed to cruising altitude and speed, Tommy handed Pietrosanti's ring to Vincent and settled down to read *Newsweek*.

———

From his vantage point in an office building across from the cargo berth of the *Quattro Stagioni*, Special Agent Tom Whelan picked up the mobile phone and dialed the number of Assistant Attorney General Willard Thornton. He'd waited as long as their patience would allow. "Nothing," he said. "They didn't show."

"Do you think they got delayed someplace?"

"No."

"Do we know they left Georgetown?"

"I got a call from the stakeout at the house two hours ago, and then from the checkpoint on the expressway when they went by. That was the last contact. You know we didn't want to spook them with a tail. We knew when they were leaving and where they were headed. Should have been good enough."

"Maybe they're taking a long way around. Changed their route. Something like that." Thornton's voice testified to wishful thinking.

"I don't think so. The ship is about to weigh anchor."

"Well, stop her, goddamn it."

"Okay, but the dock's been covered with agents all night. We've got a dozen boats out in the harbor and channel. No one's seen anything approach the ship or move on the docks."

"Give the order to stop the ship. Hook up with Customs and tell them you want every inch of that ship searched. Have them tell the captain we had a tip about a drug shipment."

"Drugs going *out* of the U.S.?"

"Look, the son of a bitch doesn't need a logical reason. Just order it. Then meet me downtown."

"Whatever you say."

———

The following week, Willard Thornton arrived at the Justice Department at his customary six A.M., passed through the metal detector, and crossed the lobby to the elevators. After getting settled at his desk, he looked up to see one of his legal assistants, a young woman, standing in his open door. "Good morning, sir," she said.

"Good morning," Thornton replied. "In early."

She laughed. "Leaving late is more like it. I've been here all night on the Robbins case."

"Then go home," he said.

"I intend to. Coffee, sir? I made fresh just a half hour ago."

"Yes, thank you. I didn't stop for any this morning."

When she returned with the coffee, she lingered for a moment. "What's that?" she asked, referring to a box on his desk. It was the size of a shoebox and was wrapped in brightly colored gift wrap. "Somebody's birthday?"

"Not that I know of," he said. "Was sitting there when I arrived." His phone rang. "Go ahead, open it," he told her as he reached for the receiver.

She slowly, carefully undid the wrapping, folding it neatly to be used another day. Inside was a shoebox with the lid secured by white string. She removed the string and lifted the lid.

"God!" she gasped, dumping the box onto the desk.

Thornton leaned over and looked inside. He saw the body of a pigeon with its eyes poked out; the ragged remains of a human tongue; and the gaudy replica of the ring that had once been Charlie Pietrosanti's good-luck charm.

XXXIX

A Week Later

"You had the courage to tell me the truth, Paulie."

Santo sat in his favorite red leather chair and sipped a glass of scotch, neat.

Paul Dante nursed a similar drink on the sofa. He'd chosen his words carefully. "You were the one with the courage, Santo. It took a ton of it to do what you had to do with Genaro." Santo had told him only that the Orsini matter had been resolved. It didn't take much imagination on Dante's part to translate what Santo had said. Orsini was dead. No details, thank you.

"How is Lucia taking it?" Dante asked.

"The security of the family comes first," Santo said. "She knows that."

Dante understood that meant it was not going well with her. Once again, time would be her only medication. He wondered if even that would help.

"She doesn't know he married her to be an informer. I spared her that. She should at least think he loved her."

"I'm sorry about the way this whole thing turned out," Dante said. "It's a nasty business."

"I never said it wasn't," Santo replied.

"I was talking about life," Dante said.

"So was I." He took a sip of his drink.

"Vincent is well?"

"Yes. He would prefer to be here, but that isn't possible. We have ways of communicating. He still has many good ideas for the family."

"I'm sure he does." Dante hesitated before saying, "I hate to ask this again, Santo, but I really want to know about Charlie Pietrosanti. You said Vincent told you he hasn't seen or spoken with him since the flight. Is that all he said?"

"Pretty much. You know men like Pietrosanti. Slimy. We'll never hear from him again."

"He's got a kid in Vegas. I just feel better knowing he's okay and still supporting the kid."

"I can't tell you more, Paul. I don't know more. When you came to my house the night before Vincent left and told me Pietrosanti had arrived in Washington, and that you had him hidden away someplace, I was angry. But you talked sense. You took a chance bringing him here."

"I left him in the car until I had assurances Vincent would buy the deal."

"And he did. Look, forget about Pietrosanti and Genaro. That's in the past. I have enough problems with now. I'm told Justice is considering using what Genaro leaked them about Vincent and the family to build a RICO case against me. The drug runners continue to operate with impunity. Many problems, Paul. I wish Vincent were here to help."

"Strange," Dante said.

"What's strange?"

"What this whole Orsini thing has done to me. You know, Santo, that I've always been a flag-waver. I joined the Marines when I probably should have stayed home with my mother and sister. I joined the MPD because I believed in what I was doing." He laughed softly. "I'm so fucking red-white-and-blue I won't even drive cars made outside the U.S. But when the government—*my* government, *the* government I put my ass on the line for most of my life—gets in bed with people like Orsini to make a score—well, I have to wonder."

"The job offer's still open," Santo said.

Dante eyed his one-time benefactor. The signs of recent hurt were still etched into his face, the dark circles heavier beneath his eyes. "Again, no thanks, Santo," Dante said. "I'm an independent spirit. I'll never amount to much, but what little I have will be my own creation." He drained his glass and stood.

"You don't mind showing yourself out, do you?" Santo said.

"I know the way."

Dante approached his friend and held out his hand. Santo started to rise. "No, stay, stay," Dante said. Santo remained seated as they shook hands.

"Keep in touch, Paulie," Santo said. "I'm going to need someone who'll give it to me straight."

"Call any time," Dante said.

They sat side by side at Booth Nine in Cuffs, the one farthest from the bar. There was a healthy number of after-dinner drinkers keeping Pete shuffling drinks, and Shelly wandering around exercising her authority. Dante was happy for the activity, for the diversion.

Sol, the waiter, and Lucette, the waitress, came to the table.

"Yeah?" Dante said.

"I got to take a few days off," said Sol. "My sister, she's got cancer and needs treatment."

"I'm sorry to hear it, Sol," Dante said. "Take whatever time you need. You need some bread, ask."

Sol shook his head.

"So?" Dante asked.

The fat waiter gave what substituted for a smile. "In New York," he said, "we say Italians who own restaurants don't give a shit for nobody who works for them. Not you. I'll get back as soon as I can."

"Do what you have to do," Dante said. Julia's smile of approval wasn't lost on him.

Sol walked away. Dante said to Lucette, "Bring us a coupla gins on the rocks."

The waitress laughed. "You don't drink gin," she said.

"I know, but say it."

"Two Beef-eee-teurs on the rocks?"

"I love it when you talk dirty," Dante said.

"Had enough of me yet?" Dante asked Julia.

She stared at hands cupped about her brandy glass. She raised her eyes to meet his. "You dumping me, Paulie?"

His eyes saddened. "You think I should?"

"No," she said, her voice from the back of her throat.

"It doesn't get any better," he said. "And that's not a line from a beer commercial."

"I don't expect that it will."

"It'll scare you sometimes."

"It already has."

"I've got a few enemies."

"But you've got one friend."

He smiled. "Dump you? I may be dense, but I'm not stupid." He took her face in his hands and bathed her in kisses.

Some Time Later—Camp Rappahannock, Virginia

It was early morning, presunrise, the time when Willard Thornton felt most in control of his faculties, a time when the great commanders, the great business leaders were alert, attentive, ready for action while the others, the losers of the world, were still shaking loose the cobwebs.

He had lost a battle with Vincent Benedetti—he preferred to view it as a strategic retreat—but single battles didn't determine the outcome of the greater conflict. Vincent Benedetti was simply missing in action. But he would be found sooner or later. Law-enforcement agencies around the world had been alerted. All friendly countries had promised cooperation. And there was leverage with even the unfriendlies now that their isolation was more pronounced after the thaw in the Cold War.

There had been the predictable political fallout. But if Vincent wasn't in jail as the plan had anticipated, at least he was away from the center of Benedetti authority—an adversary weakened.

The underboss, Santo, was now in charge, but he seemed to be a less formidable foe, at least from Thornton's perspective. The emphasis of the department would, of course, now shift to him.

Granted, considerable effort had been expended to put Vincent away—to neutralize him, so to speak. That effort had been somewhat wasted. The Benedetti family, under Santo Benedetti's direction, would be more alert to law-enforcement efforts now that the old understanding with Hoover, the misguided "arrangement" of thirty years ago, had been unalterably breached. Going after Santo would take new initiative. But that was what Thornton's staff was for. It would give them something to keep them busy. And it could be used politically, create new photo opportunities, new sound bites. The PR men could run with it. The public consciousness was there to be manipulated.

The failure to make a RICO case against Vincent Benedetti had not resulted in as much negative publicity as Simonsen had said it would. It was to no one's advantage—not Thornton's, not the attorney general's, not the President's—to dwell on the negative. The spin-controllers created the needed explanations and moved beyond damage control. It was time to press forward and to win the election. They all had jobs to preserve.

Thornton tucked his thumbs into his red suspenders, leaned back in his chair and studied the guest who sat on the couch behind the lodge's coffee table. Riccardo Diaz sipped his coffee and made a face of disapproval.

"You understand," Thornton said, "that D.C. is off limits. ¿Comprende?"

"Yes," Diaz responded, "I understand."

Thornton got to his feet, came round the desk and approached the drug lord. He held out his hand. "Then we have an agreement?"

"Of course," Diaz responded, taking the assistant attorney general's hand, then releasing it.

Thornton smiled. "Well then, I have to get back to town."

For a big man, he has a handshake like a woman, the Colombian thought. He drained the rest of his cup, winced at the weakness of the brew, got up and left with *his* arrangement.